Deception's Snare
The Arching Hunger Series
Ruan Willow
Writing as
R.U. Ann

Table of Contents

Deception's Snare (Arching Hunger, #5)..1
Wingless Hunger, Book 1, Chapter 1 | Gabriella 7
Chapter 2.. 17
Chapter 3.. 25
Chapter 4.. 37
Chapter 5.. 49
Chapter 6.. 61
Chapter 7.. 73
Chapter 8.. 81
The Siren Who Couldn't Sing, Book 2, Chapter 1 | Gabriella 89
Chapter 2 | Gabriella 97
Chapter 3 | Gabriella 107
Chapter 4 | Gabriella 115
Chapter 5 | Leif..127
Chapter 6 | Leif..137
Chapter 7 | Leif..149
Chapter 8 | Leif..161
Rejecting Queendom, Book 3, Chapter 1 | Nocter..................171
Chapter 2 | Gabriella's Yearning 179
Chapter 3 | Nocter 187
Chapter 4 | Gabriella 197
Chapter 5 | Nocter 209
Chapter 6 | Gabriella 217
Chapter 7 | Nocter 225
Chapter 8 | Gabriella 237
Chapter 9 | Nocter 245
Chapter 10 | Gabriella 255
Overcoming Heartache, Book 4, Chapter 1 | Gabriella..........263
Chapter 2 | Nocter 273
Chapter 3 | Gabriella 285
Chapter 4 | Nocter 293

Chapter 5 | Gabriella 307
Chapter 6 | Nocter 317
Chapter 7 | Gabriella 335
Chapter 8 | Nocter 347
About the Author..355
Thank you! 359
Ruan's other books | and novellas: 361
Anthologies and Award Nominations 363
Other links:...365

ISBN 979-8-9917605-7-7
Paperback version

Published by Pink Infinity Publishing LLC

R.U. Ann is a pen name for Ruan Willow for Romantasy, paranormal/magical/dark/horror tropes.

Edited by Sally Bend
https://www.sallybend.com/
Parts also edited by And Naughty Nook PR
Website: www.naughtynookpr.com[1]
Cover Design by Candice Clark, author of the series "Thick as Thieves" Thick As Thieves (2 book series) Kindle Edition[2]
Buy the Individual Books in the Arching Hunger Series
Wingless Hunger, Book 1 https://books.ruanwillowauthor.com/winglesshunger
The Siren Who Couldn't Sing, Book 2
https://books.ruanwillowauthor.com/thesirenwhocouldntsing

---

1. http://www.naughtynookpr.com/

2. https://www.amazon.com/dp/B0CK7RXG4F

Rejecting Queendom, Book 3
https://books.ruanwillowauthor.com/rejectingqueendom
Overcoming Heartache, Book 4
https://books.ruanwillowauthor.com/overcomingheartache

This book is certified Human Authored by the Author's Guild 8079692.

Dedication

This book is dedicated to lovers who play in and out of the bedroom, those who never stop playing, and those who desire to please their partners and get off on getting their partner off, plus celebrate who they truly are because that's how it should be. Mutual pleasure is mutual bliss.

This book is an erotic romance, specifically erotic Romantasy, please read and enjoy it knowing this is the genre it is in.

Marinate in your sexuality daily.

There is no hunger greater than that from a lonely heart.

Wingless Hunger, Book 1

Wingless Hunger, Book 1, Chapter 1
Gabriella

Gabriella lifted her nose to the air; the musky scent of something manly had teased her into hoping. She swore she'd gotten a whiff of a man a moment ago, but it was gone already. She slumped her shoulders and leaned against the blade of grass, a sigh escaping her lips. If only the inkling had been correct, then she'd be happy, but instead, she was still lonely, and horny. She gazed up at the sun streaming through the leaves and wished she'd not lost her wings. If she still had them, she could fly up and look around for the man. If her libido was creating phantom masculine pheromones, she was in big trouble. She believed in manifesting, but to manifest an actual living, breathing, and extra horny man? That seemed a feat even her lost magic couldn't have accomplished.

Even that tiny, delicious man-aroma had peaked her libido, and she'd enjoyed the stretching of her skin that had resulted. Now, she was back to normal, just like that, and unfortunately, it was without any satiation. She stood up and waded through the knee-high moss, her feet padding along the damp dirt. Perhaps she could eat something and that would satisfy her, but she doubted it. She wasn't really hungry. Well, at least not for food.

The roar of the waterfall increased as she stepped closer to the water's edge. That sound was always soothing, and since it never stopped, it was a source of renewable energy for her body and soul.

Her loins really yearned for a man, though. She hadn't had one grace her section of the woods for an entire month now and she was ravenously libidinous for the lush warmth and ecstatic rush, of a man rocking her body into a climax.

She released another sigh as she tried to sing, but her heart wasn't in it. She chided herself. How many times had that worked, though? Just about every time.

She opened her mouth and sang one line of her favorite song, then hummed it. She turned her head sharply from side to side, sniffing the air for any scent of the man she'd sensed earlier.

She shook her head. Nope. There was nothing. Bummer.

Perhaps when her cousins visited next week, they'd bring a man with them for her. They'd promised they'd visit, but she seriously doubted it was possible. It had come to her in a dream, so it was wishful thinking. All of it.

She laughed at herself. That was a ridiculous notion. If they had a man, they'd have spent his libido and he'd have stayed behind, not having enough energy to come with. They weren't anything less than voracious when it came to lovemaking. So, there was no hope there, even if her premonition was right.

She sang another melody as she spied a tree with a few red leaves. This signaled the start of autumn. It made her sad because, once the snow flew, she'd likely not get any visitors, so she'd go sex-hungry all winter—if she even survived it. This man just had to be real.

She continued to sing as she strolled along the edge of the river. At least the singing was lifting her spirits. She sang louder and twirled in the light breeze that had just swept up along her skin. It felt crisp and clean, so refreshing. She lifted her voice higher, sending the lovely tone to the sky.

She froze in her tracks. There it was again. Her heart leapt before she could chide it. She took in a huge breath of air, her brain analyzing it for the scent of cock. Right as she turned her head to the northwest, she caught the aroma of him again. She jumped and clapped with glee. He smelled incredible, sweat mixed with testosterone and aftershave. Then she got a whiff of cum, and a shiver swirled through her body.

Her body twitched before she felt the amazing feeling of her body stretching.

After she recovered from the growth spurt, she began to sing again. She walked in the direction she sniffed him from and sang as loud as she could. As she elevated her voice to a crescendo, she got a strong sense of him. He was surely walking her way now.

She began to jog, but not too heavily because she didn't want it to impair her ability to sing. Another tremor swept her body, and she grew another few inches. Her excitement was peaking as she paused to let the latest change finish while she hummed. She kept her voice churning during the growth, even though it taxed her. The nearness of him was energizing her, so the resolve would replenish her gusto easily.

She belted out the melody in the loudest singing voice she could muster. It worked. She grew another foot without any effort. The bodice of her dress slipped away from her breasts, and they bounced out. She could feel he was getting closer to her as she grew another blip of six inches. Her heart beat faster as she took a step onto the path, wondering if she should wait on the path or continue through the woods.

She drew in another deep breath, his manly smell directing her to walk down the path. The roar of the waterfall had waned, which was a danger sign of which she'd better heed warning. She didn't want to fall out of her zone again. Last time it had been so hard to get back home safe, being she'd been so tiny again. No matter, though, she was still within range, and she'd just go a bit further.

She strolled along as she sang, and with each step she grew a tiny bit more. Her breath caught as the scent of him blossomed.

She planted her feet and swiped her tattered dress from her waist. She really should have removed it when she felt the first twinge of growth. Now she was down another dress. No matter, with winter coming, she'd have plenty of time to sew more.

She filled her lungs with a big breath and sang louder yet. Her body rolled with the final wave of growth, and she reached her full size of five feet, ten inches. It felt incredible to be so big again. It always amplified her libido when she was big, too, which was a scrumptious sensation, but it also gave her a very ravenous feeling. She always welcomed it, though, for the beautiful pleasure that generally ensued when she got with a man.

She sighed. She needed this man, and she needed him now.

She lifted her eyes from the worn path and caught her first glimpse of him walking in the distance. Her heart leapt and she put all her efforts into her song to draw him nearer. Her nipples hardened and her labia lips plumped. He smelled horny, too. A zing of excitement bolted through her clit as the full force of his sex drive hit her sense of smell. It was earthy, fresh, and had notes of apple in it. Then she noticed the slightest aroma of beef jerky. Oh, his cum would likely be delicious. She couldn't wait!

She allowed her full sense of sexuality to bloom in the air around her, hoping her pheromones would entice him to continue on the path as much as her voice was. This could be it, and she'd be luxuriating in his arms soon.

Being this giant was such a treat. The breeze felt fresher, more exhilarating, as it caressed her naked flesh. The forest was full of aromas she never noticed when she was tiny. The leaves smelled of free greenness, the dirt carried the aroma of fertility, and the mushrooms, oh, she could tell where every one was. They were hers for the easy picking when she was big. She longed to stop off for a quick snack of them. This would blaze her desire higher, but she couldn't risk losing her prey, so she strolled along singing her song.

Her heart stopped as he seemed to have stopped moving in the distance.

She narrowed her eyes and shrieked, "No! Oh, no! Don't leave!" She began to jog as she sang desperately. She couldn't lose this cock, she needed him badly.

She sang as loud as she could, her breasts bouncing as she moved along the path ever faster. Her hopes began to crash as he continued walking away from her. These were desperate times, and she'd have to pull her strongest move out of her toolbox. She stopped and moved to the thick grass on the side of the path. She settled her body into the low vegetation and spread her legs. Closing her eyes, she took in a long breath, drawing in all the nearby forest air, and it both calmed and energized her all at once.

She reached between her legs and parted her wanton pussy lips with one hand while playing with her right erect nipple with the other. This was easy. Smelling the man had her so horny, she knew she was heading for the most epic climax, and her anticipation had her ready to pounce on this chance.

She dabbed her fingers into her slit, enjoying the wetness her body was gifting her loins. She slid her wettened fingers up to her clit and began to rub, paying extra attention to her other nipple, pulling it and tugging it as she writhed. She was so ripe, her fast finger caresses brought her quickly through the climb of her climax. As she rubbed, she hummed. Then, as she sang one line of melody, she spanked her swelling clit with her fingers, then rode its burgeoning nub harder. She was free with all her sounds, cooing, moaning, sighing, exclaiming, not holding back a single verbalization she felt like releasing. It heightened her arousal. She squirmed on the patch of grass, her eyes falling closed as she soared into the meat of her orgasm. Her body began its usual curl, and she released her sounds of pleasure in all their unmasked glory.

She fell silent as the orgasm peaked. Her fully grown body felt orgasms stronger, yet another benefit of being big, and her spirit soared into the sky, her soul dancing in the breeze above her. Even if he never came all the way to her, she was so elated to be able to climax at her full size once more. This fed her libido and her heart, and she sunk into a reverie. She closed her eyes, the peak making her sleepy.

She slipped her fingers into her mouth as her eyes fluttered open. She jumped, realizing why her climax had been so gargantuan. The man was about six feet from her. His jaw dropped open, and a look of lusty surprise filled his eyes.

"Wow! I mean...not wow, but... are you okay?" he stammered out, his eyes a kaleidoscope of concern, confusion, and wonderful lust.

She laughed and the light, airy, sultry sound of it surprised even her. "Oh, yes, I'm wonderful. Never better. That was so damn good."

He chuckled as he seemed to relax more. "Oh, good. I saw you laying there and was worried you were hurt or something." He laughed again. "Though you didn't sound hurt at all." His expression was very knowing. "You sounded rather...happy."

She sat up and her bare, pendulous breasts swung like small melons. She sat cross-legged in the grass as she pressed her hand to her upper pubic mound. This always launched her into more clitoral aftershocks. Her body twitched as she savored the bursts of pleasure, while trying unsuccessfully to hide her indulging grin.

"You okay? Not having a seizure, are you?" he asked as concern took over his gaze. It almost seemed as though he said it to tease her.

She laughed. "Um. No. Hardly." She paused. "Aftershocks." She grinned at him as he seemed to relax again.

"I must have eaten a bad mushroom." He shook his head as he took a step away from her, an unsure look on his face.

Her excitement bloomed. If he'd eaten wild mushrooms, he'd be even more virile. It was time to strike. This revelation sent her passion for him into overdrive. She quickly stood up, her breasts moving wildly, then settling. She restrained herself from lunging at him.

He couldn't take his eyes off her boobs, and it was thrilling for her to be seen in this way. "Definitely a bad mushroom." He looked both horny and bewildered at once. "This is a seriously hot fantasy, though."

"I'm real," she stated boldly. She embellished further, flourishing in a flirty tone adding, "You aren't dreaming. I'm Gabriella."

He looked as if he'd been smacked in the face, but then a jovialness took over. "I'm Leif."

What a perfect name for such a sexy man! She scanned his body, loving the thickness of his muscular thighs, the contour of his toned arms, and the slighter widening of his biceps. His eyes were a warm brown that belied sparks of some hunger blazing inside him. His hair was dark blond with a slight wave on the top, his hair shorter above his ears. His lips were full and rosy, and she longed to taste them. His nose was straight and regal looking, and his jawline begged her fingers to peruse it.

"You're naked," he said, his voice full of shock.

She guffawed and nodded. "I am indeed." She couldn't dare tell him she'd shredded her dress as she grew.

He smirked as he adjusted his backpack. "I must be high. This doesn't happen to me." He ran a hand over his jaw as he raised his left eyebrow. "This is something I'd dream. Coming upon a beautiful naked woman masturbating herself to climax in the forest. This just doesn't happen," he repeated. He blinked a few times as if to try to focus.

"I'm very real." She took a step towards him but held her hands clasped together.

He took a step back, raising his hands. "Are you cold? Do you have any clothes?" He glanced frantically back and forth.

She couldn't tell him. She had thousands of beautiful dresses and rompers, which were all way too small for her at the moment. "No, I'm not cold," she insisted with her eyes as much as her tone.

He dropped his backpack and slipped his sweatshirt off. He handed it to her with a small grin. "I'm hot anyway from hiking. Why don't you wear this?"

She liked being naked, but to help him not feel like a pervert talking to a naked woman in a forest, she took the sweatshirt and slipped it over her head. Her breasts filled the sweatshirt, making the bottom hem higher in the front than the back. She could feel air on her pussy lips and lower ass cheeks. "Thank you," she said sweetly.

He seemed more relaxed once she had the sweatshirt on. He pulled his water out and offered it to her.

"Oh, how kind. Thank you. I'm so parched after singing so much." She poured the water down her throat without touching her mouth to the opening, but she longed to taste something his lips had been on. She could smell the essence of him on the plastic, and it made her clit twitch. The cool liquid was lotion to her throat. She drank as much as she dared to, not wanting to short him any for himself.

"Wow. That was you?" he asked, looking startled. "It was so beautiful." He looked dazed as he watched her pass back the water bottle. "It was mesmerizing. I was drawn to come and see."

"Yes," she cooed. "And that was exactly what I needed. Thank you," she stated with notes of shyness. She hadn't sung like that in quite some time. She unclasped her hands, but rejoined them, folded together in front of her belly. Her womanhood was still throbbing from her last O, but she most definitely wanted more.

He shook his head as if realizing something jarring. "Are you alone?"

She nodded. "Yes."

His demeanor kept shifting. One minute he was looking at her with lust, then the next he had a look of concern. "Were you hiking too?" He glanced around again.

"No." She shuffled her feet. "Well, sort of."

"No backpack, water, or shoes?" He looked so perplexed, she felt bad for him. "Or clothes?"

"I'm a nudist. I like to be all natural in the woods," she said. It was the best she could come up with without freaking him out.

He smiled back. "Yeah. I can understand. I feel extra... primal in the woods, too." His smile was friendly and charming. His hands looked strong and capable.

She tried to calm her heart, but he was too sexy for her to chill out, plus she knew time was ticking. The sexual energy she smelled brewing inside him piqued her libido higher. She reached up to touch him, and he jumped back.

"Oh, I'm sorry," she said. "It's just been a long time since I've seen a man."

He shook his head while blinking his eyes quickly. "It has?" He looked off into the woods. "Are you sure you're alone?"

"Yes," she said with authority.

"And are you okay? Legit, for real, okay?"

His concern was sweet, but what she really wanted was his cock inside her. These were delicate matters, so she settled on another approach. "There's an amazing waterfall over that way," she said, motioning towards her home. "Care to see it?"

He nodded. "I've been hearing it. Yes, I'd love to see it. Is it far?" He harbored a slight hesitation, but when she smiled warmly at him, it left his demeanor.

She shook her head. "Nope." She put her hands on her hips, because she had to do something with them. "Just follow me." She started off into the woods, glancing back to ensure he was following.

Chapter 2

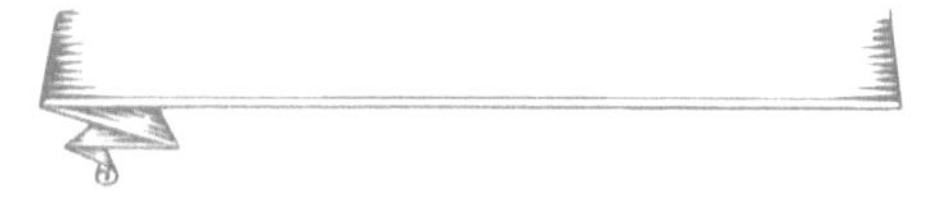

"You walk in there barefoot?" he asked, astonished.

"My feet are tough-skinned," she explained.

"Wow. They look delicate and perfect," he commented.

He followed her into the woods.

She caught a hint of his erection growing. The trace of it on the tip of her nose was titillating. She fought her urge to ask him to touch it, and kept walking through the vegetation instead. He might flee if she moved too quickly, just as the last man she'd come across had. Her wiles of seduction usually worked on men, but the last one had run away as if she'd stabbed him. That had her a bit gun-shy this time.

"It's right through these trees up ahead, not far now." She mused at the breeze that caressed the globes of her lower ass cheeks, her face flushing as she imagined what he might be thinking watching her walking with a half-covered butt. It didn't help to quell her desire for him one single bit.

"Have you been in the forest all day today?" he asked, his tone inquisitive, and still a bit confused.

"Yes, I sleep here." She cringed. That might be too much to say.

"Oh. I see. That makes sense then. Where's your camp?" He clearly liked this answer.

"It's close by." She gingerly stepped through the thick forest, holding branches for him to catch so they wouldn't smack him in the face. "It's thick through here."

"Thanks," he said appreciatively. "It really is. I'm so happy I have bug repellant on." His hiking boots crunched the twigs and dried leaves as he made his way. "I can't believe your feet aren't getting all cut up."

"I'm okay. I've developed thick soles going barefoot." She knew that wasn't a usual thing for humans, so she made a mental note to consider working on making herself a pair of believable shoes in the future. If the men didn't believe she was real, they wouldn't fuck her.

She paused in a clearing and ripped the sweatshirt off over her head. "Whew, I'm getting hot," she exclaimed. She tied the arms of the sweatshirt around her waist, lamenting that her ass would be covered up so he couldn't see it anymore. She glanced down. At least he could see her breasts now.

"Wow," he sputtered as a slow appreciative smile grew across his face. "Magnificent."

She returned his smile. "Thanks," she said coyly. She fluffed her blond curly hair to create a bit of a fan for her back. "Ah, this is much better." She started the trek again towards her waterfall. She was truly excited to show it to another man. She'd considered snagging a woman jogger who had traveled along the path the other day to see if sex with her caused the same effect, but she just really loved cock, so she'd chosen not to try to seduce her. This man was a blessing, and she needed to not mess this up, so she restrained herself. Control of her urges was what she needed to harness. What she really longed to do was grab him, start kissing him, and hopefully they'd end up with her riding his cock before he spun her and fucked her doggy. If that could happen, she'd be in heaven. But while many men liked to hook up, she also knew some were suspicious of a random naked woman coming on to them too strong in the middle of a forest. She released a sigh and suppressed a giggle. The thoughts of fucking him were making her pant.

"Are you just doing a day hike?" she asked over her shoulder.

"Yeah, I am in town visiting my mom and wanted to explore the woods. I used to walk this park years ago, but I've never gone this way before."

Ah, that made sense then why she'd never smelled him before. "Oh, that's very nice."

Once they reached the river, the waterfall wasn't much further. Her heart pounded as she neared the water's edge.

He came up behind her and whistled. "I can hear the roar. I can't wait to see it."

She glanced at him and his eyes were on her tits. It was delicious to have his eyes fixed on her naked boobs. "Do you like them?" she asked, gently shaking her tits for him.

"Them?" he asked, then scoffed. A nervous laugh teetered out of him. "Oh, your breasts? Yes, very much so." He laughed again, heartier this time. "Boob man, here," he said while pointing his forefinger at his chest. "And yours are exceptionally beautiful." He released a sigh. "All of you is exceptionally beautiful." He shook his head. "I'd swear I was dreaming if I knew I wasn't. Coming upon a very beautiful naked woman pleasuring herself on the edge of the path. That just doesn't happen every day in my world." He looked as if he'd been given a gift he wasn't sure he'd get to keep.

Of that, he was very right. Though she didn't come upon men like him every day, either. "I don't find many like you either." She'd had a few guys eagerly fuck her without much provocation at all. Leif was proving to be more of a challenge.

"So, you do stay here in the woods then, for an extended time? Alone?" he asked, his tone skeptical.

"Yes," she said, wondering when he'd get past his reluctance. She stayed true to the path. Being in the lead wasn't as much fun to her. He was only looking at her bare back and legs. She turned slightly to give him a slip of her right nip. "I live here." They were now inches away from her home, but he'd never see it. She'd chosen a nice protected spot to build it, so no one would step on it.

He followed her, and they walked in silence for the next three minutes. When they reached the clearing near the waterfall, she turned and pointed at it.

"Oh, wow. That's gorgeous. What a gem to find." He pulled out his phone and began to take pictures of the waterfall.

"Want a pic of me in front of it?" she asked casually.

"Yes, oh, I'd love that." His face fell into a quirky look. "No one will believe my story, even with a pic of you in front of it. They'll think I altered it."

"Photoshop?" she asked with a snicker. She'd learned that word from her cousins who lived in the city. Her zone had been assigned long ago. She'd been whisked away and plopped in the woods, and she'd had to stay. She hoped to one day be able to visit them in the city again, but their leader would have to lift her punishment for that to happen. She fretted over the fact that time was slipping by too fast, and it set her heart in a minor panic. At thirty-four, she feared she'd never find someone, especially being confined to these woods. She'd be a lonely old twat hermit, and die after a lonely, sexless, man-less life amid the bugs, dirt, and trees. It sounded like pure misery.

She shed the bad thoughts and posed in front of the water, alternating between silly poses and sexy ones.

"I could do this all day," he mused.

When he leaned back, his shorts tightened, and his erection became visible. Happiness filled her. He was turned on. It made her jubilant. This might happen after all.

It was time to be bold. She swiveled her body and bent over. Grasping a butt cheek in each hand, she spread her buns. "How about this?" she asked.

He burst into raucous laughter. "Holy shit!" he shouted. "It's," his voice trailed off, "fucking perfect."

She wiggled for him to make her butt jiggle and her breasts bounce.

"Oh, fuck. No one will believe me without this. Care if I video you?"

"Please do," she said. "It's much harder to fake a video." Well, she didn't really know, but it seemed so to her. She shook her butt for him, swaying to the rush of the water from the falls.

"You're incredible. If this is indeed the result of a wild mushroom, I need to go back and pick some more to bring back home." His low chuckle rumbled in his masculine body, starting from his belly and radiating out of his eyes. It was like honey in sunshine, coating her in warmth.

She swiveled and began to stride towards him, her eyes ablaze with zest. "It's not from mushrooms, Leif, this is real."

"Maybe you're going to transform into a demon next and steal my soul," he mused, a snicker laced throughout his sentence.

She jerked with repulsion. "I'm no demon." This sentence crushed her. She'd been nothing but inviting and pleasant to him.

"Oh, I'm sorry. That was a joke."

She frowned, trying at the same time not to.

"Oh, well, shit. The last thing I want to do is offend you. I'm truly sorry."

He looked sorry, so she softened her hard glare.

"Okay, maybe I should just go. I do have to get back. My mom is having a dinner party and I'm the guest of honor."

Her heart leapt into her throat. "No!" she said with way too much desperation.

He froze in place. "Well, I could come back, and we could talk more tomorrow." He looked like he liked the idea.

Her heart sank and tears welled in her eyes. She was failing. This couldn't be fixed.

She held her torso tightly, her arms under her breasts like a vise. "You won't be able to find me."

"Oh, I have a pretty good sense of direction. I can easily find this same spot tomorrow." He slipped his phone into his pocket.

"I'll shrink away," she said while staring at the ground. Many ants were busy milling around a pile of sand. They were usually the size of a dog to her, but now, once she shrunk again, they'd likely be a dinosaur to her.

He cocked his head at her, his eyes going wild. "Shrink away?" he asked cautiously, looking very much like he wanted to run away from her.

She'd been hoping they'd just fall into each other's arms in passion and have sweet hot sex on the shore of the river. She was losing her touch. In the past, she had no problems enticing men hiking by to fuck her.

"Yup. You won't be able to even see me." She couldn't keep the absolute desolation out of her voice. "At all."

He frowned. "Are you sure you're okay? I can help you get to a hospital or something?" He had lost his passionate gleam, and it was replaced by a look that said she was crazy as a drunk bat flying into a tree.

She balled her fists and shook them downward. "I'm not crazy," she said in desperation. "I just need you to fuck me."

He jumped back. "You can keep the sweatshirt." He began to back up and he looked scared. "I should go."

"I'm not crazy. I'm a fairy." She tried to curb her anger, but she was failing miserably.

He laughed heartily. "That, I believe."

She put her face into her hands as she fought tears. "I'll shrink if you leave, even smaller than I was before."

Being on the verge of tears seemed to erase his fear of her, at least enough to keep him from charging off like he'd seen a ghost. "I'd really like to help you. Will you let me?" he asked kindly.

"The only help I need is from a cock up my pussy, but I need to come." She pleaded him with her eyes because her tone wasn't helping.

"Are you magic?" he asked, but he looked amused as he said it. "I thought fairies had magic."

"I'm not magic, I'm just ...me." She dropped her arms to her sides and fell to her knees. "I'm begging you. Please, will you have sex with me?" Friendliness and bluntness hadn't worked, so she moved on to complete desperation. "Please. And I'll suck your cock, too."

He rubbed his hands together, his eyes taking on a mood she didn't like. "Look, I really think you're gorgeous. You're beautiful, stunning. Unbelievably hot. But I can't take advantage of a woman in a state like this. I'd never be able to forgive myself."

Great. She'd found a noble man. Just her damn luck. She was offering up her body and he was exercising his morals. What she needed was a horn dog, someone who matched her sexual energy, a man who wanted to rail her until she screamed. He was a knight in shining armor, and what she needed was an unscrupulous, depraved, hypersexual bull. Why couldn't he just be someone who wanted to get off?

She glommed on to some hope as she spied the tiny, tattered top half of her dress, half covered up by a dead leaf. She bent down and snatched it up as he raised his arms in defense.

She laughed heavily at his reaction while holding up the little bodice of her dress. "See. This is my dress. I was wearing it when I got the first whiff of your scent."

He shook his head. "Look, I've really got to go. I'll send help for you," he stated as he backed away from her.

"It's true. I'm not lying. I'm a fairy, but I've lost my wings. And your idea of help won't help me. I can't leave."

"Wait, is someone keeping you here? Forcing you to stay?" He pulled out his phone as a major expression of concern took over. "I'll call 911. We can fix this. I can help you." The look of panic on his face didn't look easily erasable.

She raised her hands quickly. "Please, don't do that. Let me explain." The desperation in her voice was not attractive, and it tore down all the seduction she'd tried to build with him. "You may not believe in me, but I exist. I'm a fairy. I'm not fully human."

"I'm calling," he said plainly with authority and began to punch numbers into his phone.

She lunged for him and knocked the phone out of his hands. It landed hard on the forest floor.

"Hey," he blurted, bending to pick it up. "Watch it. That's my phone." His eyes danced with anger.

This soothed her because it showed he had some passion. She could appeal to it now.

She had to spill it now. Tough to do knowing he'd be even more likely to run. "I will shrink away if I don't have sex within five hours from when I started to grow." She sat on the ground with a plop. "I didn't make up the rules."

"This is either some kind of joke, or you're insane," he insisted. "Look, I'm just going to go. I'll call the police, and they will come find you and help you."

She fingered her tiny dress. "I won't even fit in this dress anymore I'll be so tiny, so I guess it doesn't matter that I ruined it." She figured it didn't matter anymore, seducing him was out of the question at this point, so she let her tears fall. Her shoulders shook as she sobbed for a few minutes. She hugged her legs, putting her head on her knees.

Chapter 3

"Aw shit," he muttered softly. "Honey, I'm sorry. I'm just trying to help you." He approached her, his caution seeming to take a hiatus.

"I'm not crazy. And I wouldn't hurt you." She sighed. "I'm just in need of sex."

He sat next to her. "I sense that about you, that you wouldn't hurt me. You are very sweet. It's why I'd like to help you." His tone had switched again to compassionate.

"The only help I need is your cock riding my cunt." Being crass was essential when her life depended on it. And men liked dirty talk. Well, so did she, but that was beside the point.

"Okay. I'll play along. Maybe the only way to help you right now is to buy into what you are saying. Go ahead. I'm listening." He leaned back on his hands and crossed his ankles. "I'm all ears."

She giggled with relief through her tear-stained cheeks. "When I smell a man, I start to grow."

He chuckled. "Kind of like when I smell pussy, my cock grows."

She swiveled to face him, pointing at his face in a repeated motion. "Yes! That's exactly it! I can't stop it. I just start to grow. I'm actually a tiny little fairy, but when I smell a man, I grow to a full-sized human. And once I start to grow, if I don't have sex within five hours, I will start to shrink and shrink, smaller than I started." She peered at him. "See why I need the sex?"

He nodded with a silly expression on his face. "Man cum is magic?" he asked jovially, as if it was a ludicrous idea. He also seemed to like it.

"Yes, sort of. I need their cock in me, though, and I have to come, too. This is why I got so small. It keeps happening to me where I can't fulfill the full requirement, and I keep getting smaller. This will be the smallest I've ever been if you leave without fucking me." She threw her hands up in the air. "I just don't get it! Am I not sexy anymore?"

He scoffed heavily. "Not sexy? You may be the sexiest woman I've ever seen in my life."

"Fairy," she corrected.

"Well, you look like a regular human."

"Only I shrink." She played with her toes. She'd painted her toenails with fresh blueberry paint the other night, so they were a delectably deep purple. "Okay, how about I show you my house? It's actually getting a bit big for me."

"Let's stay here and you tell me more," he requested.

"Okay." She had little recourse other than to comply with his wishes. "I'm forced to stay here to finish my penance." She slumped her body. "I was a bad fairy, and I lost my wings. Now I have to stay here until my leader deems I've completed my punishment."

He laughed with delight, clapping his hands. "That's fantastic. And is he a fairy godfather, too?"

"You're mocking me," she said, her face set in a pout.

"Okay, I'll be serious. Let me get this straight. So, if you have sex, this magically fixes you? And you stay big?"

She nodded heavily. "Yes, that's it." She was disappointed he still didn't seem to buy into it.

"This may be the best pickup setup for a hookup that I've ever heard of. It's at least the most creative." He shook his head as his expression was aghast, but still very intrigued. "So, you have to fuck, or you shrink to the size of a bug?"

"Yes, precisely. And if I keep having sex, I stay this big."

"Every five hours?" he asked incredulously. "I could man up to that, but wow."

"Yes, and this is why I keep shrinking back down. The man leaves. I try to explain it to them, but they run off. And when I smell a man, and grow big, and don't have sex, I shrink even smaller. I'm afraid I might eventually just disappear." She didn't care if he thought she was crazy, she needed him to believe her for his cock.

He clapped his hands. "This is fun. I like this game. You have quite the imagination."

"You finally believe it's not the mushrooms you ate?" she asked, grinning.

"Not entirely," he said with humor. "It seems very fitting. Or I've been thrown into an alternate universe, which I don't really believe in any more than I believe in tiny fairies who need sex to stay human size."

She fought the urge to get mad at him and jumped up, then slid herself onto his lap to straddle him. "Do you believe in this?" She ran her hands into his hair as she pushed her breasts into his face. "Boobs have powers."

He grinned up at her. "Yes, they do, and yours especially do."

She leaned down until their foreheads touched, their eyes staring into one another's. "I can light up your world and make you come harder than you ever have in your life," she said with such intensity, she couldn't imagine him turning her down. "Just fuck me."

"I like your spunk. But I'm not the kind of guy who uses women, unless we've been together and established a trusting and loving relationship and she has the kink for it." He pressed his lips together.

"Oh, just use me already," she said heatedly.

His eyes were genuine and kind as a chuckle shook him. But she could feel the truth in the rod of his erection pressed to her pubic mound.

"So, you are too good to fuck me with that thing in your pants? I feel you, you're hard as fuck," she accused.

"Yeah, I'm hard as fuck. You're damn right I am. I told you, you're the sexiest woman I've ever had the pleasure of being in the presence of, so it's a damn shame you're bat shit crazy."

She hopped off him, wanting to pummel him. She gave an anguished guffaw and took a firm stance. "I'm not crazy! I'm telling you the truth."

"How about this? I wait here, and if you start to shrink, I'll fuck you." He laughed heartily like it was the most ridiculous thing he'd ever heard.

She perked up with hope, raising her hands. "Yes, that's a good plan."

"You're serious? You'd wait around here with me for five hours?" he asked in disbelief. "That's dedication."

"Well, it will be less than five hours now." She sat next to him as things were looking up for her. "But I thought you had the dinner?"

"Oh, I do. That's true, but it's not until seven tonight." His face turned whimsical. "Do you have an imaginary clock on your wrist to know when five hours is up?"

She seethed with annoyance. "No. I know you don't believe me, but I can feel the passage of time. I have about four hours or less before I start to shrink."

"Okay. That's the deal. If you start to shrink after four hours, I'll fuck you. But if you stay the same size, I'd like to take you back to my mom's house and help you get the help you need." He cocked his head at her and raised his eyebrows. "Deal?"

She nodded heartily. "Deal. I'll take it." She slithered towards him and knelt next to his legs. "But to stave off my yearnings, can I at least sniff your cock up close? Naked?"

"Shit," he exclaimed. "You want to smell it? That alone might make me come if you have your face that close to me. I'm pretty fucking worked up."

"I know, as am I. Maybe we can just play around." This was absurd! They should be fucking!

He waved his hands as he shifted his position. "No, no, no. We can't do that." He glanced around. "If someone came upon us, I'd been seen as a perpetrator."

"No, you wouldn't. I'd tell them I wanted it."

"Gabriella, you are naked and talking crazy nonsense. I'd be seen as the bad guy and get charged." He patted his cock through his pants. "You can sniff me, but my pants stay on."

"Until I start to shrink, right? Then they come off?"

He released a burst of laughter. "Yeah, okay. Then they come off," he said, nodding.

"You will have to fuck me quickly and make me come fast if we wait til the last minute, just so you know. But I'm pretty ripe, I will come fast. Just rub my clit a lot, talk dirty to me, and fuck me into rag doll status and we will be all good."

He cackled. "Okay. That sounds like a plan. You might be the best woman in the world."

"Right, except I'm not a woman. I'm a fairy."

"This might be the longest four hours of my life, but I think it might be the best four hours."

"Aww, that's a wonderful thing to say. You're forgiven." She nestled herself between his legs, prying them open further as she settled in. She laid her face at his groin, her nose pressed to his boner.

"Fuck," he whispered. "This is going to be really touch and go."

"If you come, you'll make more by then." She inhaled deeply, allowing her happiness at smelling his dick to glow on her face. "Ah, that smells so wonderful. I haven't been this close to a man's cock in a month, and not like this. I get to savor you."

"You need to stop that." He shifted.

She propped herself up in alarm and looked into his eyes. "Stop what?"

"Saying and doing things that make me like you too much." He stroked her hair. "You have beautiful hair, too."

She laid her head on his thigh and breathed deeply again, enjoying him. "And you have a very delicious-smelling cock. It looks nice and thick, too. Is it?"

He whooped out a laugh as he threw his head back. "Good mushrooms. Good mushrooms. You have got to be the best. Cock worshipping me in the middle of the forest like this. This is like every man's dream."

She twinkled her eyes up at him. "Yeah? So then why aren't you taking advantage and fucking me already?"

His face fell serious. "I already told you. I'm not that kind of guy."

"You don't hook up with women, you mean?"

"No, I do. But I don't hook up with crazy women who I find naked and masturbating in the forest, who might not be in their right mind. Maybe you took mushrooms? Drugs?"

"No," she spat, smacking his thigh with her fist. "I'm not crazy. I don't do drugs or shrooms." Well, not entirely true, but telling him that right now wouldn't help the cause, so she stayed mute about that topic.

"Okay, I promise to stop saying it. Tell me about something else." He stroked her cheek affectionately.

"I like that touch," she cooed as she snuck her nose up to the fabric covering his shaft again. She opened her mouth and licked his fabric-encased hard-on.

"Fuck," he muttered as he shifted away. "That's not helping me settle down." He sounded annoyed, but breathlessly so.

"Admit it, you're tempted." She dragged her fingernail along his shaft from tip to balls.

"Oh, hell yes, I'm tempted. I'd love to ..." his voice trailed off.

"Oh, tell me!" she insisted. "I want to know what you're thinking. And you like sex? And what's your favorite position? And do you like something called pizza?"

His jubilance was apparent in his voice. "You're such a delight. So pure. You're a rare gem."

"Awww, if you don't stop saying perfect things, I'm not going to be able to resist you for four hours." She released a chuckle. "I'll tell you my thoughts if you tell me yours after."

"Okay, I'm game."

She reached for his thigh. "If we can't fuck, and you won't take your cock out for me, I'd like to hump my pussy on your leg." She smiled mischievously.

He roared with laughter. "Damn if you aren't the most amazing person I've ever met in my life."

"Sometimes, when I pleasure myself in the five-hour timeframe, I can get it to last longer. But, come to think of it, I want it to go faster, not lengthen it. So, I'll have to wait." She paused and propped her chin up on her arm, so her face was hovering above his groin. "And fairy. I'm a fairy."

"Okay, best fairy."

"Your turn. What are you thinking about doing to me right now? And make it sex-related. None of this getting me help business."

He drew in a deep breath and hung his head. "This might be against my best judgment to tell you, but, yes, it's definitely sex-related."

She shook her head wildly. "No, it's not, I promise you. It's perfect."

"I'd love to kiss your mouth, sliding my tongue in deep to caress and taste you. Then I'd love to fondle and suck your tits. I'm a tit sucker, so I'd suck you until you slapped my head away. You'd probably get sick of me paying attention to your nipples. Then I'd travel down your body and play with your pussy. I'd eat you out, make you come, use you, then make you come again." He grinned proudly. "I'd be relentless. There's nothing more of a turn-on than making a woman climax, multiple times."

His words thrilled her, her heartbeat chugging faster, pulsing the blood through her veins. "And call me things like your dirty whore, slutty wench, horny bitch, and dominate me, fuck me doggy, too?" she asked eagerly, practically salivating at the thoughts. She'd been fantasizing about such things for the past month.

His eyes danced with sparks, showing his exuberance. "And you just keep getting better."

"I'm so turned on I might start on fire," she said in a seductive wanton voice.

"I can sympathize with that," he retorted. "Maybe we should take a stroll, so we don't rip each other's clothes off and fuck too soon?"

Well, that made no sense. That's exactly what she wanted, but she was stuck. In order to get him to comply, she needed to go along with his wishes. Or she might get so small this time she blipped away into some other nothingness or an alternate universe that had no sex at all. She didn't want that!

She pulled herself from the deep, mesmerizing, masculine scent of his aroused cock and sat on the ground.

He stood and lent her a hand to help her up.

She accepted it and, with them both standing, she noted he was taller than she was, but not grossly so. Their bodies would fit nicely together, tangled in many different sexual positions.

"We're a good height match. And can we do something called reverse cowgirl, too?" she mused with desire.

"Yes," he said as he shook his head, a great big lecherous grin claiming his mouth. "I was hoping my cock might chill if we walked around, but if you keep talking like that, there's no chance."

She grabbed his hand. "Come, let's go closer to the falls. I can take you under them, too. There's a rock ledge that goes beneath it. It's incredible. A must-see." She pulled him along, her heart singing with joy to be able to share her falls with another. "Oh, this is so fun!" she squealed as she tugged his hand to get him to go faster.

He began to jog with her, but kept hold of her hand.

Her breasts flopped in their heavy mass as she hurdled herself along, keeping hold of his hand made her heart warm.

When they reached the falls, the roaring of the water filled their ears.

"Watch where you step," she called loudly.

He nodded as he released her hand to get a grip on the rock. "This is so amazing," he shouted back.

"It is. And it gets better," she assured.

The spray of water speckled her flesh, the droplets cooking on her hot skin, and making her body cool to a more tolerable temp. The refreshing, cooling effect led her to sigh deeply. She glanced back at Leif, and he had an expression of happy awe. She loved sharing this with him. Her special place. She hadn't taken any other men this far. She had to remind herself not to get too attached to him. He'd have to leave. He likely had a whole life out there in the world and he'd never be able to live here in the forest with her. If she could leave, he might still not even want a fairy. He was so handsome and kind, her heart ached for more of him.

"I'd love to fuck right here someday," she said as she stuck her hand in the water spray.

"Yeah, that would be something," he said as he crept along behind her, hugging the wall a bit more than she was.

She paused and turned to face him. "One kiss beneath it? While we're here?" she asked, not hiding the pleading from him.

"Okay," he agreed as he pulled her to him.

She gazed up into his eyes and he smiled down at her.

He bent his head lower as she raised her face up higher until they joined their lips, both their mouths opening and tongues entering. He pulled her fully tight to him, his clothed front pressing to her nude one, smashing her breasts against his chest. They fell into a deep kiss, their tongues twinning, caressing, tasting each other. Their moans were muted by the sound of the water, but she still enjoyed what she could hear of his groan as they kissed. It got her going.

Her desire for him swelled as they kissed intimately, his hands pressing her back to him. His cock was a fat mini bat between them, and she wanted so badly to unveil it behind the curtain of the water. It would be heaven to suck it as the water rushed beside them.

Her loins screamed at her, his mouth tasted so incredible, his body was comforting and strong wrapped around her, and her brain didn't fight it. She needed his cock. She needed him. She'd beg.

She caressed down his body and cupped his hard cock with her hand. Giving it a hefty squeeze, she pulled away from the kiss. "Please," she begged. "Please, please, please, just fuck me right here beneath the waterfall. No one will ever know." She pleaded with her eyes. "I promise it would be the best sex of your life."

He released her and took a step back. "Gabriella," he said slowly.

"But you are turned on, I can tell. I'm turned on. I want it. You want it. Just give in." The feelings of desperation were thickening in her after their kiss. "That was an amazing kiss. I felt our electricity, didn't you?"

He nodded slowly and grabbed the wall behind him, leaning against it. "Yes, I did."

"Then why stop?" She should stop nagging him. This wasn't helping one bit. "Okay," she replied as she shook her head. "Let's just have fun. Come this way." She squelched her yearnings for him and pressed onward.

The hollow of the small cave was up ahead. She'd had so many fantasies of sex in the cave that approaching it with Leif in tow had her brain wired for sex with him even more. She was doomed. Her horniness was clouding her judgment. If she scared him off, she was screwed. "There's a really awesome cave ahead," she called back towards him.

"Nice," he replied.

It might be too much work to stop herself from coming on to him, but damnit, she was going to try. He wanted things platonic, but she needed to change his mind.

Chapter 4

She spied the cave ahead and made a beeline for it. Her skin was refreshed with speckles of water from the falls. As she entered the cave, the nook's dampness enveloped her, and she felt slightly chilled. By the time she sat, her skin was littered with goosebumps.

Leif sat next to her, the rush of the water filled their ears, but it was a bit muted by being in the cave. She had always thought this would be the perfect place to have sex, and thoughts of being intimate with Leif choked her ability to talk.

"You cold?" He put his arm around her.

She shivered. "Yeah, guess I am." Having him touch her sent her already-charged libido into overdrive. She was so ready to pounce on him, she could scream. And now he was touching her? Oh, fuck. She was in big trouble.

"Still cold?" he asked, gazing into her eyes, his face giving her a plethora of his inherent nature to be considerate.

She nodded and her body shuddered. "I'm wet."

"Yeah, you sure are. I have an emergency blanket. I can get it out for you." He started to open his pack. "I wish I had grabbed the sweatshirt for you."

"No, don't waste the blanket. I'll be fine in a minute, once my skin dries." Her nipples were as hard as pebbles, and she smiled when he dropped his eyes to them.

She had to hand it to him. Most men would have ravaged her at her request, but he was different, stubborn, but all that was quite intriguing. She had never met a man like him.

"So, this waterfall, quite the find." He smiled down at her as she snuggled into him.

"Yeah, it's been a source of entertainment, renewal, and joy for me while I've been here." She flexed her feet, admiring how the paint job on her toenails was holding out longer with her new formula. The last one had washed off in half a day.

"I can imagine that." He squeezed her against him. "Gotta warm you up."

She bit her tongue. She had about a million ideas of how he could do that. Not many that he would be willing to do, though. "I love waking up to the sound, but the smaller I've gotten, it's been harder and harder to hear as I wake."

He shook his head, his eyes full of amusement.

"I know, I know. You don't believe me." She hung her head as darkness loomed to claim her brain. She couldn't blame him, she was quite an anomaly.

"It's not that."

"Liar," she shot back, but she smiled to keep the mood light. She could at least try to not be a doomsayer for fuck's sake.

"Tell me more about how you came to be." He'd said it without jovially mocking her and it stroked her just right.

"My mom was a fairy, and my dad was a human. My grandmother was a siren, that's how I can sing like that."

"Your singing is what drew me to you. It was like I couldn't resist it," he said with a chuckle.

"I know. It's always proven quite effective. That's the siren in me."

"Is that like cross-species mating?" he asked, a twinkle in his eyes.

"Yeah, I guess you could say that. I haven't met another like me, ever, and I've met some wild folks." She wasn't able to tell him, though. He'd really think she was crazy if she started spinning those tales.

"Got it," he said, shaking his head.

"How about you? You haven't told me much about you. I'm dying to know." She gave him a pleasant smile as she waited.

He smirked as his eyes drifted up to the ceiling of the cave, then back down to her. "I went to school for business and finance, and now I work from home as an analyst. My company is out of Arizona, so my office has to be in my home. I travel about once a month. I love to hike and be outdoors, especially since my job keeps me indoors. I work out lifting weights, use the treadmill. I like to cook, and eat."

"Girlfriend?" she asked with trepidation. Maybe that's why he was being so reluctant with her.

He shook his head. "Nope. My last relationship ended a year ago. I haven't dated much in that year either." There was a tone of forlornness in his words.

"You sound like an amazing catch." She wasn't sure how much more of the closeness with him she could take without them launching into more. Her patience was stretched to the max, and she feared she might go too far.

He shrugged. "I don't know. I guess I'm just me."

She shivered again as she tried to calm her urge to tackle him.

He hugged her tighter, which didn't help.

"So, your mom. She lives here?" She watched him intently as he blinked.

He drew in a breath and released it before speaking. "Yup, I grew up here for part of my youth. Hiked this park, but never graced this waterfall. I can't understand how I never heard it before. It really makes no sense." He released his hug and opened his pack. He pulled out a granola bar and opened it. He broke it in half and offered her a piece.

"Thanks," she said, taking it.

They chewed in silence as the water flowed before them incessantly.

"When we get back to the woods, I want you to mark a tree with my height. Then I can show you when I'm shrinking." She hopped up and paced the cave. "We can keep track." She jumped as the urge to move made her jittery.

"You okay?" he asked, concern filling his voice.

"Yeah, I've got too much energy. I need to walk."

He stood and brushed off his backside. "I'm game. Show me the rest of it."

She led him along the cliff to the other side of the falls, then brought him back again. Once they reached the other side of the falls, the sun basking on her wet skin filled her with warmth. She twirled in the sunshine, a big smile on her face.

"You are a breath of fresh air, I have to say that. I'm glad we met." His eyes were brilliant with genuineness. "Whatever happens."

Not wanting to buy into that bad premonition, she dashed to a nearby tree. "Here." She stood next to the tree with her back to it. "Have a knife in that backpack? Mark my height with it."

She pressed herself to the rough bark, the sharp scratchiness of it pressing into her flesh. She drew in a breath of the fresh scent of the forest as he watched with an amused look.

He retrieved his pocketknife from his pack and pulled the blade out. He stepped close, his blade drawn, and she held her breath.

All she'd need to do was stick out her tongue and she could lick him. She inhaled his rugged man scent. It made her head swim, and her body want to writhe with his, their limbs entangling. Her breathing was so rapid as he leaned in closer, he couldn't miss it. They were close enough to kiss again.

He met her eyes, and an eruption corrupted her calm. Her heart beat so hard and fast, her spirit raged, wild and ready to burst. She parted her lips and placed a hand on his bicep. She saw his fire mirror hers in their mutual gazes, but instead of responding with his lips, he cut the bark above her head. She allowed her eyes to plead with his, but he only stepped away after he'd finished cutting the bark. He sheathed his blade with a grin.

"You think this is silly," she said, her voice low and downtrodden.

"I think I like you, and I want to stay here with you for a while." He grabbed her hand, and they began to walk.

They certainly weren't playing naked and the beast, yet, but she could sense a beast mode at the ready within him. If only she could trigger it. If all she'd done wasn't working, though, she had no more ideas to unleash it in him. She gasped away her panic as she held her arm up for him to stop moving.

"Look," she whispered, pointing off into the distance. A mom deer and her doe were frozen in place and watching them.

"Oh, wow," he whispered back. "Beautiful."

The four of them watched each other in silence as the birds tweeted in the tree limbs above. The deer were the first to move after they'd all been immobile for several minutes.

"That was incredible," Leif said as he watched the mom and baby leave.

"Yeah, I've been watching them. They come around here for a visit once a day." She held on tight to his hand. The strength of it was both sweet and comforting. "I'm kind of surprised you're still staying here with me."

"I want to make sure you're okay." He paused their trek. "Will you leave with me? I really can help you." He paused and stared intently in her eyes. "I want to."

She shook her head. He didn't understand. Not yet, anyway. She couldn't physically leave. There was a shell surrounding her area, and if she tried to leave, her body would bounce back. She'd learned that early on in her incarceration. She wondered if that would be proof for him, but it hurt to approach it, and she was hoping not to have to endure the pain of being thrown back. But it would certainly be good proof of what she said. She didn't want to usurp her energy in that way either. She was saving it up for when they'd fuck. She smiled to herself.

"I like that smile," he said, giving her hand a squeeze.

"You wouldn't like what prompted it," she said in a teasing voice.

"On the contrary, I can guarantee you I do."

That was doubtful, but it remained to be seen. His arousal was still a yummy aromatic odor that she rolled around in, enjoying being so near to him. He wasn't craving her body sexually, but he couldn't stop her from enjoying that on her own at least.

"So, you aren't human, but you look human," he said, trying but failing at keeping his skepticism out of it.

"Right. I'm part human. Fifty percent human."

"If you are a fairy, where's your magic? Aren't fairies supposed to be magic?" His eyes flashed with curiosity.

She stopped walking and frowned. "I was stripped of my magic. And I don't know how I'm supposed to get it back." She tried to stop the flood of memories of her trying everything she could think of to get it back. It fell upon her like a bag of bricks, making her physical frame dip back.

He reached to steady her. "Whoa! I'm sorry, I didn't mean to bring up a bad topic."

She shook her head to clear the urge to cry and smiled through her silent agony. "I'm okay. It's just a lot."

"Okay. Got it."

For someone who didn't believe her, he was being so kind. She grabbed his hand, and they began to stroll along again. She had a plan. She led him towards the small pond at the far end of her pen. She motioned him to hurry, and they raced along the path she'd created from her many wanderings to the pond.

"I want to show you my secret place," she called back to him as they both jogged.

When they reached the clearing around the pond, she dropped his hand. "Swim with me?" she asked coyly.

He laughed with humility. "This is how you get me naked."

She sent him a devilish stare, the lusty gleam brandishing in them like a bright shooting star. "Maybe," she said as she dipped her toes into the water.

"Clever," he retorted.

She waded in and then spun to face him. "It feels amazing. It's much warmer than the waterfall." She walked in backwards, watching him as he mulled it over. How could he possibly resist skinny dipping with her? "I promise, I won't make a pass at you."

He shook his head, a wide grin plastered on his face. "I can't believe I'm turning you down so much. My friends would be knocking me over the head with stones to wake me up."

A giggle rumbled from her belly as she sank into the pond, the water warm and calming. "It feels incredible. You should come in." She held her breath, her eagerness on edge as he set his backpack down. "It's so good," she cooed invitingly. The weightless feeling of the water was a luxury she always savored.

"Maybe I will. I could use a cool down." He began to remove his shirt, then he moved to slide his shorts down.

She held her breath as excitement at perhaps being able to see his cock flooded her. She couldn't keep her eyes off him, watching his every micro-movement.

He snuck his fingers into the waistband of his underwear, and she gasped, biting her lip. As he unveiled his cock, she bit her lip with more force, and an involuntary sigh flowed from her lips.

"Oh, yes," she muttered as his hard rod swung as he shifted his weight. Nothing could have looked more blessed.

He raised his arms. "I never said I wasn't aroused by you."

She might need to have him tie her wrists behind her back with a weed because not reaching for his cock once he was in the water near her seemed impossible. "I might not be able to behave after seeing that," she cooed seductively.

"This doesn't mean we're having sex," he said, shaking his head. "My friends would kill me if they knew I said that." The laugh he released was boisterous, and it made him even manlier.

She simply smiled at him. "I adore seeing it."

He waded into the water, his cock disappearing beneath the water as he sank in. His face melted into relaxation as he swam towards her. "You're right. This feels incredible. Nothing like the feeling."

"Nope, nothing," she agreed. She couldn't stop her smug look from making an appearance.

"What's that look for?"

"I got you to take your cock out," she tittered with a snicker.

A laugh rolled easily out of his mouth, his eyes ablaze with flirtation. "That you did."

She swam away from him, gracing her favorite part of the pond where the view beyond the trees showed the dip of the valley beyond. She had longed to walk down into it to see what secrets it held. Maybe someday she will earn that privilege.

"What do you do for a living?" he asked as he swam near her.

She had no idea what to say. She just lived. She existed. She foraged for food, made fires, cooked, sewed clothes, sang, masturbated, and slept. There was nothing else she could do. She was honest. "Survive." Memories of her first days in the forest haunted her once more. Agonizingly painful days of trying to figure out what she could eat, where she'd sleep, and how she'd protect herself, if need be, choked her into silence. She'd been resourceful and figured it all out. She'd not gotten poisoned by anything she ate, but she'd learned what to eat that made her feel good, and what didn't. In those days, she imagined her fairies coming for her when she was to be set free, and finding her dead from having eaten the wrong plant.

"Don't we all," he retorted. "I'm sorry, I didn't mean to pry."

"Oh, it's all good. I was just thinking about how hard my first days were here in the forest. I had no idea what I was doing."

"It must have been a little scary," he said with compassion.

"Yes, it really was." It wasn't enough that he was sweet, kind, and sexy, but he was so considerate too. If she were more of a doubting one, she'd think she was dreaming him up rather than vice versa.

She reached out and poked his shoulder.

"Water tag?" he asked jovially.

"Just confirming you're real and I'm not imagining you." She swam away from him with a teasing glance as he reached for her.

"I think I need that too."

She moved further away from him, maybe he needed more enticement.

They swam in the cool pond for several minutes before a cloud smothered out the sun.

She gazed upward. "Oh. It's looking dark all of a sudden. I hope it doesn't rain."

"Where do you go when it rains?"

"My house, or the cave behind the waterfall," she stated plainly. She rarely went to the other cave because it was too close for comfort to the edge.

"Hopefully that's not a rain cloud." He eyed up the sky above with concern in his eyes. "Maybe we should get out."

She agreed and nodded as she led the way out of the pond. With both of them wet and naked, her arousal at seeing his package unsheathed and moist had her so hot. She wanted to tackle him to the forest floor and ride him, but he'd made it very clear what he would and wouldn't do. She'd learned long ago that consent was everything, and also one of the sexiest things about a hookup was that willingness and desire to take the plunge into ecstasy with another. She set her chin in resolve. She'd wait until he was ready.

She strolled out as her nipples hardened in the slight breeze that swept up.

He handed her his sweatshirt again and she slipped it over her head. "Thanks. Just until I dry."

She watched him dress with longing. She just couldn't help herself.

"What's next?" he asked cheerfully.

"A snack. Let's go this way. I know a berry bush that had blueberries that were about ripe the last time I went past it. Unless the wildlife got it, we should have a decent fresh snack of them."

He followed her lead and when she dashed ahead, he kept up. Her graceful legs carried her like a leaf on the wind. As she reached the blueberry bush, she glanced up at the sky. "Seems to be lightening up again. Maybe it won't rain after all."

"Right, I hope not. It must be scary being out here in a storm."

She picked some blueberries and handed them to him. "It is, but I've found ways to stay covered." Her little house she'd spent a month on was one shelter, but not having it at first had been very scary. She'd hunker down under a shrub at the base of its trunk and ball up until the storm was over. Mostly, she'd stayed dry beneath the vegetation. Her leader had warned her of the coming cold weather, so she was quite nervous about surviving that, but she clung to the hope that she'd be freed by then. The problem was, she was in the dark about it all. She had no clue about garnering her freedom. She also had no idea of what she'd need to do to get ready for the cold weather. The blind hopelessness of her situation often paralyzed her.

"These are really good," he said, chewing.

"Yes, there's nothing like fresh picked ripe berries."

They chewed the sweet morsels of fruit as they looked into each other's eyes. Satisfying her hunger beside another person was something she hadn't been able to enjoy for quite some time. She bit into the fruit, enjoying the feelings of camaraderie as the flood of sweet juice bathed her tongue as she watched him eat. Her heart warmed as she observed his happy face as they shared the berries. She'd only remotely gotten this lovely feeling since living in the forest when she'd made the men come, when they'd made her come. Her smile strengthened. She loved being able to give him something good from her section of the forest. It was glorious to be able to offer him something too, and something other than her body. It wasn't about payback, it was more about sharing it with him.

He began to pick some berries right alongside her, but instead of popping his handful into his mouth, he fed them to her one at a time. His eyes brimmed with a happy, satisfied glow. A slow realization came over her that he seemed to enjoy taking care of her. She'd not had a boyfriend quite like him before. She chastised herself. He wasn't her boyfriend. She needed to stop her brain from going there. All of her past ones had wanted to be taken care of by her, they'd wanted her to feed them, pleasure them, and cook food for them. Leif was different, and she couldn't stop her heart from latching onto him even harder.

The bewilderment must have been apparent because he jerked his head back as a big grin flickered across his face. "Ever been fed by a man like this?"

She shook her head as she held up her handful of berries towards him. "Nope. Never." Perhaps her father had fed her like this, but she didn't have specific memories of that, plus this was not the same. It was a level of caretaking she'd instinctively felt compelled to offer others, but receiving it gave her a sense of being important, too. "They taste better from your hand than mine," she stated coyly.

"Yeah, I can understand that," he replied, a flicker of contemplation crossing his gaze. "I like taking care of you."

This sent a pang of impatience through her as she was reminded of her fate. Why couldn't he fuck her then and give her an orgasm? That was most certainly taking care of her.

The cloud overhead darkened the forest, and a crack of thunder struck the peaceful calm.

"Uh, oh," she cried. "We're in for it!" She knew this scene well.

They shifted their eyes to meet, both bulging with something ominous, just as the rain began to pour on them.

She squealed and grabbed his hand. "This way!" She yelled over the sound of the sheets of rain flooding them. The only close by shelter she knew of was the one place she didn't want to go.

Chapter 5

She pulled him along, jumping over logs and dodging trees and saplings that thrashed in the wind. The forest floor was slick with wetness within minutes. She started to slip, and he secured her from behind. Gasping, she allowed him to hold her as the rain poured on them. As he released her, she swiveled and gazed up into in eyes.

For the briefest moment, she swore he was about to kiss her, despite the torrent sheets of rain pelting them. Her heart sank as he pulled back.

She turned and pointed towards the left. "There's a small cave this way," she raised her voice to shout over the sound of the heavy rainfall.

She hurried as the water fell heavily upon them, almost slipping again on some mud.

The familiar unwelcome buzz reverberated against her body as she closed in on the cave. The closer she got, the more her ribcage shook. Her heart pounded as she winced, the sound a hum in her ears that was so loud it drowned out the sound of the rain. She ducked into the cave and the sound became muffled a little.

"Whew. Oh, thank goodness," she said panting. "That was awful." She laughed as she touched his drenched sweatshirt now encasing her breasts. "So much for putting on dry clothes." She did her best to try to ignore the threat of the buzz, but she knew her distaste shown on her face.

He shook his arms and water drops fell. "Wow, that was wild." His hair drooped over his forehead making him look even cuter.

"I knew it looked dark, but I didn't expect that torrential downpour." She shuddered.

He glanced around the cave. "Small in here. But much drier."

"Yeah, it will keep the rain off of us at least." The force of the nearby boundary invisibly repelled her like a sudden burst of a shockwave, but she stood her ground. She took a step back as she resisted, but then fell forward as if she'd been pushed.

"Oh, be careful. Step in a hole?" he asked, scanning the floor of the cave.

"No," she bit her lip, not wanting to tell him the truth.

"Let's sit," he suggested.

"Yeah," she agreed. That might be easier for her to resist the pushback of the boundary.

She moved to sit, but fell forward.

"Are you okay?" he asked, his voice brimming with concern. "Maybe you need more food?"

She shrugged as she planted her butt on the stone floor. "No, the berries were enough." She hesitated to say more, but he looked so expectant. "It's just that we're near the boundary and it's sending me warning pings."

He swiveled his head to stare at her. "You're kidding, right?"

She shook her head. "No. If you want proof, watch this." She stood up and backed up to the far wall of the cave, fighting the pressure as she moved. When she relaxed her stance, the force slammed into her and she fell forward, barely catching her balance.

"Shit," he stated in surprise. "No, shit?"

"If you needed more proof, there you go. I can't go much further. If I do, it will throw me in the air." She recalled the first time she'd tried to leave the forest. It had sent her flying so hard that she fell on her back and had gotten the wind knocked out of her. She'd carefully walked around mapping the very edge of her pen that day, and the bruises she'd suffered every time she got too close reminded her for days not to try to walk out again.

She shivered and tears sprung into her eyes.

"Come here, I'll warm you up," he insisted with his arm raised.

She slid in right next to him, savoring his warmth and closeness immediately. She hiccupped, which she always did when she was excessively nervous. Being with Leif helped somewhat, but he couldn't take down the barrier any more than she could.

He squeezed her closer and she melded against his body, his strength obvious in his hold, not to mention the muscles of his arm around her.

"I needed this. Thank you." She calmed, and her shivering stopped.

They watched the rain fall outside the mouth of the cave, the streams of water trickling a short ways into the cave, then traveling down to the lower side of the cave.

"I hope this stops soon." Then she regretted saying it. In his arms was exactly where she wanted to be.

"Yeah, at least it's not too cold out, or we'd be even more miserable right now."

She shuddered at the thought. It was another reminder to her, knowing the cold days were coming soon. And she was trapped to endure them. Then she wasn't sure she'd survive. She kept hoping her leader would have pity on her and come and release her before the cold weather took hold. He couldn't be that heartless. What she'd done wasn't that bad to warrant such torture.

"I'm not sure how cold it gets here," she said nervously.

"You aren't from here?" he asked incredulously. "I guess I just assumed you were from here, too."

She shook her head. "No."

They sat not talking, while listening to the rain pelt the earth.

She yawned. "Geez, the water sounds are making me sleepy," she chuckled at herself. "I'm a weakling. I've gotten used to afternoon naps."

"Oh, I love naps." He paused and rubbed her shoulder with his fingers. "Should we take one? I mean, why not? It's raining anyway. We could recharge."

She nodded, feeling strange that she felt so comfortable with him, comfortable enough to consider sleep. But she wondered if she'd be able to let her guard down and actually fall asleep. That was the question. But no matter if she didn't, closing her eyes would feel incredible. "Yes, let's do it."

He situated himself on his side, without getting too close to the rain, or the back wall of the cave. He motioned for her to snuggle in, and she pressed her full front to his. Within less than a minute, she felt his cock begin to thicken.

He cleared his throat. "Might be hard to sleep with that."

"For you and me both!" she said with exuberance.

She snuggled her head into his chest and closed her eyes. Listening to his breathing, feeling his hard-on pressed to her body, and hearing the rain, which seemed like it was getting lighter, and she drifted off to sleep.

SHE WOKE AND PULLED away from Leif, quickly sitting up. The rain had stopped, and the sun was shining again outside the mouth of the cave. Her first thoughts were about how much time had passed. Was she shrinking yet? She most definitely was sensing the passage of significant time the more she became fully awake. She looked at her legs. It was impossible to tell from looking, but she didn't yet feel the usual tugs on her body when she shrank.

She sighed in relief. That was a good sign.

"You okay?" Leif asked as he sat up next to her.

"Yeah, I'm just wondering how long we were asleep." She couldn't shake the worry, though. Her time was running out.

Leif pulled his phone out and tapped it on. "We slept for an hour and a half."

"Wow. That was a good nap." She stood abruptly and ran to the entrance of the cave. She peered out, then stepped into the sunshine. "Oh, this feels wonderful." She stripped the still-wet sweatshirt off and twirled in the warmth of the sunshine.

Leif joined her. "Yeah, it does." He eyed her up and down. "Not giving my cock a chance to ever settle down, are you?" he asked with a scoff.

"No! What I need is you aroused, remember?" Blue balls might get him more willing to drain them.

"Oh, I couldn't forget, Gabriella. That's literally not possible." He took the sweatshirt from her and shoved it into his backpack.

"You could hang that on a tree in the sunshine to dry. I'll show you a good one for it." She sprinted off across the forest towards the clearing near her little home. The breeze and flickering sunshine tickled her flesh as she zoomed along, her breasts flopping freely as she dashed. She could hear Leif following close behind her, his feet smacking the ground. The burst of exercise energized her and she felt unhinged as she coasted along.

When she finally reached the clearing, she pointed to a low bush. "Toss it on there. It will dry quickly in the hot sun."

He did as she suggested, and then approached her. "Quite the storm, but now it's the calm after." The leaves were still wet in the lower trees and bushes, reflecting the bright sunshine back upwards.

"It feels so fresh now. I love it after the storm is over." She was hungry again. "Let's find something to eat." Being big was so much more work because she ate bigger portions of food. That had been one drawback to when she'd grown big, but it had happened so infrequently, and never lasted, that she'd never had trouble with not having enough food. She had stores of acorns, seeds, and dried flowers stored up and buried in the dirt to last for a while. She hoped.

"I have some protein bars." He unzipped his backpack, rummaged inside, and pulled out four. As he handed two to her, he asked, "Need more than two? I have four more in here."

She shook her head. "No. You should save them. I think two will be enough." She took the bars from him with a wide smile. "Thank you. I haven't been taken care of like this for a very long time." She couldn't get over how comforting it was to have Leif around. It made her calm, yet excited at the same time. She grabbed his hand urgently. "Let's eat them by the river."

They walked hand-in-hand until they reached the river. She led him to a sunny patch near the edge of the water, and they sat on the plush grass. It felt warm and moist beneath her bare ass cheeks.

She knew Leif must be feeling the effects of his blue balls by now, but he didn't seem ready to launch into a hookup with her yet, which was very concerning. But once he saw her shrinking, then he might believe her and agree to have sex. It frustrated her because he was clearly aroused, but he wouldn't act on his feelings.

She tore into the bar and sank her teeth into it. The first bite was immediately gratifying, and she chewed behind her happy smile. They ate in silence. After she was done, she leaned back on her arms and raised her face towards the sun. "Mmm. Very delicious. I'm full and in the sun. That makes me so happy."

He caught her glance and nodded. "Yup. Very true."

She frowned when an unpleasant distracted look settled on his face.

"I'm going to have to leave soon, Gabriella. Will you come with me?" he asked, a pained, skeptical look on his face.

She slumped her shoulders. "What time is it?" She knew, but she wanted him to know also.

He pulled out his phone. "It's five thirty."

She jerked back. "Let's go to the tree. I should be shrinking by now. Then you'll see."

She hopped up and ran the short distance to the tree he had marked her height on. At first glance, her heart sank. To her eye, she didn't look shorter than the cut mark. She lined up her body against the tree, her whole being filled with worry.

"I'm shorter, right?" she asked, as her heart pounded. She just had to be shrinking by now. She should be.

He leaned in closer and touched the cut above her head, his fingers on her scalp. "Nope. You're the same height, honey." His eyes were filled with tenderness and compassion as he trailed his forefinger down her cheek. "Come with me, I can help you. I want to help you. Please, Gabriella."

She balled up her fists and stomped, her eyes clouding. "I don't understand this. Every time I shrink, and this time I'm not?" She paced back and forth as he watched. "This makes no sense. This has happened every single time." She wracked her brain trying to think of what she'd done differently this time to not be shrinking. "I'm not crazy!"

"I don't know," he said in an unsure tone. "Maybe we just start walking and see what happens." He shrugged.

She knew exactly what would happen. She'd be flung backwards. But then he'd believe her more. She thought for sure after the cave that he'd believed her.

"We could just start walking, and not stop until we reach my car, and then you could come with me to my mom's house." His eyes brimmed with kindness as he chuckled with mischief. "But we will need to stop at a store so I can buy you some clothes. I don't think my mom would be happy with me bringing a naked woman home to her."

She nodded. That made sense. Her brain spun and her logic struggled to keep up. She surely could not meet his mother naked, though, he was right. She shook her head rapidly. "It won't work, though, I'm telling you."

"Let's try," he urged gently, reaching his hand out to take hers. "I promise I won't force you to come with me if you change your mind."

She supposed this would confirm it for him, so she shrugged her shoulders. "Okay."

He grabbed the hanging sweatshirt and they started across the denser part of the forest. They dodged trees, bushes, rotting logs, and finally reached the path they'd first met on. She glanced ahead, knowing exactly where she'd get tossed backwards. It wouldn't take long for them to reach that spot, and this pointless exercise would be over.

They walked, holding hands. The sun was hot, and the breeze was light. The blacktop began to feel too hot beneath her feet and she squeaked, dashing for the grass. "Damn, that's getting hot on my feet."

He moved to the edge and reached for her hand. "I'll walk on the edge, and you can stay on the grass."

They walked along, exchanging glances every thirty seconds, both of them smiling.

"I like this," he said with a full grin.

She returned his expression. "Me too," she said demurely. It wasn't a lie. She felt so cozy being near him, her hand in his. There was no place she'd rather be. But she was voting for not walking to the edge of her range.

Before long, they neared the spot she knew she'd get snagged on. The dread grew in her with each step. She knew it was going to hurt. As they got closer, she slowed her movements.

"What's wrong?" he asked as wonder filled him.

"We're getting closer, and I know it's going to hurt when I bounce back, so I'm kind of scared." She planted her feet and stared at the tree she knew passing by would put her in the danger zone.

"It's right there. Twenty feet ahead." She gazed at the forest, knowing that, to him, it looked like every other section of the forest. "I know, it looks the same, but I can feel it. And I just know."

He turned to face her. "If you don't want to come with me now, it's okay." He stared her squarely in the eyes. "How about this? I leave, go see my mom, then I will go buy you some clothes, and bring them back tonight?" He looked so sincere.

Him offering his time and money to help her was very sweet. It touched her in a way she hadn't felt since years ago at home when her mom used to make her meals and take her places.

She drew in a big breath, then released it. "Okay. That might be best." Her heart sank. This meant he was leaving her soon. She instantly wanted to cry, but masked it by smiling. "You're so kind to offer all of that to me." Only she knew it wouldn't do any good. But on the other hand, it would be nice to have at least one big outfit she could wear whenever she did get big again. Her worry escalated. "But if you can't find me, please just talk so I can find you, in case I'm really small when you come back. I'll probably sense you when we are near each other again." She hoped she would, but being smaller, she really had no clue how close he would need to get for her to sense him.

"Gonna sing for me? I'd love to hear you sing again."

She nodded. She pressed her nude body to his front and draped her arms around him. "One kiss before you go?" she pleaded with her tone, and with her eyes. It very well could be her last.

His mouth slid into a sexy grin. "You bet." He wrapped his arms around her, too.

She lifted her face upwards, parting her mouth.

He opened his mouth, and they were nearly touching just as she was closing her eyes.

They collided, smashing their mouths together, his tongue finding the inside of her mouth quickly. Their tongues caressed each other, their bodies moving in rhythm together as their kiss deepened.

She moaned as her arousal was peaking, and moaned louder yet as she felt his cock thicken against her belly. Having his mouth engaged with hers was the lightning she'd been missing. It was as if she'd never really kissed anyone before. Not like this.

He groaned and she erupted. It manifested as her mauling his biceps, his back, and grabbing his scalp. She needed all of him at once.

His hands groped her backside, her lower back, and held her head. He was as frantic as she was.

Their hands were everywhere on each other, hungry, wanton, ready to ignite into more.

He pulled away. "Whew, shit!" he gasped. "It's really hard to stop. But we have to."

"Why stop?" she pleaded. "We want each other. We both want more. Please, let's."

He shook his head. "I'll be back, Gabriella. I promise you."

"What if you can't find me? I fear I will shrink so small this time I might disappear." Her voice was so desperate, how could he even consider leaving her?

"You won't," he assured as he backed away, down the path, away from her.

It hurt so bad. Watching him insist on going, and then following through with it, tore her heart to shreds. It was agony to see him leaving. With every fiber, she wanted to rush him and grab him, convince him to stay with her, but as he crossed by the big pine tree just before the boundary, she knew she had lost all her power. She was nothing more than a leaf on the strength of the wind, victim to the weather. And she had no way of assessing what the forecast was. She'd have to just live it, blind, alone, and waiting desperately for something she didn't know would ever actually happen. He could get hit by a bus and die. He could get in a car accident and be sent to the hospital, get amnesia, and forget all about her.

Her mind spiraled to all the worst things, and she ran into the woods, not daring to look back. She couldn't watch him walk away any longer. She couldn't bear it. Tears streamed down her face, and she cried out to the sky, her arms outstretched, her heart breaking and aching all at once. She wondered where her blood would flow once her heart was fully broken.

Chapter 6

She walked along slowly, seeking the tree Leif had marked her height on. Once she reached it, she stood with her back to it and reached up, dreading what she'd feel with her fingers. The notch in the tree was now two inches above her head. She crumpled forward as tears and a horrid-sounding yell burst from her body.

"Why now?" she screamed into the forest. "Why not when he was here?" She fell to the forest floor and curled into a ball, waiting for the rest of the shrinking of her body to consume her. How long would it take this time? Would she blip out of existence? The terror of it all filled her, but most of all, the terror of not being with Leif again sent her into a wild panic.

She stood up and paced about rapidly, her flee instincts taking over her logic. She needed to do something. But she'd already tried everything she could think of the last few times she shrank, and it never stopped the process. If he didn't hurry back with the clothes, not only would she not fit in them, she might be smaller than a pebble. Or worse, gone!

She jumped up and down, shaking her hands. She was screwed. She screamed again, the tone of agony in her cry consuming her with how desperate and alone she sounded. How could she go from feeling so full, satiated, and perfectly cozy to this wretched way? How could she go from feeling loved to... she paused and froze in place. Loved? Was that legit? She doubted it. That was ridiculous. What she needed was sex, his cock, and to climax.

She gasped harder, wanting to deny she'd had the thought, but she couldn't. She'd thought it. But more, she'd felt it. Still felt it. She shook her head as the realization that an ember of something had been born in her belly. It was something she couldn't deny. He couldn't love her if he couldn't see her. Her breathing kicked up another notch, her stomach hurt, and her thoughts muddied.

There was nothing worse than believing in something she'd never get again.

She cradled her body, shivering and shuddering despite the warm sun on her flesh. The warm sun that had just gifted her and Leif a lovely protein bar picnic by the river now did nothing to warm her up.

She felt a tugging and unfurled her body to lay flat. She was shrinking at a faster rate than normal. She hurried to stand against the tree and sure enough, she'd already lost another few inches.

Despair claimed her and she began to run back to the path. Maybe she could see a speck of Leif off in the distance. She rushed through the woods only to have her hopes dashed. He was long gone. All that was in her vision ahead was an empty path, to somewhere she couldn't go to find him.

She tried to calm herself by rubbing her arms. She sat on the grassy patch beside the path, wrapped her arms around her bent legs, and rocked. She closed her eyes and sniffed the air, hoping to catch a whiff of his scent.

She cleared her mind as best she could and took in a deep breath. She popped her eyes open. There! There it was! She smelled him. He hadn't left the park yet.

She leapt to her feet and her heart began to burst with joy as she sang. She sang with all her body, heart, and soul. If she did it loud enough, surely he'd come back.

Another tug gripped her, and she felt herself shrink again. It was a significant shift, and her heart dropped.

"Damnit!" she screamed. "Not so fast!" she pleaded. "Give me a fucking chance!" she screamed.

She planted her feet and began to sing again. This time the added desperation helped her lift her voice higher. Surely, he would come now, if he were near enough to hear her. She sang for several minutes, but when she didn't see him returning, she slumped to the path, her body sagging into a pile.

After a few minutes of feeling sorry for herself, she walked back to her home. It would be way too far to walk if she waited to cover the distance being small. She'd not make it by nightfall. She drudged along, making her way, sensing that with how fast she was shrinking, he'd not make it back in time.

She sat by her tiny house and set her mind to knowing she'd have to just sit and endure helplessly shrinking until she was small enough to go inside. She'd fling herself on her bed and cry until nothing happened, then she'd cry some more.

She heard a voice that sounded like Leif in the distance, but she figured she was imagining things. Her wishing so hard had her by its maniacal paws. She'd officially gone insane.

But the voice grew louder and sounded worried. She rose to her feet and began to walk in the direction she heard it coming from.

It was Leif!

She burst into song. Her heart soared and she all out ran towards him, still trying to sing as she ran. Her heart pounded and glee filled her. He was coming back! Her singing had worked.

They collided, their mouths opening and engaging in a short burst of a French kiss. He was breathing so heavily, he was having difficulty kissing her, but put his mouth back on hers.

She pulled away after several minutes of their breathy mouthlock. "You came back!" she cooed. "Come, I want to show you."

"I heard you. I was almost to my car. And then your voice sounded sad, then it stopped. So, I ran back," he said between pants, still unable to catch his breath.

She snatched his hand and pulled him towards the tree. "Come. I will show you. I'm shrinking fast. We don't have much time."

She hurried along, feeling the extreme urgency of showing him her new height to be of the utmost importance. It was imperative that he see the evidence for himself. She swore she'd felt a blip of growth as they kissed, and she wanted to confirm it.

At the tree, she lined up beneath the cut mark and felt the bark above her head.

She screeched. "I'm bigger, but not as big as when you were gone." She looked at him with widened eyes. "It's you. Your presence is doing this. I know it!"

He leaned in to examine the cut in the bark. His face grew puzzled, and more so as he fingered the slit in the tree.

"How the hell ..." He looked down into her eyes with his own full of astonishment. "If I hadn't made the cut myself, I'd be doubting this right now." His face showed how confused he truly was.

She grabbed his torso and stared into his eyes. "See! Now do you believe me? Make love to me, Leif. Right here, right now. You will save me from shrinking into nothingness. Please!" she pleaded. "It's true. You can see the proof for yourself."

He held her face between his hands. "Yes, and I can tell you are shorter when we are close. I first noticed it when we kissed, but I thought I was crazy for thinking it."

He pulled her against him, and they fell into a hungry kiss again. This time he showed more aggression in his kissing. He'd clearly held back before, and he kissed her with greater fervor, his eyes as ablaze as hers. He seemed to be unleashing his true desire for her.

She groped his body as he palmed her bottom. He squeezed her butt cheeks as he smashed her body harder against his. His erection felt full and packed against her soft belly. She wanted nothing more than to have it caressing her insides, reaching into her where she couldn't touch herself.

His kisses traveled down her neck, allowing his passion to be felt by her. It was beautiful. It was so delicious to see the hunger in his eyes and to see him indulging in his lust for her.

"Yes, yes, yes," she chanted as he suckled all down her neck and began to plant ardent kisses on her chest.

He groped her right breast, fingering her pert nipple, pinching it, and tugging it away from her body.

She leaned back in response to his tugging, her mouth remaining open in a soft moan.

He savored her bare flesh with his mouth, suckling his way down the round mound of her breast, across the pink puckered skin of her tightened nipple, then took the peak of it into his mouth. He sucked hard, elongating her nip to the back of his throat. He deep-throated her nipple as he played with her other one.

She writhed against his body as he fed on her nipple.

When he took his teeth to her tit, she winced, giggled, then sighed while cradling the back of his head against her breast.

He released her nipple, then licked along the valley of her cleavage to mount her other breast, quickly licking the map of her tightened nipple flesh to consume her peak. He did the same nipple play on that breast as she caressed his head, leaned back, and clung to him as he shifted in his suckling of her.

He smacked his mouth on her nip only to retake it back up into his mouth.

After another few minutes of tit-sucking, he came off her breast and stood up to his full height to kiss her again. They kissed as their desire for each other grew in their more ardent grabs.

"I can't get enough of you," he murmured into her flesh.

She mewled, "Yes, can't get enough of you."

She clawed at the top of his shorts trying to undo the button. It popped free and she sought the tag of the zipper, then quickly yanked it down. She grasped the waist of his shorts and gave a tug. They fell to his knees, he shifted his legs, and they fell to the dirt below.

They continued to kiss, their sounds of enjoying each other filling the air. His hungry grunts made her clit pulse and thicken.

He took a step back and removed his shirt. As he stuck his fingers into the waistband of his underwear, she raised her hands up.

"Please, can I do it?" she asked seductively, the fuck-me glow in her eyes shining like a beacon.

He grinned with relish. "Please do."

She stepped forward and curled her fingers into his underwear, and slowly dragged them down to pop his cock out. It swung once it was free of the fabric. She lowered them to the ground and knelt in front of him, so her face was even with his raging boner.

"Mmmm, I want it," she said, her eyes shifting back and forth across his erection, her fingers twitching with her want.

She grabbed his shaft with one hand and his balls with the other. She played with his balls, watching his face for signs of enjoyment. She pressed a little harder as he expressed himself in a louder groan. She cupped his balls, then began to move her hand along his shaft, collecting his precum as stroking juice with each up and down motion.

She worked harder when she saw his eyes rolling back. She wanted him to have so much pleasure from her hands that he'd feel as if he were flying.

She leaned closer and took his cock head in her mouth, amazed still that he was finally giving in to her pleas. They were going to fuck; she was practically crawling out of her skin with eagerness. She forced herself to be patient and savor his cock, licking her tongue all around his frenulum.

"Oh, Gawd, yes," he said with a manly moan, pressing his fingers along her scalp.

This is what she craved too, to make him cry out in pleasure. She sucked his cockhead while alternating her other hand to play with his balls and stroke his shaft.

After a few minutes, he pulled himself out of her mouth by stepping back. Then he took a return step back, grabbed her shoulders, and pressed her to lean back.

"You need to come," he said with determination. "Right? You need to come?" He snickered with a single nod of his head. "Hell with that, I'm making you come."

"Yes, and with your cock in me, too." She smiled demurely. "I like it hard."

He grinned wickedly and dove into her spread thighs. He wasn't gentle as he rushed her pussy. He moved with insistence, as if their lives depended on him, and she cried out when he latched onto her labia lips with a strong force. He sucked along her outer lips while manhandling her thighs.

She squirmed trying to get his mouth on her special hot spot. "Please," she pleaded as she fondled his head.

Like a scoundrel, he stole into her sensitive area and blessed her with a full suction of his mouth over her clit.

She arched her back and yelled as he sucked her bean with conviction. She closed her eyes as her body thrashed through his clit worshipping, and when he began to play around with her slit, she cried out louder.

"Yes, please," she murmured lightly tossing her head back and forth, her eyes rolling back. "Oh, fuck yes." She moaned, and was openly expressing her pleasure when he applied the perfect pressure to push her along.

He maintained that satiating suction while pressing two fingers into her. Her pussy was responding with wetness, and his fingers slid right in. He rode her hole with his fingers while sucking her and she ramped up her climactic hill in a rush. She was tipped over the edge into her orgasm, and her body instinctively began to curl around his head. Clawing at him, her sounds escalated. She grasped at his hair, pulling it in chunks as the orgasm wave radiated out of her womb and spread across her body, making it twitch and sputter.

Relief also flooded her as she had sensed no further shrinking tugs. The combo of relief and orgasmic bliss was a level of euphoria she'd never been blessed with before. And she was hooked.

She moaned in elation, then fell silent as the peak of the orgasm stretched into a second peak as she reached a full climax again.

She'd submitted to the pleasure he was giving her, and now all she needed was his cock in her so she could climax again. This time she was enjoying the process, and not so much focused on the end result. She wanted her lovemaking with Leif to go on and on.

He rose off her pelvis, the skin around his mouth and his nose tip wet with her juices. He descended between her spread legs and readied his cock to enter her. His eyes glowed with fire and excitement.

She didn't hold back either, their desire for each other mirrored between them.

"Fuck me, Leif," she said with intensity. "Fuck me with all you've got."

He didn't say a word, but gave her a salacious gleam, and lined up his cock to touch the flesh of her entrance. He pressed himself inside her, the penetration of his head into her slit causing them both to groan.

It was the most incredible feeling to have Leif's cock finally in her and she welcomed every speck of his sex drive. She wanted to see all of it, all of his yearnings, all of his horny drive.

"Give it to me, Leif, I want all of it. All of you." She didn't mask her feelings blaring in her eyes. "Don't hold back a bit. I'll love it all."

He began to ride her body, pumping his cock in and out of her ever faster with virile vigor. Her moans mingled with his, then peppered with his growls as he sped up, then slowed down his thrusting.

They fucked missionary until Leif pulled out.

He wiped his mouth and licked his lips as he backed up on his hands and knees. With his eyes glued to hers, he oozed a robust dominance that soothed her inner self. "Doggy," he said in a gruff voice.

She scrambled to position herself on her hands and knees and eagerly waited for him to penetrate her again. She trembled, so ready to receive him inside her again.

He caressed her hips and ass, then gripped her more forcefully. "Going to ride you hard until you twitch."

She believed him. "Yes, please, put it in me," she cooed as she dropped her head down. Her breasts hung below her, and as he aligned himself with her, she swayed her hips to entice him further with her wet holes.

She lowered her front half down further to open her slit up for him more. He pressed his cock to part her sealed lips and inserted himself.

He began to thrust himself against her ass at a fast rate, the smacking sounds of him slamming into her ass filling her ears. He rode her hard and fast, grunting as he pounded. The rhythm of him rocking her body shoved her to a place where her dreams met her hopes. This was it.

He reached around her right hip and began to play with her clit. She moaned louder and he pressed her swollen womanhood with faster rubbing.

All the stimulation clicked into that perfection she needed, and as he rammed into her harder and rubbed her clit faster, her arousal rose up and her climax was won. She'd reached that coveted point of no return. She shuddered as he kept up his steady strength and she soared into the full peak of her big O. She rode the wave, feeling so very grateful he'd returned to her.

As she calmed, he gripped her hips with both hands and thrust into her with such force that she once again fell limp like a flaccid doll, her head and shoulders crashing to the forest floor. Her face rubbed the dirt as he fucked her into his own climax. When he released his seed into her, his cock moved inside her easier with the increased wetness, until he began to soften.

He pulled himself out of her and dove to the ground beside her. She crumpled to the earth herself, feeling fully spent, and ideally perfect. She felt solid that she was surely her full height now, and that was all Leif's doing.

They both lay still, panting, for thirty seconds before he reached for her.

"Come here, baby. I need you." He pulled her body flush with his and they melted into each other.

She felt the same, but was too overwhelmed to speak.

The sun still beat down on them, but it was lower in the sky.

"You did it," she said softly. "You fucked me into an orgasm. I feel full size."

He stretched his neck to look more squarely at her. "You're, okay? We stopped it?"

She nodded. "Yes. We did. You did."

He laughed with relief. "Oh, well, fuck. I seriously didn't believe you." He tossed his head back as he shoved a hand through his tousled hair. "I wanted to believe, but come on, this is truly unbelievable."

"I know it is," she said pressing her lips together. "But there are so many mysteries we don't even know about in this world that are even far more unfathomable than little ol' me."

He touched her cheek. "Your face is dirty."

She mused a giggle. "Yeah, that's evidence of how good you fucked me."

He scoffed. "All the evidence I need is that look on your face."

She reached up and touched his cheek. "And yours." She held his face as she peered into his eyes. "You wanted me the whole time, didn't you?"

He released a big laugh. "Hell yes, I did. I admitted that, remember? But I couldn't do it. Not like that."

"Well, you did now. You're an amazing man and an amazing lover." She nestled her head against his shoulder and played with his chest hair. "That was the best sex I've ever had. And I'm not lying."

"Yeah." He snuggled her flush against him. "You are magic."

She squirmed slightly in his arms. "We're magic, together," she corrected.

After a few minutes of silence, he broke it. "So, what happens now?"

"I don't know," she said sadly. "I'm still stuck here. But now you can come see me, and find me, because I won't be tiny."

"Won't you shrink again?"

"You will have to keep coming back and fucking me!" she exclaimed with a laugh laced in her words.

"Well, I can certainly do that. But maybe I just stay."

"What about your mom?"

"How about this idea? I go home, I'll go buy some camping stuff, then come back. We can sleep together in the tent. My mom will just think I decided to camp." He had a calm relaxed look. "My mom will understand," he assured.

She rose up on an elbow. "Are you sure you want to do that, though?"

He nodded with assurance in his eyes. "Yes. I'm very sure. We'll figure this out together, Gabriella." He sat up. "But I'd better get going. It won't be daylight forever."

"Right," she said as she sat as well. "I'll be here. Obviously." She shrugged. She felt happy. Truly happy. "And you'll buy me some big clothes still?" She regretted she couldn't offer to help pay for it. "I'll suck your dick and give you sexual favors if you do." She gave him a flirty teasing smile.

"Sold! But I have a feeling you'd do all that either way," he said with a laugh.

She smiled wide. "You're right."

He kissed her on the lips and held her face. "I will be back. Don't leave."

"I can't leave." She cocked her head as an amused expression overcame her.

"Ok, we'll try to figure that out too." He stood up and began to dress. He pulled the damp sweatshirt out of his bag and tossed it to her. "You can hang that to dry more. But I'll be back with better clothes for you soon."

He grabbed his wallet out of his backpack and tucked it into his pocket. "I'll leave my pack so you can eat the bars if you're hungry." He paused. "Dang, I've got to buy food too, don't I? I'd better run." He waved and took off in a jog through the obstacle course of the woods, heading toward the direction of the path.

She felt confident he'd be back soon, though she couldn't help but feel a bit like a burden. She was high maintenance to the max. But at the same time, it was so incredibly cozy to have someone like Leif who wanted to do things for her.

Chapter 7

She played with a strand of grass absentmindedly as she stared off into the distance. She couldn't stop hoping every second that she'd catch a glimmer of Leif returning. She wished she could help him carry the gear at the very least. How would he carry it all by himself? Her fears were getting the best of her, making her jittery. Every forest sound startled her, which was never usually the case.

Relief had settled upon her after the sex, but there were so many other problems that she had a hard time staving off falling into hopelessness. Leif had many tasks to accomplish that could easily go wrong. Plus, time was still of the essence, too.

If Leif never came back, she wondered if she'd stay big, or would she start to shrink again? Was it the land that was cursed, or her?

A bird cawed to her left and she jumped. She hadn't felt this out of sorts since she'd first arrived. Her brain swarmed with worried thoughts. What if Leif changes his mind? What if Leif can't find her again? What if she starts shrinking before he's back? What if Leif dies?

She smoothed her cheeks with her palms. She was letting her anxiety make her irrational. There needed to be a better way for her to spend her time waiting than staring at the river as worry consumed her. She set off for the berry bushes with plans to pick some for them to add to whatever food Leif brought. It was super fun to think of having another person with her in the forest, especially a sexy man who seemed to care about her. She was thanking her lucky stars that Leif had followed her voice to begin with.

After several hours of picking berries and gathering kindling, she made a pile of her spoils. She was happy to not have to be collecting bugs to eat. She'd never gotten used to that and had cringed as she'd crunched on their bodies. Plus, she didn't like taking their lives from them. She hopped up and began to pace, the motion of the air swirling around her as she moved swiftly brought a scent of Leif.

She jumped up in the air and cheered. He was coming back! She dashed beyond the drying sweatshirt and kept sniffing the air, tracking him like a dog to ensure it wasn't the sweatshirt with his scent on it that she'd noticed.

Nope. It was really him! It got stronger as she approached the path.

She burst onto the clearing near the side of the path and directed her eyes off into the distance. She cheered again as she noticed something moving along in the distance. It looked bigger and wider than Leif, but then she supposed that was the gear.

She danced in place and began to sing, her voice calling to her new lover like the sun licks the land upon a sunrise. She elevated her voice with joy as the tiny Leif got bigger and bigger.

As he approached, she noticed he was pulling a wagon. That made sense, but then she felt worse, because he had to buy everything plus a wagon that might never get used again. Her heart leapt as she sang and watched. But he'd done it. And that was monumental. Nothing else mattered except that Leif was on his way to her.

After several minutes, he finally arrived with an overpacked wagon hauling the bogged-down load behind him.

"There's my beautiful fairy siren woman," he said with a happy grin. "Looking sexy as ever."

She scoffed with a smirk. "Well, I am naked," she said tittering a laugh.

He dug in the wagon and pulled out a plastic bag. He opened it and pulled out an emerald green, deep purple, and magenta sundress. "I had fun shopping for you."

"Oh!" she squealed. "I love it! It's beautiful!" She snatched the silky dress from his hands and slipped it over her head. "It's just about perfect."

"It looks stunning on you." He beamed. "I had to do hand motions to describe your size to the saleswoman in the boutique."

"You went into a women's clothing store just for me?" The gesture made her insides melt. She'd assumed he'd have just bought her boring hiking gear to wear from the store he bought the tent from. But for him to go to an actual women's clothing store floored her.

"Yeah. Well, I wanted help with your sizing, so I figured that was the best bet." He ran his eyes up and down her body. "It suits you. I knew it would match your eyes." He pulled her into a hug and kissed her on the lips. "The woman said if I'd been shopping for my mom, a sister, or an aunt or something, she'd have asked me out considering I was in such a store to buy things for a woman."

Hope grew a glittery sheen inside her heart. She was someone to him. "Really? Wow! That's really incredible." She'd assumed her chances of finding such a relationship as this once she'd been sent to the forest were over. She couldn't stop staring back at him with awe in her eyes. "You're incredible."

"I think you're incredible." He kissed her on the nose. "Now, let's get this tent set up before it gets dark on us." He returned his attention to the wagon, then pulled it to the edge of the forest. "I guess we'll have to carry it all in."

The wagon was piled with a tent, a sleeping bag, several bags of food, and water.

She glanced inside the clothing bag. He'd also purchased a pair of pants, shorts, a tank top, a sweatshirt, and shoes for her. "You've spent a fortune on all this." Her guilt started to rise.

"Hey, I wanted to. Plus, we'll reuse the tent, sleeping bag, and the wagon." He grinned brilliantly at her. "When we camp again."

'We' resounded in her head. Her heart burst with new hopes, new excitement for the future. One with Leif, no doubt, and with determination to find a way out of her pen.

They quickly set up the pop-up tent, laid out the double-wide sleeping bag inside, set out some bottles of water alongside, then readied to start a fire.

"I bought easy stuff to eat, mostly dehydrated camping meals, but I also snagged some beef jerky." He produced a bag plump with dried beef.

"Oh, I haven't had anything like that in ages." She eagerly took the bag from him and the first sinking of her teeth into the tasty dried meat coated her with feelings of luxury. "I feel so spoiled."

"You deserve it." He looked proud. "I'm just so happy I can provide this for you after all you've been through."

"Was your mom mad?" She chomped on another piece of dried beef as he messed with the fire.

"No, I told her I'd make it up to her by making her dinner. I bit my tongue. Wanted to tell her about you."

Gabriella wondered what his mom would think if she knew the truth. But she shoved that worry aside. She didn't think things could get any better, until she remembered her prison would prevent her from ever meeting Leif's mom and stop her from even dating Leif. He'd have to come to her. There'd be no dinner or movie dates, no walks through a park, no stops for an ice cream cone. Those hopes were dashed for her.

"You don't look the way I thought you would," he said softly.

"Leif, I don't think you really believe me that I can't leave. I've tried. It's not possible." She watched the fire crackle and pop as it took off. The defeated feeling of being incarcerated was blaring its control over her again.

He patted her leg. "I know, but now I'm here. I'm very resourceful, and I never give up."

That did make her feel better, but she knew he believed in a pipe dream. He had no special powers to break down the invisible walls, no more than she did anymore. If her powers returned, maybe, but there was no sign of that.

They made a dinner of camping meals and bananas, which tasted like heaven to her, and they finished the meal with a cookie each. She grinned at him through the dimming sunshine. He was perfect. This was all she needed forever. But she couldn't trap him with her. He needed more than she could offer.

"When are we going to bed?" she cooed, her libido awakening now that they'd eaten, and she had the joy of just staring at her man. She couldn't stop her wishful thinking knowing a comfy sleeping bag was waiting for them not more than fifteen feet away.

He scooted towards her, his arms reaching for her. "I'm ready. But first I want to kiss you by the fire."

The flames flashed against his flesh as she settled herself upon his lap.

"Now that's what I'm talking about," he murmured, as his hands claimed her back.

He caressed her backside as he pulled her into a kiss, which deepened quickly. Their mouth sounds ruined the calm of the evening, but her sex drive was nothing but calm. She writhed on his lap, savoring every bit of herself against him, his arms cradling her, his cock thickening against her pubic mound. Primal stirrings stoked her passion for him higher and soon she was sliding her hands up his shirt.

He mirrored her by slipping his hands up her sundress. "Your nipples look incredible beneath this dress," he whispered before kissing her neck. "Confession. I didn't buy a bra on purpose."

She giggled as she writhed, loving every one of his touches. "I don't remember the last time I wore one."

"Good. The dreadful things should all be burned worldwide." He cupped her breast and squeezed it. After a good groping, he held her tight to him and stood up, carrying her towards the tent.

She tightened her legs around his hips, her hands clasped behind his neck.

They kissed as he walked slowly, their sensual touches growing ever more ravenous, igniting their mutual desire for each other.

He set her down at the tent entrance.

She bent over to grasp the zipper for the door, and his hands went right to fondling her ass. She giggled and shook her hips in response to his grabs as she pulled the zipper up. They fell inside in a rush, their arousal matching as they aggressively devoured each other's bodies with their hands.

Leif broke free to zip the door closed, then promptly reached for the hem of her sundress, pulling it off her in one quick swoop. With a wicked expression, he dove into her breasts, his tongue licking, tasting, and running around her flesh. He consumed her right nipple, suckled, then moved on to her left.

She worked at getting his clothes off, but he was so busy sucking her titties, that she was unsuccessful. She giggled as she played with his hair as he continued his mouth play on her breasts.

"I can't ever get enough of your breasts. I'm obsessed," he whispered against her flesh before he ate her nip once more, his hands pressing on her back. He paused to strip his clothes off in a flash, then came right back at her with a lewd grin.

She leaned her head back as he tit-molested her, his body draped over hers. She squirmed and cried out as his free hand pressed the cleft of her pussy. As he worked his fingers downward, her moans escalated. She allowed her voice to show exactly how she felt as moans, sighs, and nonsensical word utterings fled her lips.

He began to pump his fingers inside her wet hole, a primal grunt bursting forth. He worked her clit hard as he stimulated her nips, each getting a fair turn. She sank into the luxury of a man determined to make her climax. She rode that slick hill with lightning speed and launched into a delicious orgasm. Her body shook with pleasure as she rode the high like a pro.

As her body settled, her twitching stopping. He pulled his fingers from her pussy and rose off her tit. He lightly slapped both her hips with his open palms and said in a gruff order, "Doggy."

With the sex hormones now swimming in her body, she dreamily rolled over and got up on her hands and knees.

"Yeah, head down, babe. Going to rail you, make you my cumslut. I want your cum on my fat cock before I creampie you."

The gruff dirty talk packed a punch to her desire, and she obeyed with delight, dropping her head so her cheek rested upon the plush sleeping bag.

He secured her hips between his hands. Then, as one hand left her body, she knew he was about to guide his beefy manhood into her waiting cunt.

"Yes," she cooed. "Want your cock in me, Leif."

He entered her, and they both groaned out with deep enjoyment. It felt so fucking good.

He began to ride her, the sound of their bodies colliding filling the tent. The flickering of the fire outside the tent added to the magic as they fucked. He grunted and groaned. She loved that her body gave him as much pleasure as it gave her. She savored him rocking her body. She reached beneath herself and rubbed her clit ferociously, bringing her climax quickly.

Her torso curled the little bit it could as her pussy walls took charge, sending their yummy contractions. Her internal walls clamped down on his cock as she came, and he yelled out in response.

"Oh, fuck," he said as he took his full pleasure from her with a few more thrusts.

He groaned as he came in her.

He leaned back, which pulled his cock from her body, and they both crashed down, side by side.

"Wow," she said while staring up at the tent ceiling. "That was incredible."

He laughed lightly. "Yes, babe, it really was. I'm flying now. Whew! My heart is pounding."

"Same." She snuggled up to his body. "I feel all floaty." She nuzzled her face to his flesh. "I didn't think I'd ever be this happy."

He held her close and kissed her on the forehead. "Neither did I."

They lay in silence, the exhilaration of her climax continued its soothing majestic roam of her body. Nature's natural sleep aid was taking effect as she allowed her eyes to fall closed.

Chapter 8

She opened her eyes to daylight. She glanced around and found she'd rolled a few feet away from Leif during the night. She immediately chastised herself for not dousing the fire. They could have burned to crisps if it had grown, but there were no licks of flames to be seen through the sheer fabric of the tent. She laid still until the need to pee consumed her, then she slipped out of the tent.

The freshness of the morning consumed her as she made her way to a place out of the walkway to release her pee. The newness of the mornings had always given her hope, even when she'd all but lost it. This morning her hopes were on a ridiculous high and she shoved all the doubts to the side. Those doubts were for later in the day, not meant to mar her morning vibes.

When she returned to the tent, Leif's eyes were open. "Good morning, beautiful."

She slid into the tent, noticing his hard-on.

"Yeah, I'm always hard in the mornings," he said with humility. "But this morning, I want to get straight to getting you out of here." He started to rise.

She slid alongside him, admiring his cock. She placed a hand on his belly to press him back down. "Well," she said, while teasing her forefinger along his shaft, "I can blow you and make you come quick. Then we can get to work on that." She'd been sex-starved for so long that she couldn't waste a good boner. "Will you let me?"

"Well, I won't say no," he said with a laugh as he fully settled against the sleeping bag, shoving an arm under his head.

She pounced on his cock and began to suck. His primal groaning egged her on and she sucked harder while stroking his shaft.

He played with her hair, then pressed into her scalp firmly as his moans hit a peak.

His cum blasted into her mouth and she did her best to swallow it, despite her gag reflex rearing its ugly head. She managed to not gag, then popped off his cock, whipping her fingers across her mouth to collect the excess cum.

"Shit, that felt damn good. Maybe I need to return the favor," he said, starting to rise.

"No, let's get out of here. Then do that," she said. She was starting to buy into his belief that she wasn't stuck there.

"Yeah, I'll make you come twice as hard in my hotel room tonight."

"You aren't staying with your mom?"

"No, well, I was sleeping on the couch, but we can't fuck on the couch and not risk her coming out, so I reserved a hotel room for the rest of the week." He looked proud of himself.

She loved that idea, but then immediately fell into a dark worry. What would happen at the end of the week when his stay here was over?

"Should we pack up everything or leave it?" She looked around for her dress, then slipped it over her head. She snagged the walking sandals from the shopping bag and slipped them on. They were a touch big, but securing the strap tighter helped.

"I think we just get you out, and I'll come back for the stuff. Getting you out is what matters. The rest could be replaced." He looked around and found his clothes. She watched him as he started to dress, a smile plastered on her face.

She appreciated that he seemed as urgent to get her out as she felt.

Once they were both clothed, the sleeping bag was rolled, and they ate a bit of breakfast. She felt ready to try leaving, though the pain of the throw-back her body might likely endure as she tried to leave gave her a sick feeling in the pit of her stomach. She tried really hard to embody Leif's enthusiasm that it would work, but she knew the realities. She'd had to heal from the bruises of the proof of her prison, so it was starting to become too much of a fallacy to just buy into the closer they got to trying it.

They walked away, the tent still up, like a shrine. Leif had insisted, just in case they ended up back there for the night.

In her new dress and sandals, she crept along behind Leif, her hand in his. It felt odd to walk through the woods with shoes on, and she'd forgotten how nicely shoes provided protection. Her soles had toughened up so much that she'd easily walked across the rough terrain daily. She felt secure and cared for with shoes on though, especially ones from Leif.

She smiled at him genuinely as he glanced back at her, because it came from her heart. An equally genuine smile returned by him warmed her even more. However, she couldn't shake the feeling that pain was still imminent.

As they approached the section of the woods that neared the boundary, she tensed. She glanced around, and not a single thing looked different. But she certainly felt different this time with Leif leading her. She clenched her teeth, baring down for the smackdown that was coming, but it didn't come. As she followed him, she felt no familiar ripple of ominous energy. Nothing.

He dropped her hand and adjusted his backpack. The force of a wave came at her, but not nearly as strong as before, which was quite odd because she was sure she was about a step or two away from the block.

She took three more steps, then her nose slammed into an invisible wall. Panic consumed her and her heart dropped. "Oh no!" she exclaimed. "It wasn't there, but now it is." She reached her hand up and touched the invisible shield. Leif was still by her side. But as he took a step to look at her, he crossed the line.

"You can't go further?" he asked in astonishment, his jaw remaining open after his words left his mouth.

She shook her head. "No, I can't. This is as far as I can go." She reached her hands up and moved them along the wall. "I'm not this good of a mime." Panic exploded in her further and tears sprang to her eyes. "Leif," she cried. "I'm still trapped." She glanced around and the trees all looked the same. Leif looked the same. The sky was still blue, the sun was still shining, but she couldn't move forward. "This is real." She kicked the wall and her leg sprang back. "Ow!" she hollered.

He reached for her and grabbed her hand. "I feel nothing, Gabriella." His eyes shone with concern and love.

"It's not as strong of a force as before. In the past, it literally threw me many feet backwards. I got all banged up as I mapped along this wall. And anytime I've gotten close, the force has reminded me it's here." She shifted her eyes back and forth. "But it's different this time." She felt the invisible wall with her hands, searching for a hole in it, a crack, or a weak spot, something she could punch through. But her kick hadn't done any damage, so it was likely her fist was to be even less effective.

Leif grabbed both of her hands. "Gabriella, look at me."

She darted her gaze about as panic seized her further. There was no doubt that things were different with Leif present. They'd measured her before they left camp, and she was still her full height, and it had been way more than the five hours since she'd orgasmed. "What if I'm still trapped?" The despair in her voice broke her own heart.

"I'm going to try to pull you through." He looked back and forth across her face, trying to maintain eye contact. "Hey. Baby. You've got to look at me. I've got you. Okay?" When she met his gaze, he continued. "We can do this. I'm going to drag you through it."

She resisted his slight tug. "What if you can't?"

"Let's try," he said, nodding, his exuberance becoming contagious.

She grimaced. "What if it hurts? What if it just pulls me back in?"

"I'm going to hold you, and keep holding you until we are very far away. I'm not letting go." His eyes were stern and determined.

In a flicker of hope, she believed him. She nodded. "Okay," she said meekly, allowing hope to bring a small smile to her face.

"Yeah. That's it. You're strong, Gabriella. And I've got you. Let's do this. Come on." He pulled stronger on her hands and her fingers entered the wall.

Sparks crackled and her heart stopped. "Do you see that?" she asked in a voice full of fear, her eyes as wide as they could go.

He nodded. "I see it. I believe you." His eyes didn't lie.

She wasn't crazy, and he did believe her. It felt so good to be believed. She allowed his stronger tug to pull her further through. The electricity licked her skin, leaving a stinging zing across her as it snaked along. Thankfully, she didn't feel burned by it. She held her breath as Leif pulled with a greater force, her forearms were now through the wall.

"Oh, it's working!" she shrieked, as jubilation birthed inside her. As her elbows exited, her hope thickened. "Yes," she said softly, never taking her eyes off of Leif's.

He smiled back, his grin growing wider as more of her body passed through. "Yes, baby, it's working. You're coming with me."

Her slide through the barrier was gradual. Leif's arms flexed, his muscles firming into bulges as he worked her body through it. He gritted his teeth as her breasts entered. His eyes shifted as his effort increased when her full torso was immersed inside.

She considered taking a step to help the progress. As she carefully moved her leg, her knee jutted forward, and it was more like wading through quicksand than the nothingness of air. The invisible wall lightly scratched her skin as she edged onward.

"Almost there," he grunted as he planted his feet firmly against the ground. He wore a stern expression and tensed his body, bearing down his muscles. "Ready?"

She nodded, her eyes filled with faith. "Yes," she said softly.

He gave a significant yank.

As she burst free from the barrier, they both began to fall, but he righted himself and enveloped her in his arms. The sky flared purple and pink, and silver lightning bolts jack-knifed across the sky in angry-looking streaks. The wind blew her hair wildly around her face as a slight roar filled the air.

Leif held her tightly to his body as chaos swirled around them. She tucked her head against his chest, closing her eyes firmly, bracing for what might come.

The roar waned and she fluttered her eyes open. The world had shifted again to look like the normal forest. She dared not move, her breathing still rapid, and her heart still raging, pounding quickly.

Leif began to walk while holding her cloistered to his body, as if claiming her as his. After some mini footsteps where their forward movements seemed too miniscule, he moved parallel with her so they could easily walk together side by side. He briskly led them towards the walking path.

"Get as far away as fast as possible," he muttered as he glanced backwards, his eyes laden with caution. When he looked back at her, his eyes shifted to triumph with their blooming success.

She couldn't agree more. Her fears calmed, and her heart soared as she delightfully sank into the happiness he exuded.

When they were what seemed like a good distance away from it, she walked freely beside him, still clinging to his hand. It felt too good to be true. The air felt fresher, and she could breathe more easily, but, honestly, she was scared to fully buy into her freedom. She slowed her stride as she noticed a slight rumbling on her back. The tickle shifted into a throb. The throb shifted to a fluttering. As the sensation increased, she stopped walking, filling with awe as she caught Leif's eyes.

He didn't let go of her as the tips of her wings erupted from the flesh on her back.

She allowed the joy to flood her eyes as she filled with the rush of feeling complete again. "My wings! They're coming back!" They rolled out of her back, unfurling in a glorious splendor, the fabric of her dress holding them until it gave way and ripped.

Leif's eyes went wide as he watched the wings exude from her body. "Holy fuck," he muttered in disbelief. He shifted the dress down her back so they could fully expand.

She fluttered them, then settled them back close to her body. "Oops, I ripped another dress." She laughed with glee. "And I really liked this one, too."

"Wow, I'm speechless. But they make you even more beautiful." His gaze on her was a delight.

"It feels so incredible to have them back. You have no idea." Despite the wonderful return to her natural state, dark urgency swelled in her. "Let's go. I want to be far away from here, so I'm not drawn back in." Though she wasn't even sure distance mattered.

He nodded. "Yes, good idea."

They clasped their hands tightly together and began to dash down the path. As she ran, she noticed her fingers began to tingle as they used to whenever she cast her magic. With a heart full of new love, new hope, and the desire for new adventures, she sprinted along with Leif at her side. The future was down the path.

The Siren Who Couldn't Sing, Book 2

The Siren Who Couldn't Sing, Book 2, Chapter 1
Gabriella

"You were just going to leave me there until I was old and gray?" she demanded even as she tried to cower out of respect.

"Now, Gabriella. You were to figure your own way out. I had faith in you." Nocter's stern expression was laced with a discipline she didn't want anything to do with.

"I didn't know the rules. How was I supposed to get out when I knew nothing?" She screwed her face into an expression of disgust.

He glanced her way and made direct eye contact. "You found them out, didn't you?"

"It was a test?" She snorted, making the water in front of her face move in a little wave from her exuberant exclamation. "Mentors aren't supposed to abandon their mentees." She pouted, unable to quell the fire in her eyes.

"It had to be this way." He grabbed her chin and stared intently into her eyes with even more intensity. "You are unique. You require extra."

She wiggled back from him. "Why have you summoned me here?" she asked. She crossed her arms under her bare breasts as her hair flowed in the water with her sharp head shake.

"This isn't about sex, my dear."

"Well, then, what do you want?" She swam backward, jerking out of his reach. She wouldn't be with him anyway, so this was ludicrous.

"I only want what's best for you." His eyes were lit and electric blue, mirroring the cloudless sky above as he expanded into the water, as if turning to mist, and then vanished.

A current swept her up and began to carry her toward the shore. She fought it, trying to swim back. She wanted answers, but it was no use. She was carried along in the giant underwater wave until she was tossed onto the dry part of the sandy beach she'd entered the ocean at not more than thirty minutes ago.

She stretched out flat on the hot sand, letting it pepper her skin, and sighed. "Well, what the absolute hell was that?"

She blinked against the strong sunshine beating down on her and wondered how she was going to get back to Leif's house while naked and without a car. She also wondered if she would start to shrink again. The shrinking had simmered down and been very minimal, if it even happened at all. For the past few months she'd been living with Leif, and it had been wonderful not to fear that she and Leif weren't fucking enough. But she wanted to have sex with him. That was no real big effort, it was a want. But it also kept her human-sized, so it was a win-win.

She sat up and glanced around. She saw no one. She'd picked a deserted beach to enter the ocean on purpose, so as not to freak out someone who saw her disappear into the water, and because she'd be naked. That's how Nocter always wanted it. She was thanking her lucky stars she was alone because she hadn't expected to be expelled from the sea nude without notice. She had falsely assumed her departure from the big water would be on her terms. She was beginning to realize not much was on her terms with her life, as she'd assumed it would be after escaping her pen in the forest. She was still a prisoner of sorts if Nocter could just nab her any time.

She hopped up and strode to where she had her phone and clothes hidden. The bush where she had put her clothes looked wrecked. Her clothes were no longer there. She dropped to her knees and frantically searched for her phone. She squealed when she found it. Luckily, whoever stole her clothes hadn't seen her phone. Who steals clothes? That's just weird. She sat behind the bush to hide her nakedness from anyone who might wander onto the beach. She was very tired from her swim down to meet Nocter. She certainly hadn't planned on visiting the ocean depths today.

She opened her phone and called Leif. "Leif, thank goodness. I'm on the beach and I'm naked. Can you bring me some clothes?"

He burst into laughter. Once his laughing subsided, he joked, "And we've gone back in time. I'm to rescue you with clothes in hand again?"

She fumed, though she liked his flirty teasing. "Yes, I'm afraid so. Just a different landscape."

"Where are you?" he asked with amusement in his voice.

"That small hidden beach by Seaways. You know, the one off highway one that we stopped off at once?"

"Ah, yes, I know it. I'll snag some clothes and head there." He chuckled. "Don't move."

"Very funny," she said in mock annoyance. "Just hurry."

"I will. Love you, babe. See you soon." His amusement in her predicament irked her, though it was funny. She was just in a mood.

"Bye, love you too."

She stared off across the beach. It was a beautiful day and, thankfully, not too chilly. Her skin was dry now, but even when it had been wet, it was warm enough out that she hadn't shivered. Being stuck behind a bush naked brought back memories of being stranded in the forest. She hadn't been able to leave then, either. Granted, this would easily be fixed once she had clothes on and could move about freely again.

Life had been going so great, she'd had to pinch herself to make sure it was real. The time she'd been with Leif had been over-the-top wonderful. They'd gone on dates, had sex at least once a day, made meals together, and she'd even ventured out alone on some days for a short walk while Leif was at work. She wanted to contribute to their life together, so she'd decided to try to find a job too, not that she was acclimated to life on land yet, and one free of any invisible walls. She knew she could adapt, though. Being a unique being, a fairy-siren-human, and like no others she knew, she'd had to adapt to things all her life.

What Nocter had said haunted her. He likely had more so-called well-intentioned plans for her that really just felt nefarious, despite what he said. 'Require extra', he had said, and that was meant to make her feel special? Well, it just made her feel manipulated, and to what end?

The time crawled by and she couldn't stop her mind from speculating about what Nocter had planned next. And why did he need to have a plan for her, anyway? She was happy with Leif and starting a good life with him. Wasn't that enough?

She played with her toes, wiggling them, admiring the nice paint job Leif had done on her toenails last night. She smiled. They had endured the long, agonizing waiting to have sex while they dried, which had been rather intolerable to them, turned on as they were. But funny as well, since they had both ended up laughing at how extreme their dirty talk got. It had actually been fabulous foreplay fodder, and the sex after had been explosive. If there was one thing she loved, it was a horny man who loved to make her come, and Leif had both of those traits in spades. He was her ideal man, as if she had dreamed him up and got to manifest him. He was perfect, and each day he'd become more perfect. She was waiting for the fallout of that, but so far it hadn't come.

She counted the birds as they flew by and watched the big waves lick the shore as they slurped the sand, then died. She had enjoyed her swim into the deep, as unexpected and unpleasant as the end of it was. She knew she was a rare creature, her mix of mystical beings, but did that mean Nocter had to treat her this way? She didn't feel special; instead, she felt punished for being unique. And he was acting entitled.

She saw movement off in the distance in the parking lot and her heart fluttered. It was a white truck, which was what Leif drove. It had to be him. She peered off into the distance, squinting her eyes to see if it was him. She couldn't tell. It's not like someone else with a white truck couldn't be driving by and decide to stop. She glanced around her, searching for a better place to hide, just in case. Being naked at a beach that wasn't designated as a nude beach could get her in trouble. She was learning the ways of Leif's world, but they were often perplexing to her. Everyone was so weird and almost scared of nudity. She was always nude in the sea. And why did people drive far away to work when they had so many things to do just at their homes? And why did people even own cars? Why did they need to travel so far? But then she also realized they had no wings or magic, so they needed some things to give them magical abilities, like cars.

She grinned deeply. Leif had magic. But his magic was with her and with sex. He was quite gifted in his abilities to be carnal with her, which she delighted in. Back in the forest, she'd get that delicious slice of life from passersby who'd stop and engage in primal nude practices with her, but she'd also come to realize those interactions were hollow. She only knew this after being with Leif, however. The other times were just acts of sex. They were both horny, both would come, and her needs to stay human-sized got met. But it was short-lived, and she'd shrink back down to the size of a peanut again after the passage of time.

The truck parked and the person got out. The physique outline looked like Leif's body and she rejoiced, jumping up and squealing. Her breasts flopped as she bounced out of her semi-hiding place and dashed out across the sand, her feet kicking up sprays of it as she zoomed along. Her man was coming to her rescue again, with clothes, so she wouldn't be the weirdo naked one. Hero always looked good on him, and she instantly wanted to have sex with him on the beach. Maybe they could do a quickie.

He made his way to her, his grin appreciative and he looked at her hornily. "What a wonderful way to find you," he teased. "Nude and on the beach. You look gorgeous."

She giggled. "Yeah, who steals someone's clothes? I'm just grateful they didn't steal my phone, too." It hadn't occurred to her until now that she should have perhaps been afraid, naked and alone. The thief may have still been present and watching her from a hiding place, with ill intent on his brain. She assumed it was a man, but she knew that it was also possible it was a woman who had taken her clothes. Why they did it was the real thing to ponder. "Makes no sense, honestly." She fluttered her wings as she made a leap through the air, landing one foot in front of Leif.

"Whew, you've got me hard as a rock." He looked at her with amorous intent.

She glanced at the bag in his hand and groaned. "Oh, no. I meant the other black bag. That's the one that has my cocktail dress in it."

He burst into laughter. "Seriously? I brought you formal wear to a beach?"

She sighed as she took the bag. "Well, it's still clothes. At least I won't be naked and get that arrested thing."

He chuckled at her, but then his grin faded and worry took over his face. "Yeah, we don't need you getting arrested and putting you in the light of the world. They'd cart you off to a lab somewhere to study you." His frown deepened. "That's actually no joke. That would happen, Gabriella, if someone in my world found you. You have to be careful."

She rolled her eyes. "So you've told me fifty times." She'd faced so many dangers Leif didn't even know existed in the world. A little 'getting arrested' didn't scare her one bit.

She slipped the sparkly dress over her head and smoothed it down her body. The sunlight caught all the reflective parts of the dress, and she shone as brilliantly as the sun, and that still didn't touch the way she felt inside.

Chapter 2
Gabriella

No sooner was she dressed than Leif pulled her into an embrace. He leaned down with an open mouth, readying to kiss her as his eyes seethed with lust.

"I aim to take that right back off you," he said as the scowl of a scoundrel stole any façade of innocent intent. "Sex on the beach is a drink, but coming on the beach will quench you better."

She had zero doubts about that as he kissed her with promises of deeply pleasing her dancing as flirtation in his eyes, her tongue caressing his as it ventured further into her mouth.

After pressing his arousal firmly to her bodice, her lust swelled. "Fuck me, Leif. Right here, on the beach, with the sounds of the waves in our ears."

He swept her off her feet and carried her closer to the big pillar of stone near the water's edge. It was like the rest of the cliff had left it behind in its crawl onto land because it stood solitary and regal, its peak a sharp point at the top, which would make it very difficult to stay on. The roar and crash of the waves traveling in to land satiated her need for the sea. She longed for the sea, and when she had been trapped in the forest, the longing for it had been agonizingly painful. The river and the waterfall had helped, but they were nothing compared to the ocean. The sea was as much a part of her as the land was, but she really needed them both near to feel right. When she had been in the forest, she had often wondered how far from the sea she'd been cast. The salty breeze had been too far for her comfort.

Leif stared into her eyes, his hair tousled by the beach breeze and his eyes bright with want and warm with love. He was so sexy she couldn't look away. There was nothing better than sex with him. She'd never have thought this was possible until she'd met him. He had been different from the start than the other men she'd met. She counted herself not just lucky, but somehow saved by meeting him. Sure, it was true that he saved her from herself, and from the forest, but there was something larger there that loomed above them that she couldn't quite name, but felt every day they were together.

"You are the most gorgeous creature on the planet. I want you so badly right now, want to fuck you into the sand until you come so much you fall asleep cum drunk."

She cackled. "I am a creature."

He grinned lasciviously at her. "I know." He laid her down on the sand and gently cupped her wings in his right hand. His shirt showed his muscles nicely, and she enjoyed the curve of his biceps as they contoured in a taper down to his wrists. He had large hands, and when he held her wings, she felt both comforted and aroused at once.

"That feels incredible," she cooed as he gently pressed his fingers into her wings in an alternating pattern.

"Did I mention that I love that I can arouse you even more just by touching your back?"

"Oh, you've told me a few times," she said with delight.

"Nipples, wings, and clit all tied together. No one but you gets this triple."

She nodded. Likely he was right. When she'd lost her wings in the forest, she'd missed the extra pleasure her wings had brought her. That was extra cruel of Nocter to make them vanish in the forest pen.

Yet another reason to hate him. He knew her wings gave her more pleasure. She tried not to fall into fuming over his cruel ministrations over her life and will. Who did he think he was? He was not a God, but the fucker sometimes took liberties he wasn't due. Age-gap romance gone bad was his plague on her. And it wouldn't die its due death.

She pushed Nocter forcefully out of her head as she gazed into Leif's eyes.

His hands caressed her body, his fingers bouncing along the bumps of her dress. She cringed, thinking about how she might never get the grains of sand out of the nooks and crannies of this bejeweled dress, but she already knew the sex with Leif would be worth it.

Leif leaned down to kiss her again. The warmth of the sun combined with the feel of his lips on her flesh, making her close her eyes when he kissed her neck. Plus, his head was no longer acting as her sun block. She groped his strong arm. She loved feeling him up blindly as she traveled her hand down, savoring the length so she could press her hand to his hand as he cupped her pussy. She loved to hold him as he held her that way. She pressed on the back of his hand to apply more pressure over her sensitive folds. He grinned widely before snaking his tongue inside her dress in search of swiping across her nipple.

Her nips were at full peak as he pressed his hand into her womanhood, expertly fondling that juice-slicked space between her thighs. He was a caring, capable lover who had obsessively studied her body and arousal patterns, and he proved it every time they were intimate. He just got it right. She squirmed as he squeezed and relaxed his hold on her repeatedly. When he abandoned her pussy to caress her body, she whimpered a complaint. Not that she disliked that he went right for her pussy, nor that she lamented any of his touches, but she was ready to get primal and feel his length sliding in and out of her. She loved foreplay, but being naked on the beach for so long had been so sensual that her passion was already half-cocked before Leif had even arrived.

"Fuck me," she pleaded.

"I will," he assured her as he bared her right breast and admired it with a hungry gaze. "I've never fucked you on the beach before. I need to savor you a bit."

Savor? She wanted to be rocked into waves of orgasm after orgasm, and he was lazily tasting her like an appetizer. She smiled a devilish smile and went straight for his cock with her hand down his pants.

He grunted when she grabbed his hard cock, his body lurching with a yummy masculine groan. She knew how to get him into a fiery blaze of uncontrollable passion.

He promptly tore her hand right out of his pants.

"Uh," she protested as he pursed his lips at her, his eyes narrowing.

"Not yet," he scolded as the full weight of his tease met his eyes.

"Not fair," she said with a pout.

He chuckled and rolled onto her, smashing his open mouth upon hers.

As they tasted each other in a prolonged, lush French kiss, she became aware of the sounds of the ocean beside them. They consumed her as she allowed her sensuality to dance with Leif's. She danced in spirit above them, her twirling self a soul dancing with the spontaneity of their union, bringing bliss to her body and brain. She'd felt this out-of-body experience with Leif before, but on the beach, it was intensified. There was nothing in her life to top the feeling as a part of her coasted weightlessly above her. An out-of-body experience with sex was something she'd only been able to do with Leif, and it was indescribable. Perhaps it was her fairy magic that facilitated it, but, regardless, she was grateful for how it heightened sex at times. She'd tried to explain it to Leif, but it had been no use. Mere words couldn't convey the elation she felt at being loved and aroused by Leif at once. It was like no other magic on the planet.

He bared her breasts and nuzzled them, then traveled his way down her body with kisses until his mouth met her scrunched-up dress. He grasped the hem of the dress with both hands and began to drag it down her thighs, his intent to remove it clear. She lifted her butt so he could free it from her ass, then she wiggled as he tugged. He smiled like a hungry man ready to eat as he took the dress fully off her.

She lay naked in the sand, grateful it wasn't so hot today that she felt burned. The air was the perfect temperature to be naked on the beach, yet she knew the second she entered the water she'd cool, but not too much, because her mermaid-like biological processes would kick in.

Right now, she was focused on her human characteristics as Leif groped her body with ardent hunger. She felt him up too, tugging on his shirt to get him to be topless. She'd work on baring his lower half soon. She desired to feel every bit of his flesh pressed to hers, then the wild abandon of sliding and writhing, him smacking into her as he thrust. She was impatient. She wanted all of him at once, his gentle side, his wanton rough side, and everything in between. He removed his shirt and she relished the display of his firm muscles.

His full lips nibbled along her tummy as he once again accosted her pussy with his hand. She curled upwards with a groan as he played his fingers along her slit in a tickle, then cupped her pussy with his full hand and squeezed.

She cried out as scrumptious waves of pleasure consumed her. "Please," she begged.

He continued to kiss and suckle her, his hand busy at her swollen cunt as she ran her hands all over him voraciously. She quickly reached for his groin again and kneaded his cock through his shorts.

He groaned out his pleasure and she ramped up the movements of her hand. She slid her hand down his belly into his shorts, and this time he didn't stop her. She stroked him, spreading his precum down the length of his cock.

His shorts were a hindrance, so she began to work at unbuttoning and unzipping them. He momentarily broke his intimate meandering roaming of her body to work at getting himself fully naked.

His cock swung down as he freed it. It was fully erect and hard, and she immediately began her hand job. He allowed her to play with his cock for a bit, then pressed himself down upon her. They charged into a strong kiss and he rolled in the sand to get her on top of him. She writhed and savored every speck of his skin on hers. Her breasts hung as she rose off him to gaze down.

"I love this," she said in a light whisper, her want for him raging inside.

He mirrored her intensity as he said, "As do I. Now get ready to come..."

"And sing like a siren?" she asked with relish.

"A satisfied siren," he corrected. He gazed upon her with want. "I found you because of that voice. It's special."

She smiled back, nodding, her eyes falling slightly closed. The foreplay had her feeling woozy and free.

He rolled them in the sand as she gasped, then nudged her legs apart and settled himself between her thighs. She knew sand was invading her ass crack and she stifled a grimace. The orgasms would all be worth wherever the sand snaked its way into. Maybe they could skinny-dip in the water to rinse the sand away before heading home. An ass full of sand on the truck ride home did not sound appealing.

He lined up his pole at her entrance and poked himself into her wet folds to coast smoothly inside her body. The first penetration was always heaven, and she groaned as her eyes fell closed. He began to ride her, thrusting his manhood into her at a quickening pace. She fondled his muscular body nonstop, enjoying the feel of him beneath her fingers. She squeezed him and made lovely soft moaning sounds as her arousal and pleasure rose.

He leaned down for a kiss and their mutual desire for each other erupted even further. Their lovemaking turned frantic and urgent. He reached down and rubbed her clit as he continued to slowly fuck her. Her climax loomed as he stroked her clit. He readjusted himself for optimal clit smacking—she adored his technique for top pleasure for her. He began to fuck her again, his movements contacting her clit so perfectly that she launched into her big O. He was working hard, his skin glistening with sweat as he worked himself in and out of her.

She writhed and moaned, her body curling and twitching as she was swallowed up by the enormity of her climax. Her body rocked through the contractions, squeezing him inside her on repeat.

He groaned and slid swiftly into his own orgasm. He remained hard and continued to fuck her through her descent, her aftershocks quickly giving way to another peak of orgasming and her body torqued beneath him.

He came again too, as the constant lulling sounds of the ocean still filled her ears. There was perfection all around them. He held her close as his cock softened while still inside her. He rolled to the side of her and held her to him as they both panted, their labored breathing evidence of their attained highs. The sunshine kept them warm as they lay in each other's arms.

"That was incredible," she said. "By the sea, yet on land, and also in heaven. And with you. I couldn't ask for anything better."

"Agreed," he stated with a savoring in his voice.

"Can we stay here forever, just like this?" she asked. Knowing it wasn't possible didn't make her want it any less.

"Yeah, I'd love that. We might get hungry, though."

She laughed. "True. And I'm already hungry now. That trek to see Nocter really zapped me." She bit her lower lip as she gazed into his eyes. "And the orgasms have me spent."

"Good, that's just how I like you to be," he said, smiling back.

"Whew!" she cooed softly. "That was a doozy."

"Yeah, and I'm curious to learn more about this whole process of you visiting Nocter." He shook his head. "Did you tell him how you've changed my life more than anyone I've ever met? How I'd be lost without you? I didn't know how much I needed you until I had you." His grin deepened. "And how much I love you."

She nuzzled her face into his chest and released a big sigh. "Same," she said. "I didn't tell him much, but it was weird because it was like he already knew." She felt watched even when she said that. Was he watching her still? Her fairy Spidey-sense was detecting something. Maybe the seer sea witch had told him. That hag was always nosing around in business she didn't belong in. She did not want to talk about Nocter in this lovely moment, though. She wasn't about to let him sour it. It was hard for her to process what he'd done to her in the forest. With the memories of how they'd once been lovers, she always felt that colored his so-called reigning rule over her. Being the leader had changed him, and not in any way she liked.

She recalled the image of his bright happy face when she'd look back as he swam, holding her partially out of the water. It was a triumphant swim he'd often taken them on after they'd had sex. The wind had been exhilarating, the sun warm, his hands around her making her feel secure as he coasted along, and her breasts bare to any ships who might have a pair of binoculars on them. And she would sing. Oh, that must have been a sight! A half-naked woman soaring along the top of the sea as if she could fly, all the while singing her little siren heart out. Well, she could fly, but not so well when her wings were wet. Nocter had been an attentive lover back then, making her reach the first big, glorious orgasms of her life. He had taught her not only self-control in her climaxing, but how to pamper herself to recharge. He had all the makings of an ideal leader. That was, until he became one, then he switched to a dreadful leader. There was no undoing what had been done. He was a new dictator with a section of the magical ocean to manage. The old sweet, loving, considerate Nocter had long been gone and dead.

"What are you thinking about?" he asked cautiously.

"Nocter. And no. I don't want to talk about it." She snuggled back into her man and shoved Nocter out of her head. She cringed when she thought about how she almost became his wife and would now be queen. But queen to a monster was no real queen at all. She couldn't forget what he'd done, which meant she couldn't trust him, and that was even before he had cast her into the forest. She'd effectively banished him from her thoughts back then, and that was just so she didn't gouge out her heart from heartache.

"Okay, you must be thinking about bad shit, and I want you to be happy. So, let's table that."

She nodded against his chest, remaining silent because talking seemed too damn hard to accomplish.

They lay there for several minutes, listening to the ocean and sunbathing.

"Better move before I get sunburned," he said with a chuckle.

"I don't have that problem," she said with a snicker.

"You're lucky you didn't get that human trait."

She laughed. "I'm lucky I'm not lavender like some of my cousins. They couldn't live in the human world like I can."

He looked back at her in shock. "Seriously? They are purple?"

She nodded. "Yeah. A few of them have tried makeup. They still look a bit off, but sort of passable." She gave him a skeptical look. "We wouldn't be able to live how we are. That's not wasted on me."

"Well, good on your genes, then," he said, sitting up. "We should get going, though I do love being here naked with you. But," he pointed to his engorging cock, "my cock is not cooperating with the plan of leaving."

She laughed in delight. "I'd love to use that again."

They heard the roar of a big engine. She glanced up sharply and noticed a big truck was barreling into the little parking lot behind them. They both scrambled to get their clothes on and began to walk, holding hands, back toward the lot. The person didn't get out of their truck, but he probably had seen them naked. No matter. That didn't bother her; she'd live naked if the human world wasn't so puritanical and full of shame. She always found it odd that humans were ashamed of their natural selves. It was like no other animal on earth was ashamed of what they were, they just existed and accepted that they did, but humans somehow had shame down pat.

As she got closer to the parking lot, she heard a familiar hum that made her heart stop cold. She shook her head. It wasn't possible. She must be imagining things. She continued striding alongside Leif, but panic filled her as the hum got louder. Then she felt the force field and devastation set in.

"No!" she cried, raising her fists to the sky. "Why Nocter? Why?"

Leif turned toward her, alarm spreading across his face. "Gabriella?" he asked, his voice full of concern. "What's wrong?"

She balled her fists and kept trudging along despite the looming danger. She defiantly pressed on until the force field wielded its power and she was thrown backward. She flew twenty feet behind Leif and landed with a thud in the sand. She screamed as she covered her face with her hands, her frustration fueling the rage in her shouts. "He's done it again."

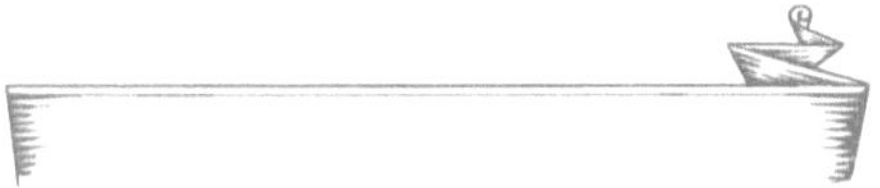

Chapter 3
Gabriella

Her ass was on fire as she tried to catch her breath. Her skirt had slid up her thighs as she scrambled to harness some dignity as she was sprawled out on the sand. She was ready to boil over, about to cry, scream, or both. How could this be? Her talk with Nocter had not indicated this. She shook her head as her eyes flared wide. She met Leif's eyes as he rushed toward her. He kneeled down, his eyes filled with obvious concern.

"What just happened?" he asked as he scanned her body. "Are you okay?"

She managed a tiny nod. "I think so." Seeing Leif's concern for her pushed her over the edge and she began to cry. His eyes told her again that he truly loved her, and lost in that love, she found relief and comfort. She loved him too. She tried to calm down, gasping as her emotions had her sputtering. "It's a force field."

Leif looked around behind him as if he should be able to see it. "Here?" he asked incredulously. "Now?"

She nodded heartily as she sat up and flapped her wings to shake the sand off them. "Yes. You saw what it did to me. It's right there. I felt it but I kept going, not wanting to believe it was real." She pointed at it, lost in a fresh round of bawling. She felt helpless. First, she was imprisoned in a forest, now on a beach? Her favorite location in the world was now to be her prison?

"Hey, I got you out last time. I'll do it again," he said confidently. "Let's go."

He stood and reached out his hand to help her stand.

"Yeah, that's true," she said, feeling better. "You did get me out last time." A tiny flicker of hope flashed. But she was shackled by the fact that Nocter would do this to her again, and when she'd been so happy with Leif on land, living a life and everything like a real human couple. Why take this from her? Jealousy? Revenge? What could be his motivation to do this awful thing to her again?

She accepted Leif's help and rose to a standing position. With her head held high, she took hold of Leif's strong hand, and they began to walk back toward the force field. Gabriella watched as the man in the truck got out and peered at them. He was likely wondering if they needed help after seeing her fly through the air as if an explosion had set her airborne.

As they neared the invisible force field, she felt the vibration first, then heard the hum. As they approached it, she felt the repulsion gripping her and it whiplashed against her body, but didn't take her this time. She smiled up at Leif as he smiled down at her with triumph across his face. It was working so far.

"See, we can do this together, just like last time." His eyes shone with confidence.

She cringed, they were at the point where she was thrown again. Would Nocter just keep locking her in pens around the world at his will and desire? His wickedness ran deep, and she wondered if he had any shred of love left for her inside his body or had it all blackened and died. She didn't know him anymore.

The force on her body increased with each step and she began to lean into it as if she were walking through drying cement. Leif walked easily and she lagged behind. She kept a death grip on his hand as he had on hers. He turned with his arm outstretched. As she swiveled to fall into his embrace, he was whisked away from her. His hand was ripped from hers and he was sent flying backward toward the shore. The second after his hand left hers, she was flung back as well. The force prevented her from seeing where Leif was, but she landed quickly enough and shuffled her body around to face the shoreline. Leif was dropped about sixty feet off shore. No doubt he was above deep water. She watched in horror as his body plunged into the sea. He did not pop back up.

She scrambled to her feet and ran toward the ocean. "No!" she screamed to its vast nothingness, nothingness that had just swallowed the love of her life. He'd drown in the currents. She had to get to him. She couldn't lose him. He could not die. Her heart wrenched into painful twists as she scanned the top of the water. She didn't see a head or a hand pop up. She saw nothing but rolling waves. Leif was gone.

She looked at the parking lot for help from the man, but the truck was rumbling away.

She ran to the sea and was thrown back. Another force field had her pinned to the beach. How could she save her man if she couldn't enter the water? She screamed as she flew back at the force field, whipping her wings on hyper speed mode only to be flung back again. She landed with a heavy thud. Her ass was killing her from this third hard drop and she knew she'd have bruises, but she wasn't giving up. Leif didn't have long, and she wasn't about to stand idly by and lose him. Her heart was breaking, and she wept as she ran again at the sea, only to be tossed back as if she were a tiny stone. This went on for a long time. Passage of time eluded her, but she persisted. She wasn't thinking straight. She could fly. Why was she just running? It was true she hadn't flown much in many months, but that didn't mean she'd lost the ability. Though she knew her wing muscles might be weak from not being used.

She fluttered her wings and rose high in the air. She flapped her wings as hard as she could and cheered as she cleared the force field and soared over the water. She easily coasted over it and was soon soaring over the water at lightning speed. The force field was only on land and not on top. It made her wonder if it had been this way in the forest too, and perhaps that was why her wings had disappeared when she'd been imprisoned there. It made sense. Nocter was no dummy. She chastised herself for not trying to get high enough to try to jump out of the forest pen. But she would have had no way of knowing it had no roof.

She quickly reached the spot where Leif had gone down. She began to sing to call to him. Her voice was pure and beautiful. A sheer magical stream of vocalization danced out of her mouth as she flew. Surely he would hear her and pop his head out of the water. She wasn't sure she could fly while carrying him, but she wasn't about to let that fear control her. Maybe together they could swim to the shore. She flew close to the surface of the water as she peered into it. She saw no signs of Leif at all. She kept singing and made her way back to where he had gone under. She dove into the water so she'd have a clearer view of the depths so she could try to locate him.

She coasted in the cool water as waves tossed her about. The current was strong and her heart fell. The current had likely swept Leif far away rather quickly, and she realized with a sinking heart that she may not be able to find him. She was too late to save him. Her heart clenched and she fought back tears.

She stopped moving altogether as she realized she was still singing but there was no sound coming from her. She gasped and tried to sing again. Sure enough, her mouth opened and she was singing, but all she heard was the sounds of being under the sea. She couldn't sing.

She swam to the surface of the water singing as hard and as loud as she could. As she burst into the air, her song belted out loud and clear. She trod water as she looked around. Confusion had her stunned, but she still managed to move her limbs in the water to stay afloat. She sang again and heard herself perfectly fine. Nothing made sense. She continued to sing and dove back under the water. Her song was muted again once she was submerged, and though she forced her vocalization as hard as she could, she remained silent. How would she call to Leif in the water if she couldn't sing under it? How would he even be able to hear her if she could only sing out of the water? He'd never hear her.

Panic set in as she thrashed about in the water. She sang as best she could through her tears, then tried to sing underwater again. It never worked. The second she went under, she went silent. She'd rather suffer a torturous death than lose Leif. She swam underwater and scanned for him. Desperation spurred her on. She had to find him. She zoomed quickly under the water using her magic and covered lots of area but didn't see a single sight of him. It was possible he'd been pulled miles away in just the time she'd been on the beach alone.

Something charged toward her off in the distance, like a torpedo, and she feared a shark had targeted her. She would not be able to outswim a shark, and with her wings being wet, she wouldn't be able to fly away to escape, either. Death would come for them both, though death likely already had come for Leif. She stopped struggling in the water and simply watched as the mass came straight for her. She might as well die too. Without Leif, she didn't really want to live, anyway. The fight in her waned as she started to sink.

The object came nearer to her and she could make out that it was a body. But human bodies don't just coast through the water like that. Humans weren't capable of such feats. She squinted her eyes as the body came closer and joy filled her. It was Leif! And he was alive! He was mouthing something and reaching for her as he whizzed by. This was a horrifying taunting. She had no chance of reaching him in time to grab him at the speed he was moving. Nocter was surely somewhere laughing while toying with them. She vowed to get back at him somehow.

The fight in her exploded and she swam in the direction he was heading. She couldn't keep up, but she could see the direction he was being moved in. She forged on, her will to rescue Leif now energizing her. She would get to him. She knew it now. This proved this was all happening because of Nocter, though. No other being on the planet could plunge a man beneath the water and cart him around with an invisible force as if he were a toothpick. Plus, Leif was still alive. This too proved Nocter was behind it. Leif shouldn't be alive after being underwater for so long. He was a carrot dragging her along to an unknown destination. And why? She knew that this was likely what Nocter wanted. And unfortunately, he was getting exactly what he designed. He had her by her ovaries and there was nothing she could do about it. He was despicable. Her anger seethed as she mustered up another burst in her speed.

She swam on, her joy at seeing Leif alive gave her magic another extra boost and she made good progress toward him at an incredible speed. Her adrenaline gave her the extra oomph and zest she needed to dart through the water, enough to where she finally caught sight of him ahead. She was gaining on him quickly, as if he'd been slowing down, except somehow, she suspected he wasn't.

She sped at an ever-increasing rate and she couldn't understand why, but she was super grateful. She was almost to him. She passed by countless fish, but they were strangely looking bigger and bigger as she moved, which made zero sense. She needed to focus and just get to Leif. He was shot out of the water ahead of her. She took in a deep breath for more gumption and swam to the top. Leif was dangling in the air like a floppy cloth doll. She began to sing her heart out. It was imperative that he heard that she was nearby. He flailed his arms in the air as he was hurtled toward the shore.

She stopped moving so she could put all her energy into her singing. She sang the same song she sang back in the forest when she called for Leif to return. Zings of hope flew through her as he waved his arms in the air, yet he still flopped about like a toy. It enraged her that he was being treated this way. It could be some unseen puppeteer moving him, but it was also possible that this was just purely Nocter's doing, mocking her invisibly from wherever he was lurking. Did he not care for her heart at all anymore? Cruelty was now his go-to?

Watching Leif be played with in the air as if he were a wisp of a dried weed instead of the man she loved wrenched her insides. She'd get revenge on Nocter somehow, some way. Her resolve to do so solidified in her as it grew bigger. This atrocity would not go unavenged. Leif was such a strong man, it was so foreign to watch him be toyed with so easily. But she, herself, had been just as toyed with by being locked in the invisible pens.

Her fury raged to an inferno as she began to swim again. She moved ten feet, swimming with her head above water, then slipped under the water again. Her ability to make sound underwater was stolen again so she struggled to get her head back above water. The coolness of the sea water gripped her as she popped her face back into the warm sunlight. Her ability to sing resumed so she slowed her swimming. She watched as Leif began to descend. She thought he had heard her, but to be sure, she kept singing, further conserving her efforts with slow swimming to allow her to handle both at once. It was agonizing how long it was taking for her to reach the shore. It seemed to be taking way longer than it should be. It made no sense. Time and space slowed as she fought hard to swim while singing. Her slow progress made her desperate, but she knew it had to be this way.

She was out of breath from both singing her heart out and swimming at the same time and had to slow her movements further.

Her magical powers weren't helping enough. Leif was dropping and then he was deposited on the shore. At least that was something; he was on land and now she didn't have to worry about him falling and breaking a bone, or worse. She shuddered. Now that she had found the love of her life, she couldn't bear the thought of not having him in her life. There was no worse torture than to think of that. She fought back tears as she slowly made her way to the shore. Her body hurt, as did her heart.

Leif was laid out flat in the sand, which worried her. He was a take-action kind of guy and he'd more likely be standing or trying to help her than lay spread lifeless across the sand. Panic bubbled in her and she feared he was overtaxed and possibly even hurting. She doubled her efforts, and after what felt like an eternity, she could finally stand upon the sand. As she walked out of the sea, Leif sat up. He didn't stand, but remained seated as he watched her emerge from the water.

He placed his hands on the sand to help himself stand up, but he was very wobbly and fell back down. He tried again and this time he succeeded. She rushed to him, her wet feet collecting a copious coating of sand as confluent as mini socks. She'd never been so happy in her life! As she approached him, however, she was filled with dread. She noticed she was smaller, and was likely a good two feet shorter than her usual height. She only came up to Leif's middle. She was shrinking? How was this possible when they'd just had sex on the beach? This shouldn't be happening.

Leif looked exhausted and his jaw dropped as she came closer. "You're shrinking," he said in shock.

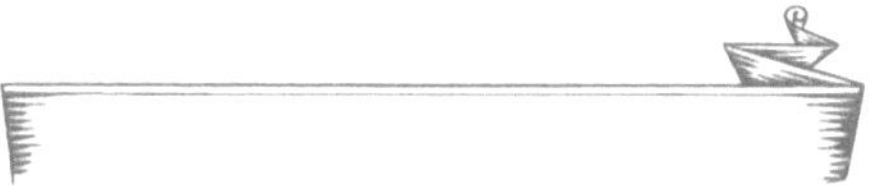

Chapter 4
Gabriella

"I am. I don't understand." Her voice was full of anguish she couldn't mask. Her shoulders drooped as she collapsed into his embrace. He smelled like the sea and himself at once, both scents of comfort to her. "This makes no sense, we just made love on the sand." She fought the tears, but they came and joined the drying sea on her face. "I shouldn't be shrinking," she said with a sob. "Not after that." It wasn't fair.

"I don't get it either." He caressed her head that was pressed to his belly.

She leaned back and looked up at him. "Are you okay? Are you hurt? Do you have any idea what grabbed you?"

He shook his head, his eyes full of confusion and weariness. "I have no idea. I saw nothing. It was like an invisible force of some sort." He sighed. "My muscles are a bit sore, yeah, but that's probably from fighting so hard to get away more than anything else."

"Did you feel any hands on you or anything like that?" Any hint of how he had felt might help her figure this out. "Did you hear anything? Feel anything?"

"No. It was like nothing was there. Only I had no control over my body." He shook his head, his eyes switching from fear to filling with love. He squeezed her tighter to him. "But I'm so relieved we're together again."

"Me too." She narrowed her eyes. "This was Nocter. It has him written all over it," she said with contempt in her voice. She glanced around. "And it could happen again. I don't think we are safe. Maybe we'd better move off the beach. I'm thinking Nocter's reach fades once we are off the sand."

"Okay," he said and took her hand in his.

They began to walk toward the forest beyond the sand. She wondered how far they'd been thrown from Leif's truck. It might be a long walk back, but going through the forest to reach the road was much safer than walking along the shoreline. She glanced back, looking for any sign of Nocter, though she knew there wouldn't be any. As they approached the edge of the sand, the hum began again.

"Fuck," she muttered. "I forgot, I can't leave." She turned to him. "You have to go, so he can't nab you again. I'll have to stay."

He looked sternly at her, a look of determination and protectiveness blaring in his eyes. "There's no way in hell I'm leaving you."

She covered her eyes with her hands and released a loud wail, then said, "Stop this, Nocter! Stop it now! Let us go!"

"Does he still want you?" Leif asked in a worried voice.

She'd only shared a little about her past relationship with Nocter with Leif, because she was certain he didn't want to hear about them. "I don't think so. If he did, I think you'd be dead."

He nodded, his expression grave. "Good point."

They turned back to the beach and started to walk back toward the middle.

She stopped. "This is as far as I can go from the forest and not hear the hum or feel the vibration."

"I don't understand this," Leif said. "Last time my presence helped you through the force field. But that's clearly not the case this time."

She plopped down in the sand and hung her head. "Nocter is not only playing chess with our bodies, but he's changing the rules."

Leif settled in the sand beside her and rested his hand on her thigh. "Well, then, we will figure this out together."

She looked at him wearily. "Horny?" She scoffed with an expression of sarcasm across her face. "I can't believe I'm asking this after all we've just been through, but want to fuck? I'm shrinking away further and further by the second here, and I'm thinking you don't want to fuck a doll-sized me." She looked at him incredulously, then laughed. "This is ridiculous, right? But we need to do it, or I won't stop shrinking until you can no longer see me."

"That just seems impossible." He shook his head in disbelief. But then, a devilish grin spread across his face. "But, you know, I could pleasure you and make you come any size you are."

"That's true I guess." She held up her hand in the air. "Match my hand and see. I've shrunk even since I've been on land."

He held up his hand and hers was dwarfed next to it. "Incredible. And awful." He grinned lasciviously. "But I'm always horny and always wanting to fuck you, so yes. Let's fuck." He pulled her close in a side hug. "Might actually make us both feel better, too, huh?"

It was just like him, looking on the bright side.

She smiled back. "Yup. Very true." She threw her head back. "I'm guessing it was all the activity and magic I just used to reach you that zapped the staying power of our last sex. I haven't used that much in eons, so I guess it makes sense. I need a constant stream of sex, as you know." She gave him a little sexy smile. "Though when I'm with you, I'm certainly not complaining about that." Blissfully, he always gave her just what she needed.

"I'm about as steady a stream of sex as humanly possible. So we're a match there," he said, pulling her to sit on his lap, which made her dress climb up to the very tops of her thighs. "My little fuck doll." He snickered.

She gave a short curt laugh back. "Literally." She bit her lower lip as she let her eyes show him her lust. "Fuck me before I disappear."

"Gladly," he said, smiling wickedly. "And I hope Nocter likes the show."

She cackled with boisterous laughter as she threw her head back. "Hear that, Nocter!" She sincerely hoped Nocter would not rip him from her when his cock was inside her. He couldn't be that evil, could he?

Leif took her face in his hands and brought her close enough so their lips touched. His eyes crackled like a freshly lit fire. They engaged urgently in a deep, hungry kiss. A kiss that said they were grateful to be together again after the whole kidnapping ordeal. A kiss that said *I want you* and *this is going to rock your world*. She held his head in her own hands and relished the swell of his cock against her bare mound. She wiggled against his loaded manhood, causing both of them to moan in arousing anticipation. She was always ready for sex, it was her mainstay baseline, as it was Leif's, which was another reason they belonged together.

They caressed each other in hungry grabs, further celebrating their togetherness. Their union would be open to the public, Nocter, whoever watched. She didn't care. Leif didn't care. This was for them and no one else; plus, it would save her once again from zipping away to being little more than the size of a bug. She couldn't help Leif if she were that small. She needed this more than for her size, though. Her desperation for Leif after almost losing him was almost bringing her to tears while her desire for him erupted. It was an odd mix, but she managed not to cry as they got more and more heated in their foreplay.

He kissed down her neck, his tongue a gifted lashing along her flesh. He tugged her dress down and her breasts popped free. Her nips peaked to hard nuggets as he played with them each in turn with his mouth. She threaded her fingers through his lush, damp hair as he held her in place with his strong hands pressing into her back. He pulled her dress further down to her belly before he claimed her by savoring her titties with licks, sucks, and nibbles.

Her dress was now a thick band around her waist. She was loving the direct sunshine upon her flesh, which was a welcome relief after the cool sea water. The water near the shore felt warmer, but the deeper parts got cold. That was the other reason she had worried about Leif. She could tolerate it with ease, but he was a full human and susceptible to the cold. A man could be the strongest in the world, but he was nothing but a blade of seaweed to the sea.

Leif's power was on land. He had the muscles to prove it. He was smart and kind and sexy as fuck. He was hers. She was his. Nocter couldn't change that. Time and space, not even death, could steal that either. It couldn't. It just was. Feelings as deep as theirs dwelled in truth and existed in a bubble. An unconditional securing of love had grown between them and she'd never felt safer in her life than she did in his love.

But then there was his passion for her, and that only served to seal the full deal. Her passion for him was just as powerful, and together, they were valiant. She never wondered if he'd pleasure her or make her come, it was his priority, his first priority, as was her safety and well-being.

He cupped her right breast as he tasted her. She wondered if her flesh tasted of the salty sea, but he looked quite happy in his tit eating so she figured it must not be distasteful to him. He dined on her tits and groped her bare ass cheeks as she ever so gently ground her pelvis, massaging his cock between them. He motioned his desire to remove his shorts, and she positioned herself so he could slide them down. His cock swung like a fat pole.

She wanted him in every part of her that was possible, so she rose up and slid down easily onto his erection. She began to ride him, her tits flopping as he nuzzled his face into them as best he could with her bouncing.

She tilted her head back, so her face was skyward and closed her eyes as she cherished the fullness of him inside her. This was in the face of Nocter as much as it was for her enjoyment. He'd played them like pawns, and it was as insulting as much as it was cruel. But this intimacy was for them and them alone.

He thrust up into her, his hips rising to meet her body. He was overcome with a fierceness that she adored as he rose and flipped her backward into the sand. She landed on her back with her legs spread and he dove between them face first. The touchdown of his mouth upon her sensitive womanhood incited her body to curl toward him as she released a sigh of enjoyment. Even her sighs were beautiful, being not that far off from her singing. She knew she had to be careful because her voice was a magnet for men and any nearby would surely come their way if they heard her. She quieted herself, only allowing the softest of mewls as he ate her out. Her body thrashed with the embodiment of a Goddess as he relentlessly brought her to climax over and over again, so much so that she was quivering and blubbering nonsensical whispers. She wanted to be loud and release all her joy to his ears, but she knew this would be a bad idea. They didn't need visitors, so she kept her sounds of pleasure downplayed and instead squeezed his biceps, caressed his face, and pressed her fingers into his scalp to signal her enjoyment.

After she'd come ten times, he readied to enter her. He grinned down at her with libidinous relish as he lined up his cock. It was his turn. He slid into her so easily and began his poundings with a force that rippled along her clit and promised another orgasm soon. She reveled in his use of her body, using her internal walls to chase his own orgasm, and quickly he burst inside her. She knew they were playing with fire, but the possibility of being bred by Leif only served to swell her desire for him more.

After he slowed his thrusting into her, he leaned back and swiveled his fingers in a circle with a wicked grin. "Let's get you as loaded up with orgasms as we can. I think it can only be protective for you to have more."

She smiled, feeling very compliant as she scrambled onto all fours to present herself to Leif's impending doggy mount. She loved his claim of dominance over her in sex. It had become one of her biggest kinks. "I like your way of thinking, though I'm not sure it works that way."

"Shhh," he muttered quickly, "don't ruin it. Just giving you a nice ocean view."

She giggled with delight. "You just want to make me come again," she said with a tease, loving his obsession with making her climax.

"And your point is?" he asked with a devious snicker as he lined himself up at her hole from behind.

He penetrated her lips and gripped her hips firmly. He began to ram himself into her at a fast pace. The force of him smacking into her bottom always sent such delicious waves of awesome sensation through her. The ever-crashing of the waves paired with his mighty backside blows as he rode her sent her soaring into another peak. She crashed, her shoulders nestling into the sand, which freed up her hand to ensure her own orgasm. She played with her engorged clit and moaned.

He grunted. "Yeah, just like that, fuck," he muttered as he voraciously slammed into her.

Her climax took hold, and her body curled toward the sand as the roar of her climax made her body shudder.

Leif released a deep growl and finished his own climax with a hearty yell.

He was panting heavily as he landed in the sand beside her, his expression a lovely display of his satiation.

She curled quickly in beside him and they snuggled to the sound of the waves crashing beneath the warming blaze of the sun.

They said nothing as they both descended from their sexual highs.

"That oughta do it," he said with confidence. "A nice solid stockpile of orgasms."

"I hope so, but I'm worried he might do it again. And why is he trapping me here? I don't even know what I've done to deserve incarceration again? I've done nothing but live with you, love you. How can he be such a monster?"

"I don't know, I don't even understand how you exist let alone anything about your world."

Her world was inside his world, unseen by most humans, unfelt or even noticed. Being that she basically looked human, she could get away with being in it like a regular human. Maybe this was why Nocter hated her, because he couldn't do what she could.

"Yeah, it's wild to me that all that goes on and humans have no clue." She had decided long ago that making sense of it all wasn't a thing she'd ever accomplish, so why try? But with Nocter, with their past, he should make sense. He didn't seem to hate her, but he wasn't making a damn bit of sense at all. His actions didn't match what she thought they had become in their relationship. He once loved her, yet he was doing all this to her. How was this possible?

"We will get you out of here. We will scour every inch of the perimeter and find a weak spot that perhaps I can pull you through."

His desire to help her had been enough last time to free her from the invisible forest pen, maybe it would be enough again if they found the right spot in the force field. She'd hang on to that hope.

He stood up. "Okay, height check. Let's see if your orgasms worked their magic."

She rose to stand in front of him. She came up to her usual spot level with his upper chest. "Yup, I'm back to my normal size." She wondered if her normal size was now actually tiny since she needed orgasms to stay big. If orgasmic bigness was her new superpower, what did that make her smallness? "I'm super grateful it worked. Now let's see if you can pull me out." She fixed her dress to cover her breasts again and tugged it down to rest on her thighs. "I'm too dressed up to be trapped on a beach." She managed a weak smile. "Ironic. I bought this dress for our planned dinner date next week at the fancy restaurant, and now it's likely trashed to the point that I won't be able to wear it out." She sighed. "If I get out of here in time to go, that is." She couldn't help but fall into doomsday thinking, especially with a new prison with apparently a new set of rules she'd have to figure out the hard way.

Maybe she could just fly out again.

"I did fly out of the last one, so that's an option too, perhaps."

Leif nodded, then triumphantly grabbed her hand with a confident smile and swung their clasped hands toward the forest. "Let's search for a loophole you can fit through, then."

He led them to the edge, and she went as far as she could to where she could feel the force field but not be flung back from it.

"Tell me if you feel a weaker force, and we'll try to pass through there."

She nodded, her heart thudding. She feared there was no such weak spot, and she was stuck. "Wait, let's try something. Can you go through alone?"

He looked at her with alarm. "I'm not leaving you."

"No, you wouldn't leave me, just, I'm wondering if we're both trapped. You don't have to go all the way through, just do an arm or a leg."

"Okay," he said, though he looked worried. "We don't know the rules. I'd rather not let go of you."

"I'll hold on to you as long as I can, but we need to know more about this new situation."

Leif nodded and strode slowly toward the forest. "Wait, let's finish the perimeter first to assess if there is a weak spot. Or like a worm hole or something."

She laughed. "Worm holes aren't real."

He snorted. "Said the Fairy-Siren-Human." He laughed freely, his eyes lit with teasing.

She laughed along with him. "True, you got me there."

They walked hand-in-hand along the edges and not a single spot felt weaker to her. It felt uniform. "Well, there goes that idea. Now let's try my idea." She wasn't about to let on to him that she was nervous about it too. He could possibly get whisked out by the force. But she had zero way of knowing. Nocter had created another microcosm for her, and this one was tiny compared to the forest one. He couldn't possibly expect her to live on this patch of sand for long. There was no food nor any way to get food. Which also told her that this was temporary, unless he wanted to watch her starve to death.

Leif released her and crept toward the forest. He looked back at her, then back toward the trees as he made his way forward with trepidation.

She mused that if he could leave, he could go and get her food and water, as long as he could get back in, or at the very least throw them to her. This would ensure her survival until they figured out how to get her out.

He extended his arms and walked like a zombie.

She laughed. "Now you need to moan 'brains,'" she joked.

He looked back and her and snickered. "I know, right?"

He sneaked on and soon he was standing on the grass.

"You can get through!" she exclaimed, clapping her hands.

He turned to smile at her with a triumphant look, his handsome face alight with happiness. And then he was whisked away into the air and flung at lightning speed off to her right. His body hurtled along the shoreline, and she watched in absolute horror as he was dropped from the height of about ten feet in the air on a beach so far away that she could barely make him out.

She screamed and ran to the edge of her invisible jail on the side closest to where Leif had been stolen away to. She ran full force. When she hit the area where the force was strong and the hum filled her ears, she gathered all her determination and all her grit and forged on with a fire inside her that blazed hot enough to likely rival a bomb. She fought the air as it clawed at her flesh. She didn't even glance down to see if the pain she felt was from her broken flesh. She used every bit of brute force strength she had, and to her amazement, she was making real progress. She solidified her resolve and clenched her teeth, balled her fists, and ran full speed ahead, then she furiously began to flutter her wings and she soared right through the invisible wall.

Once through it, she didn't stop, but kept going toward Leif. Fueled by success and hope, she moved as fast as she could toward her lover. She couldn't believe her luck at getting free. This was working and she was filled with glee. The air caressed her skin while the sun kept her warm despite the fierce breeze she created while flying onward. She didn't care who saw her; let them stare at her in awe and watch something they deemed impossible. She carried herself with her head high. She had powers and Nocter couldn't steal them from her. Well, that wasn't entirely true.

She watched Leif pacing on the shore, waiting for her. As she came nearer to him, her triumph was within her grasp and she began to sing as she flew. Her orgasmic fuel tank kept her from feeling like she was shrinking and she was overjoyed that Leif was almost within her reach once more.

Leif fell to the ground and her heart stopped, but she garnered more grit to fly faster. She watched as full terror overtook her as he tried to grip the ever-crumbling sand as he was dragged by some unseen force toward the sea.

"No!" she hollered as her panic thickened. "No, please, no!"

Leif was at the edge of the water and his scrambling to stay on land hadn't slowed at all. He was fighting so hard and failing that her heart was breaking.

She cried out as his feet entered the water and the rest of his body slid into the sea so quickly it was like his body had been greased for immediate submersion. She flew over the sea and kept going rather than diving in, her heart desperate to believe that being above the water was safer. She flew until she was parallel to where Leif had gone under but deeper yet out into the water, and dove into the sea.

Chapter 5
Leif

Panic rose in him as he was held underwater. He held his breath, but he knew he couldn't last long. The last time he was underwater, he could breathe, so he desperately hoped it would be the same this time—but he was afraid to risk it. His heart was wrenched in knots as he recalled watching Gabriella getting smaller and smaller as he was flung through the air. He felt helpless, like a wisp of a leaf in a storm. He wasn't used to feeling this weak or controlled, and he didn't like it. His anger boiled as he fought the force, but it was no use. No matter what he did, it barely even made an impact on his position. He was being kidnapped again by something, or someone, he couldn't even see.

How could he fight something he not only couldn't see, but couldn't even feel? It felt like nothingness had a grip on him, yet it was propelling him through the water. He had no special powers or strength in this realm. He was a mere pawn in some game he didn't know the rules to, nor did he know the desired destination his opponent intended for him. It was both frustrating and terrifying. His heart pounded as he tried desperately to gain any semblance of control over himself. It was in vain. All he knew was he wanted to be with Gabriella, wherever that might be. But he also knew he had no means to make that happen. She did, though, and that was his only hope.

The cool water rushed past him, carrying him to a destination he feared. His muscles hurt from fighting, but he wasn't about to stop trying. He had just found Gabriella, and she had completely changed his life. The thought of not having her in his life gutted him. He couldn't imagine living without her.

At least he wasn't drowning. Now that he'd been forced to risk it, he was amazed to find he could once again breathe just fine in the water. Despite his fear, breathing like a fish was an incredible, and impossible, feat for a human. But he wasn't fixating on his new ability long enough to be swept up into thinking all this was any bit of good. Gabriella thought her past lover was the villain doing this, but he wondered if it wasn't Nocter, but some other noxious, dangerous being? He almost hoped it was Nocter, though, because perhaps he'd have some compassion left for Gabriella. He wasn't holding his breath though. He'd be an unhappy, scorned man to lose her, and perhaps that was what was driving Nocter's nefarious doings.

He imagined Gabriella was panicking too and chasing after him. He wanted to comfort her and tell her this was all going to be okay. But he wasn't entirely sure that was the case. Someone was playing with them, and though they'd let them have sex on the beach, they might have just been playing pervert and were back to the business of evil doing now that they got their kinky fix.

He zoomed past fish and even a few sharks as if he weren't a human being. He was more like a flesh torpedo as he traveled through the water. The strong currents threatened to rip his skin. If he went any faster, he'd be a tattered bag of bloody flesh strips if he survived. Whoever was orchestrating this was powerful. Powerful enough to temporarily change his biology. An awful thought gripped him. What if what was being done to him wasn't temporary?

He was dizzy and hungry. His inability to do a single thing for himself was certainly disheartening. He imagined there must be an endpoint to all this, but he didn't think he wanted to reach it. It all made no sense, Gabriella had that right.

He closed his eyes and tried to imagine stopping. To his utter amazement, his careening through the water slowed. He focused harder, concentrating on making his body stop moving, and he completely stopped. Perplexed, he looked around. Of course, he recognized nothing. He'd never been this far out in the sea. It was sea and more sea all around him. He'd scuba dived a bit, but that was very targeted, and with a guide and a boat as a marker at the surface of the water. This was a complete mystery. He was lost. Even if he were to have his own free will, he wouldn't even know which direction to head in for the shore and which was further out into the sea. He realized that even though he was a captive, he might be better off than on his own because he had no clue where to go. But regardless, he dismissed that thought and began to swim.

He glided through the water with ease, worry plaguing him that he'd be snatched again and driven through the sea once more. Finding Gabriella in the sea was about as easy as finding a single pin in New York City. His heart was heavy, but he knew if he could at least get to the surface of the water, maybe he'd see the shore, so he'd know which way to swim. That is if he hadn't been taken so far out that the shore was no longer visible. He shivered as the fear gripped him. Maybe the position of the sun would help too. He had to keep hope, or he'd drown.

He also feared Gabriella could be shrinking again in her efforts to find him, overtaxing herself. Then she'd be even harder to find. He longed to tell her to stay put and he'd find her, but that wasn't her. She would never just sit and wait. She was a doer, an action-taker, and that was what he loved about her as well. So, he couldn't fault her, but honestly, if she stayed still, she'd stay big, and it would be that much easier for him to locate her.

He smiled as he swam. Thoughts of her made him happy. He truly did love her, in ways he'd never loved anyone ever before. He'd felt things he didn't even know were possible. Emotions, sexual highs, and the intimacy he'd enjoyed with no other woman than her. He'd been taken on a journey with her right from the beginning and it hadn't stopped or slowed down one bit, it just changed shape and form and got deeper. They got more entwined with each other every day. He'd been shocked at first, but it had been a huge stroke of luck to find her, a beautiful woman masturbating in the woods, who also desperately wanted him to fuck her. What man didn't dream of that? It was like an unrealistic adolescent fantasy, and yet it had been plopped right in his lap. He grinned as he recalled how she'd been those first days, vying constantly, trying to get his attention to have sex with her.

He chuckled. She still vied for him sexually, only now it was on a more personal level rather than just sex for the purpose of sex so she could maintain her size. She was the horniest woman he'd ever dated, which was glorious and aligned with him so well that he knew he'd never find such a match again on earth. It wasn't just the sex though. It was everything about her.

He began to swim faster, but then slowed. He knew he'd tire out quicker if he swam so aggressively. Patience was what he needed now. He was grateful he was in shape. All those days at the gym gave him the strength and stamina he needed.

He popped above the water's surface with a jubilant feeling. He took his first breath of air and instantly wondered if he went under, if he'd still be able to breathe, or if being freed of the force had rendered him back to normal. He dipped his head back under the water to check. He could not breathe. He was confident that he was now likely free of the force that had nabbed him. He swam around to face the other direction and was overjoyed to see the land in his line of sight. He could swim that easily and be back on land soon. He was surprised to be this close to the shore after all the water he had been pulled through.

He began the long swim, taking breaks every so often to either lie on his back or on his stomach, with his face in the water. Eventually, he was close enough to shore that he could stand, then he walked out of the water. His shirt had tears in it, his shorts did as well. He looked rough and would likely startle any people who saw him. For all he knew, he also looked like someone had beaten the shit out of him. He wondered if the force of the water would surface as bruises. It had hurt, so he figured it was likely. He gazed at his arms and legs and didn't see any bruises forming yet.

He glanced around, but didn't see a single soul. He had no idea where he was, either. He could be miles from his truck. Sitting on the beach seemed like a dumb idea too. In the distance, he spied a little building near the shoreline, just down the beach a bit. Maybe he'd go there and see if he could somehow get a ride or call a friend to come and pick him up. He was honestly unsure what to do. He thought staying by the ocean was a good idea, in case Gabriella knew how to locate him. He was also so hungry he could barely think logically.

An idea popped into his head as he walked along the wet part of the sand. He planned to look for another human. Then, he'd asked to borrow a phone to call his friend, Max. Hopefully, there was some sort of food in the little building. Then he could ask Max to pay for some food and he'd pay him back. Then, at least, he could think more clearly and figure out how to find Gabriella. At this rate, he was so worn out he was useless.

He walked wearily along the shore, his bare feet grinding against the sand as he strode on. He finally reached the little shack. He was relieved as he reached it because it appeared to be a restaurant. It was, indeed, a little seaside joint with outdoor seating, with wind-battered wood siding that looked like driftwood and multicolored bar stools around multiple high-top tables scattered around the outdoor deck. The deck was embedded at the edges that were swooped over with sand like it was politely coexisting with nature. He wandered inside to find a worker. A blond woman with bright green eyes and a friendly smile greeted him, despite his disheveled appearance. He supposed he looked like a homeless person living on the beach. But she was gracious to him, nonetheless. He borrowed her phone and called Max, who promptly paid for his meal over the phone and insisted on driving to meet him. This all gave him considerable hope. Though he had no idea what to say to his friend to explain his appearance and his dire predicament.

He peered out into the sea as he ate his burger and fries, hoping, in vain, that he might get a glimpse of Gabriella, which was about as likely as having an alien ship land on the sand before his eyes, but that didn't stop him from hoping. Perhaps she had some magic she could use to find him, or she could smell him or something. She had all these hidden abilities that he was always finding out about and being amazed by. She was an incredible being, a treasure, and a gift to him.

He glanced at the mostly empty restaurant. He liked being inside, away from the wind for a bit, but he wanted to be out in the open in case he heard her singing. His friend would arrive soon, and he wasn't even sure yet what the fuck he was going to tell him about it all. It wasn't like he could tell him the truth. He'd cart him off to the looney bin in a heartbeat. What had happened wasn't just crazy, it was impossible to most every human's opinion on the planet. He moved outside to wait for his friend.

When Max arrived, Leif watched his friend's face fall into shock as he gazed upon him.

"Leif? What the fuck happened to you?" he asked, looking aghast as he stood in front of him, not taking a seat at the table. His jaw dropped, and his eyes filled with alarm. "Man, are you okay?"

Leif nodded and smiled weakly. "It's a long story, one that you won't believe." He patted the bar stool next to him, trying hard to maintain a smile for his friend. The burger and fries had helped immensely, and he felt more like himself again.

"I cannot wait to hear this," Max said as he took the barstool. His sandy blond hair was being tossed by the wind, and his gray eyes were wide with wonderment.

Leif raised his hands. "I know, I look homeless. But I assure you, I'm okay. And thanks again for the meal."

Max slapped some money on the table. "Here's a hundred dollars. Don't pay me back." He smiled at Leif with determination. "I'm not taking 'no' for an answer." He looked at Leif skeptically. "Does this have anything to do with your new woman?"

Leif nodded exaggeratedly as his grin grew wildly. "Indeed, it does, but she's amazing, incredible, and blowing my mind on a constant basis." He clasped his hands together and looked directly into Max's eyes. "I'm completely whipped." He let out of burst of laughter that was louder than he had expected it would be.

Max grinned. "Okay, and is this a good thing or a bad thing?' He motioned for the waitress and ordered them both a beer.

"Thanks," Leif said. "I could definitely use a beer right about now." He took a deep breath, then slowly released it. "All I can say is it's like I'm living in a movie right now, or some wild book, and if I tell you all that really has happened, you will not only think I'm crazy, but you will think I've completely lost my mind and gone insane."

"Love does crazy things to us, my friend." He leaned back with a happy grin.

He knew Max was right, but he couldn't tell him what had gone down, not all of it. He peered into the ocean, fumbling with what to say that was at least kind of true, but didn't tell him the truth at the same time. He was at a loss for words, and they sat in silence for several minutes.

Finally, after the beers arrived and he took his first sip, he said, "She's lost. And I'm looking for her."

Max's entire body flew into an alert status, his arms raised, his expression one of panic. "Leif! We need to call the police!"

Leif chuckled. "No, it's not like that. I assure you. But I need to stay on the beach until I find her."

"This is crazy talk, Leif." He reached for his phone. "Let me call the police, or the coast guard. She isn't in the water, is she?" Max looked horrified.

Leif shook his head and held up his hand in a stop motion. "The authorities are not needed. She's okay. I just got separated from her, so I need to wait until she returns."

"I don't like this, Leif. This sounds very off." Max hadn't taken a single sip of his beer yet and looked ready to flee. "Let me help you."

"I'm serious, you have to listen to me. I know this sounds insane, but I need to stay near the beach." He raised both hands in the air as he watched Max's fearful expression deepen. "Max, I assure you, I have not gone crazy."

Max seemed to relax a little bit, but the worry remained in his eyes. "I'm worried about you, Leif."

"Can you drive me to my truck?" he asked with hope.

"Of course. Where is it parked?" Max finally took a drag of his beer.

"Near Saffron, a little secluded beach parking lot."

Max spit out his gulp of beer in a spray and widened his eyes. "Leif, that's thirty miles from here? How the hell did you get here? You certainly didn't walk." Max's worry skyrocketed as unease further took over his demeanor.

"I know. I know. And I can't tell you the full story." He made direct eye contact with Max and held it. "I need your help, though."

"This is very concerning, Leif." He shifted in his seat as he gazed out at the ocean.

Leif considered telling him the full truth, but apprehension took over. "I know it is. But you just have to trust me on this." He grabbed the money on the table and waved it in the air. "Chicken wings on you, on me?" He laughed to try to lighten the mood.

Max agreed but shook his head. "Okay. Yes. But I hope someday you trust me with all this."

Leif nodded aggressively. "Yes, man, I promise. Someday."

They shared a plate of chicken wings, a basket of deep-fried pickles, and a platter of mega meaty nachos before Max drove him to his truck. No more questions were asked. Leif was extremely grateful for his friend, who had once again proven he was a true friend.

Chapter 6
Leif

He put the money in his truck, locked it, and then turned to wave as Max peeled out of the parking lot. Max had come through for him over and above. He hated not telling him the full truth.

He needed to stay out of the truck as long as possible though, despite the wild winds that were roaring. One, to be able to hear Gabriella as she sang, and two, so she could smell him. He often wondered what part of her mix of ancestors gave her the canine-on-steroids level of smell she possessed, but both of those aspects of her had worked before in reuniting them, so he was counting on them again. He literally had no course of action other than to sit and wait for her on the deserted beach like a damn useless rock. He was counting on her coming back to the beach where the truck was, rather than the last one they had been on together.

He imagined she was scouring the sea as fast as she could go, and shrinking more and more by the second. She needed her fix of him, but he needed her present to give her that fix. He loved giving her that fix. He grinned slightly thinking about it and their last two sex sessions until he once again felt overcome with helplessness. He hated it. He was a fixer, not a beach decoration.

He sat in the sand and peered out into the ocean. He got up and strolled along the shoreline, sat back down, and attempted to doze, but failed. The hours ticked by agonizingly slowly. He waffled from confidence to panic every few minutes and the stress had him exhausted. He realized his folly in not ordering another meal from the restaurant as evening approached. He figured he'd need to spend part of the night in the truck with the heater on because it got cold at night this time of year. And he was absolutely worried about Gabriella spending the night in the water. Which was likely silly, she had spent entire portions of her life living in the ocean. He smirked. She was quite the creature, and she was his, and he was hers. No interference from Nocter could change that despite what he might be driven by. Love had linked their hearts.

About an hour later, he spied an old woman dressed in a shredded dress walking along the shoreline toward him. He perked up at first thinking it might be Gabriella, but the person had the wrong color hair and it was longer than Gabriella's—plus it looked more like sea-blown dreadlocks than her lush soft hair. He shrugged, assuming it was simply another homeless person. He glanced down at his attire and thought his appearance might tell her he was a friend to her condition.

She kept moving along, her gaze traveling between Leif and the sea, and back again. She looked harmless enough to Leif, but he avoided making too much eye contact so as not to unintentionally engage her too much.

He jumped when she veered from her course along the waterline and headed directly for him. Alarms went off in his head, but she smiled as she approached.

"You must be Leif," she said with kindness laced in her words. She was older, but also a beautiful woman with vibrant green eyes and alabaster skin, wrinkled only near her eyes.

Again, he mused she seemed harmless enough, but she also carried ominous vibes, what with knowing more about him than he knew about her.

"Yes, I am," he said hesitantly. "Who are you?"

"I'm a friend," she said quickly, her eyes flickering with good intentions.

He relaxed a little bit but rose to his feet. He couldn't be too careful.

"I have a potion for you that will enable you to enter the water safely, and once again breathe while submerged. It carries with it an ability to withstand the cold as well." She grinned widely. "It has protective powers."

Going into the ocean again seemed dangerous. And this woman could be a trick, but he did want to take a more active approach in trying to reunite with his love. He peered at her cautiously as she opened her mouth to speak again. He wasn't sure he should dare trust her, but he also knew he had very few options.

"It also contains an invisibility cloak, so you will not be seen. Only someone who loves you will be able to see you." She smiled generously.

What if she were lying? But, seriously, he chastised his hesitancy. Did he have any other options at the moment? He needed to take some sort of action, and this would, at the very least, be one. If he were in the water, Gabriella might smell him, or he might hear her singing and then be guided to her. Regardless, this gift was either the miracle he needed, or a trap that might end him.

"Who are you?"

"I told you, I'm a friend." She had a sweetness about her that was genuine. She looked to be about sixty years old, at least by human standards.

"A friend of Gabriella's?" he asked cautiously with a skeptical gaze back at her.

"Yes," she said, but it was all she said, so not very helpful.

She produced a small bottle with clear fluid in it, which could basically be water. He expected such a powerful potion to look more magical than mere water. He was fully aware that she could have been sent by Nocter to poison him. But if Nocter had wanted him dead, he'd had plenty of options to off him.

He went back and forth in his mind about a hundred times in the few minutes he studied this woman.

"I'm Listena, and I am a friend to Gabriella, and to you," she assured once more. "You can trust me."

He slumped his shoulders and stared at the sand, then out to the sea that held the love of his life somewhere in it. He didn't want to live without her, so he looked Listena in the eyes. His decision was made. "I'll take it. Thank you."

His heart clenched and his stomach constricted as he brought the potion to his lips and downed it so fast that even Listena looked surprised.

"This will help you," she insisted, then started to walk away.

"Wait," called Leif. "Don't I get to know anymore?"

She smiled at him and nodded. "You already know all you need to know to find her."

The woman began to leave again, and Leif watched her go, his panic rising despite her assurances.

If he went into the water, how would he find this beach again? He didn't have any powers like Gabriella, and he might very well be casting himself to the sea to die when staying on land might be the right answer to keep him alive. But he wasn't one for non-action, so he strode toward the water and entered it while every strand of his being told him this was a mistake. Every strand except for the ones that told him he'd do anything in the world, in the universe, to save his woman.

He swam out into the deeper water and dove beneath it. He whipped his legs in a circular motion and moved his arms in a breaststroke. So far, the potion seemed to be working. He was comfortably breathing beneath the water. He chastised himself for not asking her how long the potion would work. That was a total idiot move, but so was diving into the ocean after drinking an unknown liquid from a stranger who assured you that you'd be safe. He might be the dumbest man on the planet.

He found he could breathe underwater just as he had before with no extra effort, and luckily, he wasn't cold so he kept swimming deeper out into the ocean. He swam by schools of fish and sharks with ease, and true to what she said, even the fish didn't seem to see him. Though he wasn't sure they were even sentient like that. He had not thought his invisibility would work on animals too, but he was grateful to not be seen by the shark. He figured the shark could smell him because he got very close and lingered before moving on. Once his heartbeat calmed a bit, he tried to reason with his fear. It was no use, and he was petrified, but that didn't mean he was giving up. He was urged on by the thought of having Gabriella in his arms again. The sea might be his nemesis under normal circumstances, but right now, it was more like a partner in his journey.

After what felt like hours of swimming, he slowed and rose to float on the surface of the water. He needed to rest. Once he popped out into the air, his heart began to pound. He could hear Gabriella singing. He thrashed about trying to figure out which direction her singing was coming from. It sounded far off, but it sounded so good to hear her that his heart was ready to burst. This meant she was alive and out of the water. But it also meant he was in the totally wrong spot. The woman's intentions with the potion now seemed suspicious, perhaps to put him in peril or to set him on the wrong course. But he'd not let that stop him.

He started to swim and kept turning his head from side to side to ensure he was going in the right direction of her voice. He was exhausted, but his energy was renewed as he listened to her beautiful voice. It called to him. It was hypnotic. The allure of her voice not only touched his soul, but stirred his loins as well. There was such power in her voice that he feared she might also be drawing unwanted men to her. He often wondered if women would respond the same way to her singing, but he smirked at such a folly thing to worry about. He just needed to get to where she was.

He had to stop and rest multiple times on his trek toward the sound of her singing, but he was very grateful he didn't feel cold. His fingers looked blue, though, and it was getting harder and harder to swim. He knew his muscles were likely cramping up from the coldness of the water. He desperately needed the sun to shine again. He tried yelling in her direction, calling to her in the black of the night when he took his breaks from swimming. He might very well die of exhaustion before anything else, or the cold, despite not even feeling it.

Memories of nights with her, making dinner, making love next to dirty dishes on the couch because they couldn't wait to devour each other, and mornings waking with her in his arms occupied his brain. It was like he was dreaming of them happening rather than remembering them, and it was in a slight moment of sanity that he realized he was likely delirious.

HE AWOKE IN THE WATER. He had no clue how long he'd been asleep, but he was amazed that he was still alive. That was a miracle in and of itself, but then he figured perhaps the potion had another benefit of protection that Listena didn't mention that had kept him alive while he slept.

He began to swim again, and the sleep had renewed his drive so this was doable. He swam for as long as he could, getting closer and closer to the parking lot lights at the little beach. Her song was much stronger now too. It sure seemed like the right beach, even the way the trees lined the area, but he couldn't be sure until he got closer. Not far from the shore, he saw a figure standing in the water.

His heart leaped and he called out, "Gabriella!"

"Leif!" she called back. "I see you!" She rushed through the water at lightning speed and hurled herself into his arms.

He began to kiss her all over her face while holding her close. He was shaking, and so was she as she sobbed against him.

"I can't believe this," she murmured as she kissed him on the lips. "It's a miracle."

"You can see me! And you're alive," he said with tears forming in his own eyes. "I've been searching everywhere for you."

"You're alive!" she said, then laughed. "Of course I can see you. Why wouldn't I? You're right here." She beamed at him as relief flooded her eyes. "I've been searching for you. Let's get you out of the water."

In the moonlight, he caught sight of gashes on her arms. "You're hurt?" he asked with alarm.

"Yeah, I've had a few battles, but I'm okay." She gasped. "I can't sing underwater. I kept singing, hoping you'd hear me."

Her dress was ripped as well. They held hands as they exited the water. There was so much to say that he felt overwhelmed into silence.

Once they were on the sand, he held her close as she shivered. He still was not feeling the cold. She was a little shorter, but not as short as she had been earlier.

"Tell me what happened," he said as they made their way toward the truck. He wanted to get her into the truck and warm her up, but he knew the force field might still be in place. "I'm going to drive the truck onto the sand if you can't get through. We need to get you warm."

She smiled up at him. "I love how you always think outside the box and have a solution."

As they approached the line near the invisible wall, she stopped.

"I'm at the edge, it's putting pressure on me. It's unfortunately still there." She looked weary and forlorn, and suddenly a bit shorter.

"It's okay. With four-wheel drive I should be able to drive onto the sand with no problem, then we will have warmth and shelter for the rest of the night."

He hurried to the truck and got in, laughing to himself that anyone watching likely wouldn't be able to see him and it would look like the truck was driving itself. He floored the gas, and the truck roared onto the sand like a beast. He smiled and stopped the truck a bit closer to the shore than she was standing.

He opened his door and yelled, "Come in, babe."

He blasted the heat as she entered. He still didn't feel cold, but he welcomed the heat.

"Oh, fuck. I needed this." She settled into the seat and her eyes fell closed as she laid her head back against the headrest. "You won't believe how it's gone for me. I was basically a yo-yo being tossed into the sea and then spit back out on the sand over and over again, probably a hundred times." She opened her eyes wearily, but relief further filled her eyes. "I lost count."

He watched as she practically melted into the seat, placing her head on his lap. He caressed her hair and face. "You're safe now."

"For now," she said yawning. "But for how long?"

He preferred not to think about that. Instead, he gazed upon her beauty and marveled at her resilience.

"What happened to you?" She looked about ready to fall asleep.

"I somehow managed to will my own control over my body when I was in the water. I have no clue how I did it. But it worked. Then I swam to the shore and walked until I saw a restaurant. I called my friend Max. He came to my rescue and bought me food, gave me money, and drove me back here to the truck." He went silent as he watched her drift in and out of sleep.

"Oh, that's nice. Max. Yeah," she said sleepily. "I remember Max." She yawned.

"Gabriella, I had drifted thirty miles away."

She yawned again. "I'm not a bit surprised. I had worried it was much more than that."

When he glanced along her body, he noticed there was more space between her feet and the door than when she'd first laid down.

"Gabriella, you're shrinking and at a really fast rate."

She sat up quickly. "I am?"

He nodded. "You are, babe."

"Okay, I'm so tired." She drooped her shoulders.

"Oh, I forgot to tell you that I met a friend of yours. Listena."

She jolted awake, her eyes going wide. "Seriously? She came to you?"

"Yes, she gave me a potion and I drank it."

"Oh, shit," she spat before glancing at her body. "Smelling you must have helped me not shrink at first, but now it appears to be not enough anymore." She smiled. "You horny?"

He burst out into raucous laughter. "Yes. Always. But we're both exhausted. And hungry." He could be sicker than a dog in bed and still manage to be horny.

"And don't forget beaten up, waterlogged, and trapped." She laughed. "It's fucking ridiculous." She snuggled up against his body. "I completely lost my singing voice too and couldn't sing until I smelled you."

"Seriously? That's crazy, and incredible." He looked down into her warm eyes and relished the sparkle that she still maintained despite their dire circumstances. "Wanna fuck?" he asked in a suggestive tone with a lusty leer. "There's more room in the back. Let's move."

She laughed too. "If we must," she said jokingly. "Well, you know, I might shrink away to nothingness and all."

"Right."

They climbed to the back seat. She got up on her knees and proceeded to slide onto his lap.

"Well, we can't have that now, can we?" He gave her a hungry determined look. "But we know just how to fix it, don't we?" He loved that even with all they were going through, they both were ecstatic to reconnect intimately. He wanted to pleasure her and keep her safe. Those had become the goals for his life. All day he'd had so many moments when he thought he might never see her again, so this was a true gift to be back together, and he wasn't going to waste a second of it. "You're so beautiful. I want you."

She wiggled on his lap as a tidal wave of lust bulldozed through him. His cock filled and he couldn't wait to feel her pussy wrapped around his erection. He wanted to watch her writhe and fight her climax, then crash into it as her body shuddered with pleasure. He loved the feel of her nipples on his fingertips. Loved what his playing with them did to her, making her wet with arousal. He adored the feeling of sliding inside her, how her breathing would pause as he slid into her deep. He loved that he could make her come on repeat. He was consumed by his desire as he gazed upon her.

She kissed his neck as he cupped her breasts and played with them, bouncing them in his hands, and then squeezing them. He quickly slid her dress down to expose her breasts, then he devoured them, taking each nipple into his mouth in turn. He loved the little raised map of her skin that gathered in a pucker to make her tips erect. He couldn't get enough of running his tongue over the raised parts of her tightened areola.

She cooed softly and released little mewls that sounded like her singing voice.

Her voice was hauntingly beautiful. Irresistible.

"Give me a little of your singing," he begged as he tasted her flesh lashing his tongue across her breasts and in between. He cupped them together between his palms and licked up the cleavage line her breasts made as they were smashed together.

She sang softly as she ground her groin into his, her head dipping, her expression one of enjoyment and immersion. She ended her song and as she held his gaze in an eye lock, she demanded, "Fuck me, Leif. I need you. Please, I can't wait."

He wondered if she was shrinking again and could feel it. He urged her off his lap. "Lay back," he commanded. "I'm making you come right now. I wanna drain my balls in you, but first, you're coming."

She scampered to spread out flat across the bench seat, spreading her legs in front of him. Her expression was both wanton and excited, with a twinge of desperation in her eyes.

It turned him on even more.

Having her spread herself so openly to him was so inviting and arousing that his cock filled completely and felt extra thick. He leaned down and inhaled her musky pussy scent and it made his cock twitch in anticipation. He gripped her thighs and leaned down to lick at her slit. He poked his tongue all over her lips and then visited her clit, which made her moan and buck. He loved making her climax; he knew he'd come, that was never the issue. He could come just thinking about her. His mission was to send her into the throes of passion and pleasure to secure her size. This was his superpower.

He pressed two fingers into her slick hole as he stared directly into her eyes, their silent, ardent urges matching. Then he sucked her clit loudly with audible slurps. He again remembered he was invisible and any onlookers peering into the truck would think Gabriella's writhing as she was being eaten out was being done by a damn ghost, or she was masturbating, but without touching herself. It was a funny thought he'd have to mention to her after. His smile disappeared though as he voraciously sucked her clit, sealing his mouth around her and putting all his facial muscles into it.

She writhed then screeched as her torso curled. He held steadfast to her jerking body and kept up his suction on her clitoral head. Her sounds escalated and then she went silent as she fully arched her back, making her peaked titties the highest point of her body. He loved seeing her hardened tips pointed upwards, her back arched to its max. His cock ached desperately to be touched, to rub on something, but he held off until her body torqued into another mighty climax.

"In me," she muttered once her moans settled down.

He kneeled between her thighs and spanked her clit with his cock.

She bounced with each smackdown of his beefy manhood on her and he yanked it from her reach.

"Hey," she said, clearly feeling slighted.

"It's going in you," he said with a growl. "Get ready to be fucked until you're a cum drunk rag doll."

She smiled a grateful and excited smile, her eyes half closed.

He slid into her easily and began to thrust harder and faster. It felt incredible to be inside her, her walls gripping his cock. She was doing her pussy clenching, which drove him absolutely wild. He grunted and kept drilling away into her. He leaned up to make sure he was hitting her clit too. Her body wrenched with pleasure beneath him as he rode her to his own climax.

She moaned and quivered as she easily coasted into another orgasm herself.

His cock pumped out his cum. He relished the big load of jizz he released in her, it felt so good to be sexually spent, the evidence on her internal walls. He lay between her legs as his cock calmed down, and kissed her on the lips.

Pulling her to lie on top of him was the last thing he remembered.

Chapter 7
Leif

Leif woke to sunlight. Gabriella was asleep on top of him. When he stirred, she stirred too and woke, her eyelids fluttering.

"It's morning," she said with surprise and relief. "Maybe a new day means my barrier has worn off."

"Maybe," he said with hope. "We can hope for that. The rules keep changing on us."

"Yeah, they do. Which confirms for me this really is Nocter at work." She frowned. "Why can't he just leave me alone? We have been over for a long time."

"I don't know, babe." He kissed her on the forehead. What he was doing to them wasn't fair.

He had morning wood and knew she felt it when her little mischievous smile flared.

"I feel something," she said as she scooted down his body. "Breakfast." She slid her dress down to give him a view of her bare chest.

"And thank you for that, too." He laughed in delight as she proceeded to quickly take his hard cock in her mouth. She bobbed her mouth quickly on his turgid dick, her tits swinging. He came in a wild rush.

"Fuck," he muttered. "Whew."

She tittered boisterously. "Well, that was fast. Holy shit!"

"I'm always so turned on in the morning, but that's because of you."

"Oh, you'd wake with a hard dick regardless," she said smartly in a tease.

"Maybe, but it's hardcore intense waking up with you." He watched her play with his still-hard cock. "You up for round two?"

"Only if I can look at the ocean," she said with a wink. "Let's stock up on O's for the day, since we have no clue what's in store."

She crawled so her front half was partially in the front seat. "Doggy in the truck gonna work?" she asked without a moment's hesitation.

"I'll make it work. Might still be cold out there." He wondered if his brand of magic was still on board or not. He wasn't cold at all, but then they were in the truck, which was warm.

"I don't know, but that blow job got me really hot. I want your balls smacking my clit." She wiggled her butt, presenting it before him, and he positioned behind her, readying to plunge in.

They both groaned as he penetrated her, and with a firm grip on her hips, he pounded into her, making her tits swing and her moans fly. When he reached under to play with her bean, she climaxed quickly, her pussy walls clenching aggressively on his erection. He came inside her when she came a second time.

With his balls doubly drained, he pulled her to snuggle skin to skin.

"Well, that was delicious. And fast," she said. "And speaking of, I'm starving. Like mad raving starving. Do you think you could drive and go get us some food?"

He didn't want to leave her, but he was ravenous too. "I'm nervous to leave you," he admitted.

"I'm nervous too, but I need to eat so badly. I can't take another day like yesterday on an empty stomach. I'm near ready to pass out as it is."

He laughed. "What if I'm still invisible?"

She erupted into laughter too. "Then you get to steal, I guess!"

He chortled and they both had a good long laugh. It felt incredible to laugh with her. He was in good spirits, and his balls were emptied. It was a good day already.

"Okay, I'll go and get something. Just be careful and keep your eyes open for danger."

She scoffed. "We've never seen it coming is the problem."

He nodded. "True." He hated the idea of leaving her alone, but they did need to eat before they both fainted. He sighed and rubbed her back. "I'll hurry back."

She fixed her dress to cover herself and prepared to exit the truck. "My fairy parts are kind of malfunctioning too. I'm just a damn fucking mess."

"You look gorgeous and perfect to me." He gave her another kiss and followed her out of the truck. "I still don't feel cold. Is it cold out?"

She smirked. "A little. Your powers must still be in effect."

That took him back to remembering they had never finished their conversation yesterday. "Gabriella, who is Listena?"

She looked pointedly at him and said, "Listena is my mother."

"But your mother is ..."

She nodded with a grave expression. "Dead."

"Well, shit." He had met up with a ghost and hadn't realized it. "Has she ever come back before?"

She held up a finger. "Once." She didn't look freaked out by the fact that her dead mother had given him a magical potion, and he marveled at how insane his life had become with her in it. It was like he was legit living inside a book rather than his own life.

"Well, I can't wait to hear more about that, I need to hear more, but I'm going to get us some food first. So, we can get back to the business of getting you out of this damn pen." He secretly was hoping his new powers might somehow help him help her get free, but he didn't want to jinx it by saying it out loud. Plus, this was all the more reason to hurry the fuck up. He could wait to eat, but she'd been without food longer than he had and she looked a bit pale.

"Hurry back before I start eating sand," she joked. "I'll be here, hurling my body against the force field, trying to break through," she said with sarcasm and a raise of her hands.

He saluted. "Yes, ma'am. I'm on it. And don't get too bruised up trying. We already know you can get through." He was so grateful for the money Max had given him so he could buy something, well, perhaps steal it, if he was still invisible. For some reason, he couldn't locate his wallet in the truck, and he worried he'd lost it in the sea.

He hopped into the truck and gunned the gas to get off the sand. He realized anew that driving down the road that he might look like a truck driving itself and he got a hearty laugh as he passed a semi, and a few cars. He drove for about five minutes before he came upon a gas station. He'd know once he entered if he were still invisible or not, but regardless, he had money, so he was good to go either way.

He parked his truck on the side so it wasn't as openly visible and glanced around with caution. The place was mostly deserted, but there was one woman pumping gas. He decided to try to sneak in behind her. Not that it mattered, but it was sure to go smoother if he didn't just open the door and freak out the clerk. He didn't want to raise any unnecessary suspicions. He snuck out of his truck and waited by the door for her to finish pumping the gas. The clerk had looked his way and didn't seem to register him, so he figured he truly was still invisible.

When the woman, who was about twenty years old with blond hair and curled dark eyelashes, looked right through him, not even acknowledging him one tiny bit, he confirmed she didn't see him. Unless she was a snobby bitch. He zoomed inside the gas station on her heels and made a dash for bread and peanut butter. He shoved two big bottles of water into his pockets. He hoped they'd disappeared to the human eye. Then, he scooped up a bag of chips, some plastic silverware, bananas, and beef jerky, hugging them all tightly to his body before strolling back to the door. The woman had gone to the bathroom and was now picking out a caffeinated drink at the cooler. He waited on pins and needles as she slowly walked through the candy aisle and picked out something, then made her way to pay.

He watched both of them intently. The clerk wasn't freaking at floating bags of food and it gave him an idea. What if whatever he was carrying was also deemed invisible?

His suspicions were confirmed when neither of them paid any attention to him or the stash in his arms. He breathed a sigh of relief as his pounding heart began to calm down. He vowed to come back and accidentally pay extra someday. He thought about leaving the money, but money poofing out of nowhere was a bit conspicuous.

He easily left the gas station following the young woman. He rushed to his truck and slid in. Wasting no time, he headed back to Gabriella, speeding the whole way.

He found Gabriella sunbathing topless on a rock near the water's edge. He grinned appreciatively, seeing her bared breasts in the sunshine. She left her top down as she slid off the rock, which made her boobs bounce. As she walked toward him, his cock began to harden.

"Whew, look at you topless and oh so sexy in the sunshine." He had to admit, he'd happily fuck her again.

She had other plans. She tackled him and swiped the bag of beef jerky. She ripped it open and began to devour the dried beef. She handed him the bag, and he snagged a big handful too.

"Uhh, it feels so good to be able to eat," she said through her chewing, her head thrown slightly back as she enjoyed the food.

They sat in the sand to eat and watched the waves roll in nonstop.

"Damn, I needed that so bad. Want a sandwich?" She readied to make up some peanut butter sandwiches, using her thigh as her sandwich prep surface. She set about the work of quickly building sandwiches. They each devoured two and then laid back in the sand with full bellies.

"Food and sex. Now I'm in heaven," she said, squinting.

"Yup. And sleep."

"And no drama. For the moment." She curled to her side. "It's a false feeling though. I know we're still in deep shit."

He nodded in agreement. "We are. So, I have an idea. But let me ask you this first. Could you sing when I was gone? Did you try?"

"I did try and, no, I couldn't sing. I tried, hoping you'd hear me and come." She held a perplexed expression. "At first, I could sing out of the water, but not under. Then I lost the ability to sing completely. It doesn't make any sense. Nor does it make sense that Nocter just stopped toying with us all of a sudden. That's why I'm on edge just waiting." She frowned. "I know he's likely lurking nearby, just waiting to make his next move."

"What if I'm the key?" he mused as he rose up on one elbow.

"What do you mean?"

"Well, you're affected by me, right? You couldn't sing until I emerged from the water, I'm thinking. And when your mom gave me the potion, I went invisible, right?"

She nodded but seemed unaffected.

"Hear me out. What if, when you're near me, the powers I have, sort of, like, I don't know ...act like a cloak around you too?" He gave her a hopeful expression. He grinned triumphantly as things seemed to be making sense. "Even when I was in the gas station store and held the food, the people couldn't see the food."

She sat up quickly. "You mean, like Nocter perhaps can't see us?"

"Right." He nodded. "Precisely."

"But you were just gone, and I was alone. He'd have seen me then." She screwed her face into a pained expression.

"Maybe he was busy." He shrugged. It made a bit of sense to him. Maybe not that part so much, but the rest did.

"He would have nabbed me had he seen me alone though, if your theory is right."

"Maybe. So here are my thoughts. It wouldn't hurt to try them. What if you're invisible around me too, and if so, I could sneak out of this pen while carrying you, so my invisibility cloak covers you?"

"Well if that was the case, why couldn't we go through before?" She smirked with a raise of an eyebrow. A dirty little secret smile took over her expression. "Maybe it's your cum. It's protective." She laughed with mischief in her eyes.

He raised his eyebrows at her as he released a short curt laugh. "Ha! Right. But, also, because Nocter can sense you, even if he can't see you. You said it yourself once. But if he can sense you, but not see you, maybe he is rendered powerless to snatch you." He shook his hands and his head. "This is making more sense. Look, I know you were just alone, but maybe the fucker was busy or something and just missed his chance."

She laughed in his face. "That's wishful thinking." She laughed again. "Or, like I said, it was your cum."

He had to admit, his ego liked that possibility a bit too much. "What if you were unconscious while I carried you? So he couldn't sense you anymore."

She jumped back with a frown. "Like you'd knock me out? I don't like this plan at all." She grumpily crossed her arms over her chest.

"No," he said with hilarity. "What if you were asleep, babe? I'm wondering, what if he can't sense you when you are asleep?"

"You have quite the imagination, and wishful thinking." She hugged her knees her to chest, making her dress slide up her thighs. "That would explain why he hasn't taken either of us, though, for this long, if he can't see us." She wiggled her toes. "He can't take me when I'm far from the shore, either. All this time I've been with you, he hasn't." She threw up her hands. "But he took me to plop me in the forest when I was far from the sea, so that may not be true."

"Yes, but I wasn't with you then. Let's talk this out more. What if it's a combination of me and the distance? I mean, we've mostly been together since you've been out of the forest pen. Not all the time, but if Nocter has to make a conscious effort, then there will be times when he can't just take you, cause he's doing something else. Or maybe it's my scent in my house protecting you as well, because you still smell me there, even when I'm not there."

She shimmied her shoulders. "Your theory might hold water. But I can guarantee you that if you carry me while asleep, I'm going to wake up." She giggled. "And I still think it's your cum. You have magical cum." She erupted in delightful flirty laughter. "Just ask me, I think it's magical."

He smiled with a chuckle, then put his hands in his hair. "I'd like to think that, let me tell you, but let's focus, babe. There's got to be a way to make this happen."

"I'm open to any suggestions but I also know your potion's benefits likely have a time limit."

"Yeah, I've thought about that too," he said, then pursed his lips. "Maybe if you fell asleep in the truck, like in my lap. Then I could drive you out."

She shook her head. "The movement and the sound would wake me." She sighed visibly. "It wouldn't work."

"Maybe we should just try driving out? Would the field really stop the heavy truck just because you are in it?"

She shrugged. "We could try."

He released a big breath in a huff. He leaned back on his hands and squinted as he looked up at the blue sky. He dropped his head to meet her gaze. "Unless I hold you until you fall asleep, then I just walk out."

"That all sounds way too easy," she said fingering a curl between her fingers, her face in thought-filled awe. "And, plus, you'd get tired of holding me. It would be hard to fall asleep like that is my thought."

"But what if you got really tired, like from running around the beach, and really wore yourself out? I bet you'd fall asleep fast."

She smirked. "Maybe. I don't know. Problem with this is, nighttime is a far ways off, and I won't likely be that tired until late tonight. And by then, you may have lost your powers."

He shrugged. "All we can do is try, right?"

"Right." She looked skeptical but willing. "Okay, I'm in."

"Start running," he said with a mocking smirk and teasing grin.

"Oh, you like this cracking of the whip, don't you?"

"Kinda," he admitted with a lewd grin. "Can you be naked too?"

She scoffed and then smiled. "You're enjoying this way too much."

"And why shouldn't I? What else do I have to do?" He laid back and propped his head up on his bent arm. "Sunbathing and watching your tits flopping as you run sounds like the best passage of time, other than actually fucking you."

She put her hand on her waist and directed a pouty look at him. "Yeah, maybe we should be having lots and lots of sex to wear me out."

He loved her defiant stance, the way her pouty lip just begged him to suck it. "Maybe after you run for hours. Plus, an orgasm or fifty might make you sleepy because you will be so cum drunk and woozy." He nodded and ticked the air with a bob of his index finger. "Scheduled. Running with tit flops, then so many orgasms you fall into a deep slumber." He grinned lasciviously. "We have a plan."

"Hardy-hardy-har ha-ha-ha. Very funny." She leaned forward and shouted, "Not!"

"I think it's an ideal plan." He loved the flirting, it made him feel like they weren't trapped anymore. It felt normal.

She released a big sigh. Then seductively removed her dress in a slow deliberate strip tease. She flung the dress so it landed on his abdomen, then danced about, showing off her naked parts. "See how long you can watch me running on the beach nude before you're so horny that you chase me down and fuck me," she said in a taunting voice that damn near incited him to charge her and begin said fucking. She shimmied her shoulders to make her boobs jiggle and burst into a run, her giggles filling the air.

He smirked at her. She wasn't wrong. Seeing her nude already had his cock at a semi, and filling further by the second. He'd be fully hard in no time. It would be tough to watch her and not race to dominate her into so many orgasms that she really did feel sleepy. It sounded like a fun challenge, and one he was definitely up for. He intended to try this tactic in a bit after he watched her prance her sassy naked body all over the beach for a bit. She was a damn sexy woman, cock-fillingly so, and he'd been smitten with her upon first sight. Granted, she'd been naked then too.

His mind and heart had followed suit like good little puppy dogs. Dominating her sexually had become exquisitely exciting and opened up his sexual palate to so many new experiences that his mind was constantly being blown. She had really nestled into being submissive too, and it had been a delight to him. Their dynamic was that he was more of the leader when it came to sex, not that she didn't take charge at times. But being a strong man in the bedroom, and her acquiescence to it, had elevated his sexual prowess to heights he'd never dared imagine. He loved watching her writhe in the sweet intensity of arousal, fight coming under his direction for orgasm control and edging, and then there was the sheer massive enjoyment he got from watching her succumb to waves of climactic pleasure. He was addicted to pleasuring her.

She sang as she danced and he had to forcibly make himself stay put. Her body was massively enticing, and mixed with her singing, he was a total goner. All he saw, focused on, and heard, was her. His cock was under her spell too, and stayed hard. She was a talented seductress, as any siren was, but she had the vulnerability of also being a human. This made her his fantasy woman, and brought to his attention new fantasies he'd never even considered. She was truly a remarkable creature, and she was his to take care of. He'd knighted himself with that way back when they'd been fighting to get her out of the forest. But here they were again, fighting another entrapment, but at least now they were together. And now they knew who they were battling.

A thought seized him. He remembered last summer he'd been camping with friends and couldn't sleep so he'd bought a bottle of sleep aid at the campground general store. He was positive he'd stashed the bottle in his glove compartment because he never used the stuff normally, so it should still be there. He hopped up and waved his hands toward Gabriella, who was prancing, parading her bare flesh along the shoreline with her arms raised. She stopped and then dashed toward him.

"What is it?" she asked with concern.

"Have you ever taken sleeping pills? I mean, with your biology, can you take meds like that?" He realized that she may not be able to, or that it may be risky for her, given she wasn't a full human.

"No, I've never taken sleeping pills, so I have no idea how I'd react." She pursed her lips, then frowned. "But that's an idea. You can go back to the gas station and swipe some."

He grinned broadly. "No need. I have some in the glove compartment of my truck. I'll be right back." He ran to his truck, his heart beating, and his mind reeling with possibilities. But it wasn't without sharp edges. What if taking the pills hurt her? Or messed with her magic? What if she didn't wake up? It was risky. But they could not stay trapped on a beach, either. They needed food, shelter, and a place to take a dump other than behind a rock in a hole in the sand.

He rummaged in his glove compartment and saw the little white bottle in the back left corner. He snatched it and tossed it in the air before catching it. "Bingo!"

He left his truck unlocked with the hopes that he might be returning with Gabriella in his arms, and he wanted the easiest access to his truck possible. Then it would be a quick getaway, as far away as fast as possible to escape Nocter's reach. He doubled back and opened the door, leaving it ajar and ready to accept the love of his life.

He smiled as he hurried back to her. He handed her the bottle.

"Have you ever taken any meds at all?" he asked cautiously.

"No. Only potions and such. Mostly from my mom." She grinned. "And as you know, they work."

"More on that in a discussion in the future, but I have a plan."

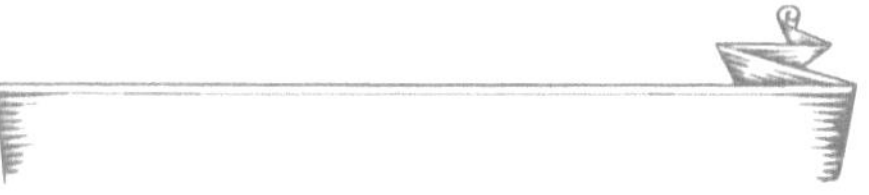

Chapter 8
Leif

"Let's hear it," she said eagerly.

He grabbed and pinched her right nip. She squealed and jumped back.

"Don't distract me. I'm trying to focus on your plan," she said with a shitty little grin.

"Don't play that with me, I know you." He raised his hand. "Okay, here's the plan. I pleasure you until you are cum drunk and feeling woozy, sleepy. But before I do that, you take a sleeping pill or two. Then I'll hold you next to the force field. And once you are asleep, I'll dash through."

She gave him a half smile. "We can try, I just don't know if I'll fall asleep like that, though." She looked at the bottle of pills. "I wonder how many I should take. Two?"

"I'd say two, yeah. I'm a bit nervous, as I see you are too. We don't know how you will react. So, we can brainstorm other ideas if you think it's too risky."

"If we don't try something, we're just stuck. I'm fresh out of ideas and we're on a timeline." She bent over to pick up the bottle of water at her feet. "Let's get to it. I'm in the mood for pizza at Roberto's in town." She grinned and opened the bottle of pills, promptly dropping two in her palm. She popped them in her mouth and took a long drag of water. "I'm yours. Make me come until I can't see straight."

He kneeled in the sand and patted it. "Take your throne, my lovely orgasm-hungry queen." He gave her a licentious look. "I'm going to make you come so much and so hard that you will be asleep in no time."

She looked filled with glee, and it made him so happy. To have a woman who loved sex as much as he did and who got so excited she glowed when it was time to have sex was a gift he'd never not appreciate. This was potentially dangerous to try though, but she was charging in full blast, which was so much in her character. He adored her for it.

"I'll take care of you, you have my word." He couldn't help but get serious as he gazed into her trusting eyes.

"I trust you, Leif. With my whole self." Her eyes flickered into looks of love and admiration loaded with trust. "Do what needs to be done."

He'd not take her submission lightly. He had a responsibility for her, both for her pleasure and for her well-being. He took pride in claiming that role.

He settled between her legs and grinned up at her. He couldn't hold his own lewd grin back. He was getting to do this, and he secretly loved it. He grasped her thighs and pinned her to the sand in his tight grip. He breathed on her sealed lower lips, and she squirmed. His excitement flourished. He tickled his tongue along the line in her flesh and she released a happy little squeal. When he took a full tongue swipe from bottom to top along her labia lips, she moaned. She grasped his hair as she pulled his face into her soft warm wetness. He was excited by her moans as he pried her lips open with the tip of his tongue. He knew her anticipation was driving her wild, and he intended to drive her even wilder with his mouth and his hands.

As he suckled the intimate areas of her flesh, moving his lips in firm grips along her skin, centimeter by centimeter, she fell nicely into allowing him to lead her. When he finally accosted her clit with his tongue, her trembling legs and her moans egged him on more. He fully fitted his mouth to her pussy and sucked hard. He pressed two fingers into her moist hole and rode them in and out of her as he sucked. Her body thrashed and bucked, but he didn't let up his pinning down of her. She wasn't squirming out of his grasp, she was going to feel every second of the heightened sensitivity, so she came hard and often. He wasn't stopping for anything, not her pleading, not her smacking his head away for a break. This was war and this was his only defense to win the battle for her.

She mewled and tossed her head from side to side. When she arched and her sounds escalated, her twitching exploded, and she came hard. Her juices met his tongue, and he ate her out more voraciously. He brought her to climax over and over again as the waves crashed and the wind played with his hair. The sun beat down on them and he hoped the warmth would also entice her to fall asleep. He wondered if it were better to hold her while she was sleepy and let her fall asleep in his arms, or if it were better to allow her to fall asleep in the sand, and then lift her up. In the end, he decided it made more sense to hold her and rock her when she seemed sleepy enough. Picking her up would likely wake her.

He pleasured her until her eyes were no longer opening, and her involuntary moans gave way to her silence. He startled, fearing he'd waited too long, and she was already asleep. He stood and scooped her up as gently as he could as his heart raged with worry. He had to be oh so careful.

She moved a little once in his arms, but then seemed to settle back into sleep when he said, "Sleep babe, I've got you."

He started to move slowly at first, wondering if she'd wake from feeling the force field pressing on her. He alternated between watching her face for signs of waking and watching the ground to be sure he didn't falter in his step, or trip on something, and drop her. He had thought he'd run with her full force to get out, but as he crept along, he felt slow and steady made more sense for keeping her asleep.

He was nearing the grass, which gave him hope because he knew they were in the area where she'd felt the force field before. She remained asleep. He carefully tightened his grip on her body in case the force field tried to pry her from his arms. He was ready for a fight, if need be. His heart pounded and his breathing ramped up as he trod swiftly along the grass and weeds at the edge of the sand. He didn't look back. Once he hit the blacktop of the parking lot, he ran full force toward his truck. Gabriella didn't flinch a single bit, even though his rushing made him jostle her.

He deposited her in the back seat of the cab and flung the door shut. He moved at lightning speed into the driver's seat, turned on his truck, and sped out of the parking lot, his tires squealing.

He tried to calm his breathing as he drove. His heart was still pounding and his head felt ready to combust.

"Gabriella?" he asked. When she didn't respond, he called to her more loudly, "Gabriella!"

He didn't see any movement from her. He tried not to panic. Maybe the dose of pills was too big for her. When he felt far enough away from the ocean, he'd stop and check on her. He was fine with her sleeping, she needed it. He just couldn't shake the fear that she may not wake up. Who knew what sleeping pills did to someone like her?

He let triumph creep into his heart a little bit. He'd done it. He'd gotten her out. He would feel so much better if she were to wake, though. He tried to stave off a panic attack, but he wasn't doing a very good job of it. His vision blurred slightly, and he felt light-headed. He focused on the road ahead and willed himself to stay the course. He needed to get her to a safe place before stopping or he'd risk losing what they'd just won.

He sped along the highway, going way too fast, but it was worth it. He'd gotten this far, he was hell-bent on making it home before stopping, despite his fears that she was not doing okay. He pulled into his driveway and got out, not wasting a single second to look around for nosy neighbors before opening her door and gazing upon her.

She was still breathing, thank goodness. Relief flooded him as he watched her chest rising and falling in a steady rhythm, and his own breathing rate started to normalize.

He gently shook her. "Gabriella. It worked. Gabriella. Wake up. Gabriella. We're home."

She didn't move a single muscle but looked peaceful as she slept on.

He shut the door and hopped back in the driver's seat. He opened the garage door and moved his truck inside. He didn't need the can of worms his neighbors would open seeing him carrying an unconscious naked woman into his house. He checked the inside door to the house to be sure it was unlocked, then propped it open. He scooped her out of the truck and carried her inside the house. He didn't stop until he was in the bedroom, and he laid her in the bed. He carefully covered her up with the comforter, deciding sleep was what she really needed.

He stayed by her side, trying to rouse her every so often when his impatience flared. She'd been asleep, out cold, for five hours. He alternated between panic and joy. He wondered if he should be taking her to the hospital, but that would expose her to the world. That was a horrible idea. He had no one to call for help, either. He tried everything he could think of to wake her, even resorted to slapping her face, but nothing worked. Then he'd tell himself to chill, and just watch her sleep, marveling at her beauty and her fearless determination that he so loved.

After another hour, he was starving so he left her for a few minutes to throw a pizza in the oven. She adored pizza and maybe she'd smell it, and then wake up. He could only hope.

He watched the birds in his backyard as he was waiting for the pizza to cook, recalling how mind-blowingly insane everything had become since he'd met Gabriella. But also, how mind-alteringly happy he'd become. His life was complete with her in it. He wouldn't change meeting her for anything in the world.

He pulled the pizza out of the oven once it was done and carried a tray with the pizza, two plates, two napkins, and two sodas to the bedroom. It smelled so wonderful, and he was so hungry. Once inside the room, he set the tray on the bed and picked up a slice. He held it under her nose.

A smile spread across her face. Before her eyes opened, she asked, "Are we at Roberto's?"

He was so thrilled, relieved, and overjoyed she was finally waking. He gazed into her eyes to see a galaxy still waiting for them to enjoy together. It was confirmed. He needed nothing else in life but her. "No, baby, we're at home."

She fluttered her eyelids, closed them briefly, sighed, then reopened her eyes. She smiled wide. "Oh, good. It worked," she said softly.

"It worked," he parroted. "And you are finally awake."

She looked confused. "How long have I been sleeping?"

"Probably about seven and a half hours. And I've been in misery every second."

"Well, never fear, my love. I'm all rested now." She eyed up the piece of pizza. "Is that mine? I'm famished."

"It's yours, it's all yours." He motioned to the pizza on the tray.

Her face was appreciative as she sat up, readying to take the first bite.

They ate the pizza in bed and then lay together snuggling.

"We made it. I can't believe it worked," she said as she fitted herself to his body. "I'm never moving again." She snickered. "Until I'm hungry or horny, that is."

"Isn't that always?" he teased.

"Yep, pretty much."

"Have I told you I love you today?" he asked. "I do love you."

She sighed and wiggled against him. "As I love you, today and forever."

"Today and forever," he repeated.

Rejecting Queendom, Book 3

Before Leif...

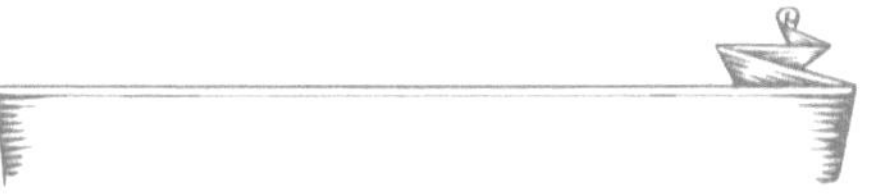

Rejecting Queendom, Book 3, Chapter 1

Nocter

He couldn't stop thinking about her. Everywhere he looked made him think of her. He couldn't focus, nor could he easily make decisions. Was this what love was supposed to feel like? The obsessive thoughts he couldn't get away from about Gabriela would have been okay if he had nothing important to do, but that wasn't the case. He had a meeting with the council soon, and they were proposing movement in a new direction that he had to weigh in on. Their current leader, King Mangen, had fallen ill, and it seemed he was not going to survive, but if they didn't act soon, someone else might swoop in and take control. He had a sneaking suspicion his peers had their eyes on him, so he needed to be in top form. He was honored to be a potential candidate, but concerned about what that would mean for his life.

He swam back and forth, pacing, as thoughts of Gabriella filled his head. He was helpless before the invasion of his love for her. He thought about how kissing her beneath the water-filtered moon last night, with the darkness surrounding them on all sides, had sent him into the throes of passion so quickly. He had been helpless to it. Her skin had glowed as bright as the moon as he caressed her nude body. She was a decadent enigma with the grace of a siren mixed with the magic of a fairy, and the human side of her gave her great creativity, lush vulnerabilities, and a crafty tenaciousness he'd rarely encountered in another. He never thought he'd be with someone like her. His parents would have been aghast at him choosing a mix like her. But sea life had settled on her well, though he also knew she was one of a few of them who could also live on land among the humans. She'd only tried it briefly, quickly returning to the sea when she couldn't tolerate the cruelty she saw. She belonged in the sea. It suited her well, but he wasn't one to tell his lovers what to do. Sure, he would play the dominant in all things intimate, but he never extended his dominance beyond that. He believed in free will for all.

But Gabriella belonged in the sea. She belonged with him.

She knew exactly how to snag him, get his attention in any state his mind was in. Images of her swimming around him as she put on a display of flirtation in the form of dancing, hypnotized him in an effective and almost menacing form of seductive courtship. When she did that, she fully consumed his brain until there was nothing left. He couldn't imagine he could ever live without her now that he was with her. He also knew he'd do anything for her. He longed to take care of her, and there was no end to his desire for her. She might just be what he dared not hope she was. Yet he wanted to be with her every moment. Devoting his life to one was certainly a daunting task to consider.

He spotted her in the distance and his heart began to race. The smile grew on his face, and he was both excited and calm at once. She was coming. He knew it would be her. It was like his heart had a sensor on it and her impending presence made it bleep. Her blond hair flowed behind her as she swam, and her breasts bounced as she moved. Her beauty was only second to the vast expanse of her beautiful heart.

As she approached, he kept his eyes glued on her. He wanted to give her not only the ocean, but the world. And she deserved it. He'd do anything for her, and she was finally beginning to understand that.

She sped up as she got closer. Her hair flowed and her face was bright, catching the sunrays streaming through the water.

Once she came nearer to him, his heart sighed. He was home. Seeing her right in front of him melted away any apprehension he harbored each and every time he was with her. He experienced a calming, like things were now right in the world, but also he savored a flaring of his arousal. It was an odd combo that he loved because it set him up to be fully focused on her. She was exactly what he wanted in a mate. Perfect.

"Hi," she cooed as she swam to his open arms. Her smile was as seductive as was her sexy body.

"Hi, yourself, sexy," he slurred back. "You are looking amazing today. Have I told you that yet?" And she did. She could turn him on faster than any female he'd ever been with. Her eyes were lit up and energetic. She looked rested and happy, and her skin was supple and firm. He couldn't resist touching her when near her.

He couldn't resist touching her all over, in fact, doing so often led to more. He caressed her body as she squirmed lightly in his arms.

"So, what are you doing today?" she asked with hope on her face. She bit her lower lip as her eyes became seductive. "Do you have time? Because I need you."

"I always have time for you." He smiled at her as he purposely denied the existence of his upcoming meeting. He'd squeeze time in for her every day, no matter what. How could he not? She was too incredible not to.

She dragged her fingers down his chest, her fingertips rising and dipping along his defined muscles. "I can't stop thinking about last night and how epic that was."

He grinned down at her, his interest peaking in repeating last night's acts. "It really was. I'm not sure we can top that."

She writhed in his arms as her gaze turned ablaze with fire. "Oh, I bet we can. It's a good goal to try for now that we've experienced that together."

"That's very true." He bent down to kiss her on the lips. "You are delicious. I can't get enough of you." He slicked his tongue along her seductive smile, which enticed her to part her lips.

They fell into a deep kiss as a current of warmer water flowed across them. They kissed and fondled each other, their arousal levels seeming to sync in ardent fervor. Nocter felt himself thicken. He wanted her.

He opened his eyes and caught sight of another approaching. His heart fell. Dang it. Bad timing. This would surely put a damper on the moment. He lifted his head to get a better look. He groaned. It looked like Finstra. He was early.

"Ugh," he muttered.

Her eyes filled with concern. "What is it?"

"Finstra is approaching." He said it as if Finstra were the beacon of doom.

"Oh," she said, her disappointment obvious.

He cringed because she knew what this meant. "I'm sorry. I do have a meeting this morning."

"You and all your new important meetings. I should have known when I started dating you." She didn't seem too sour, but she was clearly bummed. "I understand. Maybe tonight we can meet up?"

He nodded and pulled her tight to his body. He kissed the top of her head. "I will make it up to you in more ways than you will be able to count." He allowed a salacious look to take over his face.

She responded with a similar look. "Promise?" She wiggled her tummy against his enlarged manhood. "Too bad we can't use that right now." She raised an eyebrow in suggestion.

He released a quick breath. "I know. Whew, do I know." He shook his head, glancing up quickly, wondering what Finstra would think seeing the evidence of his massive arousal. It wasn't like he could just turn it off. "But the good news is I've got more where that came from. You ensure that quite well." He chuckled as she beamed a smile back. "I'll be here. Come back later?"

"Yes, good luck." She slipped out of his arms with a forlorn look and swam away.

It hurt him to send her away. However, he had no choice in the matter. He began his swim toward Finstra, taking the bait he knew he must swallow.

HE PONDERED ALL OF what the council had said as he swam back home. The news was more than he could process quickly. He wasn't sure he was ready for what they wanted. It would impact his life to the point where it would become unrecognizable if he agreed to their plan. What if he wasn't up for it? What if Gabriella wasn't? He'd never do anything to jeopardize his relationship with her. She was of the topmost importance to him. But he felt his duty string being pulled by the council. What if the Langers came in and took over and he lost their entire kingdom because he didn't act in time? He wasn't trained for this, yet he saw their point. He was truly the best candidate. But life as a king? It was true that he was strong, smart, well-liked, and very driven. He had morals and made choices with intelligence and purposeful distinction. He had cringed when Finstra had mentioned he also had a queen candidate. Candidate? That word didn't belong in his love life. She was so much more than someone to fill a role. She hadn't signed up for queendom when she'd said yes to their first date. This all seemed messed up and was moving way too fast for him. Finstra had also alluded to the fact that Gabriella would be popular with the kingdom, unite everyone, being that she was mixed. He didn't like where this was going already. She wasn't propaganda. She was the love of his life.

He sighed as he swam. His anxiety was mounting rapidly, and he needed some time with Gabriella to ground him. She always helped him in ways no one else had ever been able to. The hallmark of their relationship had been built on time spent together. He was enriched by her laugh, beguiled to happiness by her flirty nature, and yet she was a spitfire too. She was as stubborn as she was playful, as wise as she was inventive. She was spontaneous, where he held to rules. Was that why the council wanted him? To be sure, he'd need more time to think. But time was running out. King Mangen was barely hanging on by a thread.

He scoffed. If this union were to happen, the council didn't know Gabriella at all. She wouldn't play their puppet.

Marriage was not something he felt ready to embark on either, but he already knew he wanted to marry her. He'd known that for a while.

He smiled as thoughts of her filled his head. That's what he needed more of. He needed more of Gabriella. Pure and simple, all he needed was her, not these big plans the council had laid before him. Joy overcame him as thoughts of her consumed his brain. The way she moved was like cascades of warm water flowing across his body. She was a comfort, she was beauty in motion, and she excited him. She had this uncanny knack for garnering his full attention when they were together, and then also hijacking his brain with thoughts of her when he was supposed to be thinking about other things, kingdom things. Maybe that's what love was and was supposed to be. An ever-presence of a lover that never leaves you, but always warms a part of the heart; and whether it was the full showcase of being in their presence, or as in a memory, like a small lit candle, they were always there, and ultimately, all you needed. It was an ever-existing presence on some level and a resulting continual source of happiness and joy.

Gabriella would arrive soon, and he couldn't wait to spend time with her. He intended to pleasure her so much that her voice would break through to the water's surface and bleat out into the air. If he knew one thing that grounded him, it was giving her so much pleasure that she couldn't think of anything else but the ecstasy. Her voice was not only seductive, but it was also satiating, and to hear her sing was an indulgent hypnosis he constantly craved.

He was concerned, though. The days were going faster and faster. His work plate was starting to overflow into time with Gabriella. He was not going to let that happen, though. She was too important to him, and he was putting a stake in the ground. He wasn't going to let her think she was less important to him than climbing the political power ladder. It was true he loved power, but power without love was just hollow. He'd rather be dead.

He floated into his home on his last fumes. Maybe he'd take a nap before she arrived. He felt very taxed, and in order to make love to her properly, he'd need to restore his energy reserves. He settled into his bed for a little snooze with a smile of anticipation on his face. His lover was on her way.

Chapter 2
Gabriella's Yearning

Gabriella watched as Nocter approached her. His electric blue eyes shone with excitement and desire for her. She smiled as happiness filled her core. She swam in the water as fast as she could because her own desire for him had her insides popping like firecrackers. Even a short time away from Nocter felt like agony. Her heart fluttered, further churning up her need for him in a flash. He had that look he'd get when their intimate moment was about to erupt, all deliciously tinged with smoky glances filled with mischief. If returning from these meetings was going to be like this, she wanted him to attend more of them. He looked very ripe for some intimate fun.

He rushed her with his strong arms spread and she cruised through the water with the intent of crashing into him. Their mouths were upon each other in a heartbeat, blossoming into solid promises for more. Distance and time had indeed made their hearts grow fonder.

She pressed her body fully to his as she devoured his flesh with her hands. He had muscles that spoke of determination and grit, as well as undeniable capability. He was taller than her, which wasn't always evident in the water, but she was noticeably smaller than him to anyone watching. She harbored nothing standing in her way to be herself with him. She was free for the first time ever in her life.

He knew all her secrets and her genetic makeup, and he had never, not even once, looked at her with distaste. Instead, his gazes were juicy and hungry, lusty and appreciative with the perfect seasonings of teasing to entice her to flirt back. He was the ideal mate for her, a dream she'd never known she held until she met Nocter that late fated sundown, a day after losing the battle she'd fought so hard in.

He pulled back to gaze down at her.

"How did it go?" she asked, not really caring, but only because she was horny for him more than she was curious about his affairs.

"Good, it's taking a turn I hadn't expected, but I don't want to talk about that right now. I want you."

She grinned a wicked smile and bit her lip. "I want you more." She pushed the fresh worry from her head that her mother had put there recently. Listena had been burned by too many men to have anything valid to say about them. Her musings about Nocter were not useful. She was plagued by doom thinking and Gabriella would have none of that talk about Nocter. She'd left her mother in a huff after the latest warning and wondered if she could ever trust her mother's advice again.

He engaged her in a deep kiss once more. This time his meaty seductive hooks had her entrenched as he palmed her back in double-handed squeezing. He had this way of foreplay that consumed her, that garnered her attention to the point of full immersion, so that she didn't notice anything but him. He commanded that attention from her, but it was never pushy or bossy. It was just his special form of magic, and from her granting her submission to his caring and doting leadership, it was more of a lulling that she hadn't noticed until she was infatuated with spending time with him. She'd often wondered if he had planned things out, or if their relationship was all just naturally evolving into a state of trust and freedom. She hoped for the latter, because that would be a wonderful way to live a lifetime with Nocter.

She moaned into his mouth as he claimed her as his. His dominance was a sweet surrender she indulged in daily. She'd never found herself this spellbound by a lover before and when he made her climax, the whole ocean could have rippled from the strength of her internal sensations. No one had ever made Gabriella climax this gargantuanly before. She wasn't sure if it was his abilities, his meticulous attention to her, or because of their intense connection. But regardless, she loved it and couldn't get enough. She knew idolizing him might fail, but that was a notion that only lived squished down in her little right toe, and it barely had any breath left to exist. But her mother attempted to fuel that tiny blaze regularly. She frowned for a moment, then wiped her face clean. She wasn't going to think such thoughts. She was with Nocter.

He grasped her waist with both hands and lifted her up, ticking his head to the right, his sign for her to open her legs. She succumbed to the moment easily, refocusing on Nocter because his actions commanded it, always.

She spread her legs as she smiled with appreciation as he nestled between her thighs. She showed her adoration for his move with glee-filled eyes.

He smiled back with a devilish grin, then licked at her folds, opening up her desire further. She grabbed his scalp through his flowing strands of hair. The sunlight caught the yellowish-white strands, making them shine golden in the light. He took her nub into his mouth while caressing her thickening lips before pressing his fingers to stimulate her inside. She was so desperate for more of his touch, she whimpered. She watched with relish as his manhood swelled, her need for it forcing a desperate cry from her lungs.

He went at her harder and her body clenched as she burgeoned on the crest of her peak, but then didn't finish. The edging of her arousal would ebb and flow until she burst free, and he was a master of guiding her along the journey. This not finishing didn't last, though, it never did with him, and she was sent hurtling toward a climax again because he doubled down his force with renewed fervor. She cried out while gripping his head with firmness, the strength of her fingertips on him her signal. Her tipping over the edge was imminent.

He released his suction. "Wait." He whispered his command into her swelling folds.

She rolled in ecstasy as he exalted in her, glorifying her arousal as he always did before he took his turn. He was a lover who had always put her first, which had shocked and won her over from the start. He was a mighty man, and an even more smitten lover. He spoiled her, made her surpass her sexual boundaries, then he'd use her to baste his own before the massive burst of his satiation. Then he'd cradle her in love until she fell asleep. It had only taken one time of such treatment by him before she was hooked. Then the promise had held true every time since. Her faith never wavered.

"Now," he directed. "Give it to me." He retook her into his mouth and sucked her.

She cooed and squealed until her body shook with the intense rise and fall, which was both powerful and swift. She rolled in the continued wave of ecstasy, the ride gifting her the orgasm muscle memory that launched her quickly into her second peak. She whimpered when he didn't let up his stimulation. She was ready to shove him off. It was too strong to bear. She thrashed in the water until she needed him so badly she grasped for him, just before he disappeared.

She startled and then froze, her head filling with terror. Her heart pounded, her breathing was erratically rampant, and her mind remained confused. He was just gone, as if she'd only fantasized him into existence. She cried out, yelling for him as she searched for him in the sea around her, but he was nowhere to be found.

"Nocter!" she shouted to the open sea around her. "Nocter!" What horrid magic was this to steal him in the middle of their sex? He hadn't even gotten to climax. "Where are you?" Her desperation had her on the verge of tears.

Her words landed on nothing but the water around her. Sure, he'd made her climax, but she'd been cheated from gifting him his climax.

Her shoulders slumped. Maybe her mother was right.

No.

She refused to accept all that her mother had said. Nocter loved her. That was an absolute truth. She could see it in his eyes, feel it in his touch, and she held it in her heart already. It existed, and no doubts could erase it.

She slowly readied herself in preparation to leave. Maybe she'd stay for a bit to see if he'd return. What the hell was this? Were they really just going to steal him from his life whenever they needed him?

Dread filled her. What if it wasn't the council who had taken him and it was actually someone evil, someone from the Langers? Worry gripped her as she wished cell phones existed under the sea the way they did on land. Then she could have simply called him.

She dashed off, swimming in a wild burst; she needed to feel the rush of the sea along her flesh to clear her worries. She was sure Nocter must be fine. He was strong and could hold his own. Plus, having his own powers ensured he was not defenseless in any fight. She swam until her arms hurt, then she sang until she couldn't utter another sound, and then she headed for home, her heart still cradling the painful hollow left from Nocter's disappearance.

THREE DAYS HAD PASSED, and she still hadn't heard from Nocter. She'd gone to every person on the council and questioned them. No one knew where Nocter was, though she suspected something fishy about the way Finstra responded. He certainly seemed cavalier about it. She'd plowed into him with questions, but he never spilled a single detail. That was, in fact, the only thing that was keeping her from painful heartache at the loss of Nocter. If Finstra wasn't overly worried, it likely meant Nocter was just fine.

She fumed as she approached Finstra's abode. She wasn't giving up this easily. A sliver of green flickered off in her peripheral vision. The slimy beast was home.

She hollered as she approached Finstra, "Where's Nocter?"

He uncoiled into view, then rolled his eyes, his eel-like body slithering along in the water.

She eyed him with extreme disdain. How could any female in their right mind fuck that *thing*?

"Look, Gabriella," he started, rolling his eyes exaggeratedly again.

"Don't 'look Gabriella' me! You know something, or you'd have everyone and their little fishy cousins out looking for Nocter."

He crossed his thin, putrid green arms as his beady eyes narrowed. He kept his mouth closed, his barely there lips a tiny black slit on his face.

"Tell me, you ass-scented buffoon?"

He burst into laughter. "Where do you come up with this shit, Gabriella? I guess it's 'cause you've lived on land with the *apes*."

She braced herself for the insult about her part humanness. He was never one to shroud his hate for humans. "For a sliver of time," she retorted, feeling very much like shoving then pummeling his wimpy wisp of a body until he spilled what he knew about Nocter's whereabouts.

"If you don't at least tell me that he's okay, I'm going to skin that sick green hide off your backside and go feed it to the piranhas on the other side of the world!" she shrieked.

He turned away from her with a sour look. "I can't tell you anything."

"I knew it. Then you do know something!" she roared. Her blood was boiling, and she fluttered her wings too much and began to rise in the water.

"Floating off to fairyland?" he asked in a mocking snide voice.

She cooled her jets and tried her best to compact her anger. She collected her wings to lay against her back and slowly began to sink in the water again. "Just because you're mixed with an eel doesn't give you the right to pick on me." She hated that eels were revered. It gifted him with a superiority complex that he didn't really deserve based on his character alone. That, along with being on the council, made him one obnoxious ass!

"Eels are the royalty of the deep," he stated with arrogance, lowering his eyelids.

She hated the eel-sirens the most. They were all so full of themselves just because some ancient eels were epic rulers. They clung to the thin wisp of a call to fame that never really fleshed out, but they still took liberties to remind everyone of their ancestral greatness anyhow.

"Spare me the fucking B.S., Finstra!"

"It's true. You can't change history." He began to swim away.

"You bastard! You can give me a damn hint about Nocter. This is so wrong of you to not tell me. I'm in love with Nocter!" She was livid, and her wings started to flutter again.

"He will be back tomorrow," Finstra said drily over his basically nonexistent shoulder. "He's safe. He's in training."

She sighed a huge breath of relief. Nocter was fine, that's what was important, not this pompous asshole's refusal to share anything about Nocter's safety. "All I wanted to know was if he was safe. Why do you have to be such a cruel jackass? Why couldn't you have just told me this the first time I asked? You really are an ass."

"One of your stature should not make such insults to someone of my status," he said in a singsong voice.

"What is that, you fucker? A threat?"

Finstra fluttered his snake-like body in a huff and began to swim off. He called nonchalantly over his back towards her, "Don't worry, he'll be back soon to finish what he started with you. I'm sure by then he will certainly be in a state to use the release."

Gabriella seethed. So, he had been the one to take Nocter after all and he had stayed tightly lipped about it, despite knowing very well what was going on. These games were not what she wanted for her life with Nocter, but with this imitation snake involved, the bullshit was surely going to line all her paths in the future.

She scoffed as her anger filled her to the point she felt she would burst. She began to swim back to Nocter's place, hoping he'd arrive soon. Maybe she'd stay there until she saw the whites of his eyes. At least now she knew he was coming.

Chapter 3
Nocter

Nocter swam along; his body was tattered, his mind was weary, and his resolve was stretched to the max point. Turning into a king was proving to be much more difficult than he'd ever imagined. Watching King Mangen die had been one of the most painful experiences he'd endured. The poor elderly merman had been trying to tell Nocter as much as he could while every word was an effort. Every syllable became painful for the mighty King as he told Nocter all the secrets he knew. But there was a high probability that the King hadn't actually finished because his eyes had fallen into a panic as he'd taken his last breath before passing out. He was declared dead within minutes. Nocter stared at the man as the full whiplash of shock took hold of what his death meant.

After that, the montage of training started. He'd been thrown into meeting after meeting, and then, when his brain was fried, he had to prove himself in scores of physical challenges. His muscles ached, his brain was hurting from solving problems. This was not what he'd expected. He had thought he'd simply be anointed as the king once King Mangen died, in some kind of ceremony with a feast afterward. He had not expected the Olympics of tests he'd been forced to triumph in.

Sure, he could have left and said he wasn't interested. But he loved his kingdom and their way of life, so he didn't want it lost to the heathens. The Langers were brutal. He didn't want their primal, wretched, merit-based way of life to infiltrate his lands. He loved the compassion in his area, the collabs, the feelings of unity. The Langers would certainly destroy that with their fascist ways. He couldn't let that happen. And he certainly couldn't have let Finstra take his place. It was more his ancestral right to take the kingdom than Finstra's anyway, not that Finstra would ever admit that. Plus, Finstra would make a terrible king.

He sighed as his brain swirled with more knowledge than he thought he could absorb in just a few days. All he wanted was to have Gabriella in his arms. He swam faster, even though he was so tired he could barely move. He needed to get to her as fast as he could.

He reached her home and burst in. He frantically looked in every room, every corner, only to find her place empty. His heart sank. She must be off working or just on a swim somewhere. She likely was pissed he'd been taken during their intimate time. Hell, he had been pissed about that, too.

He made his way back home. Maybe he could search for her after he took a short nap. He was dragging, barely able to keep going, and a short recharge would feel so damn good. He figured she was fine, but just off doing something. She was strong and smart, more than she even knew of herself. When he finally made it, he saw her little body off in the distance and joy overtook him. She'd been waiting for him at his place. This warmed his heart to know she would wait for him in the last place she'd seen him.

A surge of adrenaline filled him, and he swam quickly towards her.

She noticed him and his heart warmed from the excitement she exuded. She rushed towards him.

They collided.

She whimpered as she placed kisses all over his body. She sighed a happy sigh when he enveloped her in his arms with several kisses, too.

"Baby, it's so good to see you," he said over the top of her head, resting his chin on her. "Are you okay?"

"Am I okay?" she asked in surprise. "You were the one stolen from me while we were having sex! Are you okay?"

He nodded. "I'm okay. Just very, very tired."

"What the hell happened? Why were you just taken like that? That's so fucked up!" she said it all in a passionate rush, not stopping for a breath.

"It was an emergency. And...I'm now the king." He felt sheepish delivering such crazy news, but it was now the truth, so he'd need to get used to it.

She flung herself away from his body in a fast swim, her eyes going googly-eyed. "You're what?"

"I'm the new king now." He smiled. He was proud to be king, despite how he'd been ushered into it at lightning speed. He still was cross with Finstra for how he did it by just blindly swiping him, and for not prepping him at all for the ordeal of it. The worst part of it all was he'd promised King Mangen he'd keep Finstra on as first advisor. That was because he knew everything, but Nocter didn't like Finstra, and he figured he'd find a new advisor once he was fully on his feet as king.

Her face was aghast, and it held no falsehood of happiness about his declaration. "You're what?" she asked again, her tone uncertain.

"I'm the king. King Nocter at your service." He bowed with a giant grin.

"Omigod," she sputtered. "You can't be serious." A small smile grew on her face.

He nodded aggressively. "It's true. I'm the new king."

She threw her arms up. "Nocter! They took you when we were fucking!" she protested, her face burning red. "They just took you and refused to tell me you were okay. Can you believe that? I asked them all, every one of them on the council. In fact, I was a pest about it." She crossed her arms across her chest as her eyes fumed. "No one would even tell me you were still alive."

He chuckled. "I have no doubts that you did. And that makes me feel good that you care so much."

She grunted, furrowing her brows further.

"I'm sorry, honey. I was under the impression they'd tell you I was okay." He was concerned over their blatant disregard for her feelings, though. They all knew she was the one he loved.

Tears welled in her eyes. "At first, I thought you were dead." A sob took over her body and she came undone right in front of him in a torrent of waterworks.

He rushed to her and held her close. "Ah, babe. I'm so sorry. You must have been so worried."

She nodded against his chest. "Yes, yes I was." She guffawed. "But I refused to fully believe it. I tried everything. Hell, I even used magic to scan the sea, which laid me out cold for several hours after. Then I swam for miles and miles."

"Wow," he said, shaking his head. "Finstra should have told you." He'd need to reprimand the guy for that. He was getting angrier about how they treated her by the second.

"Where were you that I couldn't sense you?" She released a big sigh. "I'm losing that ability, I fear. Mom told me I might eventually lose it."

"We were cloaked. I was at the King's castle. Well, at the facility next to it. I haven't gone inside the castle, yet." He pet her hair, wishing things had been different for her the past few days. "I'm so sorry you've been having to live through that all on your own." He squeezed her tight. "I won't let that happen again, okay?"

"What if it's not up to you? I don't trust Finstra worth shit." She glanced up at him with a pouty look. "He's an asshole."

Nocter chuckled, but he nodded. "You're not wrong."

"I just can't believe this. You're really the king?" She stared into his eyes, her gaze falling a bit into excitement. "That's fucking insane."

He raised an eyebrow and released a big breath in a huff. "It really is."

"Tell that little vile green fucker he's not allowed to take you during sex ever again," she declared. She swam away from him in a rush, her limbs moving in strong swift strokes.

"Oh, don't worry, I'm definitely going to give him hell for that. I won't stand for it. I'm not their puppet." He clenched his jaw as he imagined how he'd confront Finstra.

"Hope not," she said, relaxing her face and body a little. "I'm not okay with you just being whisked away from me like that with no warning, no explanation, no updates. That's just wrong. I'm your girlfriend. I matter." She balled up her fists and set her jaw in a firm line.

He nodded aggressively. "Yes, you are and yes, you do, babe." He grinned at her, loving her spitfire reaction. She was a true fighter, and she stood up to injustices, which was one part of her he had loved from the start, and actually, he found it arousing. Her strength was hot. He smirked at her, his lust rising. "You look so sexy when you're determined."

She crumpled into a giggle. "Yeah?" She swam back to him. "I like that look in your eyes. Now we're talking." Her nips constricted into tight kernel peaks, her tit flesh pebbling and gathering.

He wrapped his arms around her. "I need you, Gabriella."

"I need you," she said with heat growing in her eyes. "Let's finish what we started."

They fell into a kiss, and he caved, throwing caution to the wind as he allowed his full self to abandon everything that had just happened. He was just Nocter again, and with his girl. He held her back as they kissed deeply, his hunger for her mushroomed. He mauled her flesh, and she melted into him like putty. He rubbed down her lower back and cupped her ass cheeks, scooping up her bottom in his palms. She quickly spread her legs to wrap around his waist as he pulled her to him.

Her little hungry urgent grunts raged his desire for her even higher. He wanted her like he'd never wanted her before. His cock filled to the point it felt ready to burst as she wiggled her body against it. With his manhood sandwiched between them, he kissed with the devastation of their lost ardor. He had stolen time to make up for.

He kissed down her neck, tasting her skin, which was both flavored with a sweetness and a fierceness. He wanted to dominate her and fall back into his role as her intimate dominant, but his restraint was also necessary. She'd been through a lot, and he wanted her to feel safe, wanted, and not abandoned. Finstra had not done their relationship any favors with his blind kidnapping stunt, but he knew exactly how to repair it. He would need to set solid boundaries with Finstra now that he was the king.

He had to admit, being king was already a satiating power trip, but he also knew he needed to heed the warnings King Mangen had whispered on his deathbed. King Mangen had been a very beloved ruler, benevolent, compassionate, capable, and also ruthless in his defense of the kingdom. He would be a hard act to follow.

Nocter shoved those thoughts out of his head. Sure, he was the new king, but right now, he fully intended on pleasuring Gabriella to the illustrious peaks of her orgasmic screams. He welcomed the feelings of the seductive overwhelm to follow. He needed sex with her like he needed to breathe. Their physical unions always promised him an escape that came easily, deftly delivered, and one that was fully gratifying. He nuzzled her supple wet flesh with his ever-moving lips. His hunger for her bloomed. He wanted to give her a good ol' soul-rocking fuck, with also being gifted the honor of being inside her to his explosion, while he ensured her satiety as well. He wanted to exalt her to her sexual and spiritual heights, riding right alongside her, aiding her, experiencing the climaxes with her, yet knowing he too would find satiation. He had lofty goals with his fucking of her, and he'd never abandon that as long as he lived. She was his everything, and he intended to be hers.

He rubbed his turgid cock against her belly. The friction was utter bliss, only ever topped by being inside her body. She moaned as he crested her mound, slipping his fingers along her bare flesh. He devoured her right nipple and suckled it as he played his fingers along her lower lips. She moaned and rolled in response to his touch, spreading her legs further and gripping his hand as he massaged her pussy.

"Oh, yes, Nocter. I want you in me. Please," she slurred as her eyelids fluttered closed.

He kept working over her nipple as he spanked her clit. Her body jolted as he slapped her, and her body quickly began the familiar orgasmic curl. She shuddered as he rubbed her womanhood, pleasing her little nub the way he knew got her off. He kept up his nipple stimulation as she rode the full course of her climactic high.

Yes! Success was sweet.

He didn't wait long. He wanted her only partially descending her climax high as he penetrated her. He caressed her wings, and she moaned, rolling her body into more of his touch. He lined up his cock and pressed himself inside her special hole. He began to thrust as he fondled her wings, her cries of delight hitting a crescendo.

Her head rolled back as more ecstatic moans left her mouth. He could not get enough of urging her towards her climaxes. Her eyelids flitted as she gripped him, her body rocking into a fresh rise.

His primal urge to fuck her swelled at seeing her reaching bliss, so he pulled himself from her. He flipped her around to face away from him, his lust raging to an inferno level as bent her slightly over, and mounted her, quickly sliding himself inside her opening. He pounded into her body in a rush as his resolve dissipated, he was imminently going to lose control. He thrust into her with emblazoned passion and power and then came with a ginormous gush. He cringed, wondering if he should have pulled out. They weren't in the place to have offspring at this point, though the idea of breeding her led to his cock refilling. The thoughts of that reignited his passion for her, his mighty testosterone flaring.

She whimpered, seeming unworried about him releasing his seed inside her. If she didn't care, then he didn't, either. A baby was something he wanted with her someday anyway, so why not let fate decide? Granted, a stable union between them would provide a better nest, but he also knew they'd make it work.

She cooed as he spooned her from behind. They floated freely in the current as they stayed nestled together. One of his favorite things to do with her after sex was to just let them float along while still entwined together, with zero efforts to control their movements, location, or drift. They'd swim back when they'd gone too far. But the letting go, the savoring, the cuddling her this way was a luxury he didn't ever want to give up. It was a bit careless and reckless as the new king to have his back bared, his body vulnerable to potential attack, but danger never scared him. He desired to coddle her and protect her in his strong grasp.

He broke free eventually when he saw how far they'd drifted. They were nearing the next territory, and that posed a threat. It was time to move. He scooped her up with one arm under her legs and one around her shoulders, and swam her back to his place. She stayed snuggled into him with her eyes closed. He assumed she had fallen asleep, but then she opened her eyes to gaze up at him.

"That was incredible," she whispered. "That was a fantastic make up fuck. And afterward, being in your arms just floating along like that, well, that was pure heaven. Fuck my cunt and spoon me every day and I'll be very, very happy."

He held her tighter as he soared into his area with a flurry of flutter kicks. "It was for me too. I love you, Gabriella." He had to smile at her word choice, she was a woman with a healthy sex drive, and her love for all things dirty talk delighted him.

"I love you, too, Nocter. Thank you for that. I needed it. Really needed." She tightened her grip on him. "I need more of you."

"So did I, babe, and same," he said, wondering which one of them needed it more. He wasn't sure he knew.

He cradled her to him. He needed nothing else in this world but her, even though as the new king, he was to be given everything he'd ever need, or want. No one knew he was the king yet, but he feared that news wouldn't last for long.

Chapter 4
Gabriella

Gabriella swam with lightning speed along the top of the water, the flashes of bright sun seeming more like speckles of joy rather than bombs of blinding light. This was perhaps due to her jubilant mood. It was promising to be an excellent day. The news of King Mangen's death had not been made public knowledge yet, so she was excited to get some time with Nocter before all the insanity of being king started.

She fluttered her wings as she did flipper kicks with her feet. This combo worked like a jet pack and propelled her quickly through the water. She'd once been jealous of the sirens born with fish tails because they could swim the fastest. But others were born with wings and feet, and were more bird-like, like her. At her birth, her mother had wondered what her baby would manifest as. She often told the story of how she had thought Gabriella had just been born like the latter, the more ancient expression of the genes, that was until her magic matured. Then her mother had shared the bit about her fairy heritage. She was a true mutt, and that was proving to be a huge blessing. She benefitted from all her parts and abilities that made up her whole. She wouldn't give up one. Her mother had told her when she was young that the human part of her might lessen, or water down, as she put it, her abilities, but that hadn't proven to be the case at all. In fact, Gabriella had found the exact opposite.

She had great powers, and she possessed many more than her peers growing up because of her mix of genes. She was lucky, and with her determination and drive, she'd found many successes. Life had taught her that if she wanted the impossible, it was worth trying for.

Like Nocter, who also had seemed like an impossible claim. Her mother had warned her to stay away from him, right from the beginning. She'd grown so tired of her mother's bad premonitions. However, there was one truth that she believed, and it was that neither of them would ever be easily contained. And the plans of the council to sequester Nocter into the ruler of the kingdom would not work the way they figured it would, that much she was sure of. Her man was wise beyond his years, but he had his own notions about things. She snickered. They wouldn't likely be able to control him as king as much as they likely thought they would be able to. Forcing Nocter to do something was like trying to hold water in your hand, the cracks always had their way of leading to freedom. Nocter would not be their puppet.

She caught a current and it boosted her the rest of the way to Nocter's in a flash. Today they had plans to visit the Green Isle. It was a beautiful, submerged island covered in water plants, and hidden from the human world by a floating mass of lily pads. Maybe the humans knew about it, but likely didn't desire to inhabit it because they'd have their feet permanently submerged underwater. They'd never be able to lay down to sleep because they'd be covered in water, so the island had largely been left alone by the air breathers. It looked to them more like a vast blob of plants. But to the sea-living folk, it was so lovely to visit, and to lay at the top of the water in the pockets where there were no lily pads. They could relax yet stay submerged, and gaze up at the clouds. Gabriella and Nocter had laid together cloud-watching for hours on end. It was a haven for those in love to bask in the warm top sunshine-filled layer of the sea. Once they'd dared to have sex there and had gotten away with it. But it was a well-known place families might visit too, so they had to be careful that young eyes didn't catch their intimate fun.

Nocter had warned her that tomorrow he'd be busy, so they were taking time together before that. She was afraid his new role would impact their time together, and he'd assured her that wouldn't happen because he wouldn't let it. The day ahead felt like a rare gem where they both knew Nocter was the king, but not many others did. It was a tenuous state that would likely dissipate in the blink of an eye.

"Hi," she said as she coasted up to him. "I missed you."

He took her in his arms and held her close.

"I missed you, too."

His arousal was obvious as their bodies settled together. His knowing smile tugged at her libido.

"A quickie?"

"How about at the Green Isle?" he asked with a seductive grin.

"Perfect," she cooed, her excitement growing. "Let's go."

The swim was leisurely. They took turns leading, then chasing each other, stopping here and there to kiss. He never corralled her back when she swam further away, but would zoom to catch up. She was so happy that she imagined sparkles upon her chest, and they bloomed in the sunshine, making her body glow. She didn't want to ask about his status as king, so she shoved it from her mind. This might be their last day as ordinary, and she wasn't about to tarnish it with any verbal musings or worries. If this was a last hurrah of life as they knew it, she preferred to not acknowledge it out loud. She both feared and was excited by how right that statement would likely become. But today, was today, and tomorrow might change. What they had was a stolen pocket of time. And she wasn't going to waste a second of it.

"Beautiful," he said as he kissed her glowing flesh as they took a quick rest near the edge of the big current. "The sun looks amazing on you."

She gazed at the turbulent water. The underwater river current never waned and it was an ocean marker for all sea life. They knew to bear down and swim their hardest as they traversed it, or fear they'd get dragged into it and whisked miles away in an instant. There was no slacking when crossing that ever-running belt of water. Some claimed it was created by magic to give everyone a place to toss criminals to get them as far away as quickly as possible. Others believed the legend that it was caused by the dragging of a soul away from his lover and the lover never got over it, so the powerful fairy-siren had somehow created the slippery tunnel water. But she believed it was just another anomaly in the world that no one could ever explain away, and nothing more.

"You ready to cross?" he murmured as he nibbled her ear.

"Yep," she said, readying to kiss him if he moved his lips just a little to the right. But he kept suckling her ear, so she turned her head. "Kiss me, you fool. I want it."

He grinned at her and covered her mouth with his. They kissed long and deep, her desire for him was churning up her insides. She'd have gladly presented herself to him for some bump and grinding fun, but being they were in the open waterway near the flowage, that was a bad idea. They might get too wrapped up in the fun and get snagged into the current. Regardless, she couldn't resist fondling his meaty boner.

"Mmmm, this," she said pointedly as she then flicked her eyebrows up quickly in an obvious expression of seduction.

"Soon," he whispered into her mouth.

He grabbed her hand, and they swam towards the current. They held each other tightly as they entered the blasting flow of water. They stayed joined by their hands every time they traversed the section of water. She'd swam across it alone many times, but Nocter always insisted on holding her hand when they went through it together. His protective streak was a turn-on. He was over the top with it and like no other lover she'd ever been with. She also knew this would likely be a turn-off to her in anyone but Nocter.

She returned his eager smile, and they swam through the water stream. It tugged at her flesh, but it had no pull on her. She was a strong swimmer. She could see why many were leery of the area, though, especially parents of the young. She'd been told horror stories as a kid about the young being whisked away from their parents in the current and sometimes they were found, but others, they hadn't been.

Nocter swam in strong broad strokes, helping her along, not that she needed that, but with his muscles, he was an even stronger swimmer than she was. He had the muscles that made the females drool. He was very sought after within their section of the sea, and now that he was the king, he would be even more so. She would never have expected her life would land her dating a man about to be the king. That was a silly fantasy of youth, not any sort of reality, except for her, it was reality.

Nocter's eyes were full of fun and mischief as he pulled her into his arms once they left the strong current. "We made it," he said jokingly.

"Was there ever any doubt?" she said, a smirk taking over her face.

"Well, no. But we still made it, so we must celebrate." He bent his head down and kissed her.

She heartily returned the kiss and if they'd been somewhere safe, she'd have begged for more, but they were in the open and close to the island so the potential for others to be near was high. There were many in the sea who never cared where they were intimate, "it's the sea, and open ground for any fornication anywhere," they'd say. It was true, they weren't silly prudish humans who thought sex was dirty—was the joke they all held. They often mocked the idiot humans, those who had visited on land, and talked about how they all pretended they weren't human, and sex was just for those weak, "dirty" people, when really, they not only needed sex for the continuation of the species, but for their own health and their relationships. It was so dumb. Everyone had sex but pretended they didn't. Gabriella, being part human, never understood how the race could be so blind. Most of the occupants of the sea had low opinions of the humans, which made her partial humanness a thing of shame, which she mostly rejected. But when she'd been young, the bullying had gotten to her.

Nocter broke their embrace and grabbed her hand. "Let's go. We're almost there."

They swam together, her heart beaming with hopes to frolic among the water lilies with Nocter by her side. The island always filled her with joy. Like the kind of joy she'd had as a child. A pure feeling like doing a simple somersault in the water or finding a new colorful coral reef to explore. Each fish swimming along in vibrant colors was a gift.

When they crested the island, they couldn't see any others there. This would likely not remain the case, but for now, they had this section of it to themselves. They coasted into the brilliant sun-lit greenery and let the strands of the weeds tickle their skin.

She giggled as one frond grazed her thigh. "It always tickles."

"I should be doing the tickling." He pulled her to him, and they fell into a kiss again. He lightly trailed his fingers along her back.

They kissed as they drifted entwined in the water. The sun peeked through the cracks between the lily pads above, glazing their flesh in slivers of bright sunlight. The water was warm and being held to him was affirming. She was right where she was supposed to be. Everything was right about it. The taste of Nocter's hungry mouth was perfect, being cradled to his firm body was comforting, yet arousing, and the way his eyes promised the upcoming ecstatic delights got her heart racing.

This island would more appropriately be called makeout island, but that didn't fully encompass it because she had so many memories coming to it as a kid to explore. The place held a certain comfort for her though, and she adored adding more memories of it to the roster in her head, especially ones with Nocter.

They kissed as they floated along, their hungry moans lulling them into a reverie as much as the environment.

"Going to make you come hard," he murmured into her ear before thrusting his tongue into her ear.

She squirmed and giggled, trying to get away from the stimulation, but ultimately, she desired to be nowhere else. "Mmm, I sure hope so."

"I can't seem to get enough of you," he said against the flesh of her neck before he suckled her supple skin. He sank his teeth lightly into her and she squeaked.

"Oh," she said in shock.

"Might need to leave my mark," he said seductively.

"Mmm," she cooed back. She secretly loved it when he made his mark on her.

Her arousal thickened; she wanted him, and she didn't care who saw them engaging in their dance of mating.

Nocter kicked his feet in a flutter, slowly bringing them to the area fondly known to all as the "Expanse of Union" because of all the copulation that had been known to occur amongst its thick, partially shrouding mass of vegetation. Couples often got it on in the watery thicket, then would rejoin the easygoing flow of the rest of the island, their faces soft with the happy joy of satiation.

She was so ready to relive that set of moments.

Nocter caressed her body with firm hungry grabs, his grip making her wince when it became a bit too much.

She rolled in his touches, loving the way he claimed her body as his with his palms along her back, then quickly curving around her ass cheeks. He gripped her thighs, spreading them to allow him to nestle against her hot core. There was nothing mediocre about the way Nocter made his dominance known during sex, no question of the lush evidence of his masculinity with how he commanded the positioning of her body, and her pleasure was integral to it all.

"You're coming first," he declared as he trailed his fingers swiftly down her body.

Her need for him coiled tightly in the memory of all the orgasms he'd helped her achieve. It was like the memory of all of them took a place on stage automatically as a tool of foreplay itself. The backdrop of it all was a promise she knew he'd make good on. This was so luxurious and new to her in a lover. She cherished it so much. It had been a slow realization to her that all the incredible sex they'd had only made her want more sex with him. Sex was for her, and he never made her think it was only for him. Not once had he wavered on it and with each encounter, he proved it again. She didn't think she was ready for marriage, but if she were to choose a life mate, it would indeed be Nocter. She didn't want to think any more about that.

She shoved that thought quickly out of her head as if it burned her. She was getting too into her own head when she needed to be savoring the feel of Nocter's hands on her tummy. He suckled down her neck, pressing his teeth into her flesh again, a little harder this time.

She moaned, leaning into him, readying for his next move, which would show the world she was his.

His fingers began to broach her mound, then when he slipped a finger into her cleft she groaned out, arching her back. He rode that exquisite spot slowly at first, making circles that ramped up faster and harder quickly. Her nipples were stiffened, and he took one in his mouth as he loved on her womanly bean. She writhed in the water, making little ripples of waves.

"Yes," he murmured into her tightened nip before dragging his tongue along her wrinkled pink flesh.

She mused he'd never have to ask her why her nips never got hard because he always succeeded in arousing her enough to have them constrict with rapidity and ease. Her pleasure was his kink, and her kink was to savor that. It meant life with Nocter would never be dull or routine, it would never be the same play, but the blissful end would always be the conclusion, and their story would never end. She'd watch him watch her, loving his doting nature. He'd learned things about her that she hadn't paid attention to in herself, and in that way, and so many others, he was a magnificent lover.

She sensed the engorgement lurch of her fully ripened arousal begin in her pelvic region, despite all her ruminating, the ease with which Nocter brought her to climax announced itself with ease again. She was going to come, and soon. She couldn't stay still, the sensations had her squirming. Her breathing stepped up until she was all out panting as he rubbed her. When he inserted his fingers into her pussy, she cried out as the stimulation shot her right to the peak of her climax.

"Get ready," he instructed. "It's time. Come for me, baby. Come on. Come hard. Come for me." When he sunk his teeth into the side of her neck finally initiating the start of making his mark on her, it was a trigger, and she burst into the full sail of her orgasm.

She shouted, unable to stop her orations. The contractions traveled her body as she arched and shifted, the pleasure radiating across her torso in a set of shudders. Her exuberant moans hit a crescendo. She gasped as the wonderful sensations slowly waned.

"Again," he commanded. "Give me more."

He'd said to her once that she was his drug, and he was addicted. His obsession with her didn't scare her one bit, it thrilled her. It made their dynamic slick and easy flowing. They fed off each other and their sex. She'd not expected the glory of their fucking to be so powerful, and yet it continued to amaze and thrill her.

He pressed his teeth harder into her, biting her to fully leave his mark.

She squeaked, then twitched as the slight pain became apparent as he sunk his teeth in, but it was a murky feeling made more minuscule by the tsunami of her next orgasmic peak. He sucked her skin to the point where she knew he'd leave a slight red mark, which she'd wear proudly as a badge. Peaks number two, three, and four were often more intense for her these days. She'd come to count on it.

He released his teeth from her neck and withdrew his fingers from her. When she opened her eyes, her excitement erupted. His eyes were filled with so much desire that she startled, but this also stoked her yearning for a revival.

"Fuck me, fuck me good..." she said, hesitating on if she should utter the powerful words, words she barely allowed herself to think, but she decided to give in and said, "my king." She sputtered a few gasps, feeling overcome by wanting his seed inside her. "Drain your balls deep inside me, my king."

His passion boiled by the fire flaring in his eyes. Her submission gleefully acquiesced to his dominance as he spun her body in the water and mounted her from behind so fast, she barely had time for a breath. His grip on her hips allowed her no movement and she waited, her lower hole widening as if begging for his entrance. She shivered in anticipation.

He lined up his beefy manhood, wielding it in several spanks against her buttocks before swiftly pressing himself into her.

They both groaned deeply at the initial penetration and as he began to ride her backside, the water became turbulent around them as he pumped. He thrust into her with several fierce pounds that made her tits bounce. They fucked. They fucked for several minutes. Her ardor rose, she couldn't get enough of him.

She loved submitting to him and his needs, but only because he was always putting her needs first. She'd come to believe her man might be the smartest male on the planet. Their dynamic was so smooth, easy. They fit together as if they were made for one another. And that perfect fit was sexy and hot.

"Get it," he commanded as he sped up his movements, making her buttocks gyrate from his mighty body smacks. "Get it again before I lose it."

His claiming leadership over her during intimate times was a seductive trigger in and of itself, and she reveled in it. It didn't mar her strength, but she found it rather supported it, instead. He had her back, in and out of the sex.

She dutifully played with her sensitive spot and claimed another juicy body-shaking climax.

He grunted and rammed harder, moments later bursting inside her.

She didn't worry about the potential for breeding. It wouldn't be the worst thing in her mind to carry a king's baby.

He spooned her from behind, wrapping his arms around her. He nuzzled his face into her hair.

No one had ever made her feel as loved as Nocter. He wasn't just about to be king, he was her King already.

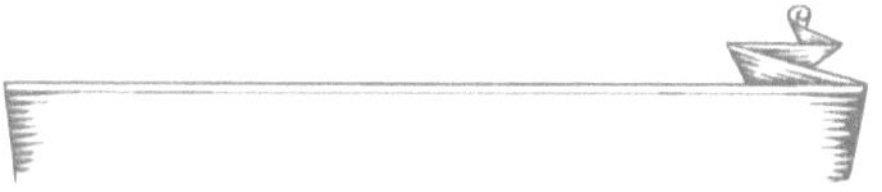

Chapter 5
Nocter

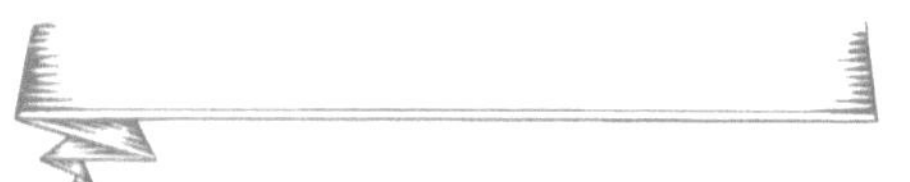

He swam along both excited and filled with dread. He liked being the chosen one, who wouldn't? But each meeting proved the task of becoming king to be more of a big deal, and more of a challenge, than the previous one. He wasn't sure he was the right person to take on being the next king, but he also agreed with them, he was the best option available. He was inevitably the only logical choice. King Mangen's heirs had all been killed. He had one nephew still alive, but he was a hermit and a recluse. The council had no one in the bloodline to choose to lead. Damn. A king. He had never aspired to this shit, but it was blaringly choosing him. One thing he was sure of, he wanted Gabriella along for the ride.

His mind drifted to the day with Gabriella on the island yesterday. The sex had been otherworldly, pointedly exquisite, and delicious. Then, adding to the perfection, the joy afterwards as they swam and explored the island had been unmatched thus far in his life, so both notions had him settling on the rightness of his decision. He was going to ask her to marry him. And soon. Becoming king was certainly a whirlwind, so apparently it would be for their engagement as well.

He smiled, imagining asking her to marry him. It excited him.

He wasn't asking Finstra's permission, but he was proving to be more controlling by the day. He'd have to keep a close watch on him. He was useful, with all his knowledge and connections, but his manipulative tactics were worrisome. No matter, he could handle the dolt. If he was king, he'd be the one fully in charge of everything anyhow. He'd use Finstra where he needed him, and nothing more. Or better yet, he'd use him and then replace him when he no longer needed him.

But there was Gabriella drifting into his thoughts again. The way her light hair flowed along her naked body as she swam, the brilliant glint of joy and mischief in her eyes. She was a fighter, and a lover, just like him. She didn't take to being told what to do, either, except during sex. He liked her independent streak, he found her strength a huge turn-on.

How would he ask her? Where would he do it? A million questions crowded his brain as he smiled deeper. This was it. It felt right and he couldn't wait to enact it. But first, he sighed, he had to deal with this damn meeting. Getting her out of his brain so he could think logically and rationally was going to be a challenge, but he knew once he was sitting in the meeting, it would command his attention.

The sky was overcast above so the sea was darkened. Turbulence was stirring the sea as he zoomed along. He'd bypass this section soon and hopefully be on the other side of it in no time. What awaited him at the meeting was likely going to blow his mind. The premonition settled on him, the occurrence was becoming a frequent prophesy.

THE MEETING HAD BEEN mostly good, except for the part Gabriella was going to despise. He wasn't looking forward to sharing the awful news with her. This was moving too fast, way too fast. It was to be announced to the kingdom immediately that he was taking over. The council wanted to do it before telling the citizens the king had passed so that everyone would take to Nocter as the new king. It was viewed that if it happened while the king was still alive, all the inhabitants of the kingdom would more easily accept it as a planned decision, rather than a knee-jerk reaction to his death. Word would start spreading by the means of the reporters scattered across their section of the sea, starting at the furthest edges of their territory and working inward. In the meantime, he was to get his life ready to launch into leading the kingdom. It seemed like a stupid and ridiculous thing to do, because he wasn't changing his course, he had his plans. He boiled as he recalled Finstra's reaction to Gabriella becoming his queen. One thing was for damn sure, he wasn't letting some pipsqueak tell him how to manage his love life. He'd be in the public eye, yes, but his love was not for sale or trade for the kingdom. He and Gabriella were a package deal. When Finstra acquiesced, Nocter had remained skeptical. The choice of who he married would be his and his alone. He fumed recalling the way Finstra had tried to steer him to considering a woman he'd never even met, for a political move. No way. Finstra was his helper, not his dictator, and he needed to make that very clear from the start.

Gabriella would arrive soon, and he hoped that she would hurry up. He was looking forward to holding her in his arms and making love to her to the tune of as many O's as he could help her flourish through. Then in the aftercare of their union, he'd ask her to marry him. He closed his eyes for a quick moment to rest.

What seemed like just a few seconds later, he felt someone touch his arm.

His eyes fluttered open to see Gabriella before him. She looked stunning, and he smiled. "I love waking to the sight of you."

"Hi," she said in a soft voice as she moved into his arms. "I didn't want to wake you, but I've been here for twenty minutes, and you still didn't rouse, so I figured I'd wake you."

"Wow. I was that conked out?" He looked around bewildered. "I must have slept much longer than I thought."

"That's okay, but I guess I was being selfish by waking you. I'm sorry." She peered up at him with her bright eyes.

"Never, I will always want you to wake me."

He held her close while stroking her hair. Ah, this was exactly what he needed. She was heaven in his arms. His arousal stirred as he gazed down at her.

"Can we just stay this way forever?" She pressed her belly to his growing erection.

"As long as we draw breath," he stated. "It's my promise."

"I'd love to use that. You up for it?"

"Absolutely and always. I'm yours."

"How did the meeting go?"

He grimaced. She had to go there, and now he couldn't *not* tell her the dreadful news. "You're not going to like what I have to say," he said with a frown.

She released a big sigh as her expression darkened. "Oh? I'm not? What happened?" She leaned backward and it separated their entwined bodies.

He shook his head. He tried to reach for her, but she swam back, shaking her head fervently. "No. Just tell me."

His heart sank. "I lost Sovereigna."

"You what?" she shrieked, her hands went flying in the air and her face flared, aghast.

"I had no choice. They're trying to evacuate the territory now."

Her hands balled into fists. "How could you?"

"Babe, I literally had no choice. I tried. There was nothing I could do. But listen, this is the important part, you've got to help. Your mother is resisting leaving. The group she organized is protesting by not budging. I need you to talk to her, convince her to leave." He pressed his lips into a thin line. "They are in grave danger."

"I fought so hard to help them survive, only to have you just give my childhood home away?" She shook her head, her eyes resentful.

"It wasn't like that, babe." Her expression hurt him to see. He certainly hadn't meant to hurt her. "Babe, they aren't safe there. I need you to talk some sense into her."

"Sense would have been to protect my home, not turn it over to the Langers like it's a peace offering."

"It wasn't like that," he protested, his heart aching for her. "I'm telling you."

"I don't want to hear it. I'm going to my mother." She swam away, then glanced back for a split second.

"Be safe," he called after her, saddened that not only did she not say goodbye, but she hadn't even said her usual, "I love you," at her departure. He'd grant her forgiveness with the grim news. It wasn't easy for her to hear it. He knew it would be the case. He hoped one day he would be able to get the section of the sea back for her, but it wasn't looking good in the negotiations. He had a plan, but it wasn't so easily enact-able in time to save it. It would have to be a pickup piece once things were underway.

He watched her swim away, his heart heavier than it had been all day. He knew there was no stopping her, and he didn't desire to stop her. He loved her tenaciousness.

HE AWOKE TO SEVERAL of the regime approaching him. He rolled his eyes. How was he just falling asleep like this? It was daytime for fuck's sake! Yet he was still exhausted, despite the naps. This was to be his life from now on, unexpected visitors constantly arriving with news that would commandeer his brain. It brought him back to his military days as a soldier and captain, but also reminded him why he retired from it. He chuckled softly at himself. Retired? As the incoming king, he was anything other than retired.

"Greetings," he spoke in a friendly inviting tone.

"King Nocter, we are here to protect you and also to inform you that it's time."

The pair at the front looked solemn. Each of the crew carried a sword and a shield.

"We are to remain with you as your personal guards, and more are coming." He tilted his head to the side, showcasing his scaled neck with red gills, which flapped slightly as he spoke. The shimmering of his green scales that traveled his chest met his flesh in a smooth transition. "Will you be preparing to move to the castle soon?"

"You mean like tonight?" Nocter had expected he'd be asked to move there soon, but he'd foolishly felt it was somehow off in the distant future. He slowly nodded as the full realization of him needing to act sank in. "I suppose I will be, yes."

"Modifications are underway for your arrival. Will your queen be joining you?"

He laughed heartily. "Well, first I need to ask her to be my queen!" He kept laughing exuberantly as they looked shocked. "I didn't realize I'd be sharing my plans with the council before I asked her to be my bride."

"We will need to have her protected, though, my king." The soldier held a very serious expression. "She will be your weak spot, so we must protect her heavily. Where is she now?" He looked around, as if he really expected her to be there.

The other five soldiers were spreading out as if ready to fight.

"Well, she's gone to persuade her mother and her crew to leave Sovereigna." He cringed as their faces went into a wild fury. "Is there something I don't know?" He watched as the other soldiers began to set up a tighter perimeter around him.

"My king, with all due respect, word is spreading of you like wildfire. You have new enemies as a result, and, so, she is not safe alone."

Worry gripped Nocter. He grimaced. "But no one knows I will be marrying her."

"That's not exactly true. Your impending marriage is in the announcements." The soldier was gravely serious, his lips in a stern line. "King Nocter, sir."

"What?" Nocter roared as he threw his arms wide. "You're announcing my engagement when I haven't even taken the step to ask her? I told the council this, expecting they'd respect my secret! Come on, this is ludicrous!" His blood boiled as he scrambled for a way to fix the PR disaster that threatened his relationship. He needed to be more mindful of what he said going forward, apparently. If Gabriella got word before he could ask her, she'd likely say she wouldn't marry him. It spoke of manipulation and obliterating her choice of free will. He knew her and this was how she'd react. "I won't have this! This must be stopped at once!" Dread consumed him as he imagined Gabriella's face as she heard the news she was to marry him, as if it were an order from the king. This was all getting so fucked up. He pointed at the smaller soldier to his right. "How fast can you swim?"

"Fast, really fast." His eyes brightened, and his expression bloomed eagerly into happiness at being singled out.

"What's your name?"

"Bleasfly, sir," said the small being.

"Bleasfly, I need you. Please swim to Sovereigna and find Gabriella. Her mother lives in the Cascades area of Sovereigna. Tell her it's urgent she returns to me, but don't scare her. It has to be her decision to return to me. You may not use any force on her." His voice boomed louder than he'd intended, but perhaps that was a good thing. "I'm serious on this. She is not to be just taken against her will."

"I'm not so sure he should leave before the others appear," the other soldier with the orange tuft on his head said. "With all due respect. Sir." He bowed while holding his weapon up. "No disrespect intended."

"I do not care. I can fight, too. I'm no stranger to battle." Nocter couldn't keep the irritation off his face.

"I know you aren't, sir." He bowed even deeper. "You have had a very respectable career."

He turned back to the other smaller soldier with his brows furrowed. "My wish is your command. Go. Bleasfly, go." He pointed in the direction of Sovereigna. "Be swift and find her. It is of top importance. The most top."

This was a disaster of epic proportions. How would he convince her this was not his doing? He could only hope she'd trust in that she knew his heart.

Chapter 6
Gabriella

Gabriella swam ahead of the soldier. She hated being summoned but understood he was just doing his duty. He was a minion of Nocter's. News of her impending marriage had been news to her indeed. How was the entire kingdom learning of her wedding before he'd even popped the question? She was angry. She felt cheated. A proposal was supposed to be between only her and Nocter, not as a rumor that landed on her ears as the new news of the kingdom. But part of her was merely excited that Nocter wanted to marry her, and that made it all okay. She'd have said "yes" if he'd asked, but she wasn't sure how to respond to a question everyone else knew the answer to first.

She had to be honest with herself, though, no matter how hard it was. She'd known for quite some time that she'd marry Nocter, if he asked. But that wasn't the point. She'd lost the joy of being asked. She would not be able to feel the excitement of the surprise, nor would she see the sweet look on his face as he asked her to marry him. This was a cruel joke fate was playing on her. This and then her mother refusing to leave her home, despite all the dangers. Her mother was as determined as she was as a general state of being, so she shouldn't have been surprised when she refused to leave. She feared for her mother as much as she now feared for herself. She was someone to be summoned. She was already a commodity rather than Nocter's lover, or wife. She smirked. She had to admit she loved the idea of being his wife and had fantasized about it often. So, she couldn't be entirely mad, but yet, she could be. This wasn't her dream proposal by a long shot.

As she approached Nocter's place, she stopped cold. He had a guard regime set up around him. This shit was fucking getting real pretty fucking quick.

"Madam," the minion said cautiously. "I mean, my Queen, are you okay? We need to continue on to safety."

"My Queen?" she parroted as her eyes expanded wide. She was already being addressed as the queen? "I am fine," she said quickly, and began to swim again. She supposed she'd play along, for Nocter.

As she passed through the line of soldiers, she watched Nocter. She couldn't mask her anger worth crap.

Nocter's face showed he was in pain. "Gabriella, I'm sorry. So sorry."

There was no usual hug, no usual love in his eyes, no anticipation or joy. She didn't like this one bit.

"I never meant for this to be this way. I had such amazing plans." He finally reached for her, his eyes softening.

She slowly let him fold her up in his arms.

"I missed you. I'm happy you're here." He kissed the top of her head.

"What, we now have to fuck with an audience?" she asked, her voice full of joking, but she knew she was also serious.

"We've done that anyway, and I know you like it." He smirked as his whole demeanor relaxed.

"Well, they're going to have to get used to watching lots of fucking, then," she allowed her eyes to show her desire for him as she continued, "because I'm not done with fucking my king." It felt good to be back in their usual way of flirting. She could only imagine what the soldiers closest to them were thinking, and she secretly loved it, whether it was with delighted lust or utter shock. Both held a special appeal in her heart, and that also was delicious.

"You'd better not be," he mused as he cupped her wings.

"Mmm, well shit, that's the way to get me going." She tried to shelve her anger, at least for the moment, lust would win.

"If I must, with an audience, but, let me first do this." He swam lower than her and following the human tradition, he bent his knees, grasped both of her hands, and stared intently up into her eyes. "My dearest Gabriella, my fiery minx, my horny partner, my lovely, beautiful lover, my sweetheart, my valiant warrior, the only desire of my heart, I would be honored if you would agree to be my wife." He smiled his most charming smile and said, "I will always bow to you, my queen."

He kept his expression flirty and playful, then he allowed it to turn serious and passionate. "My life is not my life without you in it. Please do me the honor of becoming my forever mate."

Her heart melted as she realized she couldn't let him not ask her to marry him before announcing it to the kingdom over his head like a black cloud. The most important part of it was that he wanted to ask her. But she needed him to know that she also didn't like being kept out of her own life in this way. "I should have been the first to know this." Scolding him wasn't her intent, so she quickly smiled and said, "But I can forgive your slip of the secret. Just don't do it again." She continued to smile at him as her heart began to beat wildly. A rising of joy welled up in her as he watched her with patient, loving eyes. She couldn't hold her excitement inside for a moment longer. She nodded aggressively. "Yes, Nocter. I will marry you."

He rose and pulled her into a hug in an instant. "You make me so happy, I love you." He looked so relieved that it tugged on her heartstrings. She felt right with him again, it never took much.

She allowed him to crush her against his chest as the urge to cry flooded her. "And I love you." Her tears spilled and she gasped.

"Aww, babe." He hugged her tighter and kissed her forehead. "You're not mad at me?" he asked in a curious tone.

"Oh, I'm furious with you." She released a guffaw, then sighed. "But I still love you and I still want to marry you. But don't you dare do something like that again!" She playfully punched his chest. "You're just lucky I'd decided a bit ago that if you asked me, I'd say yes."

His expression showed he was very pleased. "You're the love of my life, Gabriella. Nothing in this world can change that. And I won't do anything like this again. I promise. You're always first."

She knew he couldn't promise that, not as king, but she was happy he agreed, and declared it. "I guess I will have to get used to ears around us all the time." She eyed up all the soldiers, giving them the stink eye, even though they were looking out into the sea.

"Well, not really. The castle walls will give us some privacy."

She gasped. How had her brain not gone there yet? She would be living at the castle. "Whoa. This is getting real. I hadn't allowed my brain to go there yet."

"Well, it's going to need to be on the speed track, we have to go there now." He cleared his throat. "For safety reasons."

She startled, her eyes wide and unblinking. She hadn't considered the part where there would now be enemies who would want to hurt her as the impending queen. Claiming queendom was going to be more of a challenge than she had first thought. She hadn't just said "yes" to Nocter, but to an entirely foreign way of life. "This is going way too fast."

He nodded with knowing eyes. "For you and me both."

Her brain filled with excitement as she imagined all the sex at the castle. "Nocter, this means we'll get to fuck in the castle!"

He roared with laughter. "Did I ever tell you that I adore your libido?"

She smiled smugly. "Yes, just about every time we have sex." Her little smile grew as she began to imagine all the upcoming fun. Now she just needed to work on her mother to get her to safety.

"I'll have some of the soldiers escort you home. Grab what you need. Others can get the rest later."

She smiled. "I don't need anything but my body, and you. Nothing else is needed."

"That's brilliant. Okay, I'll get ready, and we will make our way to the castle once the rest of the crew arrives."

She followed him as he readied to go, the smile never leaving her face. She was going to be the queen, and nothing about that seemed to make sense. When they'd first started dating, he was a simple ex-soldier with a smoking hot body, a big open heart, and a libido as vast and strong as the sea itself. She'd happily bow to her king, as she already did, but only because he took such good care of her and never compromised his morals for her, until this backward proposal business. She could understand it wasn't his fault that the marriage proposal had been leaked; he could be too trusting at times, with how humble he was, and from the genuineness in his heart. He was kind, a caring one, and she knew being a cutthroat king would not be his style. Though, giving up on Sovereigna seemed a bit more cutthroat than she'd thought he'd ever be, she also accepted there might be other crucial things she wasn't allowed to know. She'd still be mad about it, but that didn't erase her love for him.

Once he was ready, she took her place beside Nocter, with all the soldiers around them, and they began the long swim to the castle. It took them a long time, but once they finally could see it off in the distance, her heart began to thud.

"This is so exciting! I've always wanted to see the inside of the castle, and now we are going to live in it!"

He chuckled. "It's pretty awesome. I still can't wrap my head around it. It's like I've been shoved into some fast-paced story and I'm the star, only I don't know my lines."

"Our lives are going to change." She was ready for it all. She beamed a smile his way.

"Yeah, they already have. And there are going to be a lot more changes to come."

"I'm in this with you," she said.

The guards stopped moving.

"What's wrong? Why are we slowing down?" Nocter couldn't help keeping concern out of his voice.

"False alarm," announced the man at the front, nodding his head. "Let's proceed."

Gabriella's fear jackknifed in her gut. "Are we really in that much danger?" she whispered the question to Nocter.

"I don't know, babe. I'm still just trying to figure this all out myself." He held his jaw firm as he gazed around them. He pulled her close. "I think we are fine. They're likely just being cautious. Any time of transition of power is vulnerable. Enemies want to strike when things are in flux."

"Sir, let's get you two into the castle. Everything is alright." The orange-topped soldier swam away from them and the whole group moved forward as a unit.

She was scared, but the castle was a dream, even from a distance. She couldn't take her eyes off of it. It loomed ahead like a shimmering opaque crystal, catching the sun's rays and spreading light out. It basically looked as if it was glowing as a result. If the inside was half as beautiful as the outside, it would be better than any of her imaginings of it. It wasn't every day that a boy like Nocter and a girl like her became king and queen. Looking at the castle made her feel better. It looked so impenetrable. She figured she couldn't help but feel safer inside its walls.

"We will need to marry quickly," Nocter stated as they crept along. "As I said, when things are in flux, the enemies often strike, so if you are okay with a speedy engagement, we can get started on preparations right away."

"I am barely remembering to breathe right now, but yes, yes to all of that." It was a dream come true to be handed so much prestige, power, and privilege. They'd be the *common folks'* king and queen, never losing heart nor forgetting the littles, everyone would be important. It wouldn't be long before they'd have children she figured, and that idea was both terrifying and exciting. They would be fresh minds to guide and nourish and she couldn't wait. Then there would be the fun of making the little princes and princesses. She snickered silently as she grabbed Nocter's butt.

"I hope the guards can handle constant public displays of affection." She grabbed both of his butt cheeks as she pressed herself to him.

One of the soldiers glanced her way with a knowing smirk. She decided instantly that he was her favorite.

Nocter grinned at her with a hungry gleam in his eyes. "Oh, I have no doubts."

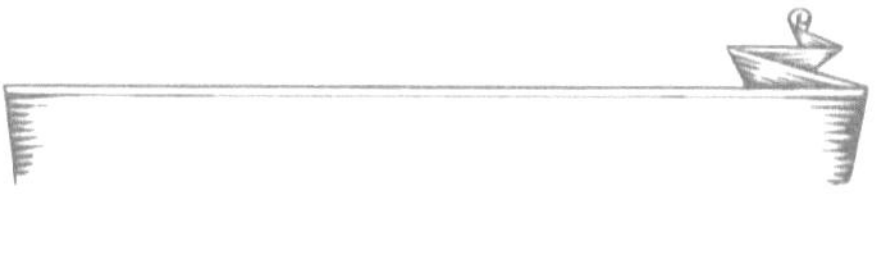

Chapter 7
Nocter

He waited in his new master bedroom for Gabriella to finish dressing. There would be no real use of the separate quarters the staff had prepared for Gabriella; he was having her in his bed from the start. No one but the staff needed to know that, though. It would be their own secret. It was a silly formality, anyway. He had smirked heavily, and with great anticipation, when he'd been shown around the king's quarters because in trunks around the room, he'd found various implements for sex. The king had clearly been a kinky motherfucker, or perhaps all the kings to date had been, each one adding their own flair of desired equipment to the sex paraphernalia collections. One chest had paddles and handcuffs among stiff pieces of driftwood that looked like gnarled mangled cocks, except they were smooth without any ridges. He had chuckled at the idea of the previous kings having artisans create fake cocks. The other gold chest had all kinds of contraptions inside. He had no clue what they were used for, but he had ideas of how to get creative with them. He couldn't wait to experiment with them with Gabriella.

His lust seethed, his cock filling at the thoughts of using them on her. Gabriella was going to be ecstatic when she found out about them all. He dug in the big one. There were dicks made of carved driftwood, complete with protruding veins, some curved at the tip, and some were clearly patterned after the privates of the monsters of the deep sea. There were magic wand looking rods that were straight and circular disks with holes in their middles, holes that likely an engorged cock would fit through, and then there were instruments clearly meant to be an adjunct to their magic. He was impatient for Gabriella to appear, but he was ready for her, his erection had decided it was definitely time to fuck in the castle. In *his* castle, where he'd live and rail his new wife daily. He had big plans, and they all ended with his cock up Gabriella at the end of each day.

The room was not modest. It was lush and the furniture was more elaborately carved than he'd ever seen in his life. The depictions on the bed's giant posts rivaled the intricacy of some of the carvings he'd seen at the bows of ships, mostly they all depicted sexy sirens or elusive seductive seeming mermaids, just like the posts of his new bed. The mattress was vast, the largest bed he'd ever seen. The fabrics on top of the bed were plush and comfy looking. Then, when he swam around the room, he found a new ornate carving he hadn't seen the last time he'd cruised this way. This room alone would take forever to explore, well, room was a weak word for the space, it was more like a large apartment or small house.

When he and Gabriella entered the castle, both of them had been shell-shocked by the shining walls, which were cerulean with streaks of muted yellow and pale blues amid a streak of purple or magenta here and there. The statues of the previous kings and queens lined the great hall, which was big enough itself to host a party. The statues were gorgeous displays of the artists' abilities, and the beauty of many of the past kings and queens. Gabriella had mused in surprised delight how their own likenesses would fill the next enclave in the hall. That was a jarring thought and fucking fantastic! They had held each other's gazes as they agreed it all was indeed magnificent.

The servants had swooped down on them instantly, insisting they rest before the full tour of the ginormous palace. Both he and

Gabriella had agreed to take it slow. Plus, they could use a romp before they strode the many halls of their new home. All the talking Gabriella had done about fucking in the castle had him really horny. He'd love to get to rail her into some big O's inside their new home before even seeing it all. He had priorities!

As they had been led to the sleeping quarters, he had caught sight of the breezeway, and that area had piqued his interest. It appeared to be a passageway allowing a steady stream of sea life to flow through the castle, but didn't seem to give them access to enter it, so the pathway served as a continual flow of fish and sharks to watch. He'd imagine both Gabriella and he would watch the miraculous animals swim by for hours on end, kind of like the televisions the human had on land, only live and real.

Gabriella entered the room breaking his dreaming of his new castle. She wore a sheer champagne-colored lace bodysuit with an iridescent pearl beaded finish. It looked like a wedding dress itself. Her cleavage was lusciously showcased in the snug fabric, and hints of her svelte figure were visible as she swam into the room. The sides showed the bare tops of her firm thighs, but kept her genitals hidden. She looked the part of a queen. It suited her well, as he knew it would. Her beauty would be seen and envied by many as queen for years to come. He knew she'd make a big difference in her role because she was just amazing. There wasn't anything the woman couldn't do. She'd be a wonderful example, worker, and advocate for the inhabitants of the kingdom.

"Hi," she said with awe, "this place is unbelievable!" She looked around the master suite and then, after a thirty-second eye tour of the huge room, met his gaze. "Wow. I can't stop looking at everything. There are treasures everywhere."

"Yup, and we haven't even seen half of this place yet." He swam to his dresser and opened a small chest. "My wizarding powers are stretched just by being here. Look in this chest, see this crystal, it's magical. And my servants told me it's a permanent ability. It won't disappear, ever. It's now a part of me. Watch what I can do now." He held his arms up and then began to disintegrate as he rapidly pixelated into tiny bits that continued to thin out until there was no trace of him left at all. Then he popped himself back to full size.

"Holy shit!" Gabriella stared at her new fiancé with her mouth agape. "That's totally extraordinary!"

"I know, right! I can go anywhere in an instant. And look at this over here. It's a book full of magic spells. This will help so much." He led her to the pedestal that the book was on. It was covered in raised iridescent swirls with a beige nugget in the middle that looked sort of like a little brain. "This will help me rule the kingdom effectively."

"That's a lot to learn about," she mused, "but very incredible."

"And the best part, apparently many of the kings have been horn dogs. There are chests and chests full of items for use in sex!"

"No fucking way," she exclaimed as she put her hand over her mouth and widened her eyes. "Seriously?"

"Yes! You won't believe what I've found. Fake cocks, restraints, things that look like perhaps cock strokers, balls on strings, paddles, straps. I mean, I can't even figure out what some of them would do."

"Well, I can't wait to experiment with you." She raised an eyebrow at him and her eyes turned to fiery quells of lust. "Let's get started, shall we?"

"We're going to have so much fucking fun!" He led her to another chest that he hadn't even opened yet. "Let's explore this one together."

He lifted the heavy lid and gasped as he saw all the ties and straps. He lifted one up and turned it over in his hands. "I wonder if any of the servants can teach us how to use some of this stuff. I can't even tell what this is," he said, shifting it in his hands.

"Me neither, but this looks like perhaps a collar for a neck, and these parts...hmmm...maybe the smaller ones are for wrists because there are two smaller ones and two larger ones, maybe for ankles. I don't know! But I'd certainly be hog-tied and at your mercy in that!"

"Mmmm," Nocter said appreciatively. "I'm thinking we need to try this out now." He flopped the straps back and forth in his hands. "I think you might be right. It's clearly a restraint. I could position you bent over so you are trapped and control you by this collar. I wonder if there's a leash?"

"Holy shit, I won't be able to move!" Her eyes filled with exhilaration and awe.

He was turned on and quite aroused seeing the excitement on her face.

"You want to try it?" he asked, trying desperately to keep his voice neutral, but he knew he wasn't exactly succeeding in hiding his interest in putting it on her. "Now?"

"Wow. I'm scared but intrigued." She smiled. Her nipples were erect, and her eyes were lit with anticipation. "So, yes. I'm in. I trust you. Let's try it. You know I love you dominating me. I will be helpless with that. It will be a good verification of how we are, and, as long as you don't do anything wrong, it will increase my trust in you."

Her trusting innocent eyes seized his interest.

He shook his head, then scoffed. "I'd never compromise your trust. You first, babe. Always." He grinned devilishly. "But we will need a signal if you want to stop. How about something you say? Something that's really easy to say and something I won't misconstrue as something else. Would that work for you?" He loved the idea of anything that confirmed he was her dominant, and that she wanted that too was totally intoxicating.

"Yes. Oh, this is going to be so sexy! I didn't know such things existed." She looked as blown away as he felt.

"Kings apparently have some very skilled artisans at their disposal. Which gets me excited about coming up with my own designs." His expression turned lascivious. "This will be my favorite leisure time activity, second only to fucking you."

She looked so happy. "I had no idea kings were so kinky. You fit right in!" she exclaimed with joy.

"I know. Makes me feel even more fit to be king, honestly." He wrapped the straps around his fist and closed it. He reached for her. "Now, let's get this on you, my sexy little siren-fairy-human. Gonna twist you into a pretzel and use you as my bitch." He allowed his dark passions to uncoil from the depths of him as he wrapped her body up with his arms.

He claimed her in a deep kiss and she fully reciprocated his heat, caressing his tongue as he probed her mouth deeply with his. He wasn't used to seeing her covered up with clothing, but it was turning him on to realize he'd get to undress her. This was something he'd never done before. It was like she was a gift for him.

He leaned back and gazed down at her. "It's crazy seeing you wearing clothes. I guess the king must wear clothes a lot, too?" he asked, wondering if he had an armoire full of clothing, too. He hadn't even opened any of them up yet.

"Yeah. It's wild. There are at least seventeen armoires filled with clothing in my quarters. But, I'm guessing that's because all the queens have not likely been the same sizes. There are some gorgeous dresses in there, though." She shook her head. "I haven't even opened the doors to the back rooms in my suite yet."

"Same here. Funny. I never even thought about how we would now be wearing clothing. I'm so used to us being naked all the time."

"Yeah, it feels weird. But I like it. It's a beautiful piece." She ran her hand over her body from her breasts to her pelvic region. "It's kind of fun, though."

"That looks like the kind of fun I want to be having right now," he slurred, running his hands down her lace-encased flesh. "It's so sexy on you. Being covered up is hot." He pursed his lips. "Now I get to unwrap you. Part by part," he said with a licentious snarl.

"Oh, please do, my king." Her eyes danced with flirtation.

"Fuck," he said with a shake of his head. "That's hot as fuck to hear you say. To hear you say those words, 'my king'," He caressed her body all over, savoring every inch of covered skin.

"Nocter, you've always been my king."

He cupped her breasts and played with her nipples through the fabric. "I love how I can see them still, but they're covered."

She grinned up at him. "I know. It's like they're caged but on display at once."

"Seductive," he whispered, taking her neck in a strong kiss.

He pressed his hands to her back as her head tipped, artfully exposing her neck further for him to devour. He grunted as he tasted her flesh, taking their closeness to the next level by thrusting his filled erection against her torso.

She moaned in sweet enticing mewls as he suckled her flesh.

He slid her robe off and it floated away. He groped and mauled her backside. "Fuck, I want you. I need you. I've been thinking about fucking you since you talked about fucking in the palace." He kissed her nipples through the lace then slid his fingers under the straps over her shoulders. He stripped the top of the bodice off her breasts. "I'm obsessed with you." He consumed her right nipple into his mouth, and she groaned loudly.

"Yes, please, my king. More," she cooed.

He slid his tongue across her cleavage and suckled her other nipple, while still playing with her right nipple with his fingers. He worked the fabric downward, sliding it to her hips. He kissed down her body as he moved the lace lower over her thighs, shins, then off her feet. He released it and it, too, floated away. He kissed her pussy mound and tickled his fingers along her labia.

She cooed in pleasure as he played with her womanhood.

As he rose up her body, he slid the strappy number off his arm and opened the collar. "You didn't pick a word yet," he mentioned with a scolding look.

"True. I didn't. How about...hmmm... how about tree?" She smirked. "I don't think I'd ever accidentally say that during sex, so it's perfect."

"Yes. And it's easy to say. I like it. Tree it is."

He secured the collar around her neck and swam back to the chest. "I need a leash of some sort. Or rope to tie on that ring." He dug for a moment, the movement making his loaded cock sway. "This is perfect." He pulled out a leash with two handles at the end, a circle at the end, and a loop along the strap of the leash. "I will have full control of you."

She giggled as he returned. "Wow. You will. My king, this is so hot." Her voice was light and airy. Then she growled. "I want you. I need you." Her voice turned even more seductive when she said, "King. Fuck me. I'm yours."

Her verbal bowing to him had his manhood well stroked. He was so ready to take her as his for the first time in his castle. He clipped the leash to her collar and allowed his intense desire to dominate her show on his face. "Yes, my queen. You are mine."

He kissed her again then gave her a playful smile before he applied the straps to her wrists. Then he spun her to face away from him and bent her over roughly.

"Oh, my!" she exclaimed as he forced her top half over. "Whoa. Fuck. This is turning me on."

"Me too," he said with great intensity. He reached around her and pulled the ankle wraps to secure them around her ankles.

He cackled deeply. "You must stay bent over. With this on, you have no options. Shit. This is hot. I'm going to rail you until you scream. Get ready to be my toy. But first, I'm making you come like a waterfall. You're my wet cum slut."

She nodded and moaned. "Yes, my king."

He floated beneath her so his head was at her pelvic region, then he grasped her thighs firmly. With the straps on her, her legs would only separate a short distance, but it was enough to fit his head between. He made a primal growl as he ground his mouth into her womanly folds.

She shrieked and grasped at his scalp, her body moving slightly as he sucked her clit hard.

He loved that her limbs were secured, and that she was at his mercy with her wrists tightly pinned together. He pressed his fingers to her lower lips and entered swiftly, moving rapidly to pump them inside her at a fast pace. When he closed in on her sensitive spot with full suction, she cried out. She tried to twist but the restraint only allowed her to move around a little. Her screams escalated as she tried to move and couldn't as freely as she normally would. He grinned. The restraints were working to get her to be even more verbal. He loved it and instantly decided he needed more exploration of this new development in her responses. And with all these implements at his disposal, he was all set to do so.

"Fuck," she muttered. "Can I come, my king? I need to."

He continued to eat her out with zero intentions of letting her come yet. He wanted her to build up as much fervor as possible. Then she would come hard.

"Please, it's too much. Oh, fuck," she muttered in desperation.

Her begging turned him on more, so he ate her out even more aggressively. After another minute of her struggling, he broke his suction. "Come when you feel it and keep coming. Don't stop until I signal."

He reattached himself to her and ate her with increased vigor.

Her body convulsed, straining against the straps. Her sounds escalated and he grinned, slightly breaking the suction he had around her clitoral head. He was obsessed with her new sounds. It was like she had to express the ecstasy somehow and it was as if it were involuntary. He adored that she was experiencing new eroticism with this restraint. That's exactly what he desired for her. These tools were surely going to skyrocket their sex to new places.

She shuddered and convulsed again. After three more rounds of her body jolting, he decided it was time to take his turn at full pleasure. She looked exhausted and cum drunk.

"Perfect," he said softly. Then in a stern, dominant voice, he said, "Now I'm going to fuck you and come up your quaking cunt like a geyser. Get ready to eat my seed, wench." The dirty talk was something they'd both said turned them on. And the more she called him "king", the more he wanted her to say it. "Beg your king for his cock."

She shuddered, then in a wanton voice said, "Please, give me your cock, my king. I want you inside me. I need you inside me. Please."

He swam around her and mounted her from behind. Having her at his mercy was certainly even more delicious the way she was fully under his control. He curved his body along with hers, yearning to make her shiver and twitch again. Hoping to elicit those utterings she could barely get out, then force her into the screams she released instinctually. Restraint was quickly becoming his top turn-on, and it seemed to be hers as well.

He played his cock along her swollen lower lips and pressed himself in slightly. He worked his cock inside her by moving his hips and he aggressively began to use her hole. He never ignored her pleasure, she was always first, but he sure as fuck took his ride from her for his own satiation. He began to thrust himself into her, hammering his pelvis into her ass. Knowing that she had to stay bent over raged his yearning to heights he hadn't enjoyed before and he slammed into her with a force that made her shout. She whimpered and groaned as he took his gratification from her sweet feminine hole. He gripped her left hip when the urge to dominate her swelled in him even higher, then he deftly took up the slack in the leash. He tugged on the handle enough to make her head tip backward, which made her chin jut out and her body scrunch up, her back deeply arching. He watched her tightened tits bob as he rode her.

He made her ass cheeks rock, and she released sounds of desperation that sounded similar to her being in pain. He pounded himself into her relentlessly, more brutish than ever, until he felt the unstoppable rise within his loins, and then he released control, spewing his first seed as king inside his queen's body. His cock pumped her full.

He grunted deeply as he kept his cock inside her, ensuring every drop of his cum would fill her insides. Then he crashed down on her body, spooning her in a tight hug. He couldn't help but hope his seed would take and that he'd just successfully bred his bride-to-be. Her being pregnant would indeed be a jubilant way to start his reign as the king.

Both of them were panting heavily. His heart was thudding so hard. It was ready to burst with love and excitement for their future together, and with the promise of countless hours of hot sex in their future.

The rough fuck left him feeling like he fully claimed her.

"Damn," he whispered. "I came really hard."

"Me too. Several times. They were really big ones." She sighed, a smile growing. "That was so fucking good, my king."

"Good. I love that." He sighed. "Hearing you call me that."

"Me too." She held his hands that were cupping her breasts. "I love you. And I love that I just got fucked by the king."

He snickered. "Yeah, the best first fuck as king I could have hoped for."

"I'll never tire of calling you that. And yeah, so many more to come. And we have chests full of unimaginable fun to explore."

"I can't wait." He kissed the top of her head. "I can't wait for a lifetime with you. We're so blessed. I love you, forever. You know that?"

"I love you forever, too. I couldn't not love you." She squeezed his arms to her body.

"You're sleeping in here with me, by the way. Your quarters can just be for you getting ready in."

"I'm not leaving."

"Good. And, just in case it wasn't clear by the way I railed you just now, you calling me 'king', drives me absolutely wild. I fucking love it." He was on top of the world.

She guffawed. "I could tell."

"Damn, whew!" He moved off her and began to remove the restraints. "You make me feel like one."

"You are one. Literally, and to me," she said as she embraced him. "Let's go to bed, lover. I'm worn out."

"Me too."

They moved to the massive bed and slid beneath the covers, holding each other as sleep loomed and claimed them.

Chapter 8
Gabriella

Gabriella woke, sensing some movement in the bed. She saw Nocter, but then he instantly poofed away, enacting his newly acquired trick. She groaned and rolled her face onto the pillow. Why hadn't he woken her up to tell her first before leaving? She'd love to know. She supposed she'd have to get used to this, him leaving at the drop of a hat. She figured this was why the ability was given to kings in this palace, because they could just zip wherever they needed to be in an instant to attend to unexpected and urgent matters. She pouted. She no longer felt first in his life, even though he said it all the time. It was going to be less true than ever. She supposed it was still amazing that he prioritized her pleasure, but as the new king, she wouldn't really be coming first that often in his new role in life. No matter. She was going to be the queen, his queen, and nothing sounded more wonderful than that. A discussion was in order though. It wouldn't take him but a second to tell her he was leaving if she were right next to him at the time. This was an expectation she'd press on him.

She stretched and released a squeal. She was nude and wondered if it was improper for her to move about the castle naked now that she had been anointed to be the new queen. She'd seen the previous queen once, as a kid, and she'd had on an elaborate jewel-toned dress that looked lush enough to be a bed. But she'd never really thought about it until now. The queen had been dressed. She'd been more obsessed with ogling the dress at the time than registering that she wasn't naked. Being awestruck by royalty would do that to her though. Now she was supposed to be royalty. It seemed fake, like some fairytale imagining rather than her new reality. She suspected she might not be as demure as most queens had been, but her fire was what Nocter loved about her, too. Her mama hadn't raised no limp sprig of seaweed, and she wasn't going to take on that persona just to be queen either. If anyone thought that fallacy, they'd better wise up!

A knock at the door drew her eyes to it. She rose and let the blanket fall off her breasts.

"Come in," she called loudly.

"My lady, I've come to check on you. Are you ready to rise? It's almost noon."

Gabriella stood up quickly. It was Marella. "It is?" She looked around. She realized being inside something with a roof had kept the sunshine off her eyes. Usually, she woke to the brightness of the sun. "Oh, dang. Seriously?"

"May I enter?" called Marella.

"Oh, yes. Of course." She'd have to get used to telling others what they could and couldn't do. She wasn't so sure she liked this development.

The woman entered. She had her head bowed.

"Hello, Marella."

The woman nodded, but still didn't look up.

"Marella. I'd like you to look at me when we talk, okay?" Her demure demeanor made her very uncomfortable.

She lifted her face and smiled a small smile. "Okay."

"Now that's much better. I'd rather speak to your face than the part in your hair." She stifled a giggle. The thought was ridiculous to her, but clearly, Marella had been conditioned to think otherwise.

Marella's shoulders relaxed more, and her eyes turned brighter. "What can I get you? I brought these things for you." She held up a robe and a bagel with cream cheese. "I'll go back for the coffee."

"Oh, wonderful. Thank you. I just noticed there are no windows in this room, so since I didn't see the sun, I didn't wake." She swam towards Marella.

"You must have needed the rest, my queen."

Gabriella turned so Marella could slide the robe onto her arm. She guffawed when she saw the restraint device on the bed. There would be no secrets from Marella.

She allowed Marella to put the robe on her other arm.

"How about I draw you a bath? Would you prefer to do it here or in your quarters, my queen?"

She found it crazy that everyone already was treating her like a queen even though she and Nocter weren't even married yet. "I think in here works. But first, I'm starving." She smiled at Marella. "And thank you." She took the plate from Marella and moved over to the table and chairs on the other side of the large room.

"I'll do that and then come back with your coffee. Shall I bring you some clothes or would you like to pick them out?"

Ah, now the robe made sense. She wasn't supposed to be naked in front of others. "Maybe I'll take a look. I'm more curious about it than caring about what I wear, though."

"As you wish," Marella said, rushing to the bathroom. "You will love this tub. It's more like a luxury pool."

Marella had fin feet, which was a sign of the fighter subspecies. It had developed in the fighter class over time. They'd had to diversify to survive so their fins split and become two. The crazy part was, the entire group of them could also walk on land so it may have developed from hardship, but the result was they were better equipped to live in the entirety of the world. There was a rumor that a group of them lived on land. Gabriella could breathe on land or in water, thanks to her mixed genes, but as strong as Nocter was, he couldn't.

She enjoyed her bagel, eating it all up before Marella even emerged from starting her bath.

"I've prepared it for you, my queen. I will be back with your coffee. Would you like juice?"

"Yes, please, Marella." She swam forward. "And, Marella, thank you. I think we're going to get along very well." She wasn't supposed to think of Marella as a friend, but she wasn't about to start following arbitrary rules.

Marella scurried off.

Gabriella watched her wondering how she had gotten a job at the castle. She'd have to ask her. As queen, she'd make changes. Nocter would be behind her choices; that wasn't a concern. But it was this damn sniveling Finstra that seemed a threat.

She entered the bathroom and gasped. It was almost as large as the bedroom area of the suite. It had three hot tubs, one was on with turbulent water flowing. The opposite wall had a hot room that Marella had already turned on for her because the heat swirls in the steamy water were visible through the glass doors. There were various chairs with holes in them in one area, plus a sawhorse with padding, a stockade frame, and some weird body bag looking kinds of things.

She laughed loudly. "Holy shit, kings were really kinky motherfuckers!"

As she walked closer, she saw a basket with handcuffs, wrist cuffs, ankle cuffs, and neck cuffs. There was a large sofa against the wall with hooks on the sides and several large triangular wedge-shaped pillows in a stack against the wall. This was more of a sexual playground than a bathroom.

The walls were covered with shells and pieces of coral, all designed by a highly skilled artist based on how beautiful they were. There was a mural of a sand dollar made of many sand dollars on the far wall and as she walked along the hall, there was mural after mural of sea life animals including dolphins, sea stars, countless fish, and jellyfish schools. The hall went on for another twenty feet and she couldn't resist swimming on to check it out.

She gasped when she entered the room at the back. It was a dungeon with plain concrete walls, complete with restraints attached to the walls and floor, chains were affixed everywhere, some with hanging locks. There were whips hung on the other wall, paddles, and a chair with multiple straps on it. She shuddered, feeling the heavy aura the room gave off. If these walls could speak, the stories they'd tell.

"Holy fuck me." She stared in awe for several minutes unable to stop staring at all the hardcore toys.

"Yeah, some kings have had these kinds of fetishes." Marella didn't seem angry or even shocked.

She took in a deep breath as her body startled. "Oh, I didn't hear you come up behind me."

"I'm sorry, my queen. I didn't mean to surprise you."

"It's okay. I was in a bit of a trance looking at all of this." She smiled. "It was like this beautiful hallway and then suddenly this torture chamber appeared. Didn't expect to find this at the end of such a hallway."

Marella chuckled. "Yeah, you should have heard the stories my grandmother would tell." She smirked, the secrets of the past were clearly locked inside her pretty little head.

"Ah, so this job has been your family's legacy then?"

"Yes, my queen. The women of my family have been castle servants for generations."

"What about the men?"

"Them too, but their endings are much more mysterious." Her face grew solemn. "Some servants in the past were forced into bondage. I was told the stories to prepare me, in case I ever worked under such a king." She relaxed. "But, so far, I have been lucky not to."

"Ugh," Gabriella said cringing. "I don't like the sound of that."

"Yeah, there's lots of history of darkness here, too, though it's beautiful, some kings were much more, shall we say, of the more sinister variety. Cruelty was hidden beneath some decadent king's clothes." She bit her lip. "Which is why everyone is so excited about you and Nocter. We all see something different in the two of you."

Well, now things made a bit more sense to Gabriella. "Got it," she said, nodding her head. Nocter could never be that cruel. It wasn't in him. Sure, he liked being dominant, but he held more of a consensual mindset than pure domination. "Well, I'd better get in that bath. I got distracted by this intriguing hallway." She glanced around the room once more, imagining some of it could be fun, with a partner like Nocter. She'd have to lead him back to this space later and read his reaction.

"How was it working for the last king?" Gabriella asked as she swam along the hall.

Marella followed closely behind, the coffee cup still in her hand. "Pretty decent. He's the only king I have worked under."

"I'm glad you didn't get one of the tyrants." She slid into the bathtub with a groan. "Ah, wow. This feels incredible."

"Can I give you a back rub, my queen?"

Gabriella released a laugh in a loud burst. "Only if you want to make me cum," she said through her laughter. "I'm not kidding. My wings are...let's say they are quite sensitive."

Marella's eyes widened. "Oh, I've heard of others like you. You are very lucky." Her smile widened knowingly.

"I know, I am. And it's all true."

"How about your feet then?"

"Perfect," Gabriella said as she popped them out of the water.

Marella reached for her feet and struggled to lay on the side of the tub and still get her hands on her feet.

"Just get in," Gabriella stated.

"Oh, I can't bathe with you. That's taboo."

Gabriella released another burst of laughter. "Oh, geez." She rolled her eyes. "One thing you need to know about me, Marella, is I don't give a fuck about rules. Get yourself in here. If you're going to rub my feet, you're getting in, too."

Marella's eyes widened.

"Are you sure, my queen? This is highly unusual."

"Get used to it, baby. I'm not your usual anything."

Marella grinned with glee twinkling in her eyes. "I can tell you that I will get used to that quite easily." She slipped into the water and took Gabriella's feet into her lap.

She began to massage her feet, working the arches, then spreading her thumbs upward toward her toes.

"Damn. I might just fall asleep again. I'm not used to being such a lazy butt doing nothing."

"There's plenty to do if you desire, my queen. But for your first day in the castle, I think this is an ideal way to spend it."

"This is so wild. Never in a million years did I think I'd be sitting as an almost queen in a king's bathtub, with a beautiful woman rubbing my feet."

"You're already a queen, my lady."

There wasn't much that could have shocked her more.

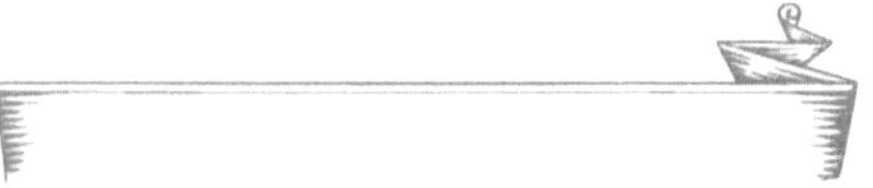

Chapter 9
Nocter

He held his breath as he harnessed the power to move. He wasn't sure he really needed to hold his breath, but he'd done it each time, so it seemed it was already a habit. He reappeared at the castle in the sitting room near the ocean stream passageway, which was the room he'd been told Gabriella was currently residing in. He wasn't sure how she'd feel knowing that someone was keeping tabs on her. He suspected she wouldn't like it.

He blinked, and just like that, he was there with her.

She laughed in delight. "That's quite the trick. Think you can do that while I'm giving you head?" She snickered as she tipped her head to the side while raising an eyebrow. "I want to play around with this new trick of yours during sexy times."

He released a belly laugh. "You're a delight babe. I'm in. How has your day been?" He descended upon her, collecting her body to him. "I'm not sure I can get used to us both wearing clothes. Though, it's kind of sexy, huh?"

She rolled in his arms while giving him a saucy look. "It is sexy. All I keep thinking about is what's beneath them." She poked at his cock, which made it thicken more.

"We might be the horniest king and queen this castle has seen yet."

She tittered a laugh. "Oh, I don't think so. I'll have to show you what I've found."

"Ohhhh. Can't wait!"

Several servants approached them with trays of food and goblets in their hands.

"This is unreal," she said as a green eel-human mixed servant handed her a goblet.

"Wine, my queen?" His smile was miniscule, but his smooth skin still made it visible.

"Thank you, Ernie."

"My pleasure." He turned to the king, who already had a drink from the large-breasted cowfish with two heads, one human and one with white and black swirls all over. She had a human breast on her human side and udders at her belly on her fish side.

"You're quite the beauty," Nocter said to the servant.

She blushed and swam back away from them, bowing her head.

"I'm shocked by all the amazing servants I've met today, Layla here included." Gabriella looked pleased.

Nocter only wanted Gabriella, but he would have happily agreed to a threesome with Layla had Gabriella deemed it her desire, too. Maybe he'd need to pose the idea to her sometime.

"We get a happy hour in front of a beautiful ocean stream showcasing the beauty of the sea to us, with gorgeous servants serving us. Are we dead and in heaven?" Gabriella took a sip of her wine.

She'd never looked more happy or more beautiful. He held her gaze and appreciated the nice deep cleavage line the purple velvet dress showcased on her chest. "And you are the most beautiful queen these walls have likely ever seen."

"Thank you. You are looking damn sexy yourself. Do you think the staff would mind if we just fucked right here?"

The two servants who had just given them drinks looked shocked but then relaxed quickly when no one made a move.

"We might be quite different rulers than what they're used to," Nocter said slyly.

"It's been pretty quiet for quite some time with the king being sick and all," Layla said in a low voice.

"I can imagine," Gabriella said.

"We've missed any sort of jubilation around here," Ernie said. "We're very excited you are both now with us."

"Thank you," Gabriella said. "I'm excited to be here too."

The room fell silent, and the servants took their leave.

Nocter sighed. "I was going to wait to say this later after we'd had dinner, but we need to move our wedding up to as soon as possible. With the help of the servants, do you think we can do this within a few days' time?" He puffed up his chest and then released a big sigh. "The kingdom needs the joy of our wedding after hearing of the king's death."

Gabriella's eyes widened and her body jolted back. "Wow. I hadn't expected this so soon."

"I know, but I'm afraid there will be many things for me to deal with in the transition, so our status needs to get set."

"Gee, how romantic," Gabriella said with an annoyed look, then rolling her eyes.

He tensed as he watched her face, a grimace overtaking his. "You know you mean more to me than a status."

Then she smiled, her expression becoming excited. "Yes. And there's much to do. But we can make it amazing."

"Babe. I need you to come to me, and nestle into my arms. I have other bad news for you."

She swam to him, her eyes filled with worry. What he had to tell hurt his heart. He'd rather keep it from her, but he wasn't about to start lying to the woman he loved. He took a deep breath and slowly released it. "I'm so sorry, babe. But Sovereigna is completely lost. And we've lost track of your mother." He held her tighter. "One reporter said she may have been killed."

Gabriella's eyes went wide, then narrowed as she cried out, "No! Please no! It can't be right."

He held her as she sobbed. It wasn't the homecoming he wanted. He held her body as it was rocked against him with her sobbing. It wasn't fair. This crushed his heart too, to watch her crumple into despair. Tears sprung to his eyes and he wept, too. A proposal, two funerals, and an upcoming wedding all in one week were too much for anyone to handle.

After they'd held each other for several minutes, while watching the fish swim by incessantly, he caressed her cheek. "What do you need? What do you want to do, babe?" His heart hurt and the stress had him wired, and seriously on edge, but being with her was having a calming effect on him overall. Holding her did something to him that soothed his soul. He had known she'd be his respite, his place of recharge in her love. The sex would help, too. He adored her relishing of all things sexual. He wouldn't trade a life with her for being king, he needed her in his life to be king.

She wiped her eyes. "I hope she's not really dead. There's still a chance she's not, right?" Her eyes flickered with desperate hope.

He nodded as every fiber of his hope pleaded with the universe that she was right. "Yes, of course. I think we will know more with time." He watched her intently. "Do you want to stay here or explore the castle?"

"Let's explore. We've sat here long enough. I need something positive, I don't know about you."

He agreed wholeheartedly. "Yes. I agree. I do too. Let's do it." This seemed simple enough to do and though he knew sex would make her feel better, he wasn't about to suggest it. Yet anyway. Better though, it should be her call tonight. He needed her to take the lead on this one and signal to him when she was ready, given the bad news.

She grabbed his hand, and they began to swim towards the east wing. "We haven't gone down this way yet." She smiled and though her eyes were red from crying, it made his heart feel a little better to see her interest.

He was worried about her. Losing her mother would be a big blow. He had hopes that she was simply hiding and not really dead. Her mother was a crafty woman and as smart as Gabriella. He wanted the best for her, but what if he couldn't protect her because he was off doing his work as the king? He needed to trust that all the guards would do their job, but whether would Gabriella cooperate with them was the question. She was not going to tame her tenacity, and in all truth, he didn't want her to. But he also didn't want to lose her. He would lose himself if he lost her. She was his heart and soul.

He smiled back at her when she glanced at him with excitement growing in her eyes. "This is an adventure! Right in our own place. This palace will take time to even explore it all. It's ginormous!"

"It is, I know!" In the pit of his stomach, he couldn't help but worry about the next thing he had to tell her. Maybe he should wait because of the news of her mother. It might be too much bad news at once and put her into a depression or something, which would be horrible with the wedding about to happen. But he also wanted to be honest with her. He didn't want her to feel like she was a prisoner in the palace, but the painful reality was that her impending queendom had put a target on her head. He wasn't sure how to bring it up. He'd have to just say it. It was going to be hard, but he needed to make her aware before they wed.

They approached the garden room and entered. Fronds of seaweed flowed slightly as they swam in. Vegetation was all around the entire room, sea flowers, fallen logs, sea anemone, kelp, and algae. Someone had taken the time to actually drag fallen trees to the palace. He was amazed at the lengths that others had gone to in order to make the palace have everything the ocean offered. Perhaps that was to create a mini world for the royal family to keep them safe in, to help them feel like they weren't prisoners, but also to help them feel like they weren't missing out by not going out into the sea like regular folk.

He cringed, wondering when he should bring up the thing he dreaded saying to her. Memories of the conversation at the meeting flooded his mind. He wasn't happy about what the council had informed him about, that Gabriella should not leave the castle, and she was never to leave it alone. They had said she really shouldn't leave at all during the current unrest. He hadn't realized becoming king would make his new wife a prisoner. He could ignore the warning and let her live her life how she desired, but that seemed stupid with all the dangers she now unknowingly faced. His proposal had made her a prisoner and he couldn't think about this without wanting to vomit. How was he going to talk with her about this? How was he going to tell her he loved her so much that she needed to stay in the castle, and be guarded for life? It didn't seem fair. It was the biggest life cheat of all to be given everything only to have free will taken away. But he was now entrenched in being king and she was stuck with him. He'd been considering stepping down but that would lead to the demise of the kingdom because surely it would then be open to severe and oppressive attacks. If the Langers, especially, knew there was no king, they'd charge in and take over the kingdom. Then he wouldn't be free anymore and neither would Gabriella, and neither would the entire kingdom. They, in fact, would now likely be the first ones killed.

He tried to stop the fear and sadness from showing on his face, but he knew he was failing the second she looked back at him.

"Whoa, what's that look about?" she asked as concern filled her face. "In this beautiful room, you can't have that kind of face. It's sacrilegious," she joked.

He didn't make a single move as he watched her come close. "I have to talk with you about something and I don't want to."

"You can tell me anything, silly." She smiled with a flirty tone.

"I don't want to tell you because I don't want to accept the reality of it, either." He fought the urge to cry as he looked into her loving eyes, which were brilliant with joy. He feared his news would kill that joy and he didn't want to watch that light go out in her eyes.

"Okay," she said with some reservation already muting her jubilance. "More bad news?"

And there it was. Her fire was dimming as worry filled her eyes. He swallowed and took her hands in his. "I love you. More than my own life. More than this kingdom. I love you more than anything I can imagine. We've come to such an amazing place in our relationship. Marriage. We are going to be married. We are going to be the king and the queen. This is a dream come true. We get to live in this incredible place. We can have children like we've talked about. We can have a wonderful life."

She grew very serious, clearly sensing the ominous tone. "But..."

He took a big breath, held it in, then slowly released it. "It pains me to tell you this and I can't even believe it's a thing. I don't want to believe it. I actually despise it." He cowered and stared upward at the ceiling for a few seconds, then met her scared gaze.

"What is it?" she asked in a voice full of fear.

"You can't leave the palace."

"What?" she shrieked. "What do you mean I can't leave?"

"There are sharks out there, and I don't just mean real sharks. Beings that will hunt you and possibly kill you if you are ever outside these walls. And before you think this isn't real, I can tell you we have watchers out there who are watching those who watch the castle.

They keep a constant vigil over the castle with their magic, and they aim to capture you and use you to get to me. They have no qualms about using you to try to twist me to give up our kingdom. By being betrothed to me, you are now ransom bait." He sat in horror on the eggshell of her silence, waiting for her fury to launch.

Her face bloomed first into fear, then quickly into anger. "No way. I don't believe this. I've seen queens leave the castle." She shook her head vehemently. "When I was younger, I saw her. This isn't right, Nocter."

"Yes, but not during times of unrest, like we have now." He hated this and vowed he'd get the kingdom to a good place so she could leave.

Tears welled up in her eyes and she shook her head. She began to back away from him.

He pursued her. "It won't be forever. This can't last, babe. I won't let it."

"This can't be. I am a prisoner here?" She looked around the room, looking so lost and confused that it broke his heart. She broke into a desperate-sounding sob and crumpled up into a ball.

He started to cry, too, rushing to hold her.

She thrashed her arms and swam away from him. "Don't."

She curled up into a ball again and floated behind the thick wall of seaweed.

"Babe, I love you. I want us to be together, but to keep you safe, we have to heed their warnings, or you could be killed."

"Rather be killed than be a prisoner," she said, slowly and with great sadness.

"It won't be for our whole lives. It can't be. I know it won't be."

"How long have you known this?" she asked in a bitter tone.

"I found out today. The council waited to tell me."

"Waited until I was inside these walls," she said flatly. "I see how this is working. Now I can't even go find my own mom."

"We will keep searching for her. We will not give up, I promise." He couldn't keep the desperation from his tone, and it was making things worse.

"Some of your promises have already died."

"Aw, baby. Please, I love you. I will fix this kingdom, mark my word. You will be able to roam freely again. I swear it on my life, Gabriella."

She swam to the edge of the thick seaweed and peered at him through the stems. Her eyes were red and so very sad, and it crushed his soul.

"I promise. This won't be your prison for life. I won't allow it."

She moved closer to him, but averted her eyes. That simple act alone was killing him. He'd never seen her like this, and it was torturing him.

"Please, look at me. I love you. I love you with all of me. I promise, this won't be your life." The sad truth was, even if they broke up, she still would have a bullseye on her. The thought of breaking up with her made him almost retch. He steeled himself off from the feeling. He walled it up. He needed to be strong for her. He would be the king to fix this awful mess the kingdom was in. And he'd do it for her.

She looked up at him and his heart leaped at the tiny glimmer of hope in her eyes. "I believe you will try. And I think if anyone can succeed, it's you." Her voice was so low, he barely heard her.

He extended his arms and pulled her to him. He held her tight. "Don't give up on me. No matter what. I love you forever and into eternity."

"As I love you," she whispered against his chest.

He believed her. And he knew it in his heart that she did.

His heart sank as he sensed the council calling. He shook his head in disbelief. This was the absolute worst timing they could have ever done. He'd wait. Maybe it was a false alarm, but the signal chimed again, and the urgent tone had been added in.

He grimaced as he said, "This is the worst timing it could possibly be. I'm sorry, babe, but I have to go. Now." He kissed the top of her head.

When she looked up at him, the look of betrayal in her eyes sent shards of ice through his heart.

The high alert sound chimed again. He had to go. He had no choice.

"I love you, babe. With all of my heart. I will be back."

He collected his power and then propelled himself out to the sea on his way to the council.

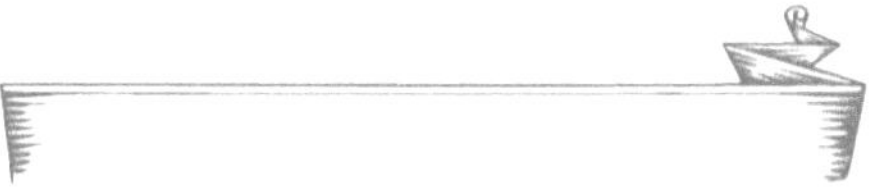

Chapter 10
Gabriella

The next few days went by quickly, likely because they were filled with all the wedding preparations. Gabriella's heart ached because Nocter still hadn't returned. She felt alone and lost. She was honestly devastated. How could she live her life as a prisoner? She was an adventurer, a soldier with fight in her heart; she was a free spirit. Staying in the castle was like not being her true self. How could she condemn herself and her children to live a life inside walls? Even a castle as incredible and elaborate as this was not the whole world. It couldn't be. There was so much more out there to see and live and experience. And she and her children would live lives coddled like little incarcerated souls, like the criminals. It made her not want to have children anymore. How could she have kids knowing she was condemning them to a jailed life?

And Nocter. She loved him dearly, with her whole heart, soul, and self. But, he was changing. And the changes weren't stopping, they were intensifying. Before all this, she couldn't imagine him agreeing to this life as a prisoner for her. So, she was trapped between unfair circumstances and her love for Nocter. She couldn't be herself around him anymore because he wasn't himself anymore. A weird formality would take hold of their relationship as she imagined it becoming transactional, and the thoughts of that future doom were making her miserable already. To be with someone she'd loved for so long, and couldn't imagine not loving, now meant she had to lose her own free will. Gone was the pure innocence of their love. It couldn't exist for the purpose of itself anymore.

The world no longer made sense to her. He was Nocter, her amazing wonderful caring lover who always wanted to take care of her, pleasure her, and have fun with her. He'd held her in his arms making her feel special every day since they'd fallen in love. But all of that was being replaced by his cold hard absence, by her lethal sentence of needing to stay in the castle, or by her impending death from simply moving around outside the castle walls. It was a death sentence without dying. She feared when they would be together, it would be a shadow of its former state. Her heart ached and she wanted to cry. Her new life was ending just as it was also starting. She couldn't stop the floodgates, and she burst into tears, her body quaking with her hopeless sobs.

After several minutes, she calmed down. The crying fit had made her feel better, but it hadn't erased the feelings of doom.

There was a knock on her door.

"Come in," she said in a weak voice, perhaps too weak because a knock came again. "Come in," she said in a louder voice.

Marella appeared, looking distraught. She was wringing her hands. Gabriella still wasn't used to having a servant wait on her, especially someone who was her friend. Over the days, she and Marella had become closer. It was with Marella she'd had a few glimmers of happiness in planning the wedding, the flowers, and her dress. It had been fun stuff, however, stuff she'd have thought she'd have done with Nocter. The other thing that made her depressed was that her mother wouldn't be at her wedding either, nor her friends, other than the servants, many of whom were beginning to feel like friends already. She stared down at the wedding dress on her body. It was gorgeous. It was perfect, well almost, it had a few more alterations Marella was going to assess and fix today.

"I've been instructed to inform you that Nocter has been pulled away into heavy negotiations." She looked so worried and with the formal way Marella had spoken, she felt her friendship was shifting into something else, too. She didn't like this feeling one bit.

She didn't like any of these horrid changes at all. None of them, and now Nocter was to be delayed in his return, and with their wedding about to happen. This was horrible timing.

"What? Are you serious? How can this be? We are to be married in three days. Will he be back?" She tried not to let her hope die.

Marella's eyes were filled with fear and compassion. "I was told that's unknown, but from the rumblings I hear, it could be a long time. I'm so sorry, Gabriella. I hate saying this to you."

Her heart split and the pain spreading through her body was too much to endure. The urge to flee filled her. However, she knew she couldn't leave and now Nocter couldn't return? This was turning into the worst nightmare she could imagine, and she couldn't wake up from it. It just kept getting worse. She was to live alone in this castle without him. And for how long?

She shook her head and held up her hands. Panic filled her body and she found it hard to breathe. "No. No. No. I can't do this. I won't live this way." She stared at the bouquet of flowers in her hands and then stood up. This was it. All the work that Marella had done on her dress was a waste of time. She simply couldn't marry Nocter, not when Nocter had no return in sight. Not with him constantly disappearing. The council had no respect, and she truly understood the dire state of the kingdom. But all that didn't matter one bit. It was clear how it was now more important than the love she and Nocter shared. But the problem was, she didn't think it was. The council would continue to just take him from her. She loved him and didn't want to leave him. She couldn't imagine her life without Nocter, she didn't want that, but being king took him out of her life before they were even married.

She sobbed deeply. It was over. "I don't want this life," she declared while dying inside. Her heart was screaming at her not to do this, to just stay and wait for Nocter because he would return, but her brain had turned cold and taken charge.

"Gabriella, he will return. It won't be forever. Finstra..."

"Oh, I don't want to hear about Finstra again. That egotistical bastard keeps taking Nocter from me, and I don't believe a damn thing he says anyway, so whatever you'd tell me, it's pointless," she spat angrily. Everything had become pointless.

Marella looked hurt and she dropped her head.

A flip switched inside her and her cold calculating side showed up. "Oh, I'm sorry, Marella. I don't mean to make you feel bad, but it's just, Finstra has lied to me before, more than once, so I don't believe anything he'd say." More than anything she wanted to stay and be Nocter's wife, but more than everything, she knew she couldn't. Her heart was too broken to break anymore.

"I understand." She dropped her eyes downward, then shifted on her feet. Then she perked up and she looked more hopeful. "But we can still finish preparations in case King Nocter is back in time."

Gabriella shook her head as her heart slid further into numbness. "No. I'm afraid there isn't going to be any wedding."

"No, don't say that, Gabriella. He can't be away forever. He will come back, and then you can marry." Her eyes were pleading with her, imploring her to be patient.

"I'm not marrying Nocter. Not anymore." Gabriella hated what she was saying, but there was no way out. It was over.

She squinted as she tried to figure out what had just changed before her eyes. She blinked as she watched the fabric of her dress pull away from her body.

"What the—?"

Marella was staring at her like she'd turned into a monster. Her eyes were wide, and her hand flew over her mouth. "Oh, my gosh!" she exclaimed as fright filled her face.

The dress was growing on Gabriella. It was enlarging away from her chest at a rapid rate. "What the hell is this?" Gabriella shrieked as her dress began to cover her face. Terror gripped her as she stared at the odd way her dress remained stiff without her body in place to hold it out. This was some dark magic coming from somewhere she couldn't see. "What the fuck is going on? Marella! My dress is getting bigger. Who is doing this to me?" She tried to look around but all she could see around her was the dress. She glanced up out the top hole of the dress where her body had been, but saw nothing. Marella's head appeared, and it looked huge.

"It's not getting bigger, Gabriella, you're getting smaller!" Marella's terrified voice boomed loudly above her, then she disappeared.

Soon Gabriella was staring at the waist of her dress, then she zipped down to the lower hem in a flash. She had to get out of the dress and get to safety. The dress was now as big as the giant skyscrapers on land in the human cities. Her heart pounded and she couldn't breathe. She looked around wildly trying to comprehend what was going on. This was some cruel mean trick. She tried her own magic to enlarge herself, but nothing worked. She remained small. She fluttered her wings, but they were ineffectual in moving her, as if she weighed more than they could propel.

She began to swim around in the vast expanse of the inside of the dress. The hem around her was so far away it would take several minutes of swimming to reach any edge of it. If only she could get there, then she could duck under it and see who was doing this to her. Then she could fight back.

Confusion filled her. She glanced around trying to figure out where she was. Sadness was in her heart, but why had she been so sad? She suddenly couldn't remember, all she could sense was the deepest sadness she'd ever felt. That scared her and her anxiety exploded.

Before she even reached the edge of the fabric around her, a big hand came from above like some five-legged headless monster. She tried to swim away from it, but the big hand scooped her up, the fingers closing around her making a dark cage of the obscenely large hand. She screamed and pelted her fists against the flesh encasing her as the darkness fully consumed her. Horror further filled every cell of her as she bit into the flesh as hard as she could, but whoever the hand belonged to didn't even seem to flinch. She was held steady. There was no way she was getting out. She didn't know what was going on, but she shouldn't be there, and where the ginormous hand was taking her was surely not where she was supposed to go.

Overcoming Heartache, Book 4

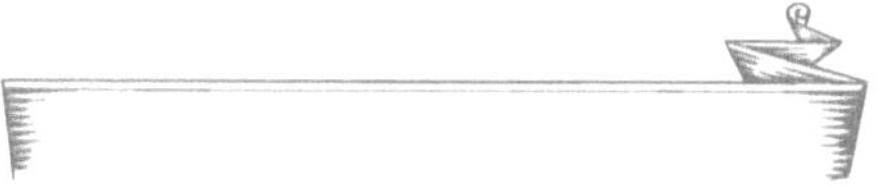

Overcoming Heartache, Book 4, Chapter 1
Gabriella

Gabriella gazed out over the turbulent sea. Flickers of memories were starting to further solidify, and they were breaking her heart. She couldn't fathom how it was all possible. It was her life, yet it was as if it were a memory of someone else's. Her tear-stained cheeks kept drying in the wind and the brutal beaming of the sun's hot afternoon rays, only to be re-wet by fresh tears. She leaned back on her hands, her fingers spread on the sun-heated rock.

How had magic betrayed her like this? Magic had always been her friend, but now she was the victim of it. Granted, it wasn't her brand of magic, but she hadn't realized how easily she'd succumb to another's power. And her entire life's course had been altered because of his manipulations. She felt cheated. Her life had been stolen, hijacked, and rewritten without her involvement. Her life had been both ruined and made better, all from one devious act.

She wanted to kill him.

How was she supposed to move forward with this new knowledge? It hardly seemed possible that she could. Her heart had frozen, and her blood was now iced in her veins. Everything had just stopped in her world, and she was too stunned to move. She had no idea what to do next.

She shook her head as the waves crashed on the shore below. She was on her favorite beach, straddling her two worlds of sea and land, realizing she'd held past beliefs that undoubtedly belonged to each, but ultimately, she belonged nowhere. Not with this resurfacing knowledge.

She spotted a woman walking along the shoreline below. As she came closer, she waved upwards toward Gabriella, like she was trying to get her attention.

Gabriella peered at the woman, studying her. Even from a distance, she looked familiar, but she couldn't be sure. She was nude and had a curvy figure. She was quite attractive, and her light brown locks were continuously tousled by the ocean breeze. She appeared to be seeking Gabriella.

The woman placed both her hands around her mouth as if trying to project her voice.

Gabriella only heard a faint sound. She wasn't sure what to do, but, since the woman kept trying to catch her attention by frantically waving and yelling, she began to descend the high cliff. She'd climbed the rock cliff with ease, her desperation egging her along the way. Surely going down would be easier. She fluttered her wings to steady herself, her impatience winning, then decided flight was better anyhow, and soared into the sky.

She watched the woman closely as she flew nearer to her, hoping she wasn't nefarious. She'd had enough evil to last a lifetime. With all the new realizations, she didn't trust anything. Not a damn thing. She had awful fears consuming her head, including the horror of the thought...was Leif even real? If everything she thought she knew was wrong, then could anything be right? No one was trustworthy, yet she knew not everyone was to blame. There was just one.

She landed in the sand about twenty feet from the woman. She had her flight mode cocked and ready to ignite at the slightest provocation. As she gazed upon the woman's face, a lightbulb was triggered. Could it be? Her heart leaped as she recognized who was before her.

"Marella?" she asked excitedly, her vision seeming to go out of focus, then back in. "Is that you?" Images of a past with Marella hit her brain, some popping up, ballooning like mushrooms, others more a slower realization coming to light, yet some others were just an impression, like a ghost. Many more memories erupted in her head with Marella in them, and they hit her awareness in rapid fire.

"Ah, Gabriella. Yes, it's me." Marella smiled and held up her arms. "Oh, how I've missed you."

The onslaught of memories fell on Gabriella like an avalanche and she suddenly felt very heavy. All the times Marella had helped her back on those uncertain days in the castle, the kindness she had extended, and the times they had had fun. Oh! All the wedding plans Marella had helped her with! The wedding that never happened.

Her heart clenched. It felt sharp, the memories brutally cutting. All of it filled her and choked her up as sobs burst from her. Marella had been her refuge in a confusing time. Seeing her now felt like a lifeboat when he really needed one.

She crumpled to the sand and held her head as she wept. It was all too much to think at once. Why hadn't she remembered her life? It was as if she were waking from a deep sleep. And, she gasped—if Marella was real, maybe it all was real...

"Oh, Gabriella..." Marella gasped as she ran to her. Her tone was sympathetic. Marella was indeed a friend.

"Oh, I don't know. I'm so confused. It really all happened?" She looked up at Marella. Every memory was pelting her with a myriad of emotions, steeling her moments to full consumption as she sank into the full memories. Every moment with Nocter, with Leif; her, alone in the forest, trying to survive and not understanding why she had been condemned to it; it all consumed her brain. The knowledge was a horror. What had happened to her was unfair and wrong. "I was taken, right out of my own wedding dress, and put in a forest jail. Why? Marella, why? Why was I taken?"

"Yes. You were, I watched it. And, oh, I don't know. I might know, but I don't know for sure. I..." She paused, seeming unsure, and slightly afraid, then continued. "But I do know King Nocter was very distraught. He was beside himself. Gabriella, he about went mad." She wrung her hands, her eyes full of worry. "Are you okay? It's been so long."

Gabriella was so confused. Nothing made sense, none of it. She had thought Nocter was the one who had put her there in that forest. If he hadn't, then who had? She was so utterly lost. "You mean...it wasn't him?"

"Who? King Nocter?" Now she looked confused, too.

When she'd returned home, it had seemed that Nocter was the evil one. He didn't tell her he wasn't. He hadn't told her much of anything at all. But if Nocter wasn't the orchestrator, who would have taken her to the forest? Who would be that cruel? Her heart ached even deeper as she imagined Nocter upset, too. They'd been deeply in love. And how had she forgotten this? It was way too powerful of a love to just be forgotten. How could such an epic love just cease to exist, like blowing out a candle? This wasn't fair. "He was?"

"Very much so. He became very hardened. You are his light, Gabriella." She pressed her lips together, looking like she wanted to say more.

Her mind spun. She said "are," as if she were still with him. She couldn't be his light, not anymore. She was in love with Leif. Her tears flowed as her heart was wrought with the agony of lost love that she hadn't even left of her own volition. She was plucked from a vibrant, caring, passionate love as if she were a pawn in a game. But she also now knew she still loved Nocter, too. She not only remembered her love for him, it was *still* in her heart. Despite all that had happened, it was like she was right back in Nocter's hug. She could feel his arms around her, their bodies so close, close enough to not feel lost. But she was beyond lost now. Everything had changed, but things were still the same.

"Come, let's get you home." Marella stood, urging her to rise by tugging on her crossed arms.

Surprise and bewilderment filled her. "Home? But Marella, my home is on land, with Leif."

Marella looked surprised and worried at once. "You mean you won't be returning to the castle?"

Marella didn't understand. She'd lived a lifetime with Leif already. She wasn't just going to leave him. She loved him very much. She needed him. He needed her.

Gabriella fell backward, landing back in the sand. "What am I supposed to do, Marella? I have two homes and two men who love me." Reconciling the truth she had come to know with a truth that was real had her head spinning, yet she felt frozen in place, unable to move.

"I'm not going to tell you what to do, but King Nocter is not himself without you." Her face grew sad and forlorn. "He needs you, Gabriella. He loves you."

She couldn't breathe before, but now she was choking. She sobbed as the knowledge of the truth squeezed her heart. Memories were filling her heart as it was constricting from the weight of now knowing it all. Reality had a death grip on her, and it had spikes. It was making her bleed. And it hurt. She wanted to be clueless again. She wished she could go back to thinking Nocter was evil and wanted to hurt her. Now she had to live with the fact that he still loved her, and she still loved him, yet she was in love with Leif. This was all too much to know, to feel, to endure. She held herself in a ball and wept. She had blamed Nocter, and he hadn't even been to blame. In fact, shockingly so, he had been heartbroken. It was so hard to process. This meant he had been as hurt as she had been. Whoever did this was a monster. How was her enemy actually a victim, too, right alongside her? She released a stronger cry. He wasn't her enemy at all, but her long-lost lover.

"He was sad?" she asked through a slight break in her sobbing. She knew the answer, but she couldn't not ask the question.

"Devastated, my lady. Utterly destroyed."

"I'm not the queen. I'll never be the queen," she said, not angry, but empathically. It was the reality. The problem was, with her memories returning, she could put herself back at any moment of her time with Nocter and she was there, living it, as if she were in the moment. "I lost memories for so long." She stared at the sand. "So many memories..."

"They are all coming back, though, right?" Marella asked with hope.

"Yes," she cried, a fresh burst of tears overtaking her. There was no way out of it. She was being forced to live it. Relive every memory, every joy, every pain, and every speck of anger. Her brain stalled on how Nocter had made her feel so wonderful, how their passion had surpassed anything she could have imagined. And the sex. Oh, holy hell, the incredible sex they'd had! She felt stabbed, tortured, the memories wringing out her soul so that every juicy joy of them became instead a sad, dried up memory of all that was lost. The loss of what was, and the love she now shared with Leif, were devastating her. Surely, all of this couldn't exist at once. "I can't handle this." She gasped and remained silent, watching the waves crash behind Marella. With every speck of her, she wished the memories would stop erupting. "It's not fair. I was robbed of my life while it still existed. Like, it was still going on without me while I was hidden away like some dirty secret, and yet I was given a new amazing life that still does exist." She was overcome with sadness, and the tears flowed. There was no reconciling all of this. It wasn't possible. "But

Nocter…I can't do this," she said in a small voice. It was like she needed to do something. She felt urgent, yet she had no ability to do anything. She was a numb lump of flesh. There would be no peace for her for the rest of her life.

Marella sat in the sand next to her, their bodies aligned and touching. She said nothing, but just sat there in silence.

The waves crashed continually on the shore. The wind came up stronger and tugged at her hair.

Marella's presence was at least comforting. But she was in big trouble. There was no way to pick Nocter, and no way she could leave Leif. Yet she still ached for and loved Nocter. This was the cruelest joke anyone could have played on her. There would be no justice from it, either. No matter who she chose, she'd have to live with the heartache of missing a lifetime with the other for the rest of her life. It was an impossible choice, but one that had already been made for her. She just had to live with it, endure the torture of knowing she couldn't have both of them. They could both love her, and she could love them, but she couldn't exist in both relationships.

"Maybe I need an amnesia spell," she said wearily, her attempt at a small smile failing. But that wouldn't be the answer. Then she'd lose both of them. But Nocter was already lost. "This is honestly torture, Marella." She leaned further into her friend. "I'm fucked."

Marella put her arm around Gabriella and side-hugged her. She sang softly, humming here and there as she slightly rocked their bodies back and forth together. She could try to rewrite history, but that shit didn't work. The body remembers. The body doesn't lie.

After what seemed like way too long to just sit doing nothing, Gabriella looked at her friend. There was only one way out of this. Nocter needed to fall in love again to fall out of love with her.

She gazed upon her friend intently. "What if you took my place, Marella? You could stand by Nocter's side and be his queen." If there was anyone she trusted to take care of Nocter and be his woman, it was Marella. Yet imagining them in the throes of love and passion made her angry. She was supposed to be there, not Marella. Her jealousy would have to sit down. There was no way out of this but to create something new. She was not ever going to leave Leif. She wanted Leif, she wanted the life they had together. She also wanted the life she'd had with Nocter, except for the part about being confined to the castle. Fears gripped her. Would she ever see Marella again if she became queen? Would she be imprisoned in the giant monstrosity of a jail if she became Nocter's queen? She wasn't sure she could condemn a woman to such a life, especially her best friend. "I don't know, but you'd be the perfect partner for him." She hated saying it, yet she knew she had to.

"Gabriella, I'm of the servants. I cannot marry a king. No one would accept it." She spoke with humility. "I can't even think of King Nocter in that way."

"But you could. I know you could. And if you spent time with him, I predict you'd fall in love." It would be an easy fix for her if Nocter could be happy. It would at least be easier to keep living if she knew he was happy, too. But to keep herself from Nocter seemed cruel and wrong, too. No matter how she looked at her life, there would always be horrible, unfixable wrongness.

"He can't fall in love with me when he's in love with you, Gabriella." She was so emphatic, and her tone told that she thought this was such ridiculousness. "He hasn't stopped loving you. He hasn't stopped waiting for you. He won't move on."

That hurt. But she knew Marella was right. Love could not be forced. Love had to grow organically, on its own; it had to live and breathe without constraints. Directing love was as impossible as capturing and holding the wind. And any wind that was blocked, soon died.

"There is no answer, Marella. I'm to suffer this the rest of my life." She sighed. "You have to go to him. Woo him, Marella, I know you can do it. You must. It's the only thing that will help. It will help him, and it will help me." Tears streamed down her cheeks and a sob took hold. She gasped through her sobs. "Please, Marella. You must try." She turned toward her and gripped her forearms, her wings fluttering on her back with her feelings of urgency. "And you must fuck him good, Marella. Oh, for the love of every drop of water in this sea, you must fuck him." She stared into Marella's eyes. "He needs it."

Marella tried to shrink back and pull her arms from Gabriella's grasp. Her eyes filled with fear as she shook her head. "No, I can't…"

Gabriella's desperation exploded. "Please," she pleaded as she held Marella's gaze. "This is the only way. It's the best we can do. Go. Be his lover if you won't be his queen. Be the best lover you can and fuck his fucking brains out." It about killed her to say it, but it was the only hope for him, and for her. She'd go to Leif, and Marella would go to Nocter.

It had to be done.

Marella nodded and stood up. She began to walk.

The pain in her heart ripped her resolve to shreds as she watched Marella go, her eyes still full of worry.

Marella turned back. "I will go and do this, but only because you asked me to. I won't lie to King Nocter. If he asks, I'll be telling him you sent me."

Gabriella wanted to screech out a loud shrill, "no", but she held it in, for if she did not, she'd have killed Marella with the first three seconds of her mighty cry. So, she flew into the air instead, as high as she could go. She watched Marella enter the sea as she skyrocketed up higher, her heart dying as her dear friend disappeared into the sea. And when she was high enough, she screeched the most horrid call she'd ever shrieked out in her life, up so high that no one but her could hear it. If they had, they would have crumpled from the ear pain, blood leaking from the sides of their head as the sound filled them and likely killed them from the inside out.

Chapter 2
Nocter

"You could kill him," Finstra slurred as he slithered through the water, his bright green body shimmering in the sunrays penetrating the sea. He whipped around and stared at Nocter with his small beady black eyes, as cold and lifeless as they were any day.

"That's not a solution," Nocter said with annoyance.

"It is a solution," Finstra said. "A very good one to the problem you have."

"To a problem you created," Nocter roared, his hair strands flapping, zapping with bolts of electricity. He'd let his hair grow long in recent days of not giving a shit. The ends of his hair crackled and flapped as his gaze still shot fire.

"Don't threaten me with electrocution. I still have a leg up on you for that." Finstra glowed, his body emitting an electric neon green sheen.

Nocter had considered killing Finstra once he'd found out he was behind Gabriella's disappearance. He had become violently enraged knowing he had kept her captive in the forest for so long, keeping her away from him, even as the sad king had desperately scoured the sea for his lost love. But he was stuck. He couldn't kill Finstra. Finstra alone was the reason he had the support of seven of the surrounding twelve regions, and a loss of him would be a big blow to his relations with those allies. He was still too new of a king, and Finstra, as vile as he was, had rapport with those rulers. He had finally been making progress on securing safety for his people, so he was hesitant to off Finstra, but his fingers itched to choke the snake every time he saw him. He'd basically set in motion Gabriella falling in love with another.

"You deserve to die for what you've done," Nocter stated. With every cell, he wanted to smother Finstra. Rage filled him, and he struggled to fight his urge. It would be so easy to kill the little worm. He could do it with his bare hands.

"I've done and will do worse," Finstra retorted with a 'tude. "The fact is you need me, King."

Nocter fumed as his fingers twitched. Unfortunately, Finstra wasn't wrong, and he fucking knew it. Finstra had ruined his life, and he was being forced to keep him alive. It was a cruel twist of fate, an impossible choice. And what would killing him do? Would Gabriella feel avenged and fall out of love with Leif? He thought it likely not. The damage was done and irreversible. He knew Gabriella, and she did nothing lightly, and would not be controlled. Likely, if Gabriella ever got close enough to Finstra, and she knew he'd done what he did, she'd kill him with her own bare hands, or her screeching death call, which had been her ultimate savior in the past. He'd seen her do it once and only once. He'd only survived because he'd cloaked himself, or he'd been as dead as the man who crossed her.

NOCTER PACED THE WIDEST hall in the palace. How was he ever going to get her to understand it all? What Finstra had done led her to fall in love with another man as if Nocter didn't even exist. And he couldn't blame her. She hadn't made any of this happen. She'd been a victim as much as he had. And she'd been led to believe he had done wrongs to her, which was the worst part of all. That alone had caused Nocter the most pain.

He wasn't one to kill another man without undue reasons, but he'd kill anyone to save Gabriella. But all Leif had done was take care of Gabriella and fall in love with her. And the biggest problem was, at present, she didn't need saving. So, there was no justice in killing Leif. Sure, he'd toyed with the man, even with the idea of offing him. But he couldn't kill a man who didn't deserve it. And he certainly couldn't blame him for falling in love with Gabriella. She was the most incredible mate in the world.

He was still in love with her himself. He desperately needed her, wanted her. His eyes filled with tears. A tragedy was what his life had become, and it had been set up so perfectly to not be that before all this, too. It was a dream come true to have the woman of his fantasies, have her love and devotion, and literally be handed the crown. It couldn't have been more ideal. How had his life fallen to such lowly depths? His golden ticket to happiness had soured and turned to blackness.

He was fucking miserable. And he couldn't even go to Gabriella for comfort or to recharge. He'd lost the only person in his life he'd do anything for. If he didn't have the kingdom to care for, he'd likely have hunkered down and just laid around until death took him. He'd have nothing to live for without his slice of the ocean to look after. He never dreamed in a million years he'd lose the love of his life and have it replaced by a population. He wasn't about to let them down, though. He was committed to protecting them, even if Gabriella no longer lived amongst them. He had hopes that one day she might return, and she needed a safe place to come home to.

He wasn't one to wallow, but he was wallowing. Luckily, he was too busy to dwell in helpless inactivity. The constant catastrophes he battled helped him move forward, but Gabriella never left his thoughts. He figured that would be the plague of his life.

If only he could get her back...

He stared off into the sea, watching far-off fish swimming along. He was sad, a sad king, and no amount of female interaction was helping. Sure, he got off, but sex was so much hollower than it had been with her. No female caught his attention enough to be more than a few times repeater to his chambers. He just moved on, again and again, hoping there might be a spark of something, anything. Perhaps it was because he was the king. Nothing would ever be genuine again, and he hated that. There would always be an ulterior motive, a pining for something, or fear getting in the way. He was doomed to never fall in love again in his lifetime, at least not for real.

So, there was killing Leif as an option. But he couldn't do it. Plus, she'd never forgive him if she found out it was by his hand. His death would mean she might consider becoming his bride again, though, but he had so much repair to do. And would she even believe him and his love for her at this point? He had played with both of them as he had scrambled, trying to figure out what to do. It became a worse disaster for him, too, and the couple had been strengthened. His game-playing had only tightened the knot of their relationship. He had been stupid and petty, but fuck, he was so pissed! He'd lost control, and that had led to his further downfall.

What was done was done.

His hair swirled as his anger sent jolts of electricity through his strands. The new development showcasing his abilities had been very effective in inciting fear in others, and he'd not really spent much time trying to control it. It was serving him well.

He swam to the sea stream room and settled in to watch the swimmers going by. At least his brain would relax watching them. The longer he sat, he settled into a greater sense of calmness.

It wasn't long before Marella appeared, looking extremely distraught.

"Good evening, Marella," he said happily, but with a twinge of worry. She was the one bright light of his days. She'd come to him and tended to all of his needs, but one, in the absence of Gabriella, doting on him like an infatuated servant. The woman was very attractive, and she was very good at serving and anticipating his needs. He also loved that she had so many happy stories about the time before Gabriella was kidnapped. He fully understood the way her face would light up when she spoke of Gabriella. The stories were soothing to listen to, and made him happy. The women had fun together planning the wedding. And he had to admit, he'd used the stories of them bathing together as fantasies to get off. But in his mind, they did way more than just swim and wash each other. They were full-on fucking.

He grinned deeply at her, trying to placate his worry, and trying harder not to think of her in a sexual way. He knew she was way more than that, but his cock had its own opinions, too. "You look like you could use some cheering up." He patted the couch cushion next to him. "Come, sit. Tell me about your day. You left the castle, I hear."

She nodded as she settled in next to him. She released a big breath and looked even more upset.

He didn't like the scared way her eyes looked, either. "Did everything go okay?"

She nodded, and her eyes cleared a little. "Yes." She paused. "Well, no. I don't know."

"Where did you go?" He wanted to comfort her in her fear, but that felt awkward, so he resisted the urge to hug her.

"I went to the shore."

He glanced at her feet. "Ah, yes, that's right. You can walk on land and breathe there." Just like Gabriella. Though he had feet, he couldn't breathe out of the water, at least not for very long without an adjunct of some sort. "How was it?"

"Yeah, I can breathe, for a bit." She shrugged. "It was...okay. I guess."

She was clearly very worried about something. He leaned back on the couch, patiently waiting for her to say more.

"The sun was out," she said with a weak attempt at a smile. "The sun feels different on the skin when out of the water." Her smile grew. "It feels hotter."

"Ah, that makes sense. No layers of water to cool the rays." He relaxed a little as she appeared to as well.

"I enjoy the warmth. It can burn, I guess. The humans can get burned from it."

"They can? How odd. When they live on the land, I had assumed their bodies could handle the environment."

"Yeah, you'd think so, since that's where they reside. Must be painful to get burned, I'm guessing."

King Nocter nodded. He'd never been burned, though he'd come too close to creatures like Finstra when they were lit, but he'd never been too close for bodily damage. "Yeah, I'd imagine it would be."

"Oh, look at that little purple fish. It's dancing along the yellow one. Like they are playing chase." Her face cleared of all traces of badness as she watched and smiled.

"Yeah, I've seen that kind of thing before. It's fun to see." He smiled back at her. He wondered how many kings had sat here beside a servant and enjoyed it. His experience might be rare.

She laughed, and her face brightened further. "And there! Is that a dolphin coming?"

The delight in her voice was a breath of fresh air. Her excitement warmed his heart, too. "Yes, they often come in groups, so be ready for the rest to appear."

He watched her watch the water stream, her face growing more excited. A spark of happiness burst inside him, and it felt damn good. Her mood was contagious, and it soothed his scrunched-up heart. "They are playful creatures, aren't they?" Marella had a genuine innocence about her, a genuineness that, if he wasn't mistaken, was carving out a special place in his heart for her.

She nodded aggressively as her anticipation never faded.

Within a minute, three more dolphins came into view. They were frolicking and swimming around each other, gliding along each other's bodies as they slowly moved along as a group.

"Ah! There!" she said, pointing, her eyes glued to the dolphins. "Oh, that's so cute!"

They stopped in the middle of the channel, and one took off, but two stayed behind. They began to swim around each other, and then the other dolphin returned to swim around them.

When the male rotated so his bottom side showed, she gasped. "Oh, holy shit! Look! He has a boner!"

King Nocter looked at the mid area of the dolphin and sure enough, he had a full cock. "Whoa, now we are getting a show here!" He laughed, and it almost felt foreign to do it. It had been too long since he'd laughed like that.

She giggled, her face slightly flushed. "This must be a mating ritual. And what's with the third?"

"Sometimes they just mate for pleasure," he said, recalling watching such scenes years ago. They were playful creatures who had sex with each other, and they were pretty open about having sex with other dolphins. All scenarios he knew weren't so fun-loving as this one, but it was nice to see their flirty foreplay. "They often look ready most of the time." He grinned at her, his loins unexpectedly springing to life at the thoughts of sex, not dolphin sex, but sex with Marella. He chastised himself. He ought to not think about her in sexual scenarios, but he couldn't stop his brain from going there, again.

Marella's eyes fell to his groin and widened. She looked away quickly and kept her focus on the pre-copulating dolphins. "They seem like they are doing some kind of mating dance or something."

Her glance downward excited him, despite his attempts to dismiss it. "They likely are, and the third may be next, or he's protecting them, standing guard so they can have time to do it safely." He smirked. "I would love it if they decided this spot was a safe place to copulate. I'd like my castle to be known for that!" He chuckled as Marella blushed a deep red.

She didn't say anything, but watched the dolphins play. They kept inching along, though, despite their slowing to engage each other. Soon they were out of sight. Marella still kept watching where they had been, as if she expected them to return.

"Well, that was quite interesting." She glanced at King Nocter, her eyes still dancing with delight. "Kind of sweet."

He knew his cock had inflated and was visible through his clothing. He didn't apologize for his arousal, but simply smiled back at her, his attempt at ignoring it. "Yeah, it sure was. They know how to have a good time."

She gazed at him, then scrunched up her shoulders as a mischievous little grin took over. "Yeah, it would seem so."

He sat next to her with his dick in a fully packed hard-on. A boner can't lie. He was turned on by her. He smirked at her. "Mind of its own," he mused. He had to address it, being it was so damn obvious.

"I don't mind," she said with a seductive slur and a flash of passion in her eyes. "It's pretty sexy. As a male, everyone knows your thoughts. Does that ever bother you?" She glanced away, then back at him again, her eyes coyly turning a bit flirty.

He chuckled. "It was hard to get used to, at first when I was young, I mean. But once it happened multiple times a day, in front of countless others, I got over it. It's most awkward when it happens in a meeting, though, I must say." He grinned deeply as a laugh built in his gut quickly. Then he released it, and the outburst left him feeling even better. "It helps being covered up with clothes now. Sometimes,

I can hide it, but other times, it draws more attention, being covered than when I was always nude." He shrugged. "Must be the novelty of wearing clothing."

"Oh, wow! I never thought about all that!" She ran her hand down her naked body. "No one knows when I'm aroused, except if I decide to show it."

"Yeah, females have that advantage, but the face tells a lot. As do the eyes." He gazed down at her, noticing her arousal. Was it bad to want her, too? She was Gabriella's good friend, and it felt almost like cheating to consider it, but he and Gabriella weren't together anyway, so that was pretty lame. When he'd vision checked on Gabriella, he'd found sights of her fucking Leif, and a lot. For which, knowing her libido, he certainly was not surprised. He'd been happy to see her getting pleasure, but it had wrecked him to know he could no longer do it. It had eventually led to him not checking up on her anymore because he couldn't stomach watching another man enjoy his mate, and her enjoy him back.

He'd assigned the checking up on Gabriella task to one of his trusted seers. He just wanted to be sure she didn't get into trouble she couldn't safely get out of. He was too much of a caretaker to not take care of her, if even from afar. Plus, he hadn't made the best decisions in his fury over her being with Leif, so it was best he assigned that to someone else. He'd beaten himself up over many sleepless nights for letting his anger rule his actions. He didn't mean to ever harm Gabriella, but his strong feelings for her clouded his judgments, and he fell prey to thoughts of revenge, which put her at risk. Never again would he do that. It had also backfired, and it seemed she began to hate him. He had been crushed by how she spoke to him that last time, and the memory of the hate in her eyes had turned his stomach too many times to count.

He couldn't trust himself. So, the task was properly shifted to someone he trusted. He was too much of a moron, and he saw it as his weakness. Her safety was too important, and his rage was too great. He needed an extra layer to keep himself in check.

He watched Marella's delicate features seem to transform as she carefully, and very slowly, laid her hand upon his thigh. He jumped as her hand touched down, not more than five inches from his turgid cock. He ached for her to grab it through his pants and stroke it. He wondered how she'd react when she climaxed, and getting lost in that reverie, he missed that she had moved her hand closer until her knuckles lightly grazed his packed meat.

"I hope you don't mind," she stated demurely.

Wow! What wonderful development was this? He broke into a burst of a cajoling laugh, mostly at himself. He instinctively raised an eyebrow before he could stop it. "Um, no. Not one bit." A sexy, beautiful, kind-hearted woman with her hand on his thigh was never going to be a bad thing in his mind. He felt guilty, but her touch was so needed. He drank in her purposeful touch.

It was true. He'd had so much sex with so many females, but without the connection of his mind to theirs, it had been basically just a little more than alone pleasuring sessions. He yearned for a deeper connection, even if it was just friendship with another.

She was coming on to him. He was used to that as king, but this time, it felt different. He'd let her make all the moves without imposing his desire on her until he was absolutely one hundred percent sure she was serious. He'd tried at first to wait for Gabriella, but when he saw she wouldn't likely return, he'd eventually taken to having sex again. And lots of it. He'd used the absolute fuck out of the sex dungeon in the back of his quarters, and he'd gone through three of the sex toy chests and tried everything in them. He'd had such high hopes for using them all with Gabriella. Even though all the sex had been lesser, he'd come hard, and often, and he'd given countless orgasms to the females, but those times had all lacked the full spicy zest he'd had when he had fucked Gabriella.

There was no love in it.

Did he dare to hope that sex with Marella would be better than all the copious amounts of loveless sex he'd had since Gabriella? It might not be like it was with Gabriella with Marella, but surely it had to be more fulfilling than all the other encounters he'd had. He worried this might be using her, for her connection to his lost love with Gabriella. He might be guilty of using their new friendship. But, in the end, it was just two people deciding to pleasure each other intimately, if things ended up going in that direction.

He had to curb his mind as his anger flared as an image of Gabriella and Leif fucking erupted in his forebrain. Rage blazed, and he tried not to show it in his eyes, but she saw.

She made a bold change and moved her hand over his hard cock. She began to move her hand across his hardness.

He calmed as he realized his rage must have just looked like desire to her. Well, he did desire her, that much was very true.

"Am I overstepping?" she asked, seeming demure, a devilish smirk taking over.

"No," he mused. "In fact, I was hoping." He grinned at her but then startled when he saw movement in his peripheral vision. "But let's move to my quarters, shall we?"

Chapter 3
Gabriella

Gabriella paced the floor as she waited for Leif to return from work. Why was time moving so damn slowly? She needed to talk to him, and she didn't want to at the same time. How was she going to tell him all of this? How would he feel about her still having feelings for Nocter? Feelings she didn't know she had, but clearly harbored in her subconscious? She didn't understand her own emotions. This really wasn't fair to the three of them. Leif had been safe in the knowledge that she hated Nocter, and now she'd have to tell him that she also still loved him? This was impossible. Who could make any sense of this? It was not logical.

She curled into a ball to keep from wailing again. She'd surely hurt some innocent human nearby if she released the wail she wanted to. She may need to fly nearly to space again to scream once more just to release this burdensome tension. It was getting too hard to contain.

Would Leif understand? Would he blame her? Even knowing it's not her fault, would he blame her for loving a man who'd done what he'd done to them both?

And speaking of that, she couldn't reconcile that either. How had Nocter changed to the point that he'd yank both her and another being around as if they were objects on chains and not living, breathing creatures? That wasn't the Nocter she knew. But yet there was no denying it all. It just made no sense to her. It was unfathomable.

If Nocter was so different, now overcome by cruel intentions, maybe it had been wrong of her to ask Marella to get involved with him. What if he hurt her? She'd never forgive herself if she put that in motion. Marella was her dear friend. She was fraught with feelings of doom.

She shook her head. This was crazy. She knew instantly once she started remembering that things were going to get messy. Very messy. Yet she still felt love for Nocter. It was too hard to make sense of this, but she also couldn't deny it. How could she make her heart stop caring? Maybe she needed a spell, some kind of magic that would kill love. Though she'd yet to hear of such a thing. Love seemed to be the one thing that prevailed, even if it weakened for a bit for the person due to circumstances, if love burned, it still burned on some level. There must be something out there, though, from some of the stories she'd heard. The trick would be to find it. All she knew was that she needed this heartache to stop, or she'd implode. Her mother would have had an idea, but that just wasn't possible anymore. Though she didn't really believe her mother was truly gone. That made no sense either.

She rocked back and forth, trying to soothe herself. This was an epic disaster, and she hated it.

After what seemed like ages, she heard Leif arrive home. She heard the usual sounds of his return, the garage door opening, then closing, the slam of the car door, and then his footsteps up the wooden stairs in the garage.

She remained still as she listened, studying the pattern of the couch upholstery because she was mere inches from it.

As Leif entered the living room, she lifted her head so she could meet his gaze.

"Babe, what are you doing? Are you okay?" His voice was full of concern.

He rushed to her and touched her arm, his eyes conveying his extreme worry.

"I'm not okay." Tears began to birth from her eyes, and a wail of anguish left her lips. She constrained it from its full potential to not hurt Leif's ears.

"What's happened?" He squatted on the ground next to her and touched her arm with both hands. He sank to the floor to sit as he held her gaze. "This must be bad."

She nodded and stared at the carpet. "So, apparently, I've had amnesia for quite some time. A spell was cast on me."

"Seriously? Oh, damn. This can't be any bit of good." His eyes showed his awareness, and his utter shock. "How bad is it?"

"The worst I could have imagined." She blew out a big breath. "I don't even know where to begin."

"Anywhere. We'll just talk through it." He took in a big breath and slowly released it, too.

"I was about to be the queen."

"What? Holy shit!" He smiled. "No way!"

"Yup. And guess who I was about to marry?" She stared into his eyes and gave a sad smirk. "Nocter."

"Fuck," he muttered, his smile fizzling. "So, he was mad and jealous, that's why he did that to us?"

"Yes. And I was kidnapped, my memories of Nocter wiped clean, and plopped in the forest to fend for myself." She stared at him. "Leif, I was literally stolen right from my wedding dress."

"Who would do this?" Leif asked, aghast.

"Finstra," she spewed with hatred. "He did this. He's behind it."

"It wasn't Nocter?" Leif looked so confused.

She couldn't blame him. She was confused, too.

"Well, he did the stuff in the ocean, but it all started with Finstra. He's the one who took me, gave me selective amnesia, and left me in the forest to die. Alone." She couldn't stop her eyes from showing him how sorry she was, then her anger flared again and her eyes became angry.

"And...if he stole you from your wedding dress, that means..."

"Yeah. I didn't want to say it, but it's true." She gasped, and a sob slipped out uncontrollably. "Oh, Leif, I'm so confused. I don't know how to feel." She sobbed harder, and her body shook. She covered her eyes and wept.

He pulled her into a hug, then settled against the couch, pulling her onto his lap.

Being in his arms was comforting, and it helped. After her sobbing slowed, she gasped. "How can I be in love with two men at once?

He caressed her back, then her hair.

"None of this is your fault." He sounded sad, but also tender.

"No, but how am I going to go on? And to find out the man I was despising is actually one I still love? What kind of mean trick fate is playing on me?"

He held her closer as she fell into a fresh burst of crying.

After several minutes, Leif spoke in a very soft voice, "So, you do still love him?"

She nodded against his chest, but kept her eyes closed. She couldn't look at him. She couldn't recall falling out of love with Nocter, unless that memory hadn't emerged yet, but she also had a fresh hate. "But I also hate him for what he did to us. And I still love you," she whispered back. Fate wasn't just cruel, it aimed to torture her. "Please, don't hate me."

"Shhh, I don't hate you, babe. Not even remotely."

But how would he feel going forward, knowing she pined for another? She couldn't say she didn't love Nocter, yet she wished she could. There was one glimmer she was hanging on to, and that was that Nocter had changed. That he no longer was the man she had been in love with. So, perhaps she just needed to reset her brain with that knowledge. She hoped this might ease the devastation for Leif. "But he's different now. I just need to learn how to un-love him, but since he's different, I have hopes that I can." Nocter certainly didn't seem like the same man, and yet her heart didn't seem to know that yet. She yearned for him and his ways. She needed his arms around her as much as she needed Leif's.

She sat up quickly as fear gripped her. "I've done a terrible thing. I sent Marella to go be with him. And I'm afraid of what will happen now."

"Who's Marella?" he asked gently.

"Oh, yeah. I forgot. You don't know her. She's my best friend." Gloom filled her, and she began to cry again. "Why would I do that to her, Leif? Why would I send her to him? Send her to someone bad? I'm so confused." A soft wail left her lungs.

"I don't know," he stated simply. "You thought it would help?"

She nodded. "Yeah. But I was thinking of Nocter, which I shouldn't have been. I should have been protecting her, not throwing her to a monster. What if he's so changed that he hurts her? I'll never forgive myself." She shook with sobs, her pain stabbing again, and with new fresh worry, it was growing.

"Tell me about Marella. If she's anywhere near as strong as you, I doubt she'll be at risk."

Her weeping slowed, and she nodded. Hope crept in a little as she gazed back at him. "She's very strong. She's an amazing woman. That's why I feel awful sending her to her be ruined." Was Nocter really that evil now?

"It might not be bad," Leif said with hope.

She laughed as a burst of a snort slipped out. "This is Nocter. Look what he did to us."

He nodded and clasped his hands together, draped over his bent knees. "True. But maybe he's not fully been turned evil." He shrugged. "He could have killed us."

"True. But, I don't know." She shrugged. Everything was ceasing to be as she thought it was. Even her relationship with Leif felt different, which she didn't like one bit. The crazy thing was she felt extreme love for both men. It didn't feel as if one love lessened the other, but she was still so unsure that she couldn't be entirely sure of anything at all. "All I can say is this new knowledge doesn't lessen my love for you. I still love you. I'm in love with you, Leif. I just don't know how to exist with these new memories, which aren't new. And the feelings, shit, it's like I'm right back with Nocter at the castle, about to marry him."

"Wow. So, tell me more about that. You were actually in your dress? How close were you to the ceremony?"

"Well, I remember I was trying on the dress for alterations. And Marella was doing the alterations. Nocter had been pulled away on urgent matters, and we had just received word that no one knew when he'd return. But the wedding was set to happen soon. I remember fearing we'd have to wait." Her memory of that day became clearer as she spoke. She paused, the newly appearing memories crushing her heart further, and then she spoke. "But, Leif, here's the thing...I'd also decided I needed to flee. I had found out that being betrothed to Nocter meant I couldn't leave the castle because it was too dangerous for me to leave. Once I was queen, this was even more true. They feared I'd be killed." She couldn't stop herself from shaking. "And I had said out loud I didn't think I could marry Nocter." She opened her eyes wider. "Oh, fuck. Finstra must have been listening." Her memories began to become even more solid. "Oh! I was going to run, Leif. I was going to leave! That's why Finstra took me, so I couldn't. But...shit, this all makes sense now. He was stopping me from leaving. But why wouldn't he tell Nocter

I was still alive?" Had Finstra been saving her from running away or just trying to get her away from Nocter? Why not just kill her if the latter?

She shook her head as she tried to figure it out.

"Wow," Leif said. "That's insane."

"Yeah," she muttered in a meek voice. Her hatred for Finstra hardened, thickening with her anger. "I guess, maybe he didn't want me to marry Nocter, but he couldn't kill me, so he just took me instead? Kept me from Nocter. But he wanted Nocter to think I'd disappeared without a trace. I bet he wanted Nocter to think I was dead, so he'd move on. Finstra never liked me. Clearly, he hates me. And I've hated him from the start."

Leif reached for her. "Come here, babe. This is going to be all right. We still have each other. We can get through this."

She wanted to believe him, but her heart still was fresh with remembered love for Nocter, too. However, she had new memories to reconcile with that. He'd put her and Leif through hell. What kind of monster would do what he did? And how had she been so stupid as to send her best friend to comfort such a horrid monster? What a stupid, selfish thing for her to do! It was as if she had no regard for Marella's well-being, but had only considered Nocter's, the one who had been so cruel. One thing was certain, why he did what he did made more sense, but how was she going to carve him fully from her heart? She couldn't just turn her love off like a switch. In truth, she should hate Nocter, but what had happened with her being taken to the forest hadn't been fair to him either, so she couldn't fully blame him, either.

Finstra had deceived them both. He had stolen their love, their life together, and their futures.

"There's no good solution, Leif. I'm doomed."

"Well, I love you, and I love you more than ever for sharing all this with me." His eyes were kind and full of love. He had the kind of unconditional love for her that she'd dreamed of.

She scoffed as she looked up at his face, connecting her gaze to his. "I thought you might hate me for saying I still have love for my ex."

He laughed at her. "Yes, true, but this isn't your everyday residual feelings going on here. Yesterday, you didn't even know you had this love, so time will tell, but I think things will work out." The worry had left his face.

"I wish I had your easy optimism."

"I'll share." He kissed her on the top of the head and held her close. "I'm not going anywhere. You have my heart."

"As you have mine," she said, snuggling in. Where would she go anyway? Certainly not back to Nocter. She loved Leif. She wanted to be with him. That was the easy part.

Chapter 4
Nocter

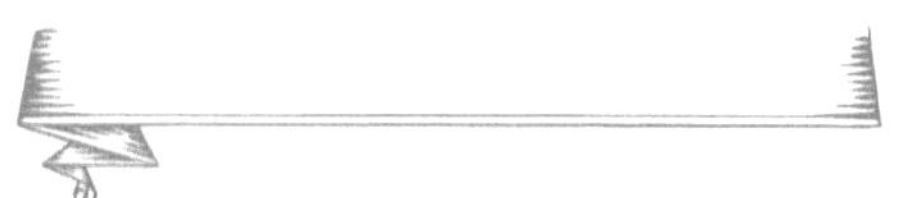

He swam, and Marella followed close behind. His heart had begun to race, thinking about fucking Marella. It was a luxury he'd never considered. To the other servants, it likely looked no different from recent days since she'd become his doting servant. It looked innocent enough, and honestly, he didn't care either way, but he did care about her. Throughout the history of royalty, it was quite commonplace for kings and servants to have sex anyhow, so it wouldn't be out of the norm. Since becoming king, he'd heard all the stories of the multiple orgies, both with kings and with queens, and all the rounds of countless hours of sex and pleasure that had taken place between the castle walls over the centuries. It was legendary in the royalty circles to know this, which was why he thought perhaps it became commonplace for the king and the queen to be clothed, so they could actually get some work done in between all the sex! The thought amused him, and he chuckled silently.

This would have fit well with how both he and Gabriella always desired sex. They were both horny as often as they took a breath. That hadn't remained dormant in him for long, even with her absence. He was a highly sexual being, and his kinks were certainly maturing, being the king and having access to so much more paraphernalia, and how that opened up so many more opportunities for sex for him. He'd had servants throw themselves at him even if he hadn't approached them. Except for Marella, she'd never done that. Until now. He'd go slow with her and wait to introduce the extra kinky things with her, though, but she'd been in his quarters enough to see the dungeon and all the gear. Hell, she'd cleaned up his toys on occasion after he'd used them on females. She had to know on some level what his tastes were.

All these thoughts were getting to him. His arousal for something sexual with Marella was peaking as he entered his chambers.

He stalled as he turned to face her, wondering what Gabriella would think of him doing this with her. But then she'd been with Leif, so why was he even worried? They were no more, it was just that he still couldn't get used to it.

"Are you okay with this?" he asked softly, waiting to approach her. "If there's one thing I will never do, it's force you. Free will and free choice make all the difference for me." He relaxed when she looked pleased. "It's a mood killer for me if it's not wanted for both of us."

"Same," she said in a gentle, but firm tone. "King Nocter, I want this. In fact, I'm not afraid to admit I've had more than one dream of joining you and the queen."

His heart leaped. This was indeed a good sign that she'd had interest in the past, so this wasn't just him pushing it.

"Gabriella gave me her blessing," she added as she swayed. "That's all I needed because I've desired you from first sight."

His heart jerked as if stabbed by a knife. His brain stalled. Wait. She was just giving him away? And Marella wanted him? All this coming at him at once sent his brain into a spiral.

"She wants you happy," she murmured as she came closer to him. "As do I."

He was warmed by the thought of them both wanting him happy, but he thought reaching happiness was completely impossible for him at this point in his life. That silly notion had died long ago. He couldn't admit that to her, though. He'd not take her offering as slighted.

He allowed his sly, seductive smile to bloom as he gazed upon her, hoping she saw the desire for her in his eyes. "I would aim to make you happy as well. It turns me on to see you climax." The many times he'd pleasured Gabriella to climax before he took his turn flooded his brain. He'd not let Marella down. He hadn't a black enough heart yet to deny his partner sexual pleasures. Despite the heartache he'd been suffering, it was surprising he hadn't fallen into that dark, blindless trap of selfishness and instead just fucked every female selfishly without a care for their pleasure. Perhaps his heart wasn't as blackened as he'd feared. This promise of an encounter with Marella had him feeling optimistic, and very turned on.

"I believe that about you. And it's very sexy. It turns me on if you are that way. The sign of a fantastic lover." Her eyes burned with passion as she approached him, her hands raised. "I'm fully in, and desiring this with you." She firmly pressed her front to his, encasing his thick manhood between their torsos. "I'm open to trying whatever you'd like."

He chuckled heartily. "Be careful with such statements." His smile grew. "I'll be taking it slow, then we shall progress as it deems worthy. I'm not one to rush. Trust between us is paramount."

"I like that you are already set on this continuing," she said in a soft coo. "I'd like that very much myself."

"Oh, I'd love nothing more than to continue down this road with you, Marella. I'm very attracted to you." He touched her hair for the first time and slowly caressed her locks. "Yes, I'm very interested in that indeed."

"Good. We're in agreement." She bit her lip, and her eyes burned even brighter. "It's been a while for me, so I'm pretty ripe."

"Oh, now that's music to my ears!" He released a low, gruff laugh after his outburst and cupped her face with both of his large hands. His passion flared with urgency. "You like that pretty mouth of yours to be kissed?"

She nodded as he pinned her head between his palms. "Very much so," she whispered, then left her full lips parted slightly.

That was all the invitation he needed. He wanted to taste her, to revel in the essence of her wet, oral hole. With each heartbeat, his desire for her grew. She was showing signs of the promise to be an easygoing lover, one who would eagerly submit, one who might be open and adventurous. That was his favorite. However, he wouldn't make assumptions yet, but if she were a dominant, they certainly wouldn't mesh. He didn't get the impression that she was a dominant woman in the bedroom, at least. It wasn't in his nature to not be the one in the lead. He had gotten to the point with Gabriella that she'd sometimes playfully guide things. It had been a fun change, but for the most part, he loved being in charge of all things sex.

He released a quick breath. He needed to hush his thoughts of Gabriella, though they came so fierce and strong, it was a challenge to silence them. He hoped Marella would fill his present thoughts enough to grab his full attention, take his mind off his lost love. The other lovers he'd taken had not. But, then again, he hadn't had any sort of relationship with any of them. He'd always imagined he'd been fucking Gabriella most of the time he'd drilled himself into them.

Marella would be different. He had hope.

He leaned his head down so their lips could meet. He hesitated for a split second as he gazed into her eyes. She was so beautiful. She was very amenable in her demeanor, and he saw no flashes of fear or negativity, so he dove in.

He covered her open mouth with his and they locked into a strong kiss that pulled his brain into the present like a charm. Her kissing commanded his attention and focus just like magic. This was something.

He slid his tongue along hers and explored her mouth. She was warm and wet, relaxed and inviting in her reception of his deep kiss. He probed her, his cock more than ready to taste her lower hole, too.

She was responsive and hungry in her kissing, and it ignited him to more aggressive moves as he groped her body. His mind wandered as he imagined what her nipples would taste like, what they would feel like against his seeking tongue.

He mauled her back, pressing her firmly to his body. She molded to him quite nicely and his loins screamed at him to hurry the fuck up and smash her. He tempered his passion, as he'd learned to do long ago, and simply kissed her neck. Just because he was horny as fuck didn't mean he should rush. Slower progression was better anyhow, the more the build, the greater his release. And hers, in particular. He was going to take his time learning her arousal sites, mapping out her erogenous zones, and teasing out her triggers. It would be so fun, and he couldn't wait.

She moaned as he suckled her neck, her head flopping to the side in submission, showing she would slip into wild abandon easily and swiftly when touched. She kept her mouth parted and moaned her appreciation as he sucked her flesh, then he applied a light pressure with his teeth. It was a daring move, and he knew it.

Her responsiveness had him wanting to make his love bite mark on her already, but he held back. He lustily enjoyed this notion and made his way down to her chest.

He loved finally being able to touch her naked body. He'd admired it so many times, but getting to touch her was exquisite. He slipped his right hand down her side, feeling her curves up as he moved his hand. He hungrily gazed upon her nude breasts, cupping the right one with his palm, then running his thumb over her hardening nipple. He'd been shown as king, many people would give him exactly what he wanted, and offer more. He liked and disliked this because, of course, he loved getting what he wanted, like anyone, but he also wanted something genuine. He craved the purity of someone wanting him for himself, and not for his status as king. Gabriella had been that way because they'd been in love long before he became king. Perhaps that added to his misery in the loss of her.

He shook his head slightly, chastising himself for thinking of Gabriella in this intimate moment with Marella. If he was to grow in intimacy with her, he needed to focus just on Marella.

They ran their hands across each other's bodies in hungry grabs.

A saucy look overcame Marella as she slid her fingers inside his smock. "Do I get to see you as you really are?" Her tone was seductive and wanton.

Her interest and her forwardness turned him on. "Yes," he said with a deepening smile. He removed his shirt, then slid his pants down, his turgid cock swinging out as it came free from the fabric.

"Oh, wow," she cooed, her eyes lighting up like the brightest stars. "You are quite the specimen. I knew you would be." Her gaze was appreciative as she scanned his body, then dwelled on his thick cock.

All the other partners he'd recently had seemed too afraid or too intimidated to appreciate him for his body and his ardor, but with Marella, her expression of apparent desire was highly gratifying. He much preferred confidence in a mate to a cower.

"I think we're going to have a lot of fun together, Marella," he said as he collected her naked body against his naked skin. He really needed a good fucking romp, and oh was he going to give it to her.

They fell ardently into a kiss again. He slid his hands down her back and cupped her buttocks, giving them a strong squeeze as he ramped up the aggression in his kiss. He wanted her, and he wanted her to know it without a doubt.

She moaned then whimpered and his cock pulsed with extreme need. She began to slide down his body, but he grabbed her arms to stop her.

"No," he said firmly. He grabbed her hand and pulled her toward the bed. "I want to savor you, make you come, then you may do that."

She smiled with so much excitement that his heart soared to a height it hadn't for a very long time.

He pressed her to settle back on the bed. As she nestled into the soft blanket, she spread her legs, a lecherous, lusty grin spreading across her face.

"Ah, yes," he said with relish. "That's what I want."

He inhaled her musky pussy scent, and it made his cock twitch. With every fiber in him, he wanted to ram his cock into her warm wet hole, but he refrained from unleashing that wildness just yet. He traced her thighs with his fingers, and she squirmed, mewling in anticipation.

This raged his desire for her more. He was ready for an attack. "You like a mouth on you?" he asked casually, as if he didn't want to lavishly eat her out. He let his eyes smolder with zest.

"Oh, yes, do I ever." She reached for his head and caressed his cheek.

The touch was affectionate, and it opened his closed-off heart a little bit. He would move with caution when it came to access to his heart, but she'd already won a peek inside.

He sighed as his eyes fell closed, but just for a moment, as he allowed her soft, purposeful touch along his cheek. The sweet calmness her caress brought was a slowing of their passion, and it lit something inside him he'd thought was dead. But that something was pure.

He opened his eyes and met her gaze. She smiled back at him with a very pleased expression as she meandered her fingers into his hair. "I don't need to tell you this. My hard nips should be telling you," she snickered while scrunching up her nose, "but you're the sexiest lover I've ever had the pleasure of being with, and get ready, because I'm the wildest ride with the biggest heart. And I like to come."

His heart burst with new energy. He released his restraint and dove into her pussy, consuming her fleshy flaps with his lips, first as a nibble, then as a full-on in-his-mouth suck.

She jolted in response as he worked his way along her folds. She jerked, making jubilant delightful exclamations when he wiggled his tongue into her hood to taste her special spot. It was the gem of her womanhood that he sought, and he attached his suction right over the top of it, securing her in place with his grip on her thighs. She was pinned, going nowhere as he ate her out.

She thrashed and fingered his scalp. Her grabbing of his hair became strong, and her sounds matched in intensity. He laid his weight upon her right leg to secure her in place and reached up to stimulate her nip.

This sent her flying into ecstasy, and she shrieked, her body torquing in the pleasure. Her sounds egged him on, and he sucked her harder.

She screamed, her back arching, making her tits rise.

He almost came as she did, her orations rising, then she fell silent as her body was rocked from her release.

He wanted more. He didn't let up, and she re-escalated in her sounds and her movements, her body jerking once again, signaling her second release.

"Please, King, fuck me. I need that magnificent cock riding me." Her wish was wanton, and her gaze still hungry.

She wanted more, and it fired him up.

He rose above her and grabbed his cock. He tapped it on her sensitive clit, and she twitched each time, her moans ticking his lust for her higher.

He pressed his cock head at her opening and penetrated her slit.

She cried out as he slowly entered her, his own groan joining the lush enjoyment sounds coming from her.

He began to speed up his thrusting of his manhood into her, going faster and harder as her sounds indicated she loved what he was doing. He fucked her like a machine, never wavering, but ramming constantly, his arousal ready to burst. He rose to an angle that he knew would hit her in the right spot, and after a short time, her body rocked out another climax.

He smiled with satisfaction at bringing her there again. Then he took her in wild abandon until his seed blasted her insides. He felt both gratified and sheepish at once. That was careless to release inside her, but he'd been so taken in, he hadn't thought about pulling out.

No matter. It was done.

When she opened her eyes, he saw the look of satisfaction that, as a dominant man, he sought. It was the mark of satiation, and it made him feel complete. It was always his goal, and the more he could make her look this way, the happier he'd be.

"Oh, King Nocter, that was so good. It was incredible." Her voice was as soft as a coo.

He grinned as he slid down her body. "But I'm not done." He dragged his tongue down her body. "I want more."

When he reached her soaked womanhood, he inhaled their combined scents. "Ah," he said with savoring. "And we need to come up with a new thing for you to call me. How about just Nocter?"

A look of surprise took over her face. "Oh!" she exclaimed. "That will feel so strange."

"Call me Nocter, and with time, I'm sure we will have more names."

He latched onto her with such fierceness that her body curled upward, and she cried out. "Oh, whoa!"

He worked his mouth over her and didn't stop until she climaxed three more times and was hitting his head with her palm.

"Oh, it's so sensitive, oh, shit," she cried in desperation, gasping.

He released her and set his chin upon her mound, smiling up at her. "Need a break?"

She fell into an easy, soft laugh. "Yes," she said, with a sigh. "I'm floaty and woozy, but wow, that was unbelievable. I've never…"

He grinned even wider. "I'm a bit insatiable. I have a hard time stopping."

She laughed and extended her arms. "I love that. Lay with me?"

He moved to cuddle in beside her. This. This was what he'd been missing. He held her close and stroked her hair. He enjoyed the sound of her breathing. When she wiggled against him, he snuggled her tighter.

She sighed, a soft, low sound escaping her mouth. "I'm sleepy," she murmured.

"I'd love to lull you to sleep. Will you stay here tonight, in my bed with me?" He let his hope live in his words, even though it felt dangerous to do so.

"Yes, I'd love to." She closed her eyes, and he caressed her cheek with his thumb, his palm holding her face. "Nocter."

He kissed the top of her head and rubbed her back until he heard the sounds of her breathing grow steady and regular.

She was asleep.

The feelings of hope and vulnerability were scary to lean into, but he welcomed them. He needed to take it slow, but this was more than he'd expected with Marella. It wasn't just sex; it was something more.

THE NEXT MORNING, HE woke and smiled upon seeing Marella in his bed. Her hair was spilled across the pillow and her breasts were spread. His awakening senses were met with arousal, joining his already existing morning wood, as he stared at her naked body. He wanted to fuck her, and fuck her good, until she was shrieking with pleasure.

He gently caressed her cheek with one finger until she squirmed and opened her eyes.

Surprise lit in them, and then she grinned. "Oh! I forgot where I was." She smiled deeper as she writhed in the bed. "And what we've done."

Her movements turned him on even more. "Oh? But now you remember?" He snuggled against her warm flesh, savoring the feel of a female in his bed again.

"Oh, do I. And it was incredible." She looked happy.

"Might need a repeat?" he asked with eagerness, rubbing his hard-on against her.

"Fuck yes I do, yes, please, Nocter." She emphasized saying his name with great relish.

"It would be my deepest pleasure, Marella." He copied her with great emphasis on her name.

Her smile deepened as she tipped her chin up.

They embraced in a kiss, locking their lips firmly together.

She kissed him as hungrily as he kissed her, and quickly, they were writhing against each other with erupting passion. Her soft moans packed his cock even harder, and he urgently wanted to be inside her.

"I want that inside me, please, Nocter. I need you," she murmured against his flesh, her need for him very evident in her pleading.

That was very satisfying to hear. "Yes, I'm going to ram you until we both come screaming."

"Yes," she cooed, then kissed his chest.

He pressed her shoulder before firmly saying, "From behind." His wicked, lusty expression got her to turn over in a flash after flickering her eyes lustily back at him. Then she stuck her butt out toward him. "Yes, yes, just like that. Going to fuck you until you're a floppy cum drunk rag." He caressed the curve of her left hip and ass cheek. He wished he could grab a restraint and secure it on her to use her body even more aggressively, but he wanted to wait until she had fuller trust in him. It was too soon for any of that kind of thing yet.

He pressed his cock at her entrance, not penetrating yet, and reached around to play with her to get her hyped up. When he sensed she was ready, he pressed his fingers inside her. She mewled and made pleasure sounds as she rolled his hips in tune with his hand motions. He began to pump his fingers into her, then pulled her juices to baste her bean. He rubbed her as she twitched in his arms.

"Yes, just like that," he instructed. "Yes, yes, yes. Come on, I want you to come," he coached.

Her legs bent up, her toes curled, and her body shook as she moaned and grunted.

Once he believed she had climaxed, he pressed himself fully into her, her groan a testament to how sensitive her genitals still were. He rode her backside, smacking her bottom with his pelvis, driving his cock deep inside her womb. She stroked herself and her orations got louder. He fucked her until her walls quaked again, squeezing him inside her walls, and then he burst his seed up inside her.

He didn't even care if she was getting bred. He needed her. He'd deal with more, if it happened. It might not.

She swiveled with a sigh, which forced his soft cock fully out of her. She smiled up at him and pressed her full front to him, mashing her breast to him. "I could get used to this."

"Same," he admitted. And for the first time in a long time, his hope grew instead of further dying.

He had a lot of meetings lined up for the day, but for now, he had a sexy, happy, willing partner in his bed. And that was more than he'd had in a long time.

Chapter 5
Gabriella

She wanted to go to the castle. She was so worried about Marella, but she wasn't sure she could face Nocter. Yet, she wanted to protect her friend. Nocter clearly wasn't himself, and she'd sent her friend into his dark lair. A week later she still couldn't stop her worry from grinding her will down. She might just tear off into the water and storm the castle.

But her fear had her also paralyzed.

Her love for Nocter hadn't exactly died yet. She wasn't talking about it again with Leif. What would be the point?

She paced and wondered how she could ever feel right again. Leif was due home in an hour, so that was her excuse for not going to the castle. Her brain kept flip-flopping between urgency to rush and drill down into the sea to find Marella, and staying away from the pain she might see, or feel, there. Leif had said he'd support whatever she decided. But that was based on that he was solid in that she loved him and wouldn't leave him. He'd said as much. And it was true!

She chewed her lip as memories of Nocter flooded her head. There were so many good memories, and as each day went on, more popped into her head. Taken alone, they'd be enough for her to dash off to Nocter and fall into his arms with ravishing delight. But her memories didn't exist in a vacuum. All the shit pile and all the amazing stuff with Leif were all there, too. It was irreconcilable. She was fucked.

She had a lasagna pan in the oven, two glasses of wine poured and set on the table, and a crisp leafy green salad waiting in the middle. They had an evening of dining and fucking planned. For that, she was very excited. When he was home, it was easy to keep her mind off Nocter and Marella.

She fluttered her wings and flew across the living room, trying to spend some of her nervous energy. She'd taken to pacing while in flight because she couldn't exactly fly outside in the neighborhood. At night, she'd sometimes soar into the sky just to remind herself she could fly. She loved her life with Leif, but she didn't exactly get to use her powers and abilities much. In the sea and on the beach, she'd used them constantly, but amongst the humans, she had to appear human, and all her wonderful traits became a dirty little secret to shield the world from. She was a weirdo in hiding.

There were times she missed living amongst her kind, but her love for Leif stamped it out. She'd never want to live without Leif. She reminded herself she'd once thought the same about Nocter.

Leif burst into the door with a giant grin. "Ah, it's so good to be home. It smells incredible in here."

She rushed to him and fell into his open arms. He smelled like coffee and his office, or what she imagined an office to smell like. It was a distinct smell, but her sense of smell was heightened compared to humans. She could usually smell Leif once he was in the neighborhood, but today she'd been too preoccupied with her thoughts to notice him approaching. "Yay, I'm so glad you're home."

"Sorry, I had to work longer. I wanted to be here with you." He looked exhausted.

"You are now," she said with a twinkle in her eyes. "Now, let's fill our bellies so you can fill me with your cock."

He grinned a lascivious grin. "You're my perfect match, babe." Some of his tension seemed to just float off him.

She nodded and blurted, "Let's eat so we can fuck."

He released a hearty, deep laugh. "I'm ready to fuck, but my stomach says food first."

"It's ready. Let me just pull it out of the oven." She kissed him on the lips and dashed to the kitchen, using her wings for a boost to hurry her along.

They ate by flickering candlelight, and she forgot all the bad and marinated in the good. Leif wasn't a king, but he was hers.

"So, tell me more about fucking," she said with a sly grin.

"Oh, I'm going to fuck you. Flip you this way and that and pound you until you spill, then I'll take you from behind like a beast!" He motioned his hands around as if he were manipulating her body. He jerked his hips upward in a thrusting motion in his chair. "I want your cum gushing out. But first I want to make out and massage your pussy. Kiss you, my kisses trailing down your neck. Might leave a mark there. Our bodies will be smacking, you will be begging, and I'll give you a hard grind. And when you cum, my cum will run out of you."

She squealed and clapped her hands as the promise of such ecstasy thickened her clit. "I love when you tell me what you are going to do to me."

"Pleasuring you is a privilege. One of life's incredible treats." He beamed a seductive smile her way.

"You're the world's best lover, you know that?" She smiled at him, but inwardly, she cringed. She'd once felt that way about Nocter. She admonished herself. However, in full truth, she wasn't yet used to having the memories of fucking Nocter back in her brain. All the amazing lovemaking sessions she'd had with him had hit her hard when they came to full fruition. They'd had some massively epic sex together. Not that sex with Leif paled in comparison, but they were different. She really couldn't say which of their styles she liked better; that was like choosing between breathing in and exhaling. But both were dominant in the bedroom, which suited her perfectly.

"I have been dreaming of pounding your pussy all day long," he mused as he squeezed the air with his hands. He scrunched up his eyes and said, "Pinning those luscious hips of yours between my hands."

She giggled and squirmed in her seat. "I'm not sure I can wait." She glanced at the dirty dishes on the table.

He guffawed. "Who said we had to?"

He stood up and strolled around the table. He held out his hand. "Shall we fuck?" He grinned with a raise of his left eyebrow.

"Yes, please," she said in a wanton tone. "And that part about bodies smacking, I need that."

"As do I," he said while pulling her into a tight hug. "I'm going to pin you down and make you come so hard you almost say your safe word."

She slurred, "Oh, please do." She sent him the dare to do it with her eyes.

They fell into a lip lock that led to loud mouth smacks.

Leif slid his hands down her back and cupped her ass. "Can't wait to pound my pelvis against this ass."

She bit her lip, and her eyes flared with fire. "You'd better," she said in a soft tone.

He kissed down her neck, then back up. On his way back down again, he took her flesh between his teeth.

She rolled her body against his bite, and the pressure of his grip, squirming slightly from the increasing pressure of his teeth. "Oh," she said, the word coming out mostly as a sigh. She flinched when he pressed his teeth together more, biting into her flesh.

He played with her right nipple as he made his mark on her neck.

She squeaked and twitched as he finished his claiming mark on her. She whimpered.

Then he licked it to soothe it.

She was sure what he'd done would leave a lasting red mark. She thought it was hot when he did it, and she loved the significance of it. She wore the little red stain on her skin like a badge each time. The crazy thing was, now she remembered Nocter doing a similar thing to her. The two of them were more similar than they were different. Thoughts of Nocter during intimate times with Leif felt invasive, though, and she tried to shove Nocter from her brain, but it was holding on to those memories like a python. It wouldn't be long now that Leif might make another mark, he'd been known to make more than one when he was in this type of mood.

He devoured her flesh across her right breast with his mouth, then moved over her nipple, taking it into his lips. He never neglected her breasts, and true to his obsession again, he suckled her nipple for several minutes, which did such good things to her genitals.

She moaned, writhing against his constant suction and tongue manipulations of her erect nip. Then he let it slip out, pert and wet, before moving over to paler flesh. He pressed his teeth together and clamped down.

She jumped with a squeak, but he had her secured against him. He sucked her breast flesh in between his teeth, then bit down while sucking, making a hickey bite mark. She shuddered as he bit down deeper.

"Oh, shit," she murmured.

He backed off her flesh and admired his work. "Nice little mark," he said with relish.

She glanced down at the reddened area of her skin and squeezed his arm. "Fuck me, please, now. I need you."

"I will, but first I need to make you cum. I want you shuddering and gasping from me eating you out. Then I'll fuck you. And hard."

Butterflies jack-knifed in her belly in anticipation. "Yes," she slurred as he took her other nipple in his mouth.

When he reached for her mound, he pressed her rounded flesh with his fingers firmly, then slid them inside her lips.

She moaned at his purposeful touch, his direct seeking out of her clit. He'd learned just the right pressures to drive her wild. He played her like an instrument, pressing lightly to edge her, then more firmly, and on the right side to drive her extra wild. There was something so comforting in him wanting so desperately to arouse to her climax before they engaged in him penetrating her with his cock. It made her feel taken care of, important, and integral to the intimacy. Hell, prioritized. Again, she cringed, remembering that Nocter had the same approach to sex. Since she'd found two mates who were similar in this way, clearly it was the kind of partner she was drawn to, or perhaps she was just one lucky female.

She felt the rise of her enjoyment fill up as he worked his fingers around her fleshy lower parts. The wet sounds of his fingers exploring her aroused her more.

He moved quickly to scoop her up and carry her to the living room. He met her gaze, his horniness flickering in his licentious expression. "Get ready, I'm not stopping at one, or five."

Excitement zinged through her body.

He laid her on the couch and pressed her thighs apart with his hands while keeping constant eye contact. "Going to suck you until you slap my head away." He lowered his head to settle between her thighs. "Grab my hair and show me what I'm doing to you."

She laced her fingers through his hair and took a grip. She liked her hair being played with, too.

He traced the tip of his tongue along her divide, then parted it, dipping his tongue into her sensitive folds. He explored her externally with his tongue, then added his fingers to tickle her arousal higher. When he pressed his fingers at her slit, she squirmed and groaned.

"Yes," she said with softness. "Please."

He pressed his fingers into her, and she tugged fistfuls of his hair. He used his mouth on her supersensitive gland and his fingers rode deeper in, pumping at an ever-increasing speed.

She wiggled, her sounds escalating, her hands entwined tightly in his hair down to his scalp. He increased his pressure and she launched. Her body rode the wave her clit sent and she soared, coasting to her sexual peak easily and with great surety. Her body shuddered through her climax, yet quickly rallied, ready and cocked for another.

True to his word, or rather his obsession, he kept on pleasuring her. She peaked again, not having fallen back to baseline with his continued attention. She scored another, then another, but still he kept on.

"Please, I need your cock in me, Leif, fuck me," she begged as she thrashed in desperation. She literally could not remain still, it was way too hard.

He pressed his fingers deep into her thighs and somehow sucked her even harder. She skyrocketed to the most massive orgasm yet, her body jittery, her gasps falling away as the overwhelm shoved her into silence.

As she began to float back down, her gasping sounds joined his suckling. She could finally hear it. It made her really fiery hot. "Please," she pleaded.

He released her and gave her such a domineering gaze that she shivered. "Oh, I'll fuck you alright, fuck you like a rag doll. Turn over. Put that butt in the air for me to ram." It wasn't a question, but a command.

She quickly scrambled to her belly and tipped her ass high in the air, and pressed her face to the crack in the couch.

He caressed her wet opening and then dragged his hard cockhead along her. He quickly pressed himself into her and got to a rapid tempo in no time. He pressed his hands into her hips and pounded away, those lovely skin-smack sounds filling the air.

She was panting as he grunted. She knew he was close, she could smell his arousal blazing hotter as he sped up his thrusting into her.

"Take my cock, every drop..." his voice trailed off as his arousal claimed all of him. He groaned, and she felt more wet inside her.

He slowed his pumping as his sounds began to settle, and laid his body upon her backside. "Holy shit, that was intense," he muttered into the flesh of her back.

"Yes, incredibly so," she said with a shudder, trying to slow her panting. Her bean felt exposed and vulnerable. She'd come again quickly if he touched her.

To her delight, he gave her a wicked growl, then he reached for her clit again, his strong arm wrapping her hip and finding the treasure. He rubbed her and she burst into another climax, bliss-filled and oh-so-damn satisfying.

Panting, they both fell down on the couch. They settled along each other's bodies. He pet her head, then finger combed her hair. "You're an amazing lover."

She sank into his statement like it was hot bath water. "As are you, Leif. You're incredible."

"I love you," he said as he kissed the top of her head.

"I love you," she mirrored back. He didn't need to ask if she had liked it, she knew he knew. And how could she not, with all that focus on her? He was her ideal man. How had she found him? It must have been fate that day that he walked into her section of the woods. But she struggled with that. Her fate had been Nocter, first. That time seemed a lifetime ago now. So much had changed, so much was better, and then, there was the stuff that was worse. Only she hadn't even known about *the worst* for very long. And what else did she have yet to remember? She was afraid of what other memories would surface. She was sort of grateful the memories were trickling in slowly, but at the same time, she was always on edge, wondering when the next doozy would pop into her brain. It was an uncomfortable feeling, not remembering her whole life. What atrocity would she remember tomorrow? Next week? In ten years? It was a cruel game, and she wanted it to stop.

"I'm not going to press you for information. I know you will tell me what you need to, when you need to. But know that I'm here for you. I'm not going to judge you. I just want you to know I love you, and I'm the luckiest man in the world to have you with me." He held her tighter.

She fought the rise of tears, but failed and they started to slip out. She sobbed against him, both from the relief that loving him brought her, and from his expression of unconditional love.

"You are the most incredible man in the world, Lief. And I love you so very, very, very much."

"It's going to be okay, babe. I promise you."

She almost believed him. Almost.

Chapter 6
Nocter

Things were stable. At least for the moment, nothing was blowing up. Daily life had settled quite nicely. He'd work, attend meetings, and come home to fuck Marella. Not a single member of the staff batted an eye at their interactions. Perhaps it was an unsaid truth that kings got to fuck who they wanted, and sometimes, throughout history, it had been the staff. He'd heard some stories, a few of them extreme, where the king had sex with them all. No one tended to say "no" to a king. No one but Gabriella. She had never had a problem telling him no, even when he was sliding into being the king. That's one thing he actually really respected about her, she was always her, and no status of becoming king held her back from speaking her boundaries, and her mind. She was bold, courageous, and fearless. All that had made her attractive as heck to him.

He smiled, thinking of her as he watched the fish swim along the stream. Marella was sleeping in, and he'd not woken her, but just let her sleep. He'd wanted sex, but that could be for later. He had woken her for sex before, but she seemed so peaceful this morning. He'd contemplated life with her as his queen. He dared to think it, though he certainly wouldn't act on it. Not at this stage anyhow, but it wasn't a no, either.

He leaned back as he heard the swish of water. Someone was coming near. He turned his head to see it was Marella.

"Hello, sunshine. You look lovely and rested." He smiled at her as she beamed.

"I feel incredible. I see I overslept." She sat next to him and snuggled into his body.

It felt so good to have a female nestled against his side for so many moments of the day again. "You did. I didn't want to wake you."

"I was surprised to find you didn't. But it did feel good to sleep in. I'm not always the best at that." She smirked. "It's in my servant genes, I guess. Time to get up and work is ingrained in me."

"You're one of the hardest workers I know." He squeezed her close. She was really growing on him, and he felt in sync with her, too. She'd lived at the castle her whole life, very rarely leaving. This notion was not wasted on him. Her entire world had been the castle. From what he'd found out, she'd only left the castle a handful of times her entire life. And once was recently, when it had been reported to him that she'd gone to the beach. The only thing that would have brought her to the beach was Gabriella.

He hadn't wanted to question her, but nothing else made sense. It had to have been to see Gabriella. He wondered what they'd talked about, and if he was a part of it. He figured that was likely true. It didn't matter. Marella had also said Gabriella had given her blessing, so he had zero doubts that the two met. He wasn't one to manipulate his partners.

Guilt spread in him daily over what he'd done to Gabriella and Leif, but he'd been out of his mind. Many would say that's no excuse for what he did, but he'd let his power go to his head, which was something he'd vowed to not do as king. He wouldn't blame Gabriella if she never forgave him. Jealousy made him cruel, and he was not proud of that. It was hard to stop loving someone and let them go without a fight. He was used to fighting for what he wanted.

He gazed into Marella's eyes as the full realization hit him of what an amazing thing he'd found with her. It had literally fallen in his lap. Though he also knew he'd never stop loving Gabriella. It wasn't in him. He'd become someone ugly with the knowledge of Gabriella and Leif's union, and he was putting his foot down to never go there again. Habits were hard to break, so he didn't intend to start the habit of letting his jealousy guide him.

Was Marella an easy choice for queen? Perhaps, yes. But that didn't mean he would be bad for choosing her. She made him feel good. She gave him leeway to allow his true masculinity to shine. In that way, she was like Gabriella, allowing him to lead in the bedroom and be a friend outside of it. And she had been all the time living in his castle, which also blew his mind. But in truth, if Gabriella were here living as his wife and queen, he'd never have even known Marella this way, though, he smirked again, he'd had many fantasies of the three of them having sex. And, plus, that comment she'd made about joining.

"What's that look for?" she asked coyly, seeming to like the suggestive suggestion in his expression.

"Oh, just the fact that we didn't get to fuck this morning."

"Well, we can change that!" she exclaimed happily.

"Yes, for sure. I do have one meeting this morning, but how about a rendezvous this afternoon?"

"I'm in!"

"Where can I find you?" he joked good-naturedly.

"Oh, I'll be around. I won't be hard to find."

He smirked. "It's a big castle, though."

"Indeed, but I know where to meet you." She gave him a flirty look.

"I'd love to find you naked and draped over something."

She laughed with glee. "Done."

He kissed her on the top of the head and zipped off to his meeting, poofing away in the zip of a second.

When he landed at the council, everyone was there. He knew he wasn't late, but being the last to arrive felt off. He shoved it out of his mind. "Hello, greetings to all. I'm ready to hear assessments."

Finstra slithered in place. "The north is secure. The west is secure. The east is iffy, as usual. And the south is turbulent, but seeming contained near our border." His beady black eyes shone. He somehow managed to look evil in every light. He was not approachable, by appearance or demeanor. Dude was just plain ugly.

Most days, Nocter wanted him gone, not to mention having to stop himself from strangling the life out of the skinny little despicable beast after he'd found out he'd been the one who had taken Gabriella. That feeling had not dimmed one bit, either. It took all this power to stop himself from carrying through with it some days. He had to watch this fucker, and had assigned watching Finstra to his best guard. Now he knew he had to keep an eye on him. "Okay, well, it could be worse. What's happening to strengthen the east and the south?"

"More guards have been placed to patrol those borders. We've upped the spy coverage to try to find out what they might be up to." Finstra rose higher, then floated back down, as if nervous.

"Good. Makes me suspicious, though. What could they be up to?" He pulled in a big breath, then slowly released it. "The natives there rarely decide to let things be, but let's hope their unrest is simply their own issue and not a desire to invade us. Our kingdom is peaceful at the moment, or am I wrong?" He could never truly relax, that was the hard part about being king. He had to always be on alert and ready to pounce, even when things were calm. His responsibilities to his kingdom were big, and he wasn't about to shirk the duties of his reign. He took this shit very seriously.

"Yes," Finstra hissed. "But Almander has something to say."

Almander was the best female warrior he'd ever had the pleasure of working alongside. When she joined the council, after her many years as a triumphant force in their army, he'd been very pleased. As a full-blood siren, her abilities were solid, and her bravery knew no bounds. She fought to the death when needed, he'd watched her do it. She was a scrapper, and never gave up.

Her long, flowing alabaster hair cascaded around her lovely, purplish flesh. "I've seen a few odd things in the east. Something is possibly brewing there. They've added soldiers to the fort nearest our border. I'm hoping they aren't attempting to mount an attack. The warriors I saw arrive are some of their most feared."

"Oh, that's definitely quite concerning," King Nocter said, his hopes crashing. "That sounds ominous. We'd better beef up that area. Do we need to pull any from other borders to reinforce there?"

"Might be a good idea," Finstra agreed. "I'll reach out to Moonsang and see if there is anything to be alarmed about."

"Perfect," Nocter said. "I'll be reachable, but if there isn't anything else, I'm taking my leave for the day."

All seven nodded their goodbyes.

He left quickly, hoping no one else would stop him with something minor. He wasn't a micromanager, they could do their jobs. He had no desire to do everyone's role for them, but Finstra was one he had to micromanage; he was a slimy one. He hated it, but it was a necessity. He'd cut him out of the council in a heartbeat if he ever saw the chance. He'd warned him to keep his hands off his partners going forward, or he wouldn't hold back his anger. Finstra had cowered and slunk away. Though, Nocter didn't trust that the vile manipulator wouldn't betray him again. His connection with Moonsang had saved the kingdom in the past, so it was too valuable of camaraderie to just kill Finstra. His fingers twitched every time he laid eyes upon the green slip of a sea serpent, however. It'd be so damn easy to off the worm.

Nocter appeared at the castle in the hallway near his quarters. He was already aroused, wondering how he'd find Marella inside. His cock hadn't taken much of a reprieve from hardening since their conversation. The meeting had killed it temporarily, but it was back, and he was feeling aggressive today. Must be experiencing a testosterone boost. Fucking Marella often satiated such urges for him, as it had with Gabriella. He couldn't stop comparing them, and he hated it. He simply couldn't turn his brain off from Gabriella, no matter how much Marella filled his brain, Gabriella rarely left it. His blood would almost boil when he'd think about her and Lief fucking. He could have easily killed Leif by dragging him through the water, but he also knew if he did, Gabriella would certainly never forgive him. He'd have killed any chance of reconciliation with her if he followed through with his desires. He didn't want her hating him, but he suspected he was too late to stop that.

His cock filled fully as he entered his chambers. He glanced around and didn't see Marella anywhere. He hoped she'd obeyed and was displayed, wanton and open, for his mounting of her. He had the hankering for a bit of dungeon play, if she was willing, which she usually was up for. He loved that about her, her constant willingness to have sex, and her actual desire for it. She'd met his suggestions of kinks with enthusiasm and intrigue. What a blessing to have a partner who so vibrantly dwelled in her sexuality, and shared it openly with him. She was comfortable enough to wear her sensuality close to her skin. This was the kind of partner he adored.

He quickly scoured the room with his eyes and his senses. He zoned in on her immediately. He could smell her scent coming from the dungeon. Perfect. Perhaps he was getting lucky, and their moods would align.

He swam quickly down the hall, his erection bouncing with his movements.

As she came into view, his gasp caught in his throat. Oh, fuck yes! Marella's nude body was arched over the circular stone in the center of the room. Her tits were pointed peaks, the curve of them a round globe giving way to her ribcage. Her belly flesh was pulled taut and her smooth mound showcased a slit divide in her lips due to her slightly spread-apart legs. He couldn't see her face because her head was lower. It seemed impossible that she was hanging on and not sliding down.

He let out a deep groan. "Oh, baby." He approached her quickly, his cock somehow filling even more.

She spread her thighs wider, giving him a view of her deepest pink layers.

His lust exploded.

She turned her head toward him as he approached, her expression full of inviting ardor. "Hi," she whispered. "I'm glad you're back."

"Me too," he said quietly as he placed a hand on her ribcage.

He ran a hand over both of her breasts, pausing to pinch each of her nips.

She squirmed as his fingers tightened on her left nip, and when he gave a rough tug, she cried out.

He ran his hands across her stretched-out body, loving the curvature of her along the round stone. "You look exquisite."

She looked like a statue embodying the sexy mystique of the sea. Her presence was intoxicating, emitting the allure of the embodiment of a sex goddess. She sighed as she spread her webbed toes slightly, making the remnants of scales over her ankles shift.

He devoured her body with his eyes, making his way around her curves, groping every inch of her he desired. "You're so fucking sexy," he slurred, his voice thick with lust.

She squirmed, making soft mewls and short expressions of surprise as he cupped, caressed, pinched, and indented her flesh with his nails.

He loved her sounds as much as he loved fucking her. He was addicted to her sounds, to making her make them. The desire to dominate her raged in him as much as his desire to make her climax. Her submission met his kink and surpassed it.

"Finding you like this is...wow," he murmured into the flesh of her breast before he took it into his mouth to suck.

He trailed kisses along her breast, moving in minuscule steps until he reached her nipple. He got a huge charge out of suckling her nipples when her back was arched. He devoured her nipple, mowing down on it like it was a tasty hunk of meat.

Her body lurched, arching further off the rock as he mouthed her areola. He played with the other one as he fed on her. Then he did the same to her other nipple.

The urge to force her to be immobile seized him. The inciting vulnerability of her being willing to play while being bound intrigued him. She indicated her willingness to try it the other night after dinner when they'd had their debriefing of recent sessions of sex. Her agreement to an act of full submission in being bound for his sexual manipulations was hot. He couldn't lie. He intended to use her, roughly, but he also intended to pleasure her above and beyond his own pleasure. The mix of their sexualities had been working between them thus far, but he hadn't gone as far as a fully secured position for her yet.

But it was now time.

One delicious urge had settled in his brain. Her being hog-tied was intensely arousing.

He yearned to next flip her body to arch the other way, to have her ass at the peak of her so he could mount her and take her from behind, without her ability to get out of it. If she would submit to that, he'd be very excited.

It would show a massive amount of trust on her part to allow this, and if she could also climax with her body secured that way, it meant she was comfortable and felt safe with him. That was a confirmation he desired. He desperately hoped he was helping her feel safe. It was the only route to full intimacy with her. Everything else would only stifle or kill their connection. He knew he had to be smart. It was her submission to him that he deeply desired. This was a roadmap to their future, too. He wanted success and mutual pleasure, not blind submission from fear.

As he kissed down her body, he squeezed her flesh between his fingers. His rough grabs, he hoped, speaking of his desire for her.

She whimpered when he pressed his fingers into her harder, and she squirmed. He loved her writhing, but he also wanted to control it, just for a brief time to see how she'd react.

He pressed his chin to her mound, inhaling her feminine scents. They were intoxicating. His need for her swelled as he pressed his fingers into her vulva lips, parting them, then he began working his way around her slit. He loved how she accepted him as he pressed his fingers inside her. It wasn't just an acceptance on her part, it was very much wanted. This pleased him immensely.

She moved her hips as he pumped his fingers into her. He then sought to feel and press her fleshy area just inside her, toward the front of her. He explored and rubbed the uneven contours there. She was moving her body, trying to get the most pleasure out of his touches, and this excited him more. Her responsiveness to his stimulations would surely lead them both to a juicy climax. He placed his thumb on her clitoral head externally, then his fingers on her fleshy area just inside her vagina. When he squeezed his fingers together, she yelled out in ecstasy.

His need to be inside her flared. But first, he desired to be inside her mouth. His cock swung in the water as he moved, his precum met his fingers as he swiped his hand across the tip of his cock. He pulled his fingers from her and made his way to her head.

She turned toward him, and he pressed his cock to her lips. She opened her mouth swiftly, and he slid in.

Securely holding her head from the back, he lightly pumped himself in and out of her mouth. He kept going until she gagged, which he savored as his cock got squeezed, then he pulled out. He gave her a guilty grin.

She laughed slightly and shook her head.

"Sorry, but I do love you gagging on me. Just for a few seconds, though. I promise." He grinned deeply and then made a gruff grunt, his mood shifting rapidly from being playful to the desire to dominate her. He reached to grab her arm closest to him. "I'm going to hog-tie you and fuck you next. Pound myself into your cumslut hole. I'm taking it. Brutally." He knew she'd stop if he got too rough. He also suspected she liked a bit more roughness. "You're taking every pound of my hips, every inch of my cock, and drop of my cum."

She moaned. It was a pleasant sound.

A strong urge gripped him, a dark one. He decided he felt brave enough to share it. "What if tied you up and let every cock in this castle use you?" He wasn't sure he would do it, but he wanted to know how far she'd go.

"Wow," she muttered, then gave a short laugh, but she didn't sound angry about this question. "I have no idea how I'd react."

"But is it a turn-on or turn-off?" He knew this wasn't the time to discuss this, but he couldn't help himself.

"I don't know." She paused her speech as he tugged her through the water. "I think…"

She didn't finish her sentence, so he just kept on with his plan. This was a topic for another time. Once he reached the far wall, he pulled her ankles and her feet together in front of her and held them together.

He gazed into her eyes for a clue. Maybe he'd gone too far. Shit.

She watched him. She didn't have an expression of fear or anger. Instead, she seemed calm.

Maybe this meant she was considering what he'd said, but not necessarily becoming angry with him.

"I think it would be hot. I'd sure enjoy coming over and over again."

He relaxed seeing that she wasn't pissed off or hurt. "Yeah," he said as he tied the rope around the ends of all four of her limbs.

He grabbed her tied parts with one hand and dragged her to the open space in the middle of the dungeon.

He would save that exploratory conversation of her as a freeuse slut for the future. He liked the idea of putting her in such a position, but he wasn't so sure he wanted their cocks inside her either. It was a conundrum he hadn't quite figured out yet.

"Well, I'm fucking you now. You're mine."

"Yes," she cooed. "I'm yours, Nocter."

"Good girl," he said with firmness. "I love it when you feel me inside you. You're my good little whore. My horny little bitch."

"Yes," she said sensually.

Dirty talk aroused her, as praise did, too, and he loved to say it all to her. "Fuck your King hard. Grind against me."

He swiveled her in the water, so her ass was the highest part of her. He wanted her more immobile though. He glanced around the dungeon for what he could affix to her to so she couldn't move and wouldn't float. He spotted a round metal ball in the corner. He'd never been quite sure what to do with this piece of equipment, but it seemed the perfect size to fit between her bound limbs and her body. He swam to retrieve it. It had significant weight to it, so he figured it would work well.

He began to work the large ball between her torso and her limbs. It mashed against her breasts.

She grunted, squirmed as if in discomfort, and then moaned as if it felt good, ending with an exclamation of surprise when he finally nudged the ball in place. It fit like a charm and made her back arch more. Her tits were sufficiently squished, but she didn't complain. He wished he could secure her head too, but he was too horny to take the time to find something that would work. He spun her in the water, her body now a casing for the metal ball.

"Beg me to fuck you," he demanded, his cock twitching with the power he felt.

"Please, give me your cock, my King, please." Her voice was so wanton, and it was so satisfying.

Her pleading while bound ticked his kink into high gear. "Good girl." As he released the ball, and it fell to the floor, he ensured she wasn't pinned beneath it so her extremities wouldn't get crushed. "You make me crave your pussy. You make me want to give you my cum."

In a strained voice, she said, "I crave your cock, my King." She gasped. "Please, fuck me with it."

She moaned as he tickled between her thighs, then progressed, pressing his fingers deep into her flesh. He worked his fingers roughly into her, but he wasn't being gentle as he prepped her for his cock. She moaned, seeming to be getting more and more aroused the rougher he played with her body.

"Good, good girl," he said, loving and praising her for so willingly submitting to his will. He worked his throbbing cock into her hole, not meaning to break his rule of always making her come first, but also fighting the urge to roughly take her selfishly, and just release himself inside her within seconds. "Your submission makes me want to fuck you again and again. You deserve a good hard fucking."

"Yes," she said. "I do. Fuck me. I need you."

"Feel me deep inside you." He began to pound himself into her against the unforgiving ball.

Her grunts were louder than usual at being stationary and banged against the hard ball.

It was so hot that he almost came.

He figured she might end up bruised, but he kept pounding away, anyway. He trusted her to say the word to make him stop.

"Feel me ram you hard and fast, fuck you raw." He thrust into her as his moans of ecstasy joined hers. "You love cock."

She grunted and tried to squirm, but being bound, she couldn't. "I love your cock," she said in a strained voice between her pants.

His heart sank as he heard the calling of the council. Not now, for fuck's sake! He ignored it and kept on using her hole. There was no way she could touch her clit, of course, but he hoped the ball might be pressing on her there, arousing her with each thrust. She seemed to be getting close to a climax, based on her sounds.

The call rang again from the council.

"Shit," he muttered angrily.

"What is it?" she asked with concern.

"It's nothing." He gripped the ball with his hands and fucked her against it, growling and grunting.

Her ass cheeks gyrated in waves as he smacked against her.

After another minute, the call came a third time, and he gritted his teeth, fucking her even harder. They could wait five fucking minutes until he came, and hopefully she did. Anger filled him with their intrusive persistence. Why were they being so damned impatient?

"Fuck," he said as he pelted her faster.

"Ah-hmm. King Nocter, we have an emergency. You need to come at once."

Nocter was aghast and furious.

It was Finstra, in *his dungeon*. And his tone was very urgent.

Nocter's anger erupted more with each second. Rage filled him, his heart was beating, his face heating. He turned slightly, while still keeping his cock inside Marella. "Not now! Can't you see I'm busy?" He yelled it in full fury, pausing the motion of his hips so he didn't accidentally hurt her in his anger. "Get out and never enter my chambers again! You're banished from entering here ever again!" he boomed, his shouts filling the dungeon.

Finstra didn't move a muscle, his eyelids narrowing over his beady eyes.

"Now!" Nocter shouted. He tried to get a grip on his anger. This wasn't the mood he wanted to be in while fucking her.

Finstra finally left, and he tried again to calm his frazzled nerves. How dare that fucker interrupt him while he was fucking Marella! Never again would he accept such insolence from his subordinates. There needed to be more respect, and he was going to drill that into Finstra. The sheer disregard of Finstra for Nocter had him reeling. The fucker needs to go.

He tried to temper his rage, but it was proving to be impossible. He knew he was in danger of fucking her brutally.

"Mmmph," she said, trying to wiggle, but not able to.

He gave in to his impulses and banged into her, not meaning to take his frustration over the intrusion out on her. She seemed to be acquiescing to his rough treatment, though, taking each powerful blow and seeming even more satiated from it. She appeared to relish his roughness as her moans escalated, and her body shifted slightly, showing her apparent ecstasy.

"Fuck me, my King, just fuck me," she begged with desperation. "Use me."

He followed her lead of permission as he rage-fucked her beast-like, her sounds of pleasure peaking. "Come on my cock and come loud like a good, pinned slut," he seethed through clenched teeth.

Her body tried to convulse as she started her climax, her body barely flopping against the ball as she was sent along her climax climb. She made louder outbursts being bound as she came.

That ticked him right over the edge. He lost control and came deep inside her pussy. He panted and gasped as he descended his high. "That's my beautiful cumslut. Good. So good."

"Mmmmm," she cooed. "I feel so floaty."

"I love that you love cock." His voice was gruff.

"I love your cock, my King."

He began to untie her bound limbs and lifted her off the ball. "I want to spank your pussy with my cock. Cock whip your pussy. Then eat you out, watch you arch as I suck your clit." He scooped her up and carried her down the hall to the bed. He laid her out, then gazed down at her with a devilish smile. "I want to watch you shake as I make you come. Grab my hair, and say 'Eat my pussy, King. Get it all.' Say it." He loved demanding this from her as he settled upon the bed.

"Yes, oh yes, my King. Eat my pussy, King, get it all," she parroted back with seductive delight.

She squirmed, making her head move back and forth on the champagne-colored pillow.

"Want to taste my cum soaked whore." He descended between her thighs and ravished her until she came three more times.

Taking the time to cuddle her, he stayed for ten more minutes. She looked sleepy.

"I have to go, take care of some things." He sighed. "I have no choice."

"Don't kill him," she said with worry. "He's just doing his job."

Nocter didn't think that was the case. Not at all. There was something much more devious behind all of Finstra's actions. And he'd make damn sure nothing like what he'd done to Gabriella ever happened again. His chambers were his sacred space, he needed it. And Finstra was not allowed to invade it, no matter what. The violation would not go unpunished. His blood boiled.

His mood simmered down as he gazed upon her, though. His heart melted. He couldn't stay mad looking at her so satiated, so fantastically cum drunk. She was beautiful! His woman in his bed after he'd made her come, multiple times. And with all the kinky acts! This was his dream! Nothing else could look more wonderful to him. "I love you," he said as he rose, then he stopped in a startle, realizing it was the first time he'd said it out loud. "Holy shit, I just said that out loud."

She bounced up and wrapped her arms around him, settling on his lap. Her eyes were lit with excitement, her expression was full of glee. She peppered kisses all over his face, then said, "Oh, Nocter. I love you too!" She bounced on him with exuberance. "I was scared to say it, so I haven't. But now that you have, I can. I love you, Nocter!"

He beamed a happy smile at her. "I love you," he said, not being able to resist saying it again.

"And I love you!"

She'd reciprocated his declaration, and for that, he was so very happy. But his heart sank, knowing he had to go. It wasn't fair to have anything darkening this glorious moment. He hated that he had to leave her after all this, but he also knew he'd pressed his luck taking this much time with her after Finstra left. The vile green being would certainly be fuming and ready to strike. But she deserved this, and he wasn't going to slight her. He didn't care. He'd just found this new feeling with her, and he wasn't going to downplay it. She was his priority and Finstra would have to get used to it.

"I'm so sorry I have to go. I'd rather stay with you and snuggle. But. I'll be back. Hopefully, this won't take long. I feel we have much more to talk about now."

She lay back in bed with a happy smile. "Yes, we do. I'll be here. I'm not going anywhere."

He knew she was right.

Chapter 7
Gabriella

GABRIELLA WATCHED THE bottom of the boat disappear as she sank in the water. Leif had insisted on coming along, but he'd need to stay with the boat, because he couldn't breathe underwater, of course. Plus, he'd rented the boat and couldn't just let it float off. That would cost thousands of dollars to replace. She'd learned that much in the human world; money was the driver of everything.

Leif had tried to think of how he could come along down into the depths of the sea with her. She could have put a spell on him, but she'd never done such a spell before, plus it just made more sense for him to stay in the boat, so he'd accepted it.

She was nervous, venturing into the sea with her destination being the castle. She was terrified of bumping into Nocter. But she figured he'd be off doing his king work, so she'd likely only find Marella there. She wondered if the servants would let her in. They all knew her, so she was banking on that. And Marella was her friend, so she hoped they'd just buy that she was coming to see her friend. They didn't let people into the castle lightly.

She needed to talk with Marella and tell her so many things. It hurt her heart that she'd sent her friend into a snake pit by asking her to go to Nocter. She'd thought it was a good idea at first. Marella was strong and smart. And Nocter needed a mate. But it was such a bad idea that she felt the strong urge to warn Marella. There were too many potential dangers ahead for Marella, and she needed her to know that being with Nocter meant life imprisoned in the castle. Granted, she already worked there, but she'd not been confined. This was a whole different level of incarceration. Dooming her friend to such a life was not what she wanted hanging over her head, and most definitely not the kind of life she wanted her friend to live. Marella deserved more. Way more.

She coursed through the water quickly, feeling grateful that her mega-speed mode had not waned at all. She torpedoed toward the castle at lightning speed, her heart pounding and filling with dread as she zoomed.

When she reached the castle, she slowed her movement, glancing around to ensure it seemed okay. That was the other reason she'd gone so fast, it was less likely for someone to spot her and follow her. She assumed her disappearance was widely known, and if she were spotted, it might cause some sort of uproar, or at the very least, a ruckus. She had one mission only, and that was to talk with Marella.

She knocked on the big knocker on the massive double door of the castle. The knocker had the face of an old male sea siren with a wide open mouth, and his eyes looked stuffed with stars. It had coils of curls for the triangular beard, and the hair on top of his head looked like a pointed hat. This all gave the knocker the overall shape of a diamond.

After a minute, the door opened.

It was Boopah who opened the door. "Hello, Madam. You have returned. Please come in." He motioned for her to come in, looked around outside, and then slammed the mighty stone door shut.

The bang made Gabriella jump and she instantly felt claustrophobic and sick to her stomach, as if she were trapped in a tiny cage rather than an expansive, ginormous castle.

"Hi, Boopah. It's so good to see you." At least seeing her old friend was helping calm her.

Boopah opened his arms and gave her a big hug.

"We've missed you. I'm so happy you've returned." His thick gills flapped as he talked, and the sheen of silvery scales all down his abdomen shimmered in the great hall lights. His eyes were round black disks with no visible pupils.

"I've missed you all too."

"Are you well, my queen?"

She snickered. How was he still referring to her as "queen"? She moved slowly, allowing the grace of slow movements to flow through her. "I'm not the queen."

"You are engaged to be the queen." He smiled at her.

"Yeah, that's no longer a thing."

"Gabriella," King Nocter said in a loud, firm voice.

The sound of his voice made her jump. When she spun around, her heart stopped. There he was, looking regal, proud, and sexy as fuck. None of that had changed. He was still her Nocter. Though, he had a new hardness to his expression he never carried before he was king. Seeing him dropped her heart to her toes and she gulped down the urge to burst into tears and rush to him, so she wouldn't do either one.

"My King," Boopah said bowing, then leaving them.

Her heart was beating so hard it was hard to speak calmly. "Nocter."

"Gabriella."

That was all he was going to say? Shocked by his cold nature, she stammered, "We were once in love." It felt awkward to say, but she also couldn't not say it.

His face softened, and his old congenial expression returned. "Yes. Yes, we were. Very much so." He also looked sad.

"Yes," she said. She was not sure what to even say.

Seeing his reaction helped her relax. Maybe he was himself somewhere in there still.

"It wasn't fair what happened." He didn't look happy as he said it.

"No," she stated, trying not to let her hate for him show. She both loved him and hated him, and it was wild to be in his presence. She felt so many conflicting emotions at once that all she wanted to do was flee. But she knew she needed to find Marella.

"No. It was wrong. So wrong. And Finstra has paid, but not enough." A look of anger erupted on his face. He closed his eyes and took a deep breath, then released it slowly. He opened his eyes to gaze into hers. "I see you are remembering things now," he said in a softer whisper.

"I am, yes. But I'm not sure how much of it I remember. Memories keep coming to me. At random times."

"How much do you remember?" His voice was soft, and caring.

She held in a sob. "I remember many times of us. Happy." Her brain tried to reconcile it all, but it made no damn sense. "Why didn't you just tell me?"

His expression turned urgently hostile, then soured into a moody darkness. "You wouldn't have believed me if I had."

There was too much to say, so she found it hard to say anything at all. It hurt her heart to see him, and it stirred her heart. She still had feelings for him, this was even more evident for her being in his presence, which was hard to mesh with her love for Leif. How could she be in love with two mates at once? Yet her love for Leif was so simple, pure, easy. Her love for Nocter was complicated, convoluted, and now tarnished, but she couldn't deny that it was still there burning as a flame inside her heart. If her love for him could survive all that had happened, it surely was even stronger than she'd thought. Seeing him fed that fire and it crushed her heart even more. Nocter had said "were" in love. But so had she. Did he not feel anything for her anymore? But why did she care? She loved Leif.

She wanted to cry. She wanted Nocter to comfort her like he used to. She needed him, but she couldn't have him. She loved him, but she was supposed to hate him. She was supposed to discard him, not crave him. And after all he'd done that was bad, she shouldn't have any love left for him at all.

But. He was still Nocter. Her first love.

And he was right before her, in the flesh. She lamented not having memories of missing him. This was crazy! She shook her head in confusion. She missed not missing him. That was hard to process, and it rolled around in her head on repeat. What an odd feeling. She had regrets of not having memories of missing him like she should have had, because she hadn't fucking known their whole love story. It was all so ridiculous. And she'd been cheated out of living something wonderful. Nocter had been cheated, as well.

It might have been easier to blame and hate him than how she was feeling now.

Her brain stalled, remembering how she'd felt about Nocter before she'd been taken. Those feelings of love were flooding her. She gasped and crumpled to the floor.

"Oh, Gabriella," Nocter said, rushing to her side.

She stood back up wearily. The compassion in his tone was breaking her broken heart.

"King Nocter," Warrior Mingy stated firmly. "There's another urgent matter. Finstra needs you. It's of very urgent importance."

"Gabriella!" shrieked Marella in excitement. "You're here!" She swam quickly to her.

King Nocter moved away as the two embraced.

"What are you doing here? Are you okay?" Marella asked with concern. "You look very off."

"King Nocter," Warrior Mingy said in a stronger tone.

"Yes, thank you. I will go. I understand." He turned to Gabriella and Marella, and raised his hands. "I must go again. I will be back. Please, stay Gabriella."

Marella pulled Gabriella toward her chambers. "Let's talk in your chambers," she suggested with a loaded expression.

Gabriella saw her happiness and excitement, and it eased her worries a little. Marella looked well, not in any way distressed. "They are no longer my chambers."

The swim to her quarters seemed to take forever.

Marella shut the door and spun to face Gabriella, her face lit with joy. "Gabriella! I'm so happy! You have no idea how wonderful things are! I seriously can't believe it!"

Gabriella blinked and bobbed her head backward in shock. "Oh, I've been so worried. I felt horrible after I realized I may have sent you into pain and darkness. I felt guilty sending you to Nocter." She couldn't stop her frown, even after seeing how jubilant her friend was.

"No! No, no, no! It's not like that at all. In fact, it's the best news ever." She stopped fluttering her hands when she watched Gabriella's reaction. "Oh, I hope this isn't going to hit you badly. But then, I guess I forgot that you don't remember everything. So, it might be okay. How much do you remember?"

She shrugged as she sat on the plump easy chair to her right. "How would I even know?"

"Ugh, that's true. You wouldn't know what you don't know." She kneeled at Gabriella's feet. "Are you happy with Leif? Like you wouldn't not want to be with Leif?"

"I do love Lief, with all my heart. I love him, and I'm in love with him." Gabriella held her face as a sob burst free.

"But..." Marella said cautiously.

"I didn't know I still had feelings for Nocter until I remembered some things."

"Oh, shit." Marella rubbed her shins. "It's okay. You've been through a lot." She stood up and wrapped her arms around Gabriella. "You aren't going to like what I have to say, then." She sighed and squeezed her friend. "But I must tell you."

Gabriella pushed her back slightly to gaze into her eyes. "No, I love Leif. Marella, I'm not leaving Leif."

"Ah, I understand. Yeah, that makes sense. But you now also remember you never fell out of love with Nocter, though. Am I right?"

She shook her head as tears streamed down her face. "No, I didn't," she said in a small voice as a sob caught in her throat. "And, yes, you are."

"Aw, honey," Marella said, pulling her back into a hug.

"Does Leif know? Does he understand?" She seemed nervous, but happy.

Gabriella nodded against her chest. "Yes, he knows. But I'm not sure I understand. I reassured him, though. I'm not leaving him. He's a very understanding man, Marella. He's incredible, if I'm being honest. I couldn't have dreamed a better man."

"Good," she said as she pet Gabriella's hair.

They settled into a prolonged silence. Then released their hug.

It was obvious to Gabriella what was going on. She looked directly at her friend. "You love him, don't you? I can see it in your eyes."

Marella froze in place and looked at the ground. She was silent for a short time, then met Gabriella's gaze. "Yes," she said finally. "I really do."

Gabriella leaned back. This might help her shut the door on her chapter with Nocter, but she doubted it. "Then I'm very happy for you. I want you to be happy. I wasn't thinking of you when I suggested you go to Nocter, and that wasn't fair of me. I had all these visions of you being tormented, hurt, in hell." She smiled. "To find you happy and in love is a much better scenario."

"It has been a wonderful joy! Every day gets better, Gabriella. I've never felt this way ever in my life!"

Gabriella enjoyed smiling through her tears, it helped them scorch her heart less. "He's amazing, isn't he?"

"Very. He makes me want to twirl through the hallways, sing through the garden rooms, and, seriously, I can't stop smiling!"

"It shows. Sweets, you are glowing." Gabriella was sad and happy at once. Another dichotomy she wouldn't be able to reconcile was her best friend living the life she was supposed to have lived while facing living the best life she could imagine with Leif.

Marella's expression turned into one of worry. "You're not upset about this? I'd understand if you were." She paused and held Gabriella's hands, gazing deep into her eyes. "Do you want to pummel me?" She cringed slightly. "Kill me?"

"No, I don't want to kill you. I'm happy for you." She grabbed her friend's hands. "Marella, I'm very much in love with Leif. But it's so hard because I never stopped loving Nocter. That's true. I also have bad feelings about what he did to us, but, now that I remember the wonderful things, I can't hate him, either. And it's true, I do still harbor some love for him." She grimaced, her emotions going hot and cold willy-nilly without any sense of logic. "Don't tell him. Ugh. This is really weird, isn't it?"

"Very. But we're friends. We can do this." She snuggled next to Gabriella and placed her arm around her. "We can still be friends. We know the reality of this. Knowing that, we can navigate it just fine. I have confidence."

"Nocter is very lucky. You are incredible. Kind. Loving. Supportive. Smart. Caring. Beautiful."

"Aww," she said with a shrug. "Back at you."

"Will you marry? And become his queen? You would make a very good queen." This stung to say out loud. But she had to ask if they were that serious. She figured they were. The love she had seen earlier in Nocter's eyes as he looked at Marella had been real. "Marella, you will be queen," she said excitedly as the full thought formalized in her brain. She was happy for Marella. A servant turned queen was about the best story anyone in the kingdom could hope for.

She shook her head. "No. We haven't come that far, though. But today, today! We both said 'I love you' for the first time! And, Gabriella, he said it first!"

"Oh, wow! That's awesome! He's really amazing, Marella. I don't need to tell you, but I do. I know him." Unless he'd changed more than she thought, most of him must still be the same. She hoped, anyway. She figured Marella would know. She'd spent time with him recently whereas she clearly had not. She might be wrong about him. She had to acknowledge that.

"He's the most amazing ever! I don't think I understood how wonderful he was until now." She giggled as she brought a hand to her mouth. "And the sex? Oh, holy shit, the sex is wildly incredible beyond my wildest dreams!"

Gabriella nodded her head as a slow licentious grin overtook her face. "Yeah, that man is a very gifted lover." She was only happy she could say the same about Leif. "He still kinky?"

Marella shook her hands quickly as a little shriek flew from her mouth. She looked cute. "Oh, yes. He's unbelievable! I've never felt this way before. He's like, I don't know…magic!"

Oh boy, did Gabriella know. And she'd miss it. She was missing her life with Nocter that wouldn't be, but she was also so excited about her own timeline of life with Leif. "Definitely magic. I assume he's still obsessed with your pleasure?"

"Yes! I've never had a lover put me first like that. He's really quite brilliant, but it doesn't feel like a game to get what he wants. It feels genuine." She sounded sure of herself, but with a slight desire for reassurance.

"That's totally accurate about him, yes." She smiled at Marella and rubbed her bare thigh. "You will have to get used to wearing clothing, though, as queen." She didn't want to darken the mood by asking about the incarceration of the castle part, but she planned to bring it up soon. Marella deserved to know that before committing herself to Nocter. Just not in the sunshine of her expressing the new love. She wasn't that cruel. Or maybe it was best that Marella knew right away? She couldn't decide.

"I wonder how the kingdom will feel having a servant of the castle turned queen?" she asked softly, meekly, like she was afraid of saying it out loud. "And, honestly, he hasn't asked me yet, so our speculation might be unfounded."

Gabriella shook her head. "I don't think so, I know Nocter." She smiled. "He's thinking it. I can assure you."

They were both startled as a laugh came from the corner. It seemed to have come from behind the biggest armoire.

They both stared in the direction with confusion on their faces.

"Did you hear that?" Gabriella asked with caution.

"Yes, I did. It sounded like a laugh." Marella stood, her eyes wide with fear. "Who's there?"

They both began to move in the direction the laugh came from. Gabriella didn't like that someone had snuck in to listen to their private conversation. "This is really creepy," she said.

As they approached the armoire, another laugh erupted, short and loud.

They moved along, their bodies aligned as they swam.

Everything went dark within a second. They were whisked away so fast that they couldn't even process what they were seeing.

When they stopped moving, things came into focus. They were sitting on colored rocks. There were fish swimming overhead. But what they saw in the distance seemed like giants. And they weren't swimming, they were walking.

"Oh, fuck!" Gabriella exclaimed, realizing they were in big trouble. "We're in the human world. We're on land." She stood up and traversed the small rocky bottom. "Come with me," she said, reaching for Marella.

Marella followed close behind. "I'm scared, Gabriella. I've never been to the human land like this before. I've only been to the beach."

"I know." She crept forward, dragging Marella along.

When they got to the end, Gabriella put her hands out to touch what was in front of her. Her fears were right about where they'd been deposited. A human boy ran around the room, a red cape flying up off his back as he moved. His mom, even more giant, appeared with a cup and a cookie. "Fuck. Marella. We're in a damn fishbowl."

She met Marella's eyes, and the terror she saw there mirrored her own.

"We're tiny, aren't we?" Marella looked horrified. "And lost."

"Yep." She nodded slowly. "Somewhere unknown in the human world, where no one will find us." It had to be Finstra again. But why?

No one would know where to look for them. They'd have no clues at all. It would be up to them to get out. The problem was, how would they get to the top of the fishbowl, and how would they traverse a large amount of land being so tiny? She could fly, but could she also carry Marella and fly? She didn't think she could.

"This is bad, very bad." This hurt. Why do this? Was Finstra so devious that he couldn't tolerate Nocter being with the mate he wanted? For fuck's sake. Someone needed to off Finstra, he deserved to be off the fucking planet. The only consolation was they hadn't been separated.

Marella's eyes were so filled with fear, Gabriella knew this was going to be mostly up to her.

Her worst fear bloomed. The question was...what if this wasn't Finstra at all, but an enemy of Nocter's? An unknown enemy would be harder to battle. At least she now had a flavor for Finstra's brand of evil. And this did smell like it, but she wasn't entirely sure of that either.

She held Marella close in a hug. "We'll get out. I promise."

Marella whimpered as she nodded her head. "Yeah," she said weakly. "You're strong, Gabriella. I believe you."

They settled back on the bottom of the fishbowl and watched the little boy running around. It wasn't going to be easy, but she wasn't going to sit down and just die either.

Chapter 8
Nocter

King Nocter returned to the castle. The meeting was short, thank goodness. He couldn't wait to see both Marella and Gabriella. Could he be the first king of the kingdom to have two queens? The thought really excited him. He couldn't not think of them that way, though. Gabriella would always feel like his, too, whether she wanted that or not. He felt responsible for her, and if he was honest with himself, he still had love for her. But this new love with Marella had him on cloud nine.

He swam throughout the castle, not finding them. He questioned the staff, but no one had seen them. His worry ballooned. Where could they be? The last place anyone had seen them was when they were going into the queen's chambers. But Nocter had fully searched there, and there was no sign of them.

"Shit," he said, a sinking feeling consuming his gut. "Finstra!" he shouted, sending out his call telepathically to the conniving beast.

Within seconds, the green slug appeared. "You rang, King?"

His fury had him seeing red. "Where are they? Where did you take them this time? And don't think I'm not going to kill you over this if one hair gets harmed on them."

Finstra rolled his black eyes and let out a puff of air. "I do not know what you mean. I did not do this, whatever you are saying." He seemed annoyed and bored. He turned to leave.

"Hey, fucker. You have not been dismissed. I don't believe you. Where are they? You know everything that happens." He grabbed Finstra by the throat, which didn't look like a throat at all because his whole body was the same width.

He coughed, then gagged.

Nocter's rage was overcoming him as he started to squeeze. "Tell me, you fucker. Where are they?"

A servant behind him shouted, "Whoa! King, if you choke him, he can't tell you."

It was Misty, the cook.

She was right. Nocter released his hold on him. He knew if she hadn't appeared, he may very well have just killed Finstra. He no longer cared that the vile politician had influence and contacts. He was not allowed to dictate and control Nocter's life like this, putting Marella and Gabriella at risk.

Finstra spat and coughed. More of the staff appeared to see what the ruckus was about.

"Where are they?" he boomed. "You tell me, or so help me, I will kill you with my bare hands in front of my staff for insolence." That was a sentence Nocter thought he'd never say to another being in his entire life, but he'd never been this full of rage before. His breathing was labored, his head hurt, and his fists were clenched. "Now!" he screamed.

"King, I didn't do this. You have to believe me." Finstra was shrinking; his tone was begging. For once in his life, he looked scared rather than arrogant and cocky. "Ask Leif. He's in a boat above, waiting for Gabriella. Maybe he saw something."

Nocter's fears skyrocketed. If Finstra truly hadn't taken them, then surely it was one of the bordering enemies, and both of them were in grave danger. They wouldn't be treated nicely as prisoners.

"Fuck!" Nocter shouted, his booming yell filling the entire room, practically shaking the vases lining the far wall. "How did this happen? With all our guards? How?"

None of the staff moved a muscle.

"Where is he? Where is Leif?" he asked Finstra urgently.

"I'll take you. It's toward the east, but over our territory."

"Were you going to tell me this? This is something you should have told me once you knew. I clearly cannot trust you. I should have known, but I thought I needed your contacts and your network. This will be the end of you. You will no longer be in my inner circle."

"King, it wasn't me. I swear to you." Finstra cowered, sinking lower in front of the king.

"Take me to Leif, now," he demanded.

Finstra swam, leading Nocter out of the castle. A set of ten guards swam along as protection.

Once they reached the boat, Nocter hesitated. He looked up at the boat. Leif looked so helpless in a tiny boat surrounded by the vast ocean. Not unlike Nocter would be if on land, but he'd die quickly on land, whereas Leif could briefly hold his breath underwater. This was going to be tough. Why would Leif even believe him at this point? Why would he trust him? Surely, he wanted to kill Nocter for what he'd done. He had no choice, so he moved on and popped to the top. He created a bubble of water around his head and surfaced.

"Leif," he said, his voice warbled by the water layer. "I can't stay like this for long," he shouted. "Someone has taken both Gabriella and Marella, right from the castle. Did you see anything? Anything at all?"

Leif's calmness erupted into anger as he backed up to the far end of the boat. "Stay back," he warned. He raised his fists.

It was getting hard for Nocter to breathe already. Normally he had more time, but his heavy breathing was taking up all his air quickly. He dipped under the water again, gasping. Once he caught his breath, he recreated the bubble and re-emerged. He needed to calm down and get Leif to understand this was urgent.

Leif was staring down into the water, his eyes roaming across the team of warriors who surrounded Nocter. His expression was still full of anger. "I only saw what looked like a cloud. It appeared on the surface of the water over there," he said, pointing off to the right. "Then it went that way. Could that have been them?" he asked incredulously.

"Yes, it could have been them." Nocter had heard of such things before. Sea wizards from a nearby section of the sea were capable of rapidly transporting others like that, as if they were weightless and almost invisible. He'd heard it could happen within the blink of an eye. They were master kidnappers, and often no one had a clue what was happening before it was too late. Likely someone had paid them. The sea wizards rarely had their own agendas, but they were known to be for hire.

"Shit," he said with a hefty amount of disgust. Well, at least they had some clues. "I'm almost one hundred percent sure of it. When was it?" Nocter hated looking at this man, the man who had stolen Gabriella from him. His blood boiled again. His rage was getting out of control. Leif hadn't taken her. He had to temper himself, Leif hadn't known, and back then, neither had Gabriella. It didn't help him enough to settle down thinking this way. All he could think about was how the man had her and was having sex with her. He knew Gabriella would not be staying with him if she didn't love him, though. If he hadn't found Marella, and his new love for her hadn't grown, he'd have surely ripped Leif to shreds with his bare hands.

Leif glared at him.

He looked as hostile as Nocter felt.

"We are going to have to work together to get them back," Leif said.

Nocter had to re-dip into the water to get a new layer to breathe in.

He gasped and sputtered beneath the water, then caught his breath. "He saw something," Nocter told Finstra. "It sounds like the work of a sea wizard."

He re-emerged from the sea with a fresh layer of water to breathe in. He shouted to Leif, "You hear me, right?"

Leif nodded, his expression apprehensive and pissed as hell. "How will we find them?"

"We need to be able to talk. Can you take a turn and hold your breath underwater?" Nocter was strong, but this was tiring him, and he needed to preserve his strength.

"Yes," Leif nodded. He dove into the water.

"I can put a breathing spell on him so he can breathe underwater," Finstra said.

Leif nodded. "Do it."

Finstra approached Leif and spun around him rapidly, causing turbulence in the area of water around him. Within a minute, Leif appeared to be able to breathe. "It won't last long. Probably a half hour or so. Do not go too deep."

Nocter had a limited ability to do this type of magic, too, but he was grateful for Finstra doing it. The act would surely have usurped more of his energy.

"Is this your doing?" Leif demanded angrily at Finstra. "I know what you did before." Then he turned to Nocter. "And you. You are both my enemies. How am I to trust you?"

Nocter nodded. "I know. I understand. But our mates are together, and lost, and they are best friends. We're going to have to work together whether we like it or not. They are in grave danger. This was likely one of my enemies, but it wasn't Finstra. He assures me." Nocter gave Finstra the evil eye. "So, he says, anyway. Soon I will know," he said in an ominous tone as he glared at Finstra.

"I don't believe you, but I see I have no choice. And you have not killed me, but have helped me breathe under the water. So, I will work with you, though I'm staying very alert." He glared at Nocter. "I don't trust you."

"Gabriella loves you. I won't lie. I still love her, but I've recently realized I have feelings of love for Marella." Nocter felt odd discussing this in front of all his guards and Finstra. "I'd like to pursue a life with her as my queen. I will not take Gabriella from you." He puffed up his chest as the full realization hit him that this was true. He looked at his guards and Finstra. "King's declaration. Sound the alerts across the sea. A queen has been kidnapped."

The kingdom would surely step up and assist, hearing this. The only problem was, once Marella knew this, would she agree to be his bride? The web was getting more convoluted. And it felt a bit too familiar for his comfort.

"Marco, you and Mecksta head back to the castle and organize a search. Send warriors here who can go on land. I suspect they've been taken out of the sea. Marella can be out of the sea for a short time, but her kidnappers may not know this. This might give us a clue of where to look for them. Perhaps in bodies of water, pools, rivers, that sort of thing. Have the seers start searching to find out if they can see anything about their location." He felt his determination firm up in his jaw. He boomed, "This is not how my mates will die."

He watched Leif as his words sunk in. Leif's anger flared higher, his brows knitting, his eyes burning with anger.

He held Leif's gaze as he said, "I still will always watch over her. Forever."

"It's not your place to," Leif stated heatedly, puffing up his chest and getting up in Nocter's face.

"I understand, but you don't get to decide that. Now, let's get a plan going. We need each other to get them back. Where will we start? The land is your domain. I'm open to suggestions."

Leif stared at Nocter as if he were vile. "How far would these kidnappers go? Is there a limit?"

"I don't believe the sea wizard's power is more far-reaching than ten miles or so inland. This will help, unless they had helpers on land. But we have to start with the assumption that they don't, then move on from there." They had to start somewhere, and this made sense. He would find them, and this time he wouldn't ever stop looking.

"Yes, I will map out an area. So, you will not be able to search on land?" Leif looked less angry and more urgent.

"No. I cannot be on land for long. As you saw. I need the water layer to breathe out of it. I will search in the sea." He glanced around at his warriors. "Can any of you breathe on land?"

"I can," a small muscular female stated. "I'm Kenlah. At your service, King."

She was a blue-skinned creature with piercing purple eyes.

He laughed. "Great, but you won't exactly blend in." It felt good to laugh, even for something so critical to their success that also seemed impossible to work.

"I can shapeshift her. It will last twenty hours." Finstra approached her. "I cannot change her eyes, though."

"That's okay. That will likely work well enough." He turned to the warrior. "Kenlah, I ask you to go with Leif." The king stared at her expectantly. "Do you accept this mission? I cannot tell you the dangers you may face."

"Yes, sir. I accept the mission. Change me." Her chin was high, and her look was fierce. "I can do this."

The only spell Nocter knew for this would potentially leave her changed, so he kept mute about it. Finstra was stepping up to help, but he may not be doing enough to get on his good side just yet. He still had a hard time believing Finstra didn't have a hand in the kidnapping.

"We are looking for what could be a needle in a haystack. We may be facing the impossible. My only hope is that they can somehow help themselves, too." The king gave her a confident look. "I believe you can do it. Lean on Leif." That was hard to say and mean.

"I will do it," Kenlah stated, tipping her head upward. "I will bring them back."

Finstra swam around her, and her skin darkened to a shade of dark brown. "I can only darken her flesh."

"This is perfect," said Leif with assurance. "It will work. She will pass for human now."

"Return to this spot in twenty-four hours if you can. We will also return here every twenty-four hours until we have found them."

Kenlah moved to near Leif.

Nocter allowed his urgency to overcome him as he hollered, "We will be successful. They will not perish from this act. I will have my queen, and you will have Gabriella. Go. May speed and strength be your partners. Let's find them."

Nocter watched Kenlah take Leif's hand as he pulled her into the boat.

The motor sound droned away as King Nocter began to swim to the first place he could think to check. This was life or death and he wasn't accepting the latter.

The End of Book 4, Novel 1.
Stay tuned for Novel 2.
Learn more about Kenlah in Novel 2.

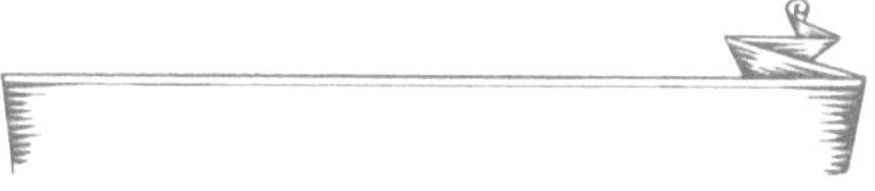

About the Author

Ruan Willow is an open door spicy romance author, sex blogger at https://ruanwillowauthor.com/ , sexuality and erotica fiction podcaster at the Oh F*ck Yeah with Ruan Willow Podcast, and an audiobook narrator/voiceover actor. She is also published on Medium, Frolic Me, Theo Reads, and Literotica. She loves spending time with family and friends, interacting with fans, cooking, sharing/chatting with and educating people about sex, reading, travel, being outdoors, swimming, learning about sex, podcasting, and more sex. Did you catch all the sex? She's giggling right now thinking about you reading all about sex. She values openness and talking about the natural act of sex. And. Yup, she loves to laugh!

Pen Names:

She writes general erotica/erotic romance/erotic rom com/menage as Ruan Willow, hotwife erotica as Ruin Willow, taboo erotica as RuAnn Willhoe, and R.U. Ann for open door romantasy/erotic horror/paranormal fiction.

Thank you!

Thank you to all my family and friends who support me. I wouldn't be where I am without you. You are all the magic and the light in my life, the love that grows in my love. I am honestly thrilled and humbled by the supportive people in my life. Love you!

To Fans:

Thank you for purchasing and/or reviewing this book!

I peddle fantasies for the purposes of your enjoyment, entertainment, and expanding your sexuality and openness. Always remember that no fantasies are bad. You should enjoy your sexuality and your fantasy life as much and as often as you can.

Thank you for reading my book! I write for myself and for my fans. My fans are my main focus though, but of course, I want to like what I write too, and I thoroughly enjoyed writing this story.

In writing erotica/erotic romance, I'm always excited for the erotic journey! I'm personally on a path of sexual empowerment, enlightenment, and enjoyment. Thank you for reading this and I'm honored to be a part of your journey as well. I strive to spin stories where the characters get to enjoy lots of pleasure, and I hope you have also gotten pleasure from reading this book. Enjoy your own journey!

I am where I am because fans have responded to me and my content, so I owe everything to you! Thank you! Thank you! Thank you! You are a blessing in my life, and you give me more joy than you will ever know. I love interacting with all of you and I will never give that up.

My stories are open door erotica and erotic romance, so they have a generous amount of sex in them, as I believe our relationships should have as well. I hope you enjoyed this novella for what it is, literature that is in the erotica genre where sex is a part of the plot, storyline, and character development. It is very different from a closed door romance, and there are different levels of heat in the erotica genre as well. Explore them all! I personally love open door romances because I want the full story of the relationship, not a partial one.

If you'd like more of my work, please see below for my list of published works on the following pages, visit my sexuality and erotica podcast, find my audiobooks, visit my website, my Patreon, visit my profile on Medium, and my linktree with all my links at https://linktr.ee/RuanWillow

Thank you for purchasing this book, I'd love to hear your thoughts in an honest review on the site where you purchased the book from. I'd absolutely love it if you shared my book with others. It warms my heart profusely when I see someone who has taken the time to review/share my book. Love you all very much!

All my best, yours truly, with overflowing love from a full heart, Ruan Willow

Erotica author, sexuality/erotica podcaster, and erotic book narrator

Ruan's other books
and novellas:

All books:
https://books.ruanwillowauthor.com/
Collections:
Howife books:
https://books.ruanwillowauthor.com/hotwifebooks
Spring Break and Stranded with Her Best Friend's Brothers Collection:
https://books.ruanwillowauthor.com/springbreakandstrandedwithherbestfriendsbrothersseries
Servicing the Work Men, Her Filthy Hotwife Adventures Series
https://books.ruanwillowauthor.com/servicingtheworkmenseries
The Sex Challenge Series
https://books.ruanwillowauthor.com/thesexchallengeseries
The Getaway Series: age gap
https://books.ruanwillowauthor.com/ruansgetawayseries
Taboo books
https://books.ruanwillowauthor.com/taboospringbreakandstrandedwithherbestfriendsbrothersplus6men
Check out the Audiobooks:
https://books.ruanwillowauthor.com/audiobooksnarratedbyruan

Standalone by R.U. Ann:

In Scarlet's House, in ebook

https://books.ruanwillowauthor.com/inscarletshouse

In audiobook

https://books.ruanwillowauthor.com/
inscarletshouseaudiobook

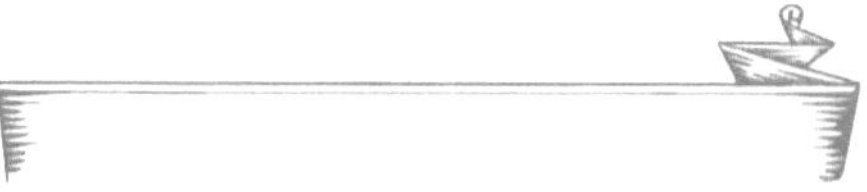

Anthologies and Award Nominations

Ruan has stories in the following anthologies:
He Will Obey (which was AWARDED THE 2020 SILVER PIGTAIL IN BEST ANTHOLOGY CATEGORY
The Femdom Coven (nominee for 2021 Golden Pigtail Smut Awards)
Inside of Ruan Willow (also available in an audiobook)
(this audiobook was a nominee for the 2021 Golden Pigtail Smut Awards)

Decadent Erotica An Anthology **3rd Place Winner in the 2022 Golden Pigtails Smut Awards for Dark/Taboo Category**
Nominations for the 2023 Golden Pigtail Awards include:
Servicing the Trash Man, My Filthy Hotwife Adventure
Dressing Room Domme
Anthology Ruan has a story Hearts and Flowers, Whips and Chains

Other Anthologies:

Halloween Anthology: Trick or Tease II
Christmas/Holiday anthology: Season's Teasings: Snowbound Seductions

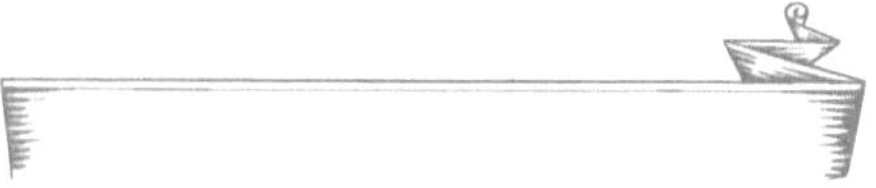

Other links:

RUAN WILLOW ON GOODREADS Ruan Willow Goodreads Author page[1]

Ruan Willow on BookBub https://www.bookbub.com/profile/ruan-willow

Sign up for Ruan's newsletter: https://subscribepage.io/ruanwillow

ARC copies are usually on BookSirens and StoryOrigin App. Check those sites for FREE ARC of books and audiobooks.

---

1. https://www.goodreads.com/author/show/21312130.Ruan_Willow